BLUE RONDO

John Lawton is the director of over forty television programmes, author of a dozen screenplays, several children's books and seven Inspector Troy novels. Lawton's work has earned him comparisons to John le Carré and Alan Furst. Lawton lives in a remote hilltop village in Derbyshire.

THE INSPECTOR TROY NOVELS

Black Out
Old Flames
A Little White Death
Riptide
Blue Rondo
Second Violin
A Lily of the Field

BLUE RONDO

John Lawton

Grove Press UK

First published in 2005 by Weidenfeld & Nicolson, London, England

This paperback edition published in 2013 by Grove Press UK, an imprint of Grove/Atlantic Inc.

1 3 5 7 9 8 6 4 2

A CIP record for this book is available from the British Library.

ISBN 978 1 61185 587 6

Printed and bound by CPI Group (UK) Ltd, Croydon, CR0 4YY
Grove Press, UK
Ormond House
26–27 Boswell Street
London
WC1N 3JZ

www.groveatlantic.com

For
Anne McDermid
(also known as Eira)

That Scottish Canadian Woman
from a valley in Wales

I can understand companionship.
I can understand bought sex in the afternoon.
I cannot understand the love affair.

GORE VIDAL

In my fanciful projections I took red hair to be the mantle of goddesses and priestesses who craved no obedience, like Ayesha, but a siren enjoining flight up into the firmament of life itself. It was the copper-headed helmet of destiny of those who would hurl their challenge against the very centre of creation and, having struck, plummet and explode upon a disbelieving world. It was lifted by the winds from the north-east, breathing like warspite Hotspur. It was the shade of the imagination's crimson twilight, punitive and cleansing, the colour of communing voluptuaries, of pre-Raphaelites, Renaissance princes, of Medicis and Titians, of Venice and Northumbria, of bloodaxe and vengeance, Percy and Borgia, of Beatrice – Dante's and Shakespeare's – of hot pretenders and virgin monarchs. A red-haired Doris Day was unthinkable.

JOHN OSBORNE

Prologue

A grim prospect greeted Troy and Bonham. Eight small boys ranged across the pavement, all looking expectantly towards Bonham. No one spoke, the expectant looks seemed fixed somewhere between joy and tears. Sgt Bonham held power over the greatest, the most mysterious event in their short lives. Troy looked down at a motley of gabardine mackintoshes, outsized jackets tied up with string, brown boots, pudding basin haircuts, bruised and scabrous kneecaps. Such an amazing array of ill-fitting hand-me-downs that only the peach-fresh faces challenged the image of them as eight assorted dwarves. Out on the end of the line, a grubby redhead, doubtless called Carrots, juggled a smouldering cocoa tin from hand to hand, an improvised portable furnace. Troy wished he had one of his own.

Troy glanced at the boys, wondering how much they heard and how much they understood. Eight cherubic faces, and sixteen hard, ruthless eyes looked back at him. Preserving innocence seemed a fruitless ideal.

'How would you like to make some money?' he said.

'How much?' said the biggest.

'A shilling,' said Troy.

'Half a crown,' said the boy.

'You don't know what it's for yet!'

'It'll still cost you half a dollar,' the boy replied.

'OK, OK,' said Troy, 'half a crown to the boy who finds the rest.'

'Freddie, for God's sake,' Bonham cut in. 'You can't!'

He gripped Troy by the shoulder and swung him round into a huddled attempt at privacy.

'Are you off yer chump?'

'George, can you think of any other way?'

'For Christ's sake they're kids. They should be in school!'

'Well they clearly have no intention of going. And they don't exactly look like Freddie Bartholomew do they?'

'Jesus Christ,' Bonham said again.

'Don't worry,' said Troy.

'On your own head be it.'

Troy turned back to the boys, ranged in front of him in a wide semicircle.

'I want you to look for . . .' he hesitated, uncertain what to call a corpse. 'For anything to do with what Tub found. OK?'

They nodded as one.

'And if you find it don't touch it. You come straight back and tell Mr Bonham, and nobody, I mean nobody, goes near it till he's seen what you've found. Understood?'

'You know, Freddie,' Bonham said softly, 'There are times when I think there's nothing like a long spell at the Yard for putting iron in the soul.'

1

Boys' Game

Short, nasty and brutish.

Troy stared.

'Go on,' said Churchill.

Still Troy stared.

'Go on. Pick it up.'

Troy hefted the gun in his left hand. Sawn off at the barrels and stock, it had become less a shotgun than an outsize handgun. He felt the weight, thought the alterations did nothing for its balance and less for its looks. 'I hope this didn't start life as one of your hand-mades,' he said.

'Far from it. I helped myself to it after a trial a few years back. The court wanted it destroyed, naturally, but I pleaded its . . . educational value.'

Churchill smiled at Troy over this last phrase. Down the tunnel Hitler and Göring watched with fixed gazes. Tempting him.

'My education, I suppose?' Troy said.

'As it happens, yes.'

'You know,' Troy went on, 'it's appalling a policeman should ever have his hands on such a weapon.' He tucked the stubby stock into one hip and fired. The first shot cut Adolf in two, the second set fat Hermann spinning. Straw and sawdust everywhere.

Churchill sighed. 'What have I told you, Frederick?'

Troy recited: 'Every shot counts. Speed isn't everything.'

'And?'

'And a wounded man can still kill you.'

'Quite,' said Churchill. 'If old Göring had been anything more than a cut-out from *Picture Post* and a sack full of straw you'd be dead now. Shall we do it again with a little more accuracy and a little less haste?'

'Again.' It seemed to be Churchill's motto, and it seemed to

Troy that he was no further on than the day Churchill had walked back into his life three weeks ago.

§ 1

In the summer of 1944 Lady Diana Brack had shot Detective Sergeant Troy in the gut. He had lost part of one kidney, and had been lucky not to lose a length of small intestine. He had been off work for six months. Six months that to him seemed far more than enough and which he ascribed as much to his superintendent's desire to punish him as to the rigours of passing the medical. Every time he reported for duty, Onions sent him home. Not long before Christmas he had finally got back into his old office, behind his old desk, and attempted to slip on the old skin he had sloughed off in June.

A week later he was back in hospital, rushed to the Charing Cross with internal bleeding as a result of a massive haemorrhage, the first he had known of which had been pissing blood. Sergeant Wildeve had picked him off the bog floor, flies gaping, cock out, slewed in a crimson slick of blood and piss.

His family came to drive him mad.

His mother sat at his bedside and distracted him from the prospect of death by reading aloud to him, much as she had done when he was young. He had been a sickly child. Now that he was a sickly grown-up, he was happy to have her read; he wished only that she had chosen something more cheery than Rimbaud's *Une Saison en Enfer*.

He could understand why. French was her first language. Like many Russian toffs, Russian, to her, had been a language for talking to servants, and, unlike her husband, she had never found it in herself to embrace the irregularities of English with the passion one could only ever muster for something so perverse. French it had been, French it was – but Rimbaud. Mother, please.

7

'*J'attends Dieu avec gourmandise. Je suis de race inférieure de toute éternité.*'

Oh, bloody hell, he thought. Waiting for God? Was that what he was doing? But help was at hand. His sister Masha had appeared at his mother's shoulder: 'There's two chaps waiting to see Freddie, Maman. As he's only allowed two visitors at a time . . .'

His mother stuck a bookmark in the pages of the battered Rimbaud and told him they would continue tomorrow.

'Anyone I know?' Troy asked.

'You'll see,' said his sister, and as she walked out Kolankiewicz had walked in, followed closely by a face that made Troy think for a moment. Churchill, Bob Churchill. Good Lord. He didn't think he'd seen Bob since his father's funeral.

Lady Troy offered a cheek for Churchill to peck. Troy couldn't help feeling she would have preferred a handshake, but that would have meant surrendering the grip on one or other of her walking-sticks. For eighteen months or so now they had kept her mostly upright and moving against the tortuous twists and stabs of arthritis. All Kolankiewicz got was a mumbled, 'Good evening.' She had never liked Kolankiewicz, but then so few people did – so few could or would get past the foul exterior and the fractured English. Besides, Poles and Russians . . . they had history. *Taras Bulba* was not a novel or a name ever to be mentioned around Kolankiewicz.

Churchill had gained weight – a family trait, perhaps. He was almost as rotund as his distant cousin Winston, and when the mood took him the same mischievous Churchillian glint could be seen in his eyes.

No one spoke as Troy's mother walked to the door, sticks clacking arrhythmically across the linoleum floor. When she had gone Churchill said softly, 'Your mother was fine the last time I saw her. Has all this come upon her since your father's death?'

Troy's father had died late in 1943. He had watched his mother slip into sudden ill-health, her limbs seizing up as the most important limb of all had been cut from her. A physical parody of her mental state. It was not Troy waiting for God, it occurred to him, nor was it a poem read for his benefit – it was his mother, and there were times he thought God could not arrive

8

soon enough for her liking.

'Yes,' he said. 'And there's little to be done. She seems almost to relish the affliction. It's her punishment for letting the old man slip.'

'You been reading that bugger Freud again?' Kolankiewicz said.

'Let's change the subject, shall we? I'm sure I don't owe this honour to your desire to argue the toss about Freud or Bob's concern for my mother's health.'

Churchill and Kolankiewicz looked at each other, and Troy knew he had hit the mark. It was indeed an honour – a visit from the greatest gun expert on Earth and from London's finest forensic pathologist. If the two of them had got together to visit him in his sick bed they must be up to something – the static between them flashed out 'conspiracy' to Troy.

'Bob has an idea,' Kolankiewicz began.

'Well, more of a suggestion, really, and it was your idea, really, Ladislaw . . .'

Ladislaw? No one called the Polish Beast by his Christian name.

'Stop there, both of you. I'm too tired and too pissed off to listen to you play Tweedledum and Tweedledee. Could one of you just spit it out?'

Kolankiewicz deferred. Churchill took the chair Troy's mother had been in, and Kolankiewicz perched on the edge of the bed.

'It's like this, Frederick. After you were shot, Ladislaw and I met up . . . When was it now?'

'Doesn't matter when,' said Troy.

'I suppose not. Anyway, he told me you couldn't hit a barn door at twenty paces and the only reason Diana Brack hadn't killed you instead . . .' Churchill paused, reddened even, as the inevitability of what he had to say next struck him.

'Instead of me killing her,' Troy prompted.

'Quite. As you say. The only reason was . . . well . . . pure luck. Wasn't it?'

Churchill looked at Kolankiewicz. Kolankiewicz looked at Troy. Troy met them head on. 'Yes. A lucky shot,' he agreed.

Lucky? The bullet that had killed Diana Brack ricocheted through his dreams and would do so for the rest of his life.

'So . . . what's your point, gentlemen?'

9

'Well . . .' Churchill fudged.

Kolankiewicz had had enough of fudge.

'Well is as well does. Next fucker who comes at you with gun is going to kill you, you stupid bugger.'

Churchill manoeuvred around the F-word by pulling out a large linen handkerchief and honking loudly, as though a good hooter blast could erase the sound of air turning blue.

'Fuck it, Troy, you know as well as I do if the Brack bitch had got off a second shot you'd be six feet under pushing up buttercups!'

'Daisies,' Troy said softly.

'Eh?'

'It's "pushing up daisies" not "pushing up buttercups", you Polish pig – and, yes, you're quite right. She damn near killed me. I've had six months to work that out. Now tell me something I don't know.'

Churchill got between them. 'When will you be discharged?'

'For Christmas,' Troy replied. 'They've assured me of that.'

'And how fit will you be?'

Troy threw back the bedclothes, hoisted his nightshirt and pointed to the four-inch scar on his abdomen.

'I see,' Churchill said. 'You'll take a while to heal. So, we'll take it gently at first, shall we?'

'Take what gently?'

Kolankiewicz answered, the steam spent, and a near-avuncular tone in his voice: 'My boy, Bob is offering to teach you to shoot. It's a good idea. It could save your life.'

'I get weapons training at the Yard.'

'Perfunctory stuff, take my word for it,' said Churchill. 'Enough so coppers don't dislocate their shoulders with recoil, enough so they can fire the odd bullet in roughly the right direction. A few weeks with me and you'll be shooting like Wyatt Earp.'

It was a good idea. Troy knew it. But he had a built-in aversion to guns. He'd only had one with him that night because Larissa Tosca had nagged him not to go unarmed. He had lived through that night. Tosca had not – although the absence of a body had always left him with more than enough room for doubt. On the nights when Brack did not rattle round in his head, Tosca did.

10

On a really bad night they met. Yes – he'd master that aversion: learning how to shoot would be good. It might even occupy his mind, an organ desperately in need of occupation, any occupation, that might evict the dead women squatting there.

§ 2

It must have been two or three days later. He was waiting on the consultant's round, waiting on his petty god and the news of his own imminent escape. His mother sat once more at his bedside, his sister, as ever, out in the corridor preferring a tacky novel to their mother's grapplings with poetry, although Masha's influence must have prevailed to some extent. When the old woman had flourished a volume of Hardy's verse, Troy's spirits had floated on visions of Wessex life and rumpy-pumpy in haystacks, only to crash to earth when she began to read 'The Voice' from Hardy's poetry of the last years before the Great War. Her accent was atrocious.

'"Woman much missed how you coll to me, Sayink zat you are not as you were. . ."'

And he realised she was about to embark on a cycle of dead woman songs – Hardy's own *Frauentotenlieder*.

'". . . Zuss I; faltering fowadd, leafes around me follink, Wint oosink sin srough ze zorn from nowidd, And ze woman collink."'

Jesus Christ. Dead women collink? What had possessed her to pick that? Innocence? Not grasping what the man was banging on about. It's about death, dammit! Hardy's murky obsession with dead women. Far, far too close to Troy's own.

Saved by the bell once more. The consultant breezed in like a man late for a dead cert at the bookie's, glanced at his chart and said, 'You can go, Sergeant Troy. Healing up nicely, wouldn't you say?' And did not wait for an answer.

'I shall let you dress,' said Lady Troy. 'Masha and I will be outside.'

From the other side of the bed Troy heard the impatient sigh of the BigMan foldinghis *News Chronicle*. 'Struth, old cock, I

11

thought she'd never stop. I don't know who this Hardy bloke is . . . but wot a miserable git! D'ye reckon everyone he knew popped their clogs?'

'Who cares? Help me out of here before I pop mine.'

Troy swung his legs to the floor, felt the first rush of dizziness and paused, staring down to where white knees peeped from under his nightshirt, pale as jellyfish.

'Awright, cock?'

The Big Man loomed over him, big and round and blue in his Heavy Rescue uniform, blocking half the light from the window, like a tethered anti-aircraft balloon floating in his flight path. Troy felt the rush of an old, familiar feeling breaking in his mind. He wondered out loud: 'You know, this has been bloody awful. I was the kind of child who got everything going, mumps, measles, scarlet fever . . .'

'Wot kid didn't, matey?' said the Big Man without sympathy. 'Bet you didn't get rickets, though, nor pneumatic fever – not toff 's diseases, are they?'

Every so often the Big Man would do this to him, remind him, whether he liked it or not, of their respective places in the layers of the big onion that was English society. Troy spent a split second wondering what pneumatic fever might be, then gave up. 'Can I finish?'

'Be my guest.'

'I was a sickly child – but nothing prepared me for this, I mean for the last six months. For all this . . . recuperation . . . all this fucking hospitalisation . . .'

'Mind yer French, young Fred, there might be ladies about.'

'. . . and if I thought . . . I mean if I thought I'd have to go through this again . . . ever . . . I mean . . . spend this much time in hospital . . .'

He had no ending to the sentence, but the Big Man did: 'If you want to avoid all this malarkey in the future, then you best do what that Klankiwitch bloke and Bob Churchill are telling you.'

'You know about that?'

'O' course. Mr Churchill and me, we go back a long way. Till when you was a nipper, I should think. He's done a fair bit of the old owsyerfather for the guv'ner, has Mr Churchill.'

Troy had given up trying to find out who the 'guv'ner' was. He was clearly the Big Man's employer, and once in a while the Big Man would refer to himself as a 'gentleman's gentleman', but declined to solve the mystery. Troy had known him intermittently since the end of last winter, when he had come across him tending a pig on an allotment carved for wartime necessities out of the former elegance of Tedworth Gardens in Chelsea. The last time Troy had discharged himself from hospital, in June, it had been the Big Man who had bundled him up like a baby and rushed him to hospital and, when it came down to it, saved his life. Troy had never been really grateful to him. It had all got in the way of an indulgent self-pity that had left him wanting to die.

'So you think I'm going to get myself killed as well, do you?'

'You can bet your best baggy underpants on it, old cock.'

The Big Man held underpants in one hand, trousers in the other. As Troy snatched them from him he remembered a phrase of Dorothy Parker's that came close to the approximation of gratitude: 'You might as well live.'

'Might as well live? Wossat mean, cock?'

'Nothing,' said Troy. 'It doesn't matter. You've won this one.'

§ 3

The Big Man wrapped him in a blanket – a parcel awaiting collection once again – and put him into the back seat of Troy's father's 1937 V12 Lagonda. The last time Troy had seen the car it had been up on blocks. Now it purred softly at the pavement, like a big cat lazing away a savannah afternoon. 'Where did you get the tyres?' he asked.

The Big Man tapped the side of his nose. One of those infuriating ask-no-questions-be-told-no-lies gestures he seemed to delight in using.

'The petrol?' Troy persisted.

'Your family pooled their coupons to give you a smooth ride home. An invalid carriage fit for a king.'

'How about an invalid carriage fit for an invalid?' said Troy remembering how he had got the car up to 110 m.p.h. on the Great North Road one day in 1938.

'Trust me,' said the Big Man.

Troy found himself in the back, next to Masha, his mother the best part of six feet away next to the Big Man, who sat behind the steering-wheel.

Masha smiled almost sweetly at him. It was one of her great cons to be unpredictable and unreadable. Troy thought there might be a *Just So* story somewhere in which a deadly creature habitually smiles at its prey. 'OK,' he said. 'Let's hear it.'

'Let's hear what?'

'Whatever it is that you're bursting to tell me. Whatever snatch of gossip is eating your soul at the moment.'

'I don't gossip.'

'Fine. Have it your way. Bitch a little instead. You can bitch for Britain, after all.'

Masha mused, lips gently parted, one hand idly conducting some invisible orchestra. 'Well . . . Mummy's raised the most enormous crop of leeks for the winter.'

'Is that the best you can do?'

'And with no keepers and no shoot the pheasants have bred like rabbits, so we have a positive plague. Cocks duelling at it all over the place. And, of course, more pheasants means more food for foxes so we have an army of little red—'

'Masha, for Christ's sake.'

'OK. OK.' (Pause) 'Speaking of cocks . . .'

'Yeeees?'

'My co-natal sibling would appear to be the object of a penetrating physiological enquiry.'

The woman was talking bollocks. Then he realised: code. A code to exclude their mother, who might have nodded off or might be listening. Co-natal sibling? Her twin, Sasha. Penetrating physiological enquiry? Fucking. Sasha had a new lover.

'Really,' Troy said at last. 'Who's she shagging now?'

'Freddie!'

But his mother had not turned. Her ears had not pricked up at the prick. Troy concluded she had nodded off, ramrod straight,

14

more upright asleep than she would ever manage waking. And the Big Man was in a happy world of his own, foot on the floor – flouting wartime wisdom – tearing along at over ninety, a tuneless tune humming on his lips. The outrage on Masha's part Troy knew to be bluffery – the fond illusion the twins cherished that, whilst flinging caution to the winds themselves, they could somehow protect him from the very people they were. There were times their catalogue of conquests bored him, times, as now, with little else to echo in the idling mind, when it was better than nothing.

'Anyone I know?' he asked.

'Nice young chap. RAF, actually. Based at Duxford. Shot up in a Hurricane. Not too bad, but too bad to fly, so he's one of those chaps with lots of rings on his cuffs who pushes little models around a map with a sort of snooker rest.'

Troy revised his metaphor slightly – they had flung caution to the hurricanes, well, at least to a former Hurricane pilot. 'You know,' he said tentatively, 'there's something awfully familiar about that description. Didn't you have a thing with a chap out at Duxford last September?'

'Sort of.'

'How sort of ?'

'Sort of yes.'

'Sort of yes with a chap who got shot up in a Hurricane and now pushes little models around a map with a sort of snooker rest?'

'If you put it like that, yes.'

'How else could I put it? What you're saying is that you passed this Wotsisname—'

'Giles Carver-Little, actually.'

'Whatever. This English toff with too many names gets passed from one sister to the other like a brown-paper parcel.'

'A brown-paper parcel? No. Not at all. More like some delicacy from Fortnum's in a little white box all done up with a pinky silk ribbon and a gold-edged card saying, "To my darling sister, all my love Masha".'

Good God, it was rich. He had often wondered if there was anything of which these two were not capable.

'I mean, if you found out about something jolly good wouldn't you tip off a mate about it?'

'Don't make it sound like a tip for the Derby. What you're telling me is that the two of you are willing to share lovers.'

'Not literally, not any more. We haven't done threesomes for a while. But yes. I mean. Bloody hell, why not?'

'Don't you think it's all a bit melodramatic? Everyone having everyone else?'

'Not in the least. I simply let my sister in on a good thing. As for having everyone else . . . isn't that just that Darwin chap – evolution,

survival of the fittest and all that?'

'Herbert Spencer,' said Troy.

Masha mused.

'No. Can't say I've had him. Don't think I've ever had a Herbert, in fact. But you can't really expect me to remember the lot now, can you? Friend of yours, is he?'

'I meant,' Troy persisted, with wasted logic, 'that the survival of the fittest was said by Spencer not Darwin, and I cannot for one moment see how you can pass off what you get up to as the ascent of the species.'

'Selective wotsit? Natural thingies?' Masha ventured.

'Shared shagging,' Troy said.

'Quite,' said his sister. 'I mean. Wouldn't you?'

Troy said nothing. Yet again the woman had gone beyond the bounds of what he knew.

They rode awhile in silence. Troy had no wish to feed whatever bizarrely amoral trend of thought might be lurking deeper in the pit that was his sister's psyche. They had crossed into Hertfordshire ten minutes ago. Home, after all, was not far away. It just seemed that way and had for a while – but as the car passed through the gateposts of Mimram (the gates having gone to make Spitfires in 1940), rounded the curving, crisply brown winter beeches at the head of the drive and the house sprang into view, Troy lost mental sight and sound of his sister. His childhood home. The rotting pile his father had bought in 1910 and had never quite finished restoring. An English country seat crossed with a Russian *dacha*. It was like a Mexican blanket, thought Troy, ragged at one corner where the artist had left loose threads and thus allowed his soul's escape from his art. His father had escaped into death, and Troy's own words to the Big Man came back to him in all their crassness – if he could get him alone he'd tell him so. 'You might as well live' seemed so inadequate in the face of all that Mimram now dragged out of him.

He turned to Masha, said, 'Home.' And thought that perhaps his inflexion had not been as intended for she said, 'Where did you think we were going?'

§ 4

Christmas came to drive him mad. Christmas at the family home seemed tailor-made to drive him mad. It was their second without his father – Troy was certain his mother counted 'dead Christmases' – one of many without brother Rod, a pilot on Tempest fighters, stationed in France, or the brothers-in-law Hugh and Lawrence, both doing their bit for King and Country. It was, Troy thought, a return to the infantile: too many women to remind him that he was the baby of the family at twenty-nine and would for ever be so. Yet it was lavish in a way few English families could extend to in the winter of 1944, for his mother raised not only leeks but potatoes in her greenhouse, fresh as June for Christmas Day, turkeys in a pen on the south lawn and Brussels sprouts on a vast raised bed in her vegetable garden. She had propped up her failing limbs and dug for victory since the first blast of war in 1939. Nonetheless he had had all the gin and charades he could take by Boxing Day, so his mother suggested to him that it might be a good idea if he invited some of his 'chums' round for a day or two. He leapt at the chance, rang Jack Wildeve and rang Kolankiewicz.

Kolankiewicz said, 'And your lessons, my boy?'

'My lessons?'

'You are bored already. Give Bob Churchill a call and get down to business.'

To his surprise Churchill readily agreed, said that he had not been to Mimram since he had personally delivered a hand-made shotgun to Troy's father in 1928.

Churchill was last to arrive, rolling up the drive at the wheel of a '34 Buick, a huge two-seater, complete with dickey seat propped open and covered in tarpaulin. He was in tweed, all set for a pre-war country weekend. The Big Man slid out from the passenger seat, still in his LCC Heavy Rescue outfit, and muttered 'Wotcher.' He unroped the snow-spattered tarp from the dickey and unloaded a pile of darkly polished, dovetail-jointed, brass-plated, mahogany carrying cases. He set them on the drive, a neat and presumably lethal pile at their feet.

'Don't expect me to hump the lot on me tod,' he said.

'You came prepared, then?' Troy stated the obvious.

'Oh yes,' said Churchill. 'We'll tackle the lot. Smith and Wesson, Colt, Winchester, Mauser, Walther, Schmeisser – get you familiar with them all.'

The Big Man picked up two cases and stomped off into the house. Churchill fished his dinner togs from the dickey seat, crumpled on their hanger. Handed them to Troy. A black tent of a jacket and capacious trousers.

'You came over-prepared, then?'

'I did?'

'We haven't dressed for dinner since before the war. But don't let me put you off. My mother will be delighted.'

'Y'know, the last time I was here your father was in . . . what shall I call it? One of his moods. Not only would he not dress for dinner he wouldn't dress at all. Spent two days in his dressing-gown . . . wouldn't shave, often as not wouldn't speak.'

'He could be like that. I've seen dinner pass with him sitting like Banquo's ghost at the end of the table.'

'And at other times—'

'You wished you knew how to make him shut up?'

'Exactly,' said Churchill.

'I can promise you a more customary evening,' said Troy. 'We are none of us enough like the old man to put you through that again.'

He spoke too soon.

§ 5

Troy's mother had gone to bed after the main course, leaving Troy, Kolankiewicz, Wildeve and one sister to finish the meal alone. She had been charmed by Churchill's dressing for dinner, something Jack and Troy chose not to do and something Kolankiewicz never would, but perhaps the presence of two such trenchermen as Kolankiewicz and Churchill had proved too much for the old lady. Troy had seen few men with the appetite of Bob Churchill. But he, at least, was virtually teetotal. Kolankiewicz could drink a pub dry. The Big Man had declined to join them on the grounds that 'an evenin' of toff chat would like as not bore the britches off me and, worse, lead to me missing me favourite programme on the wireless'. A pity: Troy had wanted to see the look on his face when he realised there was a Sasha as well as a Masha. As identical twins went, they were identical. Troy had never had any trouble telling them apart, but he'd known his own brother get them mixed up; he'd known both of them to exploit the fact for all it was worth, and, as yet, time and chance had not wrought enough differences in their characters that one could drive a playing card between them. They were, as Troy was wont to think and utter, one dreadful woman with two bodies. He decided to reward the Big Man for his churlishness by letting him find out the hard way. Masha had gone home on Boxing Day: let him 'discover' sister Sasha for himself. All the same the Big Man had been right about toff chat. Even Wildeve was stifling yawns as Kolankiewicz unburdened himself of one of the many theses he seemed to store up in a mental sack. Troy thought that conversations a bit like this, though surely less intense, must be taking place all over the country – 'when the war is over' had all but displaced 'before the war' as an opening gambit.

'It won't be the same,' Churchill was saying. 'It can't be the same.'

'You're speaking professionally?' Troy asked.

'Indeed I am. But it's your profession as much as mine.'

'What are you expecting? A sudden surge in the possession of guns?'

'Goes almost without saying. Call it the debris of war. Any war. The flotsam and jetsam. Whatever shade of government we have, whatever system we set up for the demobilisation of a million men-at-arms, we'll never get back so much as a fraction of the handguns we've issued.'

'Souvenirs,' Wildeve offered. 'All my uncles kept an old Webley in the desk drawer throughout the twenties. We boys thought it was great fun. Never saw one fired, though.'

'Lower your sights a little,' said Churchill. 'What happens to a handgun in the possession of your uncles is a world away from what happens to it in the hands of a man for whom it has become simultaneously his first taste of freedom and power.'

'Eh?'

'Bob is saying,' Troy said, 'that we can expect a crime wave as soon as our boys get home.'

'Really?'

It wasn't that Jack was thick, thought Troy, more that he was distracted. He had had the feeling for several minutes now that Sasha had been playing footsie with him under the table – the slope of her torso, the sense that she was stretching out, the seductive grin on her too, too pretty face – and as Jack's innocent 'ehs' and 'reallies' mounted he had been certain that the damn woman had winked at him.

'Jack, we've turned a million men loose on the continent. Some may come back and settle for being bank clerks or hewing coal again but as many won't. The Labour Party may talk of a quiet revolution after the war. What they don't see is that it's happened already. It wasn't necessary to politicise the working classes, it was necessary merely to turn them loose. And when they get back they may well just take what they want. Legally or not. They won't wait on a change of government, and they won't tuck their old Webleys or their "souvenir" Lugers in a desk drawer to amuse the kiddies with.'

'But,' said Wildeve, 'it didn't happen that way after the last war, now, did it?'

'That was a very different war,' said Churchill. 'Men came back hammered into the ground. It may not be for a man of my age to say this, and I certainly wouldn't say it in the presence of a serving soldier, but this generation, this English generation, has got off lightly. It could have been so much worse.'

Kolankiewicz, having kicked off this discussion, had said nothing for several minutes. His interjection cut through brusquely: 'You English. You English. The island mentality. The compromise with history. You do not know the half of it.'

'Meaning?' said Troy.

'Where were you when the war ended?'

'What's that got to do with it?'

'Humour me. I am a cranky old Pole.'

'I was three,' said Troy, with a hint of exasperation, 'and Jack wasn't even born.'

'I was thirty-two, pretty well where I am now, doing pretty much what I'm doing now,' said Churchill.

'And I,' said Kolankiewicz, 'was a twenty-year-old conscript in what remained of the Polish regiments of the Imperial Russian Army. Forced to fight a war to defend a country we hated against a country we hated almost as much. Poland has always been in the middle. So much in the middle that for hundreds of years at a time you find it erased from the atlas and all but erased from history. The war you date as ending in 1918 ended a year earlier for the whole of Poland and Russia. And in its place began another which has never ended. When the Germans put Lenin in that sealed train to the Finland Station, they had sent us a time-bomb. By 1920 I was a prisoner of the Whites. Suspected of being a Red, wanting merely to be a Pole. Stuck on a train of cattle wagons on the new border with Poland and shipped east. You may say I had not run fast enough. Quite so. A lesson hard learnt. Ever since I have not ceased to run. I have lived in the same house in the same backwater avenue in Hampstead Garden Suburb for sixteen years now – and still I run. Every day and every night I run. What do you English know of running?'

It was a blunt, almost brutal little speech. A rain of bricks and rubble clunking down around them, bouncing the cutlery and shattering the china. In a few swift sentences Kolankiewicz had demolished the edifice of argument, pulled racial rank on them all and upped the ante. There was a pause as he helped himself to more port. This time, Troy was certain, Sasha had winked at Wildeve.

'What you are both focusing on,' Kolankiewicz went on, 'are the social and criminal consequences of demobilisation. I cannot fault you on this, Bob. You are, in all probability, right. What I saw in Poland and Russia after the last war were the effects of total war on the civil population. On those who did not or could not fight, and on those who were too young to fight.'

'Total War?' said Troy.

'The phrase has been in use for a while you will find.'

'It's your use of it that bothers me. It's used to describe . . . how shall I put it . . . a mobilisation of resources . . . you're talking about it as a culture . . . as a substitute for culture.'

'If it is all you know of life, if it has shaped the values by which you live, then it is your culture. Substitute or not. I met it face to face. I said I was not swift enough to run in 1917. It would have been convenient to find myself on the German boundaries, to be part of the newly mooted Poland. *Mea culpa*, I found myself in the hell that was the embryonic Soviet Union. And, as I was saying, I found myself with a one-way ticket to Siberia. It was January. Not the kindest of months. The train ground to a halt in a mountain of snow just this side of the Urals. I never did find out where – Mumsk or Bumsk, it scarcely matters. Among my many travelling companions was another ragamuffin such as I was myself. But he was older than me, older than any of us young men being herded east. I knew him. I'd known him as a sergeant on the eastern front, under the name of Ivan Volkonsky – the name he was doubtless born with, but I also knew his *nom de guerre*. Since 1917 he had been Leonid Rodnik, a general in Trotsky's Red Army. He knew me too. His secret became a bond, as it were. The idiots guarding us would have had a prize, if only they had realised just who they had. How they caught him Rodnik never said. But, as the train sat the best part of a month in the deadly cold of a Russian winter, I got to know him rather better. I got to know his life story and he mine – what little there was of it. Indeed, I owe much of my command of Russian to his tutelage.

'Each wagon would be allowed out once a day to piss, to shit and to gather wood. We stripped the forest of kindling while the Whites watched, and fed the pot-bellied stove inside our wagon. And when we ran short Rodnik opened up his shirt and revealed what had kept him warm those weeks, a lining of several million roubles in Tsarist currency. We fed that into the stove too – I was warmed by the heat of burning money. Rodnik started to laugh. Infectious. The whole wagon joined in, hysterical with laughter at the thought of burning that which most of them would have killed for but a few years earlier.

'We starved and we fell ill, and each day the guards would take the most infirm among us and despatch them to the next world with a bullet to the back of the head. It was obvious, even disregarding the fate that awaited us on the other side of the mountain, that if the train did not get through the next tunnel soon we would all die in the same fashion. The rough justice of the judge with the rifle. You may recall the long passages in *War and Peace* when the French march their prisoners westward shooting the wounded as they go. It was not unlike. One of those moments when you seek no parallel in literature. I have never seen myself as Bezukhov. Indeed, I have never been able to read the book since. No matter.

'As dead wood grew scarcer the guards escorted us further and further from the train. Every so often someone would make a break for it and get a bullet in the back. We were lucky. I escaped without a scratch. Rodnik took a bullet in the arm. But we ran. In half an hour they gave up the search. Why waste a bullet? Winter would kill us anyway.

'On the third day we stumbled into a dream . . . no . . . a fairy tale . . . a setting from the *Gebrüder Grimm*. It was dark–an hour or so after dusk. We came upon a clearing in the forest. Tiny huts built of branches, a campfire burning, a stew of some forest creature bubbling, an array of utensils beaten out of tin, a hard circle of earth, clean and worn as though someone had lived there a while – but of that someone there was not a sign. So . . . we raised the pot and we ate. We had neither of us shown any ability to live off the land. We had starved for those three days, and for weeks before that we had lived on rations of nothing but oats and kasha. It was a matter of minutes before I saw them. They had been watching us all along. Then they came out of the trees, those hideous, blackened bodies . . . and not one of them four feet tall. A dozen children living wild in the forest. Rodnik put down his tin plate and stood to speak to them. The first child stuck a spear in his chest, another aimed at me and missed. A third crawled along the ground and sank its teeth into Rodnik's leg. We ran again. Or I ran and Rodnik hobbled, dragging the demented child along by its teeth. I leapt a ditch. Rodnik could not. The weight of the child held him down. He screamed at me, "Run," and I ran. I looked back and saw children swarming over him like flies upon a carcass. I spent a night in the forest. I circled. Determined to rescue Rodnik, if I could. Not knowing the folly of such a thought. The next day I entered the same clearing. The children were gone, the campfire burnt still. But there was no sign of Rodnik. I approached the pot, prepared once more to rob Lilliput to keep Brobdingnag alive. I picked up the beaten tin ladle, stuck it into the stew and raised a mouthful to my lips, all the time looking around for the children. And from the corner of my eye I saw a pile of long bones, and another pile of the clothes Rodnik had been wearing. And I knew what was in the pot. I knew what it was I held to my lips. I had almost eaten the delicacy known as long pig. Those children had killed, skinned and jointed Rodnik, put him in the pot and eaten him. I ran. It seems to me now that I ran all the way to England. All the way to Hampstead Garden Suburb. When I die you can shovel a spadeful of North London into my coffin, much as Chopin's friends shovelled a bit of Poland in with him. Whatever . . . I ran, and they did not catch me.

'Who knows where those children had come from? How far they in their turn had run to escape the war? Who knows how long they had lived like that, without parents, without teachers? Who knows how long they went on like that? The little cannibals of the Russian forest. Orphans of the total war. Stripped of all morality. Stripped of anything you or I might recognise as civilised values. That is total war. And I will warn you now that there is a whole generation growing up in England stripped of conventional morality. Cannibals? Perhaps that is unlikely . . . but a generation that survives by taking what it wants?'

Not so long ago it seemed – had it been last February or March in the depths of winter? – Troy had faced a bunch of urban urchins in Stepney in London's East End. He recalled

24

the mixture of innocence and greed that had flickered across eight small faces as he bribed them all to help him search a Blitz bombsite for the remains of a corpse. His old mentor Sgt Bonham had been outraged. Not simply the bribing of kids, that alone was bad enough, but the knowledge of what they might find. Troy had had no doubts. He was not corrupting youth. Youth had been corrupted long before he got there. Those boys had had the best part of five years of war. They were ten years old or thereabouts and their memories of life before the war must have been scant. They'd known little else but rationing and deprivation – wanting was their world. But, try as he might, Troy could not see the comparison Kolankiewicz was making between the savagery he depicted and the children he had met. It was still an innocence of a sort. Take away the simple fact of death – a body to whose fate the kids had been indifferent not, it would seem, out of callousness or war's familiarity but out of a paucity of imagination – take away that body and it wasn't Kolankiewicz's primitive nightmare in a Russian forest it was . . . it was . . . *The Coral Island* . . . it was adventures with Jack and Ralph. Wasn't it?

He looked round for his Jack. But Wildeve had slipped out silently. So had Sasha. Ah well, he thought, there were worse things in the world than your best friend fucking your sister. Weren't there?

§ 6

The next morning the Big Man made a makeshift shooting range in the orchard out of straw bales and cardboard. He painted up a rough series of concentric circles. A target so big perhaps he thought even Troy could not miss it. But Troy did.

Churchill tried him out first on the police-issue Webley. Troy knew – he'd been told – he couldn't hit the side of a barn door. Not with a weapon as clumsy and imprecise as this he couldn't. He stuck out his arm, fired off three rounds and missed the target every time. He paused and could have sworn he heard the Big Man sucking air through his teeth.

'Ignore him,' said Churchill. 'The only opinion that counts is mine. It's about body and posture, Frederick. Don't hold the gun as though you're offering it up for sacrifice. Pull back your arm and tuck yourself in a bit tighter.'

'But then I can't use the sight.'

'Sights on a handgun are a waste of time. The best you can do is aim your whole body in the right direction. So, swing round, full on to the target, pull back . . .'

Troy fired a fourth round that nicked the edge of the Big Man's target. He hoped he was smiling, not smirking, but getting it right, or marginally right, for the first time was enormously satisfying.

'Fire the next,' Churchill said, 'and if you hit it again make the adjustment to hit closer with the one after.'

'Adjustment? What adjustment?'

Churchill swayed gently, rolls of fat surely quivering beneath his winter tweeds, feet planted firmly in the crisp snow. He looked like a woolly Buddha performing some ritual exercise. 'Flow,' he was saying. 'I can't think of any other way to put it. The whole body flows with it. You don't steer . . . you just flow. It's like riding a bike.'

This at least made sense to Troy. That was the great thing about a childhood spent on a bike. You thought, it did. Symbiosis between boy and machine. All he had to do was to think of the gun, any gun, as a Rover bike with a Hercules three-speed.

The fifth clipped the edge again. He thought, 'in a bit', and placed the final shot in the second inner ring. And all, he thought, without seeming to have to do anything. His bike had gone round corners without him having to steer it.

'Not bad, not bad at all,' Churchill said.

'Always knew you could do it,' the Big Man lied.

'Reload. Fire off another six, and then we'll try an automatic.'

Two misses four inners.

Troy would always have a 'thing' about the American army-issue Colt .45 automatic. It was the gun that had put him in hospital. He said nothing to Churchill, picked it up and loaded.

Something must have been obvious, perhaps the hesitation,

perhaps the sense that Troy had weighed up the gun in his hand as an outward manifestation that he was also weighing up the idea.

'Anything wrong?' said Churchill.

Troy clapped a hand to his side. Roughly where the bullet had caught him.

'Oh, I see.'

'I really ought to get over it,' Troy said.

'Indeed. It's hardly more than a superstition if you think about it.'

'Quite.'

'One Colt is much the same as another.'

'I know.'

'Except, of course, that this isn't a Colt.'

'Eh?'

'Well, it's the Colt patent, all right, but Colt didn't make it.'

'Eh?'

'Well, wartime demand got so heavy they . . . they . . . franchised the manufacture. I'm sure that's the word, "franchise". If you look at the grip you'll find the name of the manufacturer.'

Troy took his thumb off the grip and opened his palm. 'Good Lord . . . Singer. Don't they make . . .'

'Sewing-machines? Indeed they do. Now, sing along with me: the sewing-machine, the sewing-machine . . . it's a girl's best friend!'

And he burst into song. A clear, accomplished baritone. Troy did not sing, but at every repetition of 'sewing-machine' he squeezed off a round.

The Big Man had begun his retreat from the matter once it was obvious that Troy was not going to make a complete fool of himself, and had felt, after less than an hour out in the cold, the pressing need of his elevenses: a Thermos flask of hot tea, a ham sandwich and that morning's pitifully thin copy of the *Daily Mail*. Once Churchill began to sing, his interest perked up again and his bass joined Churchill's baritone – a fat man's chorus: 'the sewing-machine, the sewing-machine.'

Two misses, four inners. Troy changed magazines and reversed the proportions. The gun behaved differently. It felt to Troy as though it could run away with him, get so easily beyond his control. The escaped bicycle. But he could not deny it was a more accurate gun and easier to handle once that initial runaway feeling had been mastered. With his third magazine he got all six on the target. Low-scoring shots in Bisley terms, but in Churchill terms they were 'at least going in the right direction'. They worked at it until lunchtime, alternating between the Webley and the Colt – and the inevitable fatties' chorus – ending with twelve shots apiece from the Smith & Wesson and the Schmeisser.

The Smith & Wesson took him by surprise. Long and slender, unusually heavy, with a surprisingly small bore – but it blew the target to smithereens and kicked back at him like an angry pig. In complete contradiction to his usual body-hugging technique, Churchill had him hold it at arm's length. With each shot his arm bucked as though it had been jerked upward by an invisible spring.

'What on earth is this? It feels like a hand-held cannon.'

'Pretty much what it is,' said Churchill. 'The manufacturers describe it as a big man's gun. But that's advertising for you. It's what they call a Magnum. They've been around for a few years now. J. Edgar Hoover supposedly had the first, and I believe General Patton carries one with a pearl handle. But that's Patton for you. Essentially – a .357 bullet backed up by a whopping great cartridge. If you look at the chamber you'll see it's out of all proportion to the barrel. That accounts for most of the extra weight. A small bullet propelled at high speed by a big charge. You could shoot through a brick wall with it.'

Troy stared down at the monstrosity in his hand. 'Why,' he asked, 'would anyone want to?'

'Call it stopping power. Hit someone with a round from a Magnum, they won't get up again.'

Troy put the gun gently back on the wooden case. He rather thought it had just displaced the Colt in his disaffections.

At lunch Kolankiewicz ate behind a copy of the *News Chronicle*. The Big Man still pondered his *Daily Mail*.

'Is he any better?' Troy heard Kolankiewicz ask.

'That barn door's getting a bit closer,' the Big Man replied.

After lunch Churchill said, 'I've asked him to rig up a clay shoot on one of your meadows. Have you ever used a shotgun before?'

'My dad let me – no, made me have a go with that one you

made for him. Can't say I thought much about it at the age of thirteen. I certainly didn't go back for a second crack at it.'

'It's just the thing for teaching you to sight aim.'

It may well be true, thought Troy, after twenty or more cartridges had burst uselessly against the clouds, but by the time you've sighted up a clay pigeon it's somewhere else in the sky.

'I'm sorry, Bob,' he said. 'Let's go back to handguns. I'm clearly hopeless at this.'

Before Churchill could answer a dishearteningly cheery voice could be heard saying, 'Half a mo', you chaps. I want a go.'

Troy turned to see his sister Sasha crunching down the path in her wellies, wrapped up against the cold in her habitual black Russian-doll outfit, furry earflaps flapping, toting, breech broken across her arm, their father's 1928 handmade Churchill shotgun. Something Troy had thought twice about using in front of its creator.

'Not chaps only, is it?' she said in pure defiance, meaning that if it was they could just get stuffed. She had come out to play and would play regardless of what they thought. 'I'll show you how it's done, li'l bro. Rightie-ho, Fatty, let 'em rip.'

''Ere,' said the Big Man. 'Oos she calling fat? I never been called fat before. Robust maybe, but fat? Never!'

Troy looked at Churchill. Churchill looked at the Big Man, the Big Man looked at Troy. Troy silently weighed up the precision of Sasha's epithet, decided she was right, and nodded to him. This was not the moment to explain the sisters to him. Clay after clay exploded into shards as Sasha, quite literally, showed him how it was done. Churchill, recognising a natural when he saw one, silently deferred.

'You don't follow, brer. You let it come to you. See?'

Another clay soared above them. The gun seemed to dangle at the end of Sasha's arms about waist height. Then, without any sign of haste, she raised the gun to her cheek, looked down the barrel and blew the clay to smithereens. You don't follow, you let it come to you. You don't steer, you simply flow. Was it, he thought, all going to be quite so arcane? The initiation into a Zen mystery?

'You didn't think I could do this, did you?' Sasha whispered to Troy.

'It's not a matter of think,' he whispered back. 'I didn't *know* you could do it. Is there a knack, some secret you'd care to share with me, or are you going to make it into another of your little conspiracies?'

'No,' she said, at a normal volume, head swivelling just to be certain they could all hear. 'No knack. Just the orthodox technique, wouldn't you agree, Mr Churchill? And I do not conspire. I imagine.'

'And what,' Churchill asked, walking into the trap Troy had sidestepped, 'do you imagine?'

'I imagine,' she said, sighting up another, 'that all these wretched clays . . .' another bit the dust mid-sentence '. . . that all these wretched clays are my wretched husband. And as a result . . . one never misses.'

Troy heard the Big Man chuckle, saw Churchill raise his eyes to heaven much as he did when Kolankiewicz swore.

'And,' Troy whispered, 'what do you think your wretched husband was doing while you were rogering Jack last night?'

'Don't know. Don't bloody well care! Pull!' Sasha blasted off again, then beckoned Troy in closer.

'Young Jack was deevy. Simply deevy. Why didn't you tip me the wink before? Keeping him all to yourself.'

Troy said nothing.

Over the next week Churchill took Troy from inners to bullseyes with half a dozen different handguns. The Walther, the Browning, the Mauser. His own progress astounded him. He began to wonder if he might learn to sing as well – another art at which he had long considered he had no talent whatsoever. The sewing-machine, the sewing-machine.

And his sister Sasha took him to the point where he was hitting forty-nine clays out of fifty. She struck him as a surprisingly good tutor. It put him in mind of a day long ago, lost in his adolescence. The first occasion on which black tie had meant just that. Standing in front of a mirror swearing at a recalcitrant bow-tie. It was pointless asking his dad. His dad would not give a damn about such things. Ties were part of the rules, and whilst the old man knew perfectly well how to tie a bow, he saw no reason whatsoever to initiate his son into rules when rules were made for other people, not for his son and certainly not for him. In the absence of big brother Rod, it had fallen to the sisters to intervene. He was twelve and still shorter than them. They took it in turns to stand behind him and guide his hands in theirs, weaving around his throat like the wings of birds, cool and light. For years they had thought him so young as to be hardly worth notice; they had dressed and undressed in front of him without a shred of self-consciousness. This was the first time they had 'dressed' him. He recalled with neither guilt nor embarrassment, just the sharp backward stab of memory so vivid as to be tangible, the involuntary erection he had had as Sasha – or was it Masha? – had pressed her hips into him to reach the closer.

Early in the new year Churchill said, 'I must get back to town. Can I suggest you come with me? I've a couple of customers to see, but once work's out of the way there's one last gun I'd like you to try.'

Just when Troy thought he'd tried them all. But, then, the first time he'd met Churchill he'd interrupted him in the act of stripping down a Bren gun. And they hadn't tried that.

'It's not your Bren, is it? I've really no need of a working knowledge of a Bren gun.'

'No. It's not. It's the kind of weapon I couldn't bring here. In fact it's the kind of weapon I wouldn't let out of the house. If I thought you needed lessons on a Bren I'd've stuck it in the dickey and brought it down. No, you come up to London. It's something you need to try.'

§ 7

'Again' had paid off. An afternoon's practice with a sawn-off shotgun had paid off. Down in the cellar that ran from his shop out under the arches of Orange Street Churchill pronounced himself well pleased with Troy's marksmanship.

'You may not be Buffalo Bill but, if I say so myself, I'm a good teacher and you've proved a good pupil. I'd enter you for Bisley if I knew the war would be over by next year, and I thought for a moment you'd do it.'

The end of the cellar was now a mess of straw and sawdust – Troy's cardboard assailants lay in shreds. He laid the shotgun back on the workbench between the Colt .45 and the Smith & Wesson Magnum. His sense of distaste did not pass readily.

'You're being very kind about all this, Bob, and I couldn't be more grateful for the time you've put in. But I don't think I'll ever have an affinity for guns. I'm a firm believer in an unarmed police force . . . and for the life of me I cannot conceive of the circumstances in which I'd have to use a weapon like this.'

'Nor can I. I'm a believer in an unarmed force myself. I'd hate to see London become New York or Chicago. But that's hardly the point, is it? The point is, as you so inadvertently and appropriately put it, "the life of you". If we're dealing only in known quantities, as it were, I'd've brought you up to scratch on the standard-issue handguns and left it at that. You'd be *au fait* with the Webley and not much else. The point is what a villain comes at you with, and what he can do to you if you don't react properly. It's not what you do when you fire this at one of the buggers. It's what they do to you. And if Kolankiewicz's thesis of the moral decay we can expect in post-war life is to be believed,

God knows what that will be.'

'I'll try to bear that in mind,' said Troy, forgetting already.

2

Blue Rondo

§ 8

Onions stuck his head round the office door.

'Champagne in my office. Ten minutes. OK?'

Troy sat behind his desk still scribbling notes to himself.

Wildeve was staring out of the window, watching the first hint of summer dance on the Thames in a sparkle of white light. 'It'll be Asti Spumante,' he said, without looking up. 'Was last time.'

'Don't knock it,' Troy said. 'He tries. And if he can't celebrate a thief-taking as rich as this one then things have come to a pretty pass. Serious Crime have been after Alf Marx for about as long as I can remember. If I were Stan I'd pop the cork on a few bubbles myself.'

Ten minutes later they found their way to Onions' outer office, crowded with coppers. John Brocklehurst, Chief Superintendent of the Serious Crime Squad, was on the receiving end of handshakes and backslaps. Madge, Onions's secretary, was spilling fake champagne over the carpet and getting very little in the glasses. Wildeve relieved her of the task and popped corks with the ease born of years of practice. Onions's inner door opened a fraction. Troy saw a large blue eye peer out at him, and a hand beckoned.

Inside, Onions was struggling with his uniform. 'I can't do these bloody buttons up.'

'Then don't.'

'Can't host a do like this wi'out a uniform. Don't be daft.'

Onions, like Troy, hated uniforms. After thirty-five years in plain clothes the assumption of office as the Metropolitan Police Commissioner had the occasional wearing of a uniform as one of its many drawbacks. In the unlikely event of the job ever being offered to Troy he'd decided to say no.

'Must have put on a few pounds since last time. Do I look fat?'

Troy had no idea how to answer this. Instead he gripped Onions's tunic with both hands and forced the blue serge over the silver buttons.

Onions exhaled. The fabric stretched across his belly tight as a snare drum.

'Grand,' he said. 'Grand. Are they all out there?'

'I think so,' said Troy.

'And John?'

'A bit red in the face. You know Brock, doesn't take centre stage easily.'

''Appen if he did he'd be wearing this fancy get-up, not me. Right. How do I look?'

'Fine,' Troy lied. 'Fine.'

He watched Onions step into the throng, half listened as the top copper in the land congratulated his force on the arrest and conviction of East London's 'Mr Big', King Alf – Alfred Joseph Marx – stopped listening as Onions praised the jury system, the Twelve Good Men who'd just voted to bang up Alf Marx for fifteen years. Troy rambled into mental arithmetic: Alf Marx would be sixty-seven when he got out, sixty-two if he kept his nose clean, though he was unlikely to do that, and would emerge some time in 1974, a spent force. The world would have moved on, changed around him, while time stood still in whatever maximum-security nick housed him.

Troy, standing between Wildeve and Swift Eddie Clark, felt Wildeve nudge him. Saw Onions's eyes upon him. When the blue gaze left them, Wildeve whispered, 'You were daydreaming.'

Troy whispered back, 'I was just thinking. Nature abhors a vacuum.'

'What the hell is that supposed to mean?'

'The king is dead. Long live the king.'

Champagne soon ran out. Whisky appeared as if from nowhere. Detectives drank whisky – neat, or drowned in half a tumbler of water, it seemed to be the professional drug. Madge went home. Swift Eddie parked himself in a corner with a triple and farted.

Troy and Wildeve found themselves the unwelcome recipients of Onions's pissed bonhomie; the buttons popped on his tunic, one arm around Brock's shoulders, telling him what he had told Troy an hour before. 'If you'd played your cards right, it could have been you in this damn monkey suit.'

Brock answered quietly, 'But I didn't want it, Stan. I always say it pays to know your place. My dad was a pork butcher in Nottingham.
One step at a time he said. So I make detective chief superintendent. A pretty big step, mind. Who knows where my lads'll end up?'

Onions ignored the common sense of what Brock had said and heard only the deference. 'My old man was a bloody millwright in Rochdale! You sayin' I shouldn't have taken the job?'

'I was saying nothing of the sort, Stan. I was saying I shouldn't have taken it, and I didn't. I didn't even get the chance.'

Onions pondered this. Poured himself another Scotch and failed to see that one statement or the other had to be a lie. Troy knew the truth: men like Brock were never made commissioner. Class alone might not account for it – character had a lot to do with it. And Brock, though ambitious, was not pushy, and, above all, was not the diplomat that Stan was. He'd just demonstrated the limit of his diplomacy in avoiding telling Stan that he should have said no to the job. Men like Stan did not get made Met Commissioner either, but he had. All too often the job went to the Troys and the Wildeves of the world. Men whose birth and education marked them for leadership in a country hidebound by class. Stan was a changeling – brash and Lancashire, magnificent and magisterial, pushy and proud, sly, dissembling, deceitful and manipulative. Everything Troy and Wildeve were, but with a clogs-and-cap accent and a ruthless short-back-and-sides. Jack looked like a naval officer, a minor film star in the mould of Michael Wilding or Stewart Granger. Troy looked like a demonic faun from a Diaghilev ballet. Stan looked like a trade-union leader, more Fred Kite than Ernie Bevin – an excellent candidate for one of the most devious jobs imaginable, but the wrong class to make it work for him. Brock could see the difference, Troy could, and doubtless Wildeve too, but through the bottom of his glass Stan was darkly, if momentarily, blind to it.

Half an hour later they poured him into a squad car and packed him off to Acton and the tender mercies of his daughter Valerie. Troy watched Swift Eddie and Jack Wildeve, both dwellers south-of-theriver, make their way towards Westminster Bridge. He found himself alone with Brocklehurst.

'One for the road?' Brock asked.

Troy had had one token glass of champagne and avoided the whisky. The merest hint of a hangover could put him on the wagon for weeks. 'I, er. . .'

'For me,' Brock said. 'Just for me. You and me, Freddie. There's no other buggers here. Besides, I want a drink with a man of me own rank.'

Troy could not say no now. Brock had pulled the old pals' act on him mercilessly. It meant there were things he had to say. He was probably going to cry into his glass and say things he would never dream of uttering to other ranks.

They picked up Brock's Wolseley from the motor pool, and drove almost to Troy's house, to the Chandos, a small pub on the corner of St Martin's Lane and William IV Street. If Brock and booze got the better of him, Troy could roll home from here. And it was far enough from the Yard to bank on not meeting other coppers.

Brock bought himself a beer and a shot, smiled at Troy's request for ginger-beer shandy, pulled out his fags with nicotined fingers and lit what was probably his fiftieth Senior Service of the day. It seemed to Troy that Brock always walked in a fug of fags, that they coloured his hands, his teeth and quite possibly his personality. There was, he had thought these last few years, something in Brock that had dried up and shrivelled.

'How old are you, Freddie?'

Silly question, but Troy was the youngest chief super at the Yard and accustomed to accounting for his age. 'I'll be forty-four in the summer.'

'I'm fifty-two,' Brock said. 'You start to feel it when you get to my age.'

Silently Troy thought this a preposterous remark.

'I've begun to realise. There's not much time left.'

Troy said nothing, hoping not to have to tease a single word or phrase out of the man. Brock stared into his pint letting time, of which he now seemed to have so little, tick by.

'So I made me mind up. . .'

He was looking at Troy, almost as though he was willing him to finish the sentence for him. Troy didn't.

'I'm putting me papers in. Going. Retiring. Out to grass. *Finito*.'

'Is that what you want?' Even to Troy it sounded pathetic.

'I've had enough, Freddie. I've had enough. Enough is enough. And . . . I always wanted to get out while I was ahead of the game, winning. There'll be no bigger win than today. I'll put in me papers. Pick up me pension and me gold watch. Be out by the end of next month. Sell the house in Islington. Travel a bit. Who knows? Might even meet the right woman. Get married again. You never know.'

Brock, like Onions, was a widower. Jack had never married, a practised womaniser. Troy had married one summer, three years ago. By the autumn she had left him. He had not seen her for months now. He had to bend to see Brock's point of view. Men there were for whom home was not home without an aproned body bustling around a kitchen telling you whatever time you came in that you were late and your dinner was on the table. Men there were who could not sleep without a stout body denting the mattress next to them. Coppers' wives were an odd breed, as odd as the men themselves. Troy had never wanted one. It was probably all that men like Stan and Brock craved. Afterwards, dust gone to dust, their lives were hollow spaces vainly filled by an inflated notion of 'the job'. And if Brock was through with that . . .

He was not responding. Brock was nudging. 'And you, Fred? How long do you think you'll give it?'

For a second Troy had no idea what he meant. 'Give it? You mean when will I retire? I'm forty-three – I thought I just said that. I've never even thought about retirement.'

'Next year there's got to be an election. Mebbe this year – there's still time. Labour are a dead cert to win, a shoe-in, and you'll find yourself running the Murder Squad with your own brother as Home Secretary. Do you really want that? Do you think the brass'll find that acceptable?'

Troy had scarcely given the matter a deal of thought. His elder brother Rod had been an MP since the Labour landslide of 1945 – the khaki vote. He had served as a junior minister at the Air Ministry towards the fag end of the government and held on to his seat in what now seemed like interminable years of opposition. The Conservative Party had won the last two elections, survived the enforced retirement of Churchill, the madness of Eden, and now seemed to be riding out the stop-go chaos of an old romantic named Macmillan. The prospect of Rod becoming Home Secretary had been dangled before him for three years. It was above and beneath contemplation. Not worth the time it took to work up a worry.

'I'm sure if the brass find it impossible they'll let me know.'

'They can hardly be expected to tolerate a direct line from a chief super to the Home Secretary, now, can they? It's like a short-circuit.'

'"They", as you put it, is Stan. Stan has known Rod since before the war. I hardly think he'll feel undue access is being granted to me or undue political pressure put on him with me as the conduit.'

'You're playing the innocent, Freddie. You know as well as me it's a pig's ear of a situation. A right pickle.'

'Then I'll tackle the pickle when I come to it.'

Brock grinned, sniggered, and then laughed out loud. Troy was pleased. He could not have tolerated the conversation proceeding pofaced in this direction much longer. Yet to call time on a man who'd just celebrated his greatest triumph, just announced his abdication, seemed inexcusable. He was stuck with Brock until Brock called time and rolled home.

'How are your spuds this year?' he tacked away unsubtly.

They had this in common – all three of them, Brock, Troy and Stan: they passed their free time gardening. Troy in the ancient kitchen garden of his country house in Hertfordshire; Stan on an allotment in Acton; and Brock on a strip of reclaimed bombsite in Islington. He was forever digging out broken brick.

'Oh, not a bad year at all. Lovely crop of King Edwards on the way. As tall as an elephant's eye. And you?'

'A touch of wireworm last year,' said Troy. 'If I beat it this year I'll be delighted. Plants look healthy enough.'

'Not a problem you get on a mix of brick and subsoil, but you know what to do, don't you?'

Troy didn't.

'You let it grass over this winter and turf-strip it next spring. You'll catch most of the little buggers that way. Let 'em die off in your compost heap.'

By chucking-out time – not that anyone chucked out London bobbies – they had happily compared beetroot, leeks and carrots, and discussed the virtues of Troy's prize pig. Brock lamented the confines of Islington. Perhaps when he'd had his jaunt, found Miss Right – who knows? – he'd find somewhere you could park a pig.

Troy was sober. Brock was pissed, but no amount of Troy's cajoling would persuade him he was not fit to drive. Troy gave up the ghost of the argument. After all, there was no law against driving drunk, as long as you drove within the law. Once you broke the law, crossed the speed limit, bumped another car, shot a zebra crossing, then the police could nick you, and your drunkenness, or otherwise, would without doubt be a factor in the beak's sentence, but it was not unlawful *per se*.

'Knock it off, old son. I've driven wi' a damn sight more'n this inside o' me. Islington's three miles up the road. What can go wrong in three miles?'

Troy shrugged. All coppers drank and drove. They all felt the job bought them immunity. He and Brock stood on the pavement on the opposite side of the street, heard the bolts shot on the pub doors. Brock swayed slightly. Troy steadied him and steered him towards the car.

As Brock fiddled with his keys in the door, Troy said, 'You're quite sure?'

'Sure I'm sure. Stirling bloody Moss, that's me.'

'I meant about putting in your papers.'

'Already done it, old son.' Brock tapped the side of his nose. 'Slipped 'em on old Madge's desk after she went home. Stan'll get 'em Monday morning and that'll be that. You'll be in Monday, won't you?'

'Of course,' said Troy.

'Then ah'll see yer then.' Brock moved swiftly for a drunk: he

43

clasped Troy in a bear hug, crushed him to the ribs and let him go. 'Night, old son.'

Troy walked off. Stopped, turned, watched Brock climb into the driver's seat, waved pointlessly, and walked on towards home. The blast of the bomb lifted him off his feet. He hit the pavement ten yards away. The world turned green, then black. He sank into black as into the arms of a lover. It was all so familiar. Smothering, comforting, known.

§ 9

When Troy awoke his lover was sitting at his bedside, reading. He couldn't see the book's title. It and its jacket were a blur. So was her face, but if he couldn't recognise Foxx by the shape of her legs after three years . . . He watched her turn two pages before she looked up and saw that he had woken.

Anxiety written on her face. She turned in the chair. Eyes searching for a doctor. A nurse.

'It's all right,' Troy said softly. 'I can see, I can hear and I think I can think.'

She laid the book face down on the bed and took his right hand in both of hers, the meniscant bubble of tears forming in the corners of her eyes. 'Do you know what happened?'

'Car bomb,' he said, just as quietly. 'Somebody killed John Brocklehurst. I got in the way.'

The bubble burst. Tears coursing down her cheeks. Mascara staining.

'He is dead, isn't he?'

Foxx nodded. 'Could have been you,' she said at long last, her voice buried deep in her chest.

A white-coated doctor appeared behind her, whispered to her. She let go of Troy's hand. Walked away with half a dozen glances over her shoulder.

The doctor talked and touched at the same time. Flicked on a narrow-beam torch and plucked at Troy's eyelids with her thumb as she spoke. Troy vanished in a tunnel of blinding white light.

'So, Mr Troy, you can hear and you can see. You know, that was quite a blow you took to the head. Tell me, do you know where you are?'

Troy didn't.

'Charing Cross Hospital,' the doctor said, perching on the edge of Troy's bed.

Again? That figured. He and Brock had been only yards from it when the car went up.

'In fact, you almost made it here unassisted. The blast rolled you right to the doorway. All we had to do was carry you in on a stretcher.'

'Carried in,' Troy said. 'But I'll walk out?'

'Well, you broke nothing, and that's a minor miracle in itself. A few grazes and a lump the size of a tennis ball on your head. But that's what concerns me.'

She held up a hand. 'How many fingers?'

'It's all right,' Troy said. 'I'm not going to pretend. I'm seeing two of everything, perhaps three.'

'Then we'll be keeping you in for a while. Absolutely standard with head injuries – but I doubt it'll be long. No bloodclots on the brain, no hairline fractures. Your pulse and blood pressure are quite normal. Now, you must be feeling tired. Comas are like that. You sleep an age and wake up exhausted.'

'Coma,' said Troy, rolling the word around as though trying to divine a hidden meaning. 'How long?'

'Two and a half days. It's Monday morning.'

She told Troy that she would send Foxx back to him. Troy closed his eyes. She was right. He was knackered. He thought he would spare himself the pain of the overhead light. Why couldn't they put him in a dark room? He had no idea or intention to sleep, but he did. Red flames lapped around him. His ears rang with a cacophony of bells. His eyes flashed open. An act of will. The only sure-fire way to stop a dream. To wake. The figure at his bedside was not Foxx. It was a man. Troy willed resolution. Wildeve – Jack Wildeve.

'Good,' Jack said. 'I was just about to give up and let you sleep.'

'I was asleep?'

'Yes. You've slept about an hour, I should think. I sneaked in between that rather delicious doctor you've got and your Miss Foxx. She's getting a cup of tea. Strictly one at a time today.'

An hour? Good God – it had felt like a second anatomised. Time's merest measurable fragment.

'Is there anything you can tell me?'

'I doubt it. Brock . . . got into his car . . . tried to stop him . . . couldn't.'

'Why?'

'He was drunk. Didn't give a damn. I walked off. The car blew up. It . . . sounded like it went up with the ignition . . . can't be sure.'

'Sounds about right to me,' Jack said. 'Forensic say it was done with a length of cable running from the distributor under the car to a spark plug dangling in the neck of the tank. Very crude, but effective. As soon as Brock turned the key the petrol vapour would have exploded. The tank, the feed line and the engine would have followed in an almost instant reaction.'

Not instant enough. Troy could hear in the mind's ear the struggle of the starter motor, then the bangs of the explosion, three at least before he had fallen to Earth.

'I knew he was dead. As soon as I heard . . . no . . . felt the bang.'

For a second or two as he looked at Jack, Jack swam into clear focus and Troy could read his face plainly.

'Tell me,' he said. 'Tell me the truth.'

Jack would not now meet his gaze, but to Troy he had already dissolved into Jacks. One of them drew a sharp breath and said, 'Brock wasn't killed outright. He suffered almost ninety per cent burns. Damn Terylene suit went up like a roman candle, melted on him. Melted him. There was nothing left of his face but his eyes. But they got him out alive. Tried to treat his burns. Pumped him full of morphine to numb the pain. He had the constitution of an ox. Kept regaining consciousness. Kept asking after you. All the pain he was in and he kept asking for you. He died last night. About three in the morning. It really couldn't come soon enough. There never was a chance he could live with that sort of damage.'

Troy's mind clicked on, clicked back. His brother. The end

of the war. A celebration party at their father's old house in Hampstead for Rod's first election win. His old RAF mates turning up. Two faceless men. The angles and arches of noses and eyebrows dissolved into blobs and curves. The shiny skin of plastic surgery. The gung-ho optimism of one, the scarcely containable rage of the other. Brock would have been like that. Angry. Cursing God and Man and Fate.

§ 10

The next time Troy awoke it was with the sense that time had slipped. There was a big man, no, a fat man – this man was definitely fat – seated next to the bed leafing through the pages of the *Daily Mail*. He was wearing an LCC Heavy Rescue blouse, he was bald and he was humming 'April in Paris' softly to himself. Troy strained to read the front page of the paper and found he could not decipher the headline, let alone the date. But he saw the leather elbow patches and cuffs on the Fat Man's outfit, like the piped edging of a leather suitcase, the visible tears of wear, of fifteen years' digging spuds and shovelling pig muck, and time regained its keel. It wasn't 1944 at all . . . It was whenever it was . . . ages later.

'Been here long?' he said.

'Seems like an age, cock, but . . . looking at me watch . . .' He deftly yanked a pocket watch from a breast pocket and flipped the case. '. . . I'd say about an hour and a bit. I'm supposed to phone young Jack when you come round again, and he's supposed to call your guv'ner. That Onions bloke.'

'And Foxx?'

'Foxx?'

'My . . . er. . .'

'You mean yer totty?'

Troy was quite sure he didn't. 'I mean Miss Foxx, Shirley Foxx.'

'Sent her back to your place to get some kip. She's taken this badly, if you ask me. Needed to get her 'ead down. After all, I bang on the door she can be here in two shakes of a lamb's tail.'

The Fat Man passed the paper to Troy and went to the payphone in the corridor. Troy let the paper slip. Print was a maelstrom to him. It spun and it eddied and it went down a big plughole.

'He'll be right over,' the Fat Man reported back.

'Fine,' Troy said, without feeling. 'While he's here would you mind going round to the house and asking Foxx if she'd come over? I'm sure she was here a while ago, but . . .'

'But what, old cock?'

'But I can't remember when.'

'She's been here every day.'

'And today is?'

'Wednesday.'

He'd slept another thirty-six hours or more. He felt as though sleep were a runaway train. Give in to it for so much as a second and you woke to find the world had rolled on without you . . . station after station . . . oh Mr Porter. . .

'Brock's funeral?'

'Friday, but don't bank on being there.'

Onions looked grim. As though all the sleep Troy had had was stolen from him. He had five o'clock shadow – but for all Troy knew it was five o'clock – his blue striped suit was crumpled and the bags under his eyes were as big as pheasants' eggs. He looked less like the Commissioner of the Met than the hard-working, both-ends-burning copper he'd been until promotion fell on him, like reward and punishment in a single hammer-blow.

'I'd've been over sooner . . .' he began.

'Forget it,' Troy said. 'I've not been in a state to receive you. I would not have known you were here. Do we have any leads?'

Onions sighed. 'We've nowt. But that's not why I'm here.'

'You pulled Alf Marx's mob, though?'

'We pulled everyone who's ever met him, but we've got nowt all the same. London is shtum, or London knows nowt. And, like I said, that's not why I'm here.'

'You pulled Bernie Champion?'

Champion was King Alf's long standing number two – the right arm, the heir apparent.

48

'Aye, and I sucked on half a dozen eggs while I did it. Of course I pulled the bugger. He turned up with so many briefs we had to set out more chairs. And, needless to say, he's got an alibi you could wallop with a Tiger tank. Arrogant gobshite. Blowin' up a copper on the streets of London and defying us to do a damn thing about it. He's just taking the piss, isn't he?'

'He'd hardly have done the job personally, would he?'

'No. But, like I keep tryin' to tell you, that's not why I'm here.'

Onions looked around. Pulled a packet of Woodbines from his jacket pocket. 'D'ye reckon they let you smoke in here?'

Troy smelt a rat, saw it, touched it. 'No. I'm sure they don't. Why not just spit it out, Stan?'

Onions looked wistfully at his fags, shoved them back and bit on the bullet. 'Freddie. Have you thought about retiring?'

It was pretty close to the last thing Troy had expected. At the same time it was vaguely familiar as though he could hear another, unidentifiable voice asking the same question. 'Stan . . . I'm forty . . .'

But he couldn't remember quite how old he was. Onions looked away as Troy fumbled for the numbers, but looked back with that old steely glint in his blue eyes. 'You've taken another bad blow to the head. That's at least the third while I've known you. The first sent you blind.'

That had been in the summer of '44. And it hadn't been the first.

He'd been kicked in the head by a horse at the Battle of Cable Street before he and Onions ever met.

'I recovered, Stan.'

'Then you got shot in the head three years back.'

That had been 1956. He rather thought it might have been summer too. He'd ended up in this very same hospital.

'I recovered from that too.'

'And there must be half a dozen times you've had that lunatic Pole patch you up just so it doesn't get on to your file. Things I'm not supposed to know about.'

Troy said nothing.

'But what the quacks are telling me now is about the cumulative effects of all those blows. You can't see straight, can you?'

'No. But I will.'

'It might be weeks, months, even.'

'Stan, are you firing me?'

Onions seemed almost to flinch as though Troy had struck him. 'O' course I'm not bloody firing you! I'm just trying to get you to see sense. It'd be retirement. Full pension. Mebbe even a gong. I wouldn't dream of firing you!'

'Fine,' said Troy. 'Because if you want me to retire that's what you'll have to do.'

Onions gave in to the need, pulled out his Woodbines once more and lit up. 'I'm only trying to show you where your own self-interest lies,' he said, through the first cloud of smoke. 'How long do you think you can go on taking punishment like this?'

Troy had not thought of it as punishment. The mereness of metaphor was wide of the mark.

'I appreciate that, Stan. I'm just not going to do it.' Over Onions's shoulder he caught sight of a young woman talking to a nurse. Her face was out of focus – what wasn't out of focus? – but it had to be Foxx.

Onions followed his gaze, got out of the chair and said, 'I'll be back. Oh, and you're forty-three by the way.'

As Onions passed Foxx, Troy saw them exchange words he could not hear. He saw Onions's eyes glancing back at him as he whispered.

She approached him. He reached out a hand trying to draw her into focus, trying to resolve the shimmering mirage of Foxxes into one coherent woman, and for a second or two he saw her as she was, slender, blonde, wistful, challenging – a blue-jean vision for his blurring eyes.

'I've been every day,' she said. 'They seem to want you to sleep. To, like, sleep it off.' She sat on the edge of the bed. Kissed him. Smiled. He was sure she smiled.

'Don't worry,' he said. 'I'm going to pull through.'

'I know. I've been every day. I've talked to the doctors.'

'And?'

'And I want you to quit.'

'Eh?'

'I'd like you to retire from the force.'

She said it so slowly, but still he couldn't quite get the meaning of her words, could not quite take them at face value. There had to be another layer. 'What?'

'I've had enough. I can't bear any more. Since I met you you've been shot, stabbed and blown up. That's an awful lot for three years. I want you to stop now because it's time to stop, because it's time to quit before the job kills you. I didn't come to London, I didn't take up with you just to watch you die. So, I want you to stop now.'

This was pretty much the last thing Troy had expected. But now the other voice was clear and distinct. Before Foxx had asked him this, before Stan had asked it, it had been Brock putting the same question to him that night in the Chandos, minutes before the explosion. Troy found himself uttering the same answer: 'But I'm only forty-three.'

This was pathetic. Stupid even to his ears, the second it was out of his mouth. He was forty-three. Foxx was twenty-five, or was it twenty-six? He wanted something more out of the job before he reached the same frame of mind Brock had been on that last night. She wanted the life she had ahead of her – the miracle was she wanted it with him.

'What did Stan say to you on his way out?'

She ignored this. 'I don't expect you to say yes just like that. Think on it. Sleep on it. I'll come back in the morning.'

'I can't say yes.'

'Don't say anything. Just do what I ask. Sleep on it.'

So he did.

When he awoke on what he took to be the Thursday morning, Foxx wasalready at hisbedside.

'I can't do it,' he said, as though nothing but the one question had rattled around in him all night.

She kissed him, said, 'You have to do it.'

'Why?'

'Because if you don't I'm leaving you.'

As she walked away Troy said, 'What did Stan say to you?'

She ignored this.

On the Friday she came later. He was awake and had eaten breakfast. Two doctors had already done their rounds. One had told him he had 'bounced rather nicely'. The other had said, 'You still can't see straight, can you?'

Foxx said, 'Have you thought about what I said?'

'Yes,' he said. 'And the answer's still no.'

'Then I'm definitely leaving you.'

And she did.

§ 11

On the Monday he was discharged and given over to the care of his physician. He'd known Anna Pakenham for years. They'd met, he thought, in 1940 or '41. She'd been the longest serving of Kolankiewicz's assistants out at the Hendon Laboratory. She'd put up with his abuse, his bad manners and his foul English in exchange for the wealth of knowledge he possessed. She had finished her MD after the war, served a couple of years in the fledgling NHS and soon found she was better suited to Harley Street, where she had practised these last five or six years. It had been a negotiation getting her to be his doctor. He needed her for the same reasons he needed Kolankiewicz – for the certain knowledge that Stan and the Yard would never learn one iota of what went on between them.

'It's a bit, you know, iffy,' she had said, 'taking a lover as a patient, BMA rules and all that. Medical ethics. Hippocratic stuff, gross moral thingie.'

He had said, 'You sound just like my sisters . . .'

'God forbid.'

'Never the right word if there's a thingie to be found. However, the word you want is turpitude. Gross moral turpitude. And if anyone in your practice gives a toss about it I'll be amazed. You can't tell me Paddy Fitz plays by the rules?'

'Troy, I doubt very much whether my senior partner knows there are such things as rules. Or if he does he'll have the same cavalier attitude you do, that rules were made for idiots.'

She had taken him on all the same. And when their affair had ended some three years ago she had not turned round and said, 'Get yourself another doctor.'

On the Monday morning she arrived at the Charing Cross as he was dressing, stuck her head through the screens. 'Oh, good. You're awake. You've been asleep every time I've called in. Still, you'll be needing a lot of sleep.'

'Is that a professional opinion?'

'Yes. I'm signing you off sick.'

Troy beckoned her into the privacy of the screens. 'How long?'

'As long as it takes.'

'Has Onions been on to you?'

'Yes. He wanted me to talk to you about retiring.'

'And?'

'I said I wouldn't waste my breath, that I'd sign you off sick for as long as you were sick, and after that you were his problem not mine.'

'Thanks,' Troy said.

'No need, Troy. All I did was tell the truth. If I could get you to quit I would. But I can't, can I? Now, shall we go?'

She had kept one hand behind her back as they had talked. Now she brought it forward, clutching a rubber-tipped National Health walkingstick. It seemed to Troy to be one symbol too many – it scrawled 'cripple' across his conscious mind. She read his mind. 'Look at it this way, Troy. It's too near for an ambulance. The cabbies would think we were pulling their leg asking to go two hundred yards. So it's shanks's pony and your little wooden friend. Look at it this way, you're leaving under your own steam. Not the way you came in, after all.'

For a moment Troy could hear that triple bang inside his head. For a moment he could feel the inertia of going head over heels into goodnight. Blown in could so easily have been blown out.

Anna lifted his left hand, placed the crook of the stick in it, held out her own left arm for his right.

'Leanonme.'

But he never would.

As they came down the narrow end of Goodwin's Court he saw a pile of what he thought might be suitcases outside his own door. Closer, they appeared to be the first odd components in a matching five-piece set of pink lady's luggage, the set Foxx had equipped herself with the summer they met, for a weekend in Paris and beyond.

'I think this is where I leave you,' Anna said.

'To be left by two women simultaneously. Is this a record?'

'I don't know, Troy, but it's hardly a laughing matter.'

As Anna turned and walked off, Foxx appeared in the doorway with the largest of her cases.

'Oh,' she said. 'I was sort of hoping to be done and dusted by the time you got back.'

'You're serious, then?'

'What on earth would make you think I wasn't?'

She ducked back inside, like an animal darting back into her cave. Except the cave was his cave. For a moment he could see nothing as his eyes adjusted to the light, he could just hear the sound of her banging about more loudly and more quickly than he thought necessary for the simple job of packing.

'You'll have to send some stuff on, if that's not too much trouble.'

She wasn't even looking at him. She was bent over the last of her cases, vainly trying to crush whatever square peg it was into the almost round hole. T-shirt, American blue jeans and ponytail. A sight, he thought, for sore eyes. And the only part of him that didn't feel sore was his eyes. They felt lunar, lagunar – moony and watery at the same time, as most images swam gently in front of him. Not enough to make him vomit, but enough to give the less than fond illusion that what he saw was somehow not real.

'I can't manage the LPs. Too many and too heavy.'

'You don't have to manage anything.'

Now she looked up at him, sweeping the errant ponytail from one eye. 'Eh?'

'You don't have to go.'

'Going to make me stay then, are you? You know, Troy, that might involve actually saying something along the lines of "Please stay" or "I'd like you to stay" or, if you were feeling really bold you might say, "Please don't leave me." '

Troy said nothing.

'Go on, Troy. Ask me, just ask me to stay. But you bloody well won't, will you?'

Troy said nothing.

'I thought as much. You shit, Troy, you complete and utter shit.'

Foxx barged past him and slammed the last case down on the pile just as a cabman came up the yard to say, 'You ready now, Miss?'

Troy said to her back, 'Where will you be?'

She had the two smaller cases, one in each hand, as the cabman picked up the bigger three and set off back down the yard. One more flick of her head and the ponytail took its desired place as a mane bouncing halfway down her back.

'There's a flat over the Kingly Street shop. A storeroom or two at the moment, but I'll soon get it tidied up. Well . . . as the agent said to the sword-swallower, "Don't call us, we'll call you." '

He watched her all the way to the kink in the alley, watched her till she passed out of sight. It seemed terribly familiar, but he couldn't pin down who he had watched walk out of his life in quite this way. He went inside, closed the door, resorted to the English panacea – put the kettle on – and, while he waited for it to boil, leafed through a pile of thirty or forty long-playing records she had left. Some were their joint taste – the Elgar and the Delius, the Debussy and the Fauré. Some was his taste thrust at her – Little Richard. Some was her taste thrust at him – Elvis Presley. And some was a taste she had that he'd never acquire in a thousand years: American crooners of the Ratpack variety. It seemed to him that he held in his hands the modern, the fifties equivalent, of lovers' keepsakes. If they'd been a couple of generations older, he would be finding wild flowers they had pressed into the endpapers of a book of poetry on some idyllic ramble through the English countryside in the years before the Great War – lovers from a novel by D.H. Lawrence. Instead they had music, pressed pieces of plastic, and none the shabbier for that.

§ 12

His brother phoned. 'Not good news, I'm afraid.'

'Just spit it out, Rod.'

Troy heard him sigh. To Troy it was second nature telling people that someone they knew/loved/hated was dead. Went with the job, and he had long ago ceased to use the 'spare your feelings' line. Now he merely wondered who.

'Hugh died last night.'

Hugh – their brother-in-law, husband of sister Sasha, Viscount Darbishire, umpteenth of that line. Troy had known him twenty-five years and never found it in him to like the man.

'I didn't know he was . . .' The penny dropped. 'Good Lord, what am I saying? How did he do it?'

'I wasn't aware his intention was that obvious, but he hanged himself in the garage. Surprised me, I can tell you.'

'Did it with the old school tie?'

'Freddie, for Christ's sake, the man isn't even cold yet.'

'How's Sasha taking it.'

'Sanguine, I'd say. Surprisingly sanguine.'

Half an hour later he was able to put the same question to his sister Masha.

'Barking. Absolutely fucking barking. I look at her and wonder if she'll ever come down from it. I look at her and think, Good bloody grief this woman is my twin! If Rod thinks she's "sanguine" – bloody silly word if you ask me – it's because he sees what he wants to see or he catches her in her quiet moments. Truth is she's cock-a-hoop. She's been let out of a loveless marriage. No messy divorce. No shyster lawyers.'

'Was she contemplating divorce?'

'Don't be naïve, Freddie. She was contemplating shooting the bastard. She has every day for years, as we both know.'

'And in a few days' time we will all attend his funeral, speak well of the dead and mourn him as a missed husband and father.'

'Won't we just? If I were you I'd turn off your irony button.'

Troy was right: it was a matter of days. The coroner opened the case and closed it minutes later with a discreet misadventure verdict. It was so hard in England to commit suicide as a form of statement. The general public must have at least been mildly baffled at the number of accidents while cleaning a shotgun, and quite what legitimate purpose might be served by anyone putting a rope around his neck, the other end around the main roof truss, then swinging out into nowhere must have been utterly perplexing. There had to be easier ways to reach the cobwebs, after all. And, less than cynical, Troy concluded there had to be easier ways to meet your Maker.

The funeral took place forty-eight hours later.

Hugh, Umpteenth Viscount Darbishire, was one of a breed that had become much commoner since the war – the impoverished toff. The country pile had long since become just that, a pile of bricks in a field. The family fortune had been squandered by his father, the late Umpteenth-Viscount-but-one, and Hugh had preserved as much of the style of the English aristocracy as he could, on very little of the substance. The money was all Sasha's. After the war Hugh had played on the old school tie, with which he had not thought to hang himself, and become 'something in the City', as well as, of late, picking up his measly stipend for attending the Lords and voting on things about which he knew bugger all and, worse, occasionally speaking on things about which he knew bugger all. He had never made money, so the funeral took place at Mimram, in the small cemetery attached to the village church of St Job, patron saint of one or two of the worst things in life, in the Troy family plot. Living off his wife even in death.

The Fat Man picked up Troy in the Bentley and drove him out to Mimram. It was rare to see him togged out like a gentleman's gentleman, but there was no denying he fitted the part. Black, stripes and a cavernous bowler. But there it stopped. There was no holding the passenger door open, no standing upright as though on parade. He simply told Troy to 'shift yer 'arris' and get in. It was a pleasant drive through the burgeoning English countryside in summer, and a pleasant hour spent on the joys of the Gloucester Old Spot. How Lord Emsworth could even keep Whites baffled Troy – as, indeed, he thought it must baffle all Mr Wodehouse's readers. The thought sent him off at a tangent of fantasy. Would he one day turn into Lord Emsworth? He already kept pigs and felt as though his life was a plague of sisters. What else did Fate have in store for him? The forgetfulness of the classic English duffer?

'We're there.'

'Eh?'

'We're there. You was off in one of your little dazes again.'

'Was I?'

'I wouldn't worry none. It's not the blow to yer 'ead. You've always done it. I reckon that's where you get some of yer best ideas. Just daydreamin' an' such. Now. Can you manage?'

'Not crippled yet.'

'Good. Cos I ain't comin' in with yer. Can't abide churchianity. I'll just sit out 'ere with me *Pig and Pigeon Gazette*. You just wobble yer way back when it's all over. There'll be a bit of a do I 'xpect?'

'Oh, yes, there'll be a do all right. In fact, I wouldn't be at all surprised if the funeral baked meats did not supply the wedding feast.'

'Eh?'

'Hamlet. On the haste with which his mother remarried.'

'The mad tart's thinkin' of marryin' again?'

'Not quite. But she won't be in mourning for long. If I were a betting man I'd be putting money on hours not weeks.'

Troy was last to arrive and picked his way down the gravel path to find two blokes leaning on spades in the shadow of a yew, having a swift smoke before filling in the grave. Fifty yards further on the black-clothed backs of most of his relations were visible. The brother, the sisters, the endless nieces and nephews, the short, rotund figure of his Uncle Nikolai, the taller, effortlessly elegant figure of his brother-inlaw, Lawrence. The unfamiliar figure of the vicar – Troy had not met the vicar, any of Mimram's vicars, in years. This chap could be the new incumbent or an old stager for all he knew.

He'd missed something, clearly, but the vicar was still droning on, and he found a place in front of Rod and behind Sasha's younger son, Arkady. Looking around the boy, since it was impossible to look over him, Troy saw his sisters side by side, holding hands as one might expect of sisters, twins especially, at a time like this – but what, he thought, was the large American-style carpet bag at Sasha's feet? A small handbag, slung across one arm, stuffed full of hankies, weeping for the use of, might have seemed appropriate. But then Sasha wasn't weeping. She was looking around rather blankly. She stared straight at him for a couple of seconds. No expression of grief, or joy or madness. And then it hit him. When had Sasha ever done what might be deemed appropriate?

Sasha stepped forward, stopping the vicar mid-mumble with a raised hand like a copper on point duty. 'It's time,' she said, 'to whizz past the platitudes of received wisdom and –'

From behind him Troy heard his brother's muttered, 'Oh, bloody hell.'

'– lay to rest the man I knew, rather the man we all wish he was.'

She opened the carpet bag and took out what appeared to be a pipe. 'Cultures there are,' she went on, 'that hold dear the belief that the departed, dear or not, have use in the next world for goods and chattels that have been of use to them in this. Indeed, if I am to believe my little brother, there are sects in India which prescribe that the widow should immolate herself upon the same pyre as the burning remains of her late husband. Suffice to say I shall not be entertaining you in quite that fashion. So, Hugh, dearest, puff on your pipe, be it in heaven or hell.'

Sasha lobbed the pipe into the grave, where it thudded off the coffin with a hollow bang. Troy watched what little blood remained in the vicar's cheeks drain to leave a tuberculoid hue.

Sasha took out an old cloth cap in a tweedy sort of pattern. 'Saturdays would not be Saturdays without you in your cloth cap.'

It, too, flopped down into the pit. As did a copy of last year's *Wisden*, a couple of golf balls, several novels of the Bulldog Drummond variety, a couple of old 78s by the comic singer Frank Crumit – a man who had found it in him to sing the joys of the prune and the errant ways of a golf ball – Hugh's old school tie (Troy had been wondering when it would put in an appearance), a copy of *Horse and Hound*, a pewter tankard bearing Hugh's initials, a badger-hair shaving brush . . . It was, all in all, thought Troy, a representative, if far from complete, itinerary of what Sasha hated about Hugh.

At last she pulled forth the final item. A Second World War issue Webley revolver. The unison communal intake of breath was like a pantomime breeze rattling the leaves.

'With this gun my husband single-handedly held off the entire German army at Dunkirk. To listen to him tell his war stories, as one so often had to, was to realise what British pluck and British bullshit were all about. That dear Hughdie was stationed in Camberley at the time of Dunkirk never caused the slightest hiccup in the telling of the tale.'

Sasha approached the grave as though intending to lob this last item into hell with Hugh. Instead she took aim at the coffin, and blew a hole in the lid. And as though not content with this, she then leapt down into the grave, legs spread for balance, took the gun in both hands and began to empty it into the late Hugh. By the third shot the vicar and most of the mourners had fled. Troy found himself at the graveside with only Masha to turn to.

'Rot in hell! Bastard, bastard, bastard!'

And with the sixth shot, the final cry of 'bastard', the gun was empty and so, it seemed, was Sasha. All passion spent.

There was silence. The birds had scattered. The cemetery seemed suddenly empty. Troy looked around. Rod had retreated to a safe distance, the two gravediggers peered round the yew tree, wide-eyed and gob-smacked.

'Don't just stand there. Give me a hand out, you two.'

Troy and Masha each extended an arm and pulled Sasha out. She tossed the gun over her shoulder, one last thump down in the grave, and beckoned to the gravediggers. 'Come on, you dozy buggers. I'm not going to bury the bastard myself, am I?'

Then she turned to Troy. 'Shall we go home now?' And smiled.

She slipped an arm through her sister's and wandered up the path more as though coming from a picnic than from an act of madness. Troy followed, reached into his pocket as he passed the gravediggers and bunged them each ten quid. 'Two things,' he whispered. 'Not a word to anyone, and that gun stays where it is.'

'Done,' said the diggers, with all the deference of greed, and Troy followed on, to find the Fat Man perched on the wall, exactly as he had said, reading his copy of the *Pig and Pigeon Gazette*, oblivious to all that had happened. That which might wake the dead, of which there were plenty at hand, had not penetrated his self-absorption.

'Is the do now?' he said.

§ 13

It was about an hour and a half later. Sasha was mingling among the grazing mourners as though nothing at all had happened. Rod was pouring wine on troubled waters, and Troy was looking sceptically at what he held to be a bunch of lunatics, and wondering if, perhaps, he had not been found under a gooseberry bush, when Rod's daughter Nattie came to tell him there was a policeman at the door.

'One of mine?'

'No – old Trubshawe from the village.'

'And he's asking for me?'

'He's asking for the guv'ner, whoever that might be.'

'Fine. Show him into my study. Then find Sasha, get her upstairs and keep her there.'

Troy gathered up Rod and brother-in-law Lawrence. 'I want the two of you there. But say nothing unless I give you the nod. This is copper stuff and I suggest you let me handle it.'

Neither argued. When Constable Trubshawe was shown into Troy's study, the three of them had arranged themselves like actors blocking out the set in a third-rate West End drawing-room drama, the fireplace, the desk, the french windows. Troy thought they all looked like suspects in Cluedo. All they needed was the lead piping or the dagger. Trubshawe clutched his helmet, that monstrous, absurd symbol of his authority, in one hand and shook Troy's hand with the other. Troy had known Frank Trubshawe most of his life. He'd come to the village as a constable – indeed, he was still a constable – when Troy was in his teens. All the same it was not a time to use his Christian name.

'Good of you to call so soon, Mr Trubshawe. You know Rod,

of course, and my brother-in-law, Lawrence Stafford.'

'Mr Rod, Mr Stafford,' Trubshawe said, with the hint of deference he could never quite lose after twenty-seven years as a village bobby. He sat on the edge of a chair, the helmet at his feet, his notebook out and flipped open.

'I gather there was a funeral this mornin', a member of your family, I'm told, sir.'

'We buried my sister's husband. Viscount Darbishire,' said Troy.

'I have had reports of the discharge of a firearm.'

'Really? From whom?'

'The vicar, sir. Canon Chasuble. Very distressed, he was.'

'Anyone else?'

'Oddly enough, no, sir. The gravediggers say they heard nothing, and I've not yet had occasion to talk to any of the mourners.'

'They're all here.'

'I'm sure they are, sir.'

The remark seemed almost dismissive, a conclusion foregone.

'However the Reverend Mr Chasuble can hardly be dismissed lightly, so if you'd care to tell me what happened . . .'

Trubshawe's appearance was misleading, fat, fiftyish, red-faced, bald, but nobody's fool.

'My sister did fire a gun, yes. She was hysterical with grief. But I cannot see that any law was broken.'

'Discharge of a firearm in a public place, sir. You know the Act as well as I do. Indeed, I should think you could quote me the relevant sub-paragraph.'

'A public place?'

'The cemetery.'

'The cemetery is not public, it's private – it is the fiefdom of the Lord of the Manor and merely loaned to the Church.'

Trubshawe mused on this, but seemed undeterred. 'And who might the Lord of the Manor be, if you don't mind my askin?'

'Well,' said Troy, 'It was my father . . . so I suppose it is now one of us – Rod, as the eldest son, or me, as the owner of Mimram. It's not a conversation we've ever had.'

'Indeed, sir. And I am informed at least one shot was aimed at the coffin.'

Troy said nothing.

'Which might be termed "mutilation of a cadaver", which, as I'm sure you know, sir, is illegal under the 1716 Act and again under the revisions of 1868.'

'We'll never know,' said Troy.

'How do you reckon that, sir?'

'Well, the body is now under several feet of earth. We cannot simply dig it up and look. That would require an exhumation order from either a judge or a coroner, and I do find myself wondering if, without any further corroborating evidence, we should pursue the matter to that extent.'

'Further corroborating evidence?'

'Quite,' said Troy. 'Unless you care to talk to my entire family, who are, almost needless to say, in mourning . . . you know, grief, shock . . . all that sort of thing.'

Trubshawe flipped his notebook shut without a word written. Looked from Troy to Rod and from Rod to Lawerence. Nobody spoke. A nod from Troy, and Lawrence, with his insatiable hack's curiosity, would be in like lightning, but Troy didn't nod.

'I'll thank you for your time, gentlemen,' Trubshawe said at last. 'And I'll be off.'

Troy walked with Trubshawe to the front door. He put his helmet back on, tucked the strap into a cleft between his many chins, clutched the handlebars of his bike, and said, 'How much did you slip the gravediggers, sir, if you don't mind my askin'?'

'Tenner each,' said Troy.

'Hmmm,' said Trubshawe musing again. 'That seems to be about the going rate. Certainly did the trick.'

'Doesn't pay to be stingy at a time like this.'

'Indeed, sir. Might I also ask where the gun is now?'

'In the grave with my late brother-in-law.'

'Then we'll say no more about it. Dare I say, sir, you've got away with it?'

Troy said nothing.

'But sometimes, sir, don't you wonder just how much you can get away with, and that one day maybe you won't? It's one thing, a bunch of toffs getting the best of an old-timer like me who's never made it past constable, but you play in a bigger league, don't you, sir?'

Trubshawe wasn't smiling exactly, but, equally, he seemed to be speaking without resentment, as though the point so made was of purely philosophical interest.

'Did you never fancy life at the Yard, Mr Trubshawe?'

'No, sir. I like a world where black is black and white is white. The – what would ye call 'em? – the ambergooities of your world wouldn't sit toowellwithme.'

With that he scooted up his bike, flung one leg over the saddle and rattled off down the drive.

Troy found he rather envied Trubshawe. He'd been a copper almost as long, and well remembered the days before the ambergooities of the job had made themselves obvious to him . . . when the world had been black and white or he could at least pretend that it was.

§ 14

It was only a few days later. Troy had spent the afternoon sitting in the yard at the front of his London house, pretending to read the daily papers, occasionally watching print dance like clumsy hippopotafairies across the page.

The papers seemed to have next to nothing to say for themselves. He had read all he could stand of the exploits of Lord Steele and his headline-hogging wife Sylvia – she of the gold-plated Daimler, a woman who seemed to have no other purpose in life than to spend her husband's fortune. Ted Steele was, as he reminded the press on every occasion, a self-made man. Conspicuous consumption was his wife's prerogative. Earned, not inherited. And when he'd said his piece he stood next to his wife, as the photographers flashed away, and let her prattle on. He struck Troy as a faintly comic figure, rich, vulgar and foolish, looking, at fifty-something just a bit too old for the thirty-yearold woman on his arm.

Troy supposed that they might be a symbol of the age. That was the sort of phrase his brother used, and whilst Troy hadn't the first idea what they symbolised, he felt pretty certain Rod would. He could imagine the conversation now. 'What, brer, is the symbolic value of a peer of the realm and his tarty wife dressing to the nines and visiting a coal pit in Derbyshire or opening a town bypass in evening dress and a tiara and pronouncing, as they are wont, on matters of which they know bugger all?' And Rod would look serious, rev up his argument and embark on his thesis of the self-made man. Perhaps that was all it was – the self-made man was post-war man, or at least what post-war man aspired to, a chancer who saw his chance and took it. We would all be rich if we could. Meanwhile Rod, the man of 1945, of socialism, idealism and the Welfare State, would try to convince the British of such matters as 'the common good' and fought a losing battle. The British subscribed to the Welfare State whilst sincerely hoping to be rich, and saw no contradiction. Even Ted Steele was a member of the Labour Party. Indeed, for a couple of years he'd been a Labour MP. Troy wondered if he'd actually voted Labour before his elevation. To be a paid-up Labour Party member, whilst privately voting Conservative, now that really would be symbolic of the age. That needed no explaining.

And when the newspapers slipped from his lap he had watched summer bloom in the southern sky. Even the most blurred vision could not have missed the great swirling billows of cloud blowing offstage eastward to make way for the June blue heaven.

Come evening, he had propped open the front door, stuck Thelonious Monk on the gramophone and treated those Londoners who used Goodwin's Court as a cut-through to the joys of 'Smoke Gets In Your Eyes' and 'Hackensack'.

At dusk a figure appeared in his doorway: Anna in one of her many summer dresses – this one red with the black silhouettes of flowers. 'Why are you sitting here?'

'Would you believe "It's where I live" as an answer?'

'I might. If it weren't for the fact that you have a perfectly decent house out in the sticks. There's no need to sit here being miz.'

'I am not sitting. I am, as you will observe, lying. And I'm not miserable. I am. . .'

Content was not the word. He was not content. Happy was not the word. He was not happy. He was Monkish, but he saw no point in telling her that, and let the sentence hang.

'Must be this awful music, then. I don't know what you see in it. It's all so sodding . . . well . . . miserable. Plonk plink plonk. I'm sure you'd be much happier in the country – especially now the weather's improved a bit – where you wouldn't be on your own, where you wouldn't be fending for yourself, where there are maids and a cook, and the Fat Bloke looking after your pig.'

'Is he?' Troy asked.

'Yes. I gather you rather blew him out when he offered to look after you here.'

Had he? Troy had a half-way decent recollection of this and he rather thought the conversation had gone 'You need anything, cock?', 'No.'

'I know for a fact he's looking after your pig. I had that chap he works for on the phone asking if I'd seen him lately. What's the point in having a gentleman's gentleman who buggers off half the time, was pretty much the gist.'

'I didn't know you knew him.'

'Patient,' Anna said simply, and Troy knew there was no point in even asking her for a name. She'd invoked her confidentiality clause much as one would slap down the Get-Out-Of-Jail-Free card when playing Monopoly.

'Let's go to Mimram,' she said.

'I've only just got back. It was chaos, sheer bloody chaos.'

'You mean the funeral?'

Troy had told her nothing of what happened. 'Sasha . . . well, Sasha was Sasha.'

'I think I'll leave that as cryptic as it is. Whatever she's done this time I'd rather not know. However, the house will surely be empty now. Let'sgotoMimram.'

It was not pleading, but it was little short of pleading. He had no way of knowing whether this was what she thought best for him or merely what she wanted for herself. But the obvious monosyllabic question was at hand: 'Us?'

'The two of us.'

'My brother will be there.'

'Rod never gets there much before midnight on Friday. He spends most of Saturday with constituents. I think we'd see him for Sunday lunch and that would be that. If we get there on

Thursday—'

'That's tomorrow.'

'We could have a sort of long weekend.'

'Indeed we could. It would be like—'

'Old times?'

'Sort of,' she said. 'Sort of.'

Troy let Anna drive. He did not like driving at the best of times. At the worst – and this was surely one of the worst – he was death on wheels. They rolled down the drive of Mimram House late on the afternoon of the following day. He had nodded off and slept from the fringe of the city almost to his own gates (replaced in 1955, and doubtless made from melted-down Spitfires) and woken to Anna chattering something about how much she looked forward to the light nights of summer. The raucous heaven's choir that was birdsong, the dusky leathern flap of gliding bat, the midnight goosepimpling whoop of owl, the six a.m. barking yawn of dog fox, the *basso profundo* snuffle of pig at breakfast. Fine, thought Troy, if that's what she really wants . . .

The house was empty. Clean, well-stocked but empty.

Anna knocked up spag bol for two, Troy rooted around in the cellar for a bottle of Château Quelque Chose and they sat at the kitchen table with less than little to say to one another.

'I was always happy here,' she said at last, cradling a glass of claret in one hand and swirling it gently around.

'Happy?' he said.

'You say that as though you don't know the meaning of the word.'

'I'm sorry. That wasn't what I meant. I suppose I was saying that I didn't realise how happy you'd been.'

'But I was.'

'All the same. No regrets?'

'Oh, no,' she said. 'No regrets. I mean. After all. You're married now. Aren't you?'

It was typical of Anna to see the status of his relationships rather than their substance. She'd known him and Foxx as an item ever since they had itemised. She'd dined with them at home, eaten out with them, been to the theatre with them and, a matter of days ago, had been reluctant witness to the item's demise. All of this, any of this, might have bothered her. None of it did. Instead it was the wife, the absent wife, the relic of a marriage that had lasted weeks that bothered her.

'I've never felt less married. I don't even know where she is.'

Troy had never been able to explain Tosca to Anna. They'd never met and it was conceivable that he'd never mentioned her name until that day in 1956 when he had had no choice. Even then he'd botched it. How to explain, without sounding like an utter clot, that he had involved himself with an American WAC sergeant in the last year of the war, that he had doubtfully presumed her dead only to have her reappear for the 'other side' five years later to bail him out of a jam in Berlin, and that he had returned the favour in '56 – and that a vital part of that reciprocation had been a sham marriage and a real British passport. How to explain that, alive or dead, she rattled around in his dreams to that day? Better not even to try. Better to retaliate in kind.

'You were married when we met.'

'You know very well what kind of a marriage mine is. On or off, depending on whether Angus wanders or hangs about for a while.'

'You could try taking away his tin leg.'

'And have him crawl away from me? Good God, no. I'd far rather he walked.'

'Is he on walkabout now?'

She sipped and nodded. 'Day after you got blown up. I woke up to a call from the Charing Cross telling me you were in a coma, and a note from Angus sellotaped to his spare leg saying, "The pipes are calling." '

Angus was wont to sing when pissed, and to sing 'Danny Boy' when maudlin pissed.

'So. That's it, then,' said Troy. 'He's gone.'

There was brief, sharp silence, then . . .

'He'll be back,' they chimed together.

And Anna giggled and sprayed claret across the table.

§ 15

It was implicit. Understood. Received. They would go to the same room and to the same bed. That much he knew he could not escape. Troy had taken over his father's room years ago and left the bedroom of his childhood pretty much as it was. An unconscious if obvious shrine to he knew not what. Part of what had made his relationship work with Anna was the sheer frisson of immorality – the leaping loins of adultery; the far greater part of it was that they, for want of a less neologistic euphemism, 'clicked'. He did not magnify her inhibitions or she his, and there was, he thought, little better one could ask of any relationship.

He rooted around for five minutes in his father's study – also long since his but hardly ever referred to as anything but 'Dad's study' – for a novel to read when the insomnia hit him, found an old Penguin Margery Allingham, and went upstairs.

Anna emerged from his bathroom, peeled off her dress in a single crossing and lifting of her arms, and stood before him naked. Such lack of self-consciousness never ceased to impress him but, then, they had both grown up in a world that was so self-conscious. Even its temporary surrender was a sweet taste of victory. Anna was thirty-nine. Still beautiful, still seductive, but even as the word passed through his mind he could see its futility.

She crossed the floor. Only a fraction shorter than he, she put her arms around his neck and her lips to his.

'Come on. Clothes off,' she said.

Then she noticed the book, felt it digging into her as Troy clutched it. She took it from him, glanced at the title. '*More Work for the Undertaker*. Sounds like a busman's holiday to me, reading about coppers and corpses. Or should I take the fact that you brought it up with you as a statement of intention?'

'No,' he lied, put the book on the bedside table and began to unbutton his shirt.

Anna flung open the window; he felt the night waft across his back as he discarded the shirt.

'Too hot not to, don't you think?' she said.

He pulled his trousers over his ankles and kicked them on

to the floor, sitting, now naked, on the edge of the bed. He felt the springs creak as she climbed on to the other side, her arms encircling him again, her nipples bouncing off his back, his cock rising involuntarily – but when did it ever do so voluntarily? He sat still, so rigid it was impossible not to notice.

'What's wrong?'

'I don't know.'

'Not dizzy or anything?'

'No more than usual.'

'Then it's . . . me?'

'More likely to be me, I should think.'

'Eh?'

'Not sure I can.'

She grabbed him by the cock. 'What do you mean "not sure if I can"? Troy, it's up, the damn thing is up!'

'The flesh is willing, it's the spirit that's weak.'

'What the bloody hell is that supposed to mean? I thought a standing prick had no conscience?'

'Conscience hasnopartofit.It's. . .me. . .menow. . .meas. . .'

'As what?'

The telephone rang. They both stared at it.

'I have to,' he said.

She turned her back on him, yanked down the sheets and pulled them up to her chin.

'Freddie? It's me, George.'

George Bonham. Retired Station Sergeant Bonham. Troy's oldest friend in London. The man in charge of his first nick in Stepney all those years ago.

'Jus' to let you know. Walter Stilton's widow, Edna, died today.'

Troy was taking this in. It wasn't registering much. He was more conscious of the grief in George's voice than he was of any response of his own. He'd known all the Stiltons when he was younger. He'd even been involved in the investigations into old Walter's murder during the war, but he hadn't seen Edna Stilton in . . .

'Can't talk no more. Gotta go. This has been a blow, Freddie, it really has.'

And the phone went dead.

Anna was staring at him now. Troy watched the anger in her melt. She flung back the sheets, said, 'You might as well get in,' and then wrapped him in cool linen and warm flesh.

'Who was that?'

'George Bonham. Someone I almost knew just died.'

'It's your night for being elliptical, isn't it. What am I supposed to understand by the word "almost"?'

Troy lay back on the pillow and wished Anna would ask him a question he could answer in words of one syllable and crystal clarity. 'There are times in life when you meet people who don't want to know you and scarcely acknowledge you. I dated – at least, I think that's the word–her daughter.'

'I doubt that's the word. Unless it was before 1935.'

'Almost—'

'That word again.'

'It was 1940. And round two was in '41.'

'1941? That's when you and I met.'

Was it? Was it really that long ago?

'And I don't think Edna Stilton thought I was right for her daughter.'

'Ah . . . Old Stinker's daughter.'

'You knew her?'

'No. Never met her. But I almost knew her father.'

'Almost?'

'It was my first year in Forensic Pathology. I worked on Stilton's corpse after the old boy was killed, if you recall.'

So she had.

'Let's change the subject, shall we?'

'So . . . *wunderkind* . . . what do we do now?'

'Lie here like brother and sister?'

'You forget, Troy. I know your sisters.'

§ 16

Troy passed a pleasant Friday. Doing nothing. Anna fluttered around him in another brightly coloured summer dress like some exotic insect. She was, it would seem, as she had said, happy. Happy was the word. In all the time they had been lovers his capacity to make her happy was something to which he had given not a split second's thought. Now, sex notwithstanding, he seemed to have achieved something almost effortlessly. But when he thought about it, the lack of effort meant it was not his achievement at all. It was hers.

She vanished into the village on his sister's bicycle and returned to find him sleeping on the west-facing verandah in the afternoon sun.

'The fishmonger was open. I know it's Friday, and it's corny, but would you be OK with cod and chips?'

'Fine,' said Troy.

'Good. Then perhaps you'd find us a suitable wine.'

'Tizer,' said Troy. 'Or Vimto at a pinch. That's what you'd find in a chip shop.'

'No, Troy. Nip down to the cellar and dig out a bottle of Pouilly Fumé – I've always had a taste for that Couve de Murville you bought a couple of years ago.'

Another meal in the kitchen. Another bottle of Pooh Foom. Another conversation that skirted meaning to remain inconsequential. Happy was still the word.

Around ten p.m. Anna took herself, and Troy's copy of the Allingham novel, to bed. No winks, no smiles, not a hint of innuendo. Troy knew he wouldn't sleep for hours yet so he took himself and a second bottle of Pouilly Fumé back to the verandah. He stretched out, stared into the darkness until he could see as far as the willows down by the river, listened intently until he could hear the rustling of hedgehogs in the hedgerows. He was still staring when Rod found him around midnight.

The first he knew was Rod peering down at him only inches from his face. 'Are you all right? You look awful.'

'Thanks for nothing. It's just the insomnia. Leaves me drained but I still can't sleep at will, as it were.'

'Freddie, seriously, have you thought about—'

'Don't say it. Just don't say it. Right now the world and his wife all want me to retire or resign. Don't waste your breath.'

'Actually, Freddie, I was going to say, have you thought about taking a holiday? You know, Greece or Italy.'

Rod stood over him, a bit *déshabillé*, sweaty from the day's heat, collar popped, tie at half-mast. Troy softened. 'Let's change the subject. Park your backside and tell me something of the world outside. Lately I feel like one of those pre-war wives locked in the house all day by the working husband, reliant on him for all contact with the world.'

Rod picked up Troy's glass, filled it to the brim and sat on a battered wicker chair. 'Right now my wife has gone straight to bed. Pissed off with me that I got stuck in a meeting until nearly ten o'clock.'

'Fine. Bore me rigid. I'm all ears. Who was in the meeting?'

'Gaitskell, Brown, Wilson and me.'

'The shadow-cabinet cabal?'

'If you like. We had some rather disturbing news to discuss.'

'White Fish Authority run out of chips? Ministry of Works not working?'

'No election next month.'

'Was there supposed to be one?'

'Our narks in the government were putting money on July. Looks more likely to be the autumn now.'

'You have narks in the government?'

'Just a figure of speech. We know what they want us to know, would be a better way of putting it. But I know one thing they don't know I know.'

'You just lost me.'

'October would be a good month for the PM to go to the country. Ike is coming over for a visit. Reflected glory, basking for the use of. Macmillan would be a fool not to call an election after that.'

'Ike's coming?'

'Told me so himself. Macmillan's been nagging him about it for ages. I know he's going to say yes, because he telephoned me and asked if there was any chance of getting some of his wartime pals together. Probably towards the end of the summer, August or September. He'll make a state visit. Be seen on the news with Mac at this do or that. Meet the Queen, and all that. In fact, you're finding out about it before the PM, but I'd have to have told you sooner or later. He's coming here for a weekend – we'll have the reunion bash here.'

'I see.'

'Do you, Freddie? Extra security. American Secret Service chaps. Special Branch. I know how fond you are of Special Branch.'

'Be my guest. They can hardly exclude me from my own home, can they?'

Troy could see Rod far better than Rod could see him, and the expression on Rod's face told him that he'd just said the opposite of what Rod was thinking: Rod was praying Troy would stay away.

'Don't worry, brer. I won't fuck it up for you. You make Ike feel at home. See if he can't win the election for you.'

'God knows, we've got to win this one. Bloody country's going to hell in a handcart.'

'Really? I thought we'd never had it so good?'

'Not funny, Freddie.'

'No . . . wasn't kidding. Just look at things without the blinkers of ideology for a moment. Wages are up, pretty nigh full employment, consumer hardware available by the wagonload on tick . . .'

'Freddie, as you well know, that is the problem – on "tick". We are a nation living on the slate. We have become the something-for-nothinglive-now-pay-later society. Do you know, I was watching one of those wretched game shows the other night—'

'*Take Your Pick*.'

'As a matter of fact it was.'

'And they gave away a car.'

'Yes. They gave away a car. Can't you see how emblematic that is of greed, of things coveted and not earned?'

'As I recall, Rod, the car was a Mini – you drive one yourself – and it was won by a factory-floor worker from Leicester who made the clips that keep vacuum-cleaner bags from spewing dust everywhere. I would imagine he does it nine hours a day, biff, bash, bosh every few seconds, eats soggy sandwiches out of a plastic hamper for lunch, and bikes home in the pouring Leicester rain to eat food that's come out of a tin and—'

'What is your point?'

'My point is that while you're driving your Mini, which you think is your right, you are also sneering at the consumer society and the fat, lazy prole who somehow betrays your socialist ideal of the honest working man. The fat prole, who is also the same man as the honest working man, makes all those consumers durables – Mini cars included – the free availability of which causes you so much intellectual grief. Fuckit, Rod, they make the goods, they've a right to own them. What's good for the goose. Workers with cars and washing-machines does not automatically bespeak a society in degeneration, any more than Sylvia Steele and her gold-plated Daimler. And if you go into an election with that approach they'll vote you out for the third time in a row. What I sometimes feel you never learn is that "Jam Tomorrow" gets a bit frustrating. And I rather think Macmillan's motto is "Jam Today". What else was that tuppence off the price of a pint about in the last budget? You call it pandering to the electorate. Mac calls it "Jam Today".'

Troy thought Rod might explode. Instead he picked up the bottle, topped up his glass, said, 'Drink me,' and burst into a fit of unparliamentary giggles. 'You know, you should come out with Gaitskell some night. You've got pretty much the same sense of humour. He'd be laughing himself silly if he were here now.'

'Any time,' said Troy.

Rod quaffed half the glass in a single gulp. He said nothing. They listened to the sounds of midnight, the distant chimes of the clock on the tower of St Job's.

'Have you heard any whispers?' Troy said at last.

'Whispers? Whispers of what?'

'Sasha's little escapade.'

'Oh. No . . . not a peep. I rather think Lawrence has pulled a few strings to keep that under wraps. But, then, that's why you made sure he was there when old Trubshawe came round, wasn't it?'

Troy said nothing.

'Y'know. It was necessary. I can't deny that . . . but doesn't it make you wonder what class and a bit of power can do? Doesn't it make you wonder just what we can get away with?'

'That's what Trubshawe said.'

'And, when you come to think of it, Hugh got away with murder.'

A few years back in a fit of rage Hugh had admitted to beating one of Sasha's lovers to death. It was, Troy had argued, nothing they could ever prove, and hence nothing they should ever talk about. Rod had not raised the matter even at the time of Hugh's suicide. Now they had buried Hugh, and the problem with him. Troy rather hoped they'd never have to mention it again. It was not that the Troys had a skeleton in the cupboard: they had their own private boneyard.

Rod had closed his eyes. He wasn't asleep. Troy could hear the waking rhythm of his breathing. A cricket settled on his shoulder, drawn by the light from the room behind him. Troy wondered. Suppose his brother was made of wood? What twists of conscience was the cricket whispering into Rod's wooden head?

No cricket landed on *his* shoulder.

§ 17

On the Saturday morning, as he lay in bed next to a sleeping Anna, Troy heard the pop-shuffle-grunt of an old BSA motorbike-sidecar combination approaching. He slid his arm from under her, hoping to slip out without her noticing. They had got through two nights without sex, a whole day without recrimination. All the same, he wasn't about to risk the consequences of a morning quickie. He picked up his clothes from the floor and tiptoed to a bathroom on the other side of the house. Half an hour later, dressed and shaved, he sought out the Fat Man down by the pig pens.

Every so often the familiarity of the scene struck Troy as unchanging, timeless in the way visitors to the National Trust expect things to be timeless. The Fat Man would wear, as ever, his Second World War Heavy Rescue blue blouse, almost unchanging except that it got tattier with every year that passed. His Thermos and his ham sandwich would sit on the bench ready for whenever the need for elevenses hit him, which bore no relation to what the clock actually said, and the Fat Man would be found musing on some nonsense he'd found in the daily paper and occasionally reading snippets out loud to the pig. But the Fat Man was full of surprises. Today . . . Troy had had no idea the Fat Man could juggle.

As he came down the path to the edge of the orchard, the Fat Man was deftly juggling turnips, three or four at a time. Cissie the pig was sitting about fifteen feet away, her eyes spinning to keep track of the turnips, and every so often the Fat Man would bounce a turnip off his head – just like a footballer – straight at her. The pig would snatch it from the air, crunch it once and swallow it almost whole. She had the agility of a Jack Russell or, as Troy had observed when she was a piglet, a mountain goat, climbing everywhere – Troy often thought they should have named her Hillary or Tenzing. But Cissie it had been, Cissie the Gloucester Old Spot, a breed commonly known as the Orchard Pig.

The Fat Man put another handful of turnips into the air and the pig's neck began to twist and turn as its beady eyes followed breakfast as it spun through space.

'I didn't know you could do that,' Troy said.

'I can spin plates an' all. And what I can do with a top hat, two pigeons and a rabbit you wouldn't believe.'

He launched all four turnips at the pig. Snap, snap, snap, snap, and they were gone.

'How do you think she does that?'

'Dunno, old cock. The hand may be quicker than the eye. It certainly ain't quicker than the pig. If I was younger I'd work up a turn and go on the halls with her.'

'If there were any music halls left,' Troy added.

'O' course, cock. Goes without sayin'. Now, what gets you up bright and late on this sunny morn?'

'Angst,' said Troy.

'Ants?'

'People . . . are getting at me.'

The Fat Man sat down on the bench next to Troy, opened his

77

Thermos, handed Troy a cup of sickly-sweet instant coffee, and tucked into his sandwich. The pig's eyes followed the to and fro between them, hopefully. Troy hated instant coffee, but he'd never risk saying no to it, and much preferred the days when the Fat Man brought tea.

'You just tell me who, and I'll go round with an Austin 7 startin' 'andle and sort 'em out.'

'You're kidding?'

The Fat Man spat crumbs over Troy. 'Course I'm kidding. It's that Stanley, isn't it? And it's that young woman o' yours, and it's that other young woman o' yours – your doctor? And I reckon it's your brother too.'

'That's about the gist of it. Not my brother, oddly enough, but everybody else you just named wants me to call it a day.'

'Resign, you mean?'

'Retire.'

'But . . . you're just a boy.'

It was well meant – although Troy found it hard to take that way – and he supposed that to the Fat Man, whose age was impossible to guess, bald for years and fat almost as long, he was not much more than a boy.

'It's OK. I'm not going to do it. If I give in now I'll spend the rest of my life wondering about what might have been . . . I'll become a fat, sodden whinger, full of regret and self-pity like . . .'

Like who? For fuck's sake, like who?

The pig gave up waiting for more turnips and rolled on her back squirming at an itch she could not scratch. Troy knew just how she felt.

'. . . Like . . . like *Dyadya Vanya*.'

'Daddy who?'

'Not daddy – *Dyadya*. It means "uncle". It's Russian for "uncle".'

'I didn't know you'd got an uncle Vanya. I've met your uncle Nikolai, but I don't remember a Vanya.'

'No. I haven't got an uncle Vanya.'

'Then why tell me you have?'

'He's a character in a play by Chekhov.'

'Who's Chekhov?'

'Doesn't matter. All I meant was that I'd become like Vanya – a miserable, suicidal sod incapable of blowing out his own brains or anyone else's for that matter.'

'You want to blow somebody's brains out?'

'No, of course not. That's not what I meant.'

'It seems to me, young Fred, that about three-quarters of what you're saying isn't what you mean. But this much I will say. You do what you think's best, cock. Maybe there'll come a time to throw in the towel. Who knows? t it's for you to say. And, if you want my

Butwopenn'orth, when that time comes you'll know. Believe me, old son, you'll know. In the meantime you get back into the thick of it and kick bum!'

'Bum?'

'Arse.'

'Ah, you mean . . . as they say in America, "kick ass"?'

'Oh, no, cock. Never hurt an animal.'

§ 18

'Really, Troy?'

'Yes, really.'

'But we don't have to. I don't have to. I can call Fitz and get a locum. I could take off the next fortnight, the next month if I have to. We could stay here. Dammit, Troy, I'm happy here.'

He hoped she would not cry. It would not be out of character, but it would be impossible to contrive. Anna could not and did not cry on cue.

'You can stay. It's only me. I have to go back. Not to be in London now . . . not to be in London now is to risk being edged off the map.'

'Troy, it could be weeks before you can work again. And that's not some old flame talking, that's your doctor.'

'I can't be out of the loop. Not now. A copper just got blown to smithereens on the streets of London –'

'I know! It was nearly you or has the fact escaped you?'

'– so I have to be there. Don't you get it?'

79

'No, Troy. I don't get any of it. In fact, I think it's madness.'

All the same she drove him back. Parked the Bentley in Bedfordbury, handed him the keys, would not cross his threshold, declined his offer of a cup of tea and left with an immeasurable sadness in her eyes.

§ 19

Troy phoned Scotland Yard.

'Jack?'

'Ah . . . Freddie, you read my mind. Did you know I was about to pick up the phone and call you?'

'You were?'

'You surely didn't think I was going to leave you out of things . . . just because. . .?'

'No,' Troy lied, 'of course not. What's happened? Something's happened. I can hear it in your voice.'

'Bernie Champion.'

Bernie had been Alf Marx's right-hand man for years. The investigation that had sent Alf down had found nothing provable against Bernie. Bernie was at large: the heir apparent come into his own.

'Dead?'

'No, just missing. His wife walked into Leman Street nick this morning and said he hadn't been home for three nights.'

'Then he's probably dead.'

'I think they had more tact than to tell her that, but from now on I'll be looking at every body that turns up to see if it's Bernie.'

'Jack?'

'Yeeeees?'

'Bodies. Bodies turning up. Don't leave me out of that either.'

'As if . . .' Wildeve lied.

§ 20

The days of his recuperation – and it always seemed to him far longer than it was – took on an immediate routine, such was the nature of recuperation. Yet each day Troy awoke not with the sense of a pattern established or a life well ordered, but with the distinct, the unnerving sensation that each day was the first, the first of what he did not ask – but it was a greenness and an absence of familiarity and accomplishment that disturbed him not a little.

Blows to the head notwithstanding, Troy prided himself on having a good memory. It was part of the job. And this woman standing on his London doorstep had introduced herself with 'I'm Kate Cormack. I bet you don't remember me,' – and he didn't.

About his age, maybe a bit younger, say, thirty-eight or thirty-nine, red hair, expensively cut, a Dior suit in charcoal black, an American accent quite unlike his wife's – none of the brashness of New York, more a touch of the South, perhaps Carolina or Virginia – and an impossible sadness in the eyes that, once noticed, distracted him from the beauty of a good-looking middle-aged woman. She looked much as Anna had done the last time he'd seen her. Sad without anger. The sadness of defeat.

'When you knew me I was Kitty Stilton,' she said.

Good God, so she was. And she wasn't thirty-eight, she was nearer fifty.

Troy swung back the door. Kitty/Kate stepped over the threshold. Dropped a large flat package on the hallstand. Stood with her back to him, letting her eyes readjust to the half-light of the room. She looked around, the sadness in her eyes welling as restraint of tears in the corners. The hydraulic surge of times remembered. Then she looked at Troy. He was damn certain they were remembering the same times, thinking the same things at that moment, lumbering themselves with the same burden of imagery.

'It's been a long time,' Kitty/Kate said.

Troy said nothing.

'Almost eighteen years,' she added, then, 'Are you ever going to say anything or shall I just bugger off now?'

'Seventeen years, ten months, three weeks and I sort of lose count of the days,' Troy heard himself say.

She wrapped herself round him, tears falling wet and warm on to his face. 'And there was I thinking you hadn't an ounce of sentimentality in you.'

Slowly, he set the walking-stick against the wall and put first one arm, then the other round her shoulders.

'My mum died,' she murmured, into his shoulder.

'I heard,' he said, wondering how he could have missed the significance of George Bonham's phone call, failed to anticipate that the death of Edna Stilton might well bring her daughter home, and marvelling that at some point his unconscious had tracked back to the precise date they had last stood together in this room: June 1941. Sentimentality had less to do with it than the scrambled eggs that were his brains today.

'How old was she?'

Kitty prised her head up, pulled out a handkerchief and dabbed at her cheeks. 'Sixty-nine. Not old enough.'

'Of course,' said Troy.

'Of course what?'

'Your mother and George Bonham were at school together. They'd be about the same age, wouldn't they?'

'Yes. They were. I haven't thought of George in years. Old Bigfoot. Kept us all in line. All us kids.' She screwed her handkerchief into a ball, looking down at it, then up at Troy then down again.

'I expect he'll be at the funeral?'

'I expect so. Be unlike our Vera to forget him. My little sister, in charge again. But that sort of brings me to the point, doesn't it?'

Troy sat down, hoping Kitty would follow and take some of the tension out of this impromptu reunion. Lowered himself gently into an armchair, felt his head rattle like peas in a tin. Kitty tucked her skirt deftly, sat on the edge of the sofa, mannequin-poised, and crossed her legs. 'It's the day after tomorrow,' she went on, 'and I really don't want to go alone.'

'Alone? Your whole family will be there, your husband—'

'No,' said Kitty. 'Cal won't be coming. Quite simple reasons, really, but the upshot is I wonder if you'd escort me.'

She glanced knowingly at the stick, still propped against the wall where Troy had left it.

'I mean, you are on the mend, aren't you?'

'Yes.'

'Good. Good. I know about your accident. Vera sent me all the press clippings. You were lucky. But you will, won't you? You will do this for me?'

He could hardly say no.

'I can't stay. They want me in Stepney. Shall we say two o'clock? I'll get us a cab at Claridge's and pick you up.'

'You're staying at Claridge's?'

'I couldn't stay at Stepney. It would be too . . . well, you know.'

'I was just thinking . . .' said Troy.

'I know. Claridge's – where Cal stayed during the war. It was where . . . well, you know. It was where Cal Junior was conceived.'

'Ah.'

'You didn't really think it was yours?'

'I never knew.'

'And you never asked. No, Troy, young Cal is seventeen, the dead spit of his namesake and getting ready for West Point. I've two other children. Walter—'

'After your father.'

'I had to do it. He hates the name and he's insisted on being Walt since he was six. But I couldn't let my dad's name die. And there's Allison. And she's named after no one.'

Kitty/Kate was smiling for the first time. She took an obvious pleasure in speaking of her children that seemed less than obvious when she spoke of her husband. That infinite sadness in the eyes of women like Kate and Anna was, he realised, probably put there by men like him. Men like him and men like United States Senator Calvin M. Cormack.

'Really, I have to go now. The parcel's for you. A couple of things you'll find in every American home.'

She kissed him, did not wait for him to open the door, and left. Troy watched as she passed out of sight at the kink in the alley. He picked up the package. Given the shape it could be only one thing. A long-playing record. He tore off the wrapper. Two long-playing records.

Concert by the Sea, Erroll Garner.

Time Out, the Dave Brubeck Quartet.

He'd heard records by both pianists. The last time he'd heard Brubeck he rather thought it had been an octet. These were treats. The Kitty he used to know would have dismissed music like this as 'strictly for wankers'.

He stuck the Garner on his gramophone. It was time to buy a new one. Everyone he knew was banging on about 'stereo'. Old friends invited him round to listen to their 'stereo', invariably a recording of a steam train passing to demonstrate how the Doppler effect could be achieved with two speakers. It did nothing for music and nothing for Troy. Life, he protested, was mono. He had been perfectly happy with shellac at 78 r.p.m.

Garner played witty games with his audience. He buggered about so much with the opening of each song that they were kept guessing. So much so that a cheer went up when they finally spotted what he was playing. 'I'll Remember April' – one of Troy's favourite songs – opened with a slam-dunking left hand: Troy could almost swear Garner was doing nothing more musical than bringing down a clenched fist on the keyboard. But . . . it was intriguing. He played it over and over again for the rest of the day, and then opened the lid on his piano to see if he could do it. He could. Not all that well, but he could. And for a day and a half he was blissfully happy, blissfully unaware of his injuries, and blissfully unaware that his career was over.

§ 21

He had always known he was a klutz, long before his wife had taught him the word. As a child if it could be dropped or broken he would drop or break it, and ball games struck him as a mystery. Golf in particular had baffled him until he realised that there was no ball in golf, and that the arm gestures were part of an arcane ritual of divine appeasement, probably dating back to the building of Stonehenge.

Equally problematic were shoelaces and ties. Of late, say the last twenty-five years, he had coped fairly well, with his father's oft-repeated dictum never far from his mind: 'What does it matter, my boy?'

Today he had managed shoes but how to tie his black funeral tie was escaping him. Odd: he'd managed it without a second thought for Hugh's funeral, but today he couldn't do it for love or money. Right over left, left over right, the little rabbit goes down the little hole . . . were all right in their way, but then his father's efforts to teach came back to him: his father being right-handed and Troy left, it had been like trying to learn the woman's role in a tango and dance backwards, at the end of which footloose farce his father would say, 'What does it matter, my boy? Do not wear the tie, go barefoot if it pleases you,' et cetera.

He finally achieved something so bulky that his tie looked less like a tie than a small turban lodged at his throat. He glanced in the mirror. Good God, he looked like the Duke of Windsor, a man in the fierce grip of a fashion frenzy so absurd as to be anything but unobtrusive. He was not wearing a tie, he was making a statement. If only he knew what it was trying to say to him.

'Come on, Troy. I've a cab out in the lane with the meter running.' Kitty stuck her head in through the open door. 'I thought you'd be ready by now.'

'Can't do the sodding tie.'

'You can and probably will be late for your own funeral, Troy, but let's not keep my mum waiting, eh?'

Kitty whipped it off him and, in a flurry of hand movements, retied it and pulled the knot up to his collar. A small, sensible knot, with nothing to say for itself. 'If you had sons you'd know how to tie a tie backwards. Taught both of mine, after all.'

'Where were you when my dad needed you to dance backwards?'

'Are you feeling all right?'

'You should never dance a tango with an Eskimo.'

'I couldn't agree more, but why tell me now?'

'Never mind. It's just the sort of meaningless connection that the mind makes when it has nothing better to do.'

Troy found himself face to face with Kitty, looking slightly up at her as she spoke. She paused briefly, a sad sort of smile passing briefly between them, then she kissed him once, drew back, kissed him again and said, 'Let's go.'

They crossed the City in silence. Passing the Bank of England Troy said, 'I didn't ask you where.'

'St George's-in-the-East. Next to my dad. You weren't at that one, were you?'

'No, I wasn't. If you recall, I got stabbed a couple of days after Walter was killed. I was sort of . . . laid up.'

'Ah,' she said, and looked out of the window away from him as though not remembering.

Then she said, 'It was awful in so many ways. Dead Dad – as if that wasn't bad enough, but the church was in ruins. Got hit in one of the last raids of the Blitz only a few weeks before Dad was killed. It would have been the May, May 1941. They just swept aside the rubble and carried on. I can still remember the crunch of dust and mortar under my shoes.'

Troy hadn't been to St George's since before the war. It was a Hawksmoor, but a Hawksmoor driven to the hilt. So many towers and turrets, urns and domes. It seemed to Troy that the architect had seen this first not in his sketches but in a dream, some opium-induced fantasy of Xanadu proportions. Buildings were the stuff of dreams, after all. Worse, the stuff of nightmares. It surprised him how often he dreamt of buildings and rooms and walls.

Inside the walls, the parishioners of St George-in-the-East had erected a tin hut. It looked for all the world like a chunk of a wartime RAF base plucked up by Dorothy's tornado from a field in Kent and plonked down in London, into a frame by Nicholas Hawksmoor. It was utilitarian in the extreme. Tin and asbestos walls, stacker canvas chairs and a plug-in Hammond organ. Inside, all that was visible of the glory that had been was the dazzling mosaic gold of the Christ Crucified on the end wall onto which the hut had been built. A funeral service in a glorified Nissen hut? It seemed to Troy to be another symbol of the age in which they lived.

Troy had decided it would be no bad thing if this funeral failed to resemble the last one he had been to. Not that he expected any of the Stiltons to behave like Sasha. It would be just as well if it were different in every respect. He looked at the sky over the East

End. It was ominously, pleasingly dark. They might be in for a summer cloudburst. That would be different – it would change the tone nicely.

Compared to the funeral of the late Hugh, this was on the grand scale. The Stiltons had turned out in force. Troy would have been happiest at the back, beyond the obvious questions surely being asked of 'Who's he?' but Kitty rightly would have none of it. She was the eldest child, she had to sit at the front with her three sisters, her one surviving brother and all their many spouses. But that didn't stop her whispering and pointing out every single member of her family to him.

Aunt Dolly and her inseparable friend Mrs Wisby. Troy had the dimmest recollection of meeting Aunt Dolly before the war. Brother-in-law Maurice White, probably London's best-known self-made millionaire, formerly Maurice Micklewhite, who at some point had managed to lose the first syllable of his name as neatly as Troy's own father had lost the last of his. Troy made no effort to log the list of cousinry, and diverted himself as Kitty whispered a lengthy chronicle of Kathleens and Michaels and Alberts and Marys by wondering if cousinry might not be cousintude or cositude or some such. His dad would know. It was just the sort of trivia his dad stored up in spades.

'Have you heard a word I've said?' she said.

'Yes,' he lied.

'And, of course, old Mr Bell's on the organ. You remember him? He was our lodger during the war. He still is Vera's lodger.'

Vera was Kitty's youngest sister. Scarcely out of her teens when the old man had been killed, she had taken control of the house and, with it, the lives of most of her siblings. She had a facial resemblance to her mother, but she had grown to her father's bulk – a big woman, never far from an apron or a rolling-pin.

Troy drifted off. He was, he knew full well, just window dressing. An accessory Kitty could wear on one arm. It didn't mean he had to pay attention or say anything, and with a bit of luck he might get through the whole caboodle without having to utter a word. He stood when Kitty stood, mouthed tunelessly when she sang, sat when she sat, whipped out his clean hanky when she sniffled, and the next thing he knew he was outside standing in the drizzle for the burial.

It was, by Troy family standards, all rather restrained, rather polite and rather ordered. The tearful daughters threw single roses into the grave, the son and sons-in-law stood steely and tearless, and no one flourished a revolver. In minutes, it seemed, he found himself walking slowly back from the churchyard towards the Highway in the company of George Bonham. It seemed odd having Bonham slow down for him: for years now it had been the other way round, Bonham slowed by bulk rather than age, the heavy-footed pace of a man the best part of six foot seven and, in former days, wearing his silly policeman's helmet, nearer seven foot. He had dwarfed Troy from the day they'd met in 1936. And from that day forth Troy had dodged around Bonham like a mosquito, inflicting on him ideas and actions that either appalled or baffled him without, in either case, denting his loyalty. Troy was his *protégé* – that much he understood.

'I wasn't sure you'd be here.'

'Kitty asked me. But to be honest, until she did it had never occurred to me to come.'

'Stirs up old memories a funeral, don't it? And I suppose you've got a few.'

'Since you put it like that. I was the copper called out to old Walter's murder. I saw the body before it was even cold, sprawled on the cobbles with a bullet hole in the head. I've never felt much like facing Mrs Stilton since. I certainly never felt like answering any questions.'

'Aah,' said Bonham. 'I meant memories of you and Kitty. Sort of.'

Troy knew George's 'sort of '. It was uttered as a way of toning down whatever he had just said with a hint of uncertainty. It didn't work. 'She's married, George. Let's leave the past where it belongs, shall we?'

A path ran at right angles to the one they were on into another quarter of the churchyard. A small man in a cloth cap was hurrying down it towards them.

'It's old Arthur,' Bonham said. 'You remember Arthur Foulds? Lost his missus the same week I lost mine in the Blitz.'

Arthur turned into their path and scuttled right up to them.

'Vandals!' he shouted. 'Teds and yobs and bloomin' tearaways!'

Now that Troy could see him clearly he knew him. He'd been a resident of Stepney when Troy was a fresh-faced beat bobby. Another retired docker, characteristically built like a brick shithouse. A powerhouse of muscle packed into a five-foot-four frame that had turned slowly to fat in fifteen years of retirement.

'Just the blokes I need. A couple o' coppers.'

'We're here for a funeral, Arthur. 'Sides, I'm retired and Mr Troy's not on duty.'

'But you'll at least come and look?'

'Look at what?'

'The missus's grave. My Janet's restin'-place. It's been vandalised!'

'Arthur, there's not a lot—'

Troy interrupted: 'Let's look shall we?'

Bonham glared down at him. 'By rights it's the sort of thing you report to thenickand letthem takecareofit.'

'Won't hurt to look. Besides, we're way ahead of the Stiltons. They're still standing around gabbing. Bound to be a pecking order for the cars back to Jubilee Street. Let's buy ourselves a little time.'

Bonham accepted silently. They followed old Arthur to his wife's grave. It was a mess: every plant, and he seemed particularly fond of polyanthi, had been ripped up and left to die. The earth looked less like the carefully tended plot Troy knew it must have been and more like an allotment. The fresh marks of footprints were beginning to fill with water as the drizzle turned to rain.

'It's criminal,' Arthur stated the obvious. 'And something's got to be done,' he stated the unlikely.

'A lot of it about, is there?' Troy asked.

'First time,' said Arthur. 'Been tendin' 'er grave for nigh on twenty years . . . and nothing like this has ever happened before. I come here two, maybe three times a week. And nothin' like this has ever happened before. They've no respect. That's what's wrong with young people today. Got no respect.'

He was crying now. Bonham responded: 'You leave it with us, Arthur. We'll report it to the nick and something'll be done. Trust me.'

A huge, avuncular arm embraced the shoulders of the older

89

man.

'What's the country comin' to? What's the bleedin' country comin' to?'

Neither of them answered.

§ 22

The house in Jubilee Street had been in Edna Stilton's family since it was built in 1887. Edna and all her children had been born there. It was big, plenty big enough to accommodate the funeral party – a barn of a kitchen, a dining room, a sitting room and – reserved, if not designed, for such occasions – a parlour. It was not a concept Troy readily grasped. A room that was virtually mothballed from one event, tragedy or celebration, to the next. His house at Mimram would dwarf Jubilee Street, but there was not a room he and his brother and sisters did not use.

It seemed inevitable to him that the parlour would look as it did. Rather like a mausoleum, a living, if that was the word, museum to the recent past. Was there another house in England still with antimacassars on the chairbacks? Could you still buy macassar to necessitate the antimacassar? Surely we'd all gone Brylcreem round about 1940?

The sepia portrait of the monarch hanging on the parlour wall was not of Her Majesty Queen Elizabeth II, nor was it of her father George VI: it was of her grandfather, the 'old king', George V. Troy was prepared to bet that half the homes in England that had such patriotism as to want a portrait of the monarch still had one that matched this. It was fitting. The King had dominated pre-war England. Troy's own sisters had been presented to Queen Mary as débutantes in the twenties – the Queen had survived the encounter – and the royal couple seemed the bridge between the world we lived in now, whatever it was coming to, and the world before the war, before the Great War, which we had lost. They had survived, solidly. A smaller world – fewer peacock plumes and fewer eagles – built around the brick notion of family. The result, as Troy's father had wryly observed, was that there was now nothing quite so middle class as royalty. That much we owed to King George and Queen Mary.

On the mantelpiece were silver-framed wedding photos. One of them had to be of Walter and Edna his bride, circa 1910, but he would not have known the man. The slim young copper in uniform walking out under the arch of truncheons, raised military-style, bore scant resemblance to the well-fed trencherman he had known. But he knew Edna at once. That same look in her eye. The heart of gold, the will of iron. Young she might be, but she was still the same woman who had seen off his courtship of Kitty with 'Stick to your own kind.' Troy had found no way to impress or even please Mrs Stilton.

'She didn't change much.' Kitty, sneaking up behind him, a glass of white wine in each hand. 'I insisted,' she said. 'Can't get through a funeral on tea and brown ale. Rose thinks it's extravagant and inappropriate. What did you have at your brother-in-law's wake?'

'Champagne,' said Troy. 'But, then, we're rich and we were glad to see him go.'

Kitty sniggered. 'Don't make me laugh. That would be inappropriate. Come and talk to Tel. He may be in his thirties but he's still as awkward as a teenager. Whatever the funereal equivalent is of the spare prick at the wedding he's it.'

Kitty introduced Troy to her little brother and vanished. Troy found himself listening to a somewhat bitter, neurotic life story – how the deaths of two elder brothers in the last war had freed him from the call-up, and how there had been nothing he had wanted but to join the navy. Even peacetime conscription had passed him by and declined his services when he volunteered.

'What,' Troy asked, when he could get a word in, 'did you do?'

''Prenticeship. Butcher's. Quite enjoyed it as it happened.'

'But?' It seemed the obvious and simplest nudge of a question. 'But Mo made a pile and—'

'Mo?'

'Maurice. Reenie's husband. You must remember Maurice?'

'Of course,' said Troy. 'Yes, of course I know Maurice.'

Maurice White had formed his business partnership in 1946

–White, Bianco, Weiss. A clumsy name but, if nothing else, it at least caught a fair sample of the racial mix of the East End. Bianco had gone solo by 1950, and Maurice had taken control of the company, whittling down Weiss's role. Mr Weiss was not much heard from. The masthead conveyed the importance of who did what in no uncertain terms, Maurice's name being twice the size of the other two put together. WBW had redeveloped bombsites in South Wales and Plymouth, had built towering office blocks in central London and erected prefabricated factories in Derby and Birmingham. Most appropriately for a former pilot, Maurice had bought up some of the old RAF bases in Lincolnshire and Nottinghamshire, then sat on them until he got planning permission for housing estates. WBW had made a reputation in a very short time as one of the faces of modern Britain. A modern Britain for whom the past was less than sacred. They even had the wrecking ball as part of the company logo. These days, you could drive almost anywhere in Britain and see a sign on a site somewhere that had WBW painted up in large red letters and the slogan 'Building a Better Britain'. There were plenty of people who admired Maurice as a man of enterprise, and as many more who mistrusted him as a chancer. Troy was never quite sure what the word 'magnate' meant, but perhaps it meant Maurice.

Tel was still talking: 'Mo made his pile. And suddenly it wasn't on for me to work in a butcher's down Whitechapel. I had to have an office job, din' I? I had to go and work for Mo.'

'And you don't like office work?'

'Not so much that as . . . well, it's Mo. Mo'd like to own the world. To own the world and then sell it on at a profit. That's Mo for you. The man who sold the world.'

Tel had uttered this almost *sotto voce*, and glanced around just to be certain that his brother-in-law was not within earshot. He almost was. As Tel finished his litany, Troy's eyes met Maurice's and Maurice quickly crossed the room to clasp his hand. A big man, six foot, well groomed, wearing a black bespoke suit that looked to Troy to be almost as expensive as his own, and certainly better kept.

'Freddie, long time no see. Not been boring you, has he?'

It had been a long time – Troy couldn't quite remember when or where. Maurice clapped an arm around Tel's shoulders, more proprietorial than avuncular. He exuded a bonhomie in which Troy could not quite believe. The smile was too quick, the capped teeth too perfect.

'No,' Troy lied. 'Quite the opposite.'

'Good, good. Because I mean to steal you away from him.'

Without another word to Tel, the embracing, the captivating arm moved from Tel to Troy and steered him gently to a corner. With the arrival of riches Maurice had changed his tailor but not his accent.

'I was 'opin' to 'ave a word. In fact, you're just the chap I wanted to see.'

'Ask away,' said Troy.

'I'd sooner show you.'

'Show me what?'

§ 23

Troy had tried telling Maurice that they couldn't simply duck out of a funeral. Kitty would give him hell. And all Maurice would say was that he'd have him back in good time. They crossed the Commercial Road in Maurice's chauffeur-driven Rover 90 – 'I could run to a Rolls, but that would be just flaunting it, wouldn't it?' – and over into the rough-hewn streets of Shadwell. 'You worked out where we are yet, Freddie?'

'Watney Street.'

'Yep. I grew up here.'

'And I walked it as a beat bobby.'

'Let's walk it again for a couple of yards.'

The chauffeur stopped the car, and Troy stepped out into the closing moments of Watney Market. On a good day, and most were, this was one of London's most thriving street markets. It was said that in the 1920s you could have run from Commercial Road to the Highway on the heads of the packed punters. Today was their half-day – stalls wheeled away, a mountain of paper and rotting vegetables being swept up.

Maurice turned off the market into Cridlan Street – a narrower, residential street. Troy looked around. It was a timeshift, a backward glance. Many of the houses had broken windows, patched up with cardboard; there were gaping, rotten holes in the doors big enough to let rats in; paint was peeling off every wooden surface; there was rubbish piled up on the pavements; and in the street itself kids as tatty as gypsies played football with a bundle of rags tied up with string upon a sea of broken glass. It was probably the 1930s when Troy had last stood there. It still looked like the 1930s. Time had stood still. Spawned another generation of street kids, but stood still.

'Mind the dogshit, Freddie.'

Too late. He'd stood in it and was scraping his heel against the kerb when a dashing child all but knocked him of his feet. Maurice grabbed him, yelled at the kid and steadied Troy. Twenty yards on, the child stopped, turned around, held up two fingers and said, 'Fuck off, ponces.'

Maurice turned another corner, Troy following into Wetmore Street. More kids, more rubbish, more filth.

'Maurice, is there a point to this trip down Memory Slum?'

Maurice stopped. 'Why did Labour lose the last election, and the one before?'

'I'm not going to answer that because you're going to tell me anyway.'

'Houses.'

'Fine. You'll get no argument from me. The Tories promised to build houses and Macmillan delivered a quarter of a million a year. That was our failing – my brother never stops beating his breast about it. The obvious thing. A nation that had lost hundreds of thousands of houses –'

'One in three was damaged in the war. One in three.'

'– and the party of the people couldn't deliver homes for the people. Now tell me something I don't know.'

They ambled down the street, round another corner – one more and they'd come full circle – into Holden Street, dodging broken bottles and dogshit in a bizarre game of hopscotch. Maurice stopped at a gap in the terrace, the houses to either side shored up with beams, the rendered column of the fireplaces and flues standing out like the backbone in a fossil.

'That was my nan's. Bombed out 1940. Still bombed out in '59. Now, why is that, Freddie?'

'I don't know, Maurice, but Khrushchev said much the same thing on his visit three years ago. "Why do you have bombsites? In Russia we rebuild." Now, why not cut the history lesson and tell me what's on your mind?'

'I want to rebuild. Too much of the East End still looks like this, though I doubt there's much worse than this that's still lived in. I don't want to patch it up, fill in the gaps –'

A door opened. A shoeless young woman with her hair in curlers ran out screaming. A shirtless man, braces dangling, chased after her. 'Cheese? I go out and do a hard day's graft and all I fuckin' come home to is fuckin' bread an' fuckin' cheese! You dozy tart, you dozy fuckin' tart!'

'– I want to knock it all down and rebuild. I want to get in the wreckin' ball, the dynamite and the diggers and start all over again –'

Over Maurice's head Troy could see up to the first floor of the houses behind him. In one window a pretty young woman stood smoking a cigarette, staring back at Troy. She whipped open her blouse, flashed her tits and beckoned to him with the hand that waved the fag. Troy returned his gaze to Maurice, uninterruptible in his spiel.

'– not houses like this, with outdoor khazi and no bathrooms. I want to put up tower blocks, flats for working families, with all the mod cons. I want something that stretches as close to heaven as we can get. Fifteen, twenty storeys. Something London can be proud of.'

'You mean, level it?'

'Absolutely.'

'Finish what Hitler couldn't?'

'Hitler would have been doing this place a favour if he had. I'm going to do a damn sight more than just level it, Freddie. I'm going to level it, raise it and reach for the sky.

'Well, I'd have no professional objection. As the districts of

95

London go, this one probably has the highest proportion of criminals of any. It's often been a subject for discussion when the Yard meets with the divisions. All the same I still don't see why you're telling me.'

'I need political support. I need to talk to your brother.'

'My brother?'

'Labour can't lose again. There's bound to be an election soon. Rod'll be Home Secretary any day now . . . Need I say more?'

'No. But you'll need to ask him yourself. Indeed, I can't think why you haven't. I've just remembered the last time you and I met. It wasn't at the Stiltons', it was at Rod's demob party. You flew with his squadron in '44. You know what the RAF means to Rod. Call him at the Commons. I can't believe he won't take the call.'

'Really?'

'Yes. Really. And you'll have to do it because I'm not going to do it for you.'

'We've not met since the last reunion in 1954.'

'Trust me, Maurice. He'll take the call. Besides, whilst I doubt you're a paid-up member of the Party, I'll bet that your millions have made the odd contribution to Party funds.'

'There has been a few quid. When I thought I could help out.'

'Very coy, Maurice. Can we go now?'

They turned back into Watney Street, emerging at the junction where the market met Cable Street, where the London, Tilbury and Southend Railway crossed high on its way to Essex, and the East London branch of the Metropolitan Line crossed deep on its way under the Thames down Brunel's tunnel to Rotherhithe. They stood outside the Eel and Mash shop. Maurice waved for the car, all but besieged by kids at the top of the street, and as Troy got in he said, 'Maurice – why?'

'Why? Because it's my street. It's my neck o' the woods. As they say Stateside it's my "briarpatch". It's what made me. Even the effort of getting away from it made me. It's time to give something back. We all have to give something back.'

Maurice sat back in the seat. It seemed to Troy that he was smiling contentedly. He gazed back at the grubby faces of rowdy kids pressed to the windows without concern.

'Give something back?' said Troy. 'And make something while

you're at it?'

Maurice wasn't smiling now: he was grinning.

'Goes without saying, Freddie. That's the way of the world.'

§ 24

Troy felt they'd been lucky. Kitty was ready to leave, but hardly champing at the bit. She was chatting happily to another old face from Troy's East End days – a broken-nosed, pugilistic face, but a handsome one – the boxing promoter Danny Ryan. As Maurice came in he threw a mock punch at Danny's shoulder, saying, 'Just taken Freddie back to the old street, Dan.'

Ryan smiled without any more to it than good manners. 'Whatever you say, Mo. Blow it up, paint it sky-blue pink. All the same to me.'

Maurice moved on. Kitty looked from Troy to Ryan and back again. 'So, you two know each other?'

'I knew Danny when I was a beat copper.'

Ryan said nothing.

Kitty said, 'Danny and I go back a long way. We were kids together.'

Ryan cleared his throat and spoke: 'I think we were a bit more to each other than that, Kit.'

She touched his arm gently. 'Of course we were.' And turned to Troy whilst still touching Ryan.

'But that was before you and I were . . . you know . . .'

'Of course,' said Troy.

In the cab heading back West, Troy said, 'Been your day for old flames, hasn't it?'

'I don't know about that. There was only you and Danny. And Danny wasn't there as an old boyfriend. He was there because he'd been very good to my mum since my dad died. Not that my mum would ever have asked, but if it were left to Danny she'd never have wanted for anything.'

She caught Troy smiling. 'What's so funny, Troy?'

'The use of the conditional "were". It's very American. Twenty years ago you'd've said "woz".'

'Leave it aht, young Fred,' said Kitty in pure glottal-stopped Cockney, and her hand took his and gave it a squeeze.

§ 25

'Do you have anything to drink? I mean hard booze. I don't think I could face another glass of wine, let alone another cup of tea.'

'Of course,' said Troy. 'Not much choice, but say what you'd like and we'll see.'

'Vodka.'

'No problem.'

'Not much choice' was a lie posing as modesty. Between the squat brick columns that supported the kitchen sink Troy kept his 'cellar'. Every trip home to Mimram would garner another half-dozen bottles of wine from the genuine cellar that his father had left equally to Troy and brother Rod in 1943, and which, sixteen years on, they seemed scarcely to have dented. For the benefit, mostly, of guests he also kept vodka – Polish as well as Russian to keep Kolankiewicz happy – and whisky, a couple of single malts, which had pretty much the same happiness quotient for Wildeve. And pale ale for those rare occasions when the Fat Man knocked on his door. He picked up the Russian. It wasn't as strong as the Polish. Something lurking in the memories of his youth left him scared – oh-so-slightly – of a Kitty pissed.

'I'll be staying a while. I don't know how long.'

'I understand, things to sort out.'

'No,' she said. 'Not a damn thing to sort out. Probate won't take long. Mum's will was perfectly straightforward. I'm the executor, me and her sister Dolly. There are small bequests to no more than a dozen people, a bigger one to Tel – always worried about Tel, Tel being the youngest – and the house goes to Vera.'

'Pretty unequal, then?'

'Unequal but fair. Vera's run that house since my dad died. She's never lived anywhere else. Mum would never have put her in the position of having to sell up and move just so she could divvy a share of it to Rose and Reenie. They're doing all right. Or, rather, their husbands are. Tom's got his civil-service pension. They'll be "comfy" – a very Tom word, "comfy". And, you'll have gathered, Maurice has made a fortune since the war.'

'Impossible not to. If you flick through the pages of the Sunday newspapers, there's often as not a bit of gossip about Sylvia Steele's latest abomination for charity in the home pages, something in the financial pages about Maurice, usually a company takeover or a building going up, and another bit about Danny Ryan in the sports. If you'd invited Lady Steele to the funeral you'd have scored a hat-trick. And you? What's your legacy?'

'I asked for nothing. Vera wants me to take Mum's old sewing-machine. A girl's best friend, as she insists. But that's a sentimental thing. I might even do it. But I asked for nothing. What would I want with a few quid from the estate? Cal is richer than he ever was, almost as rich as Maurice, which is surprising when you come to think of it. No one in that family has done any work – real work, I mean, not politics – since before the Civil War.'

Troy steered her back to the subject. 'But all the same, you're staying.'

Kitty drained her glass and stuck it out for more. 'There's something I haven't told you.'

Troy was quite sure there were thousands of things she hadn't told him.

'Cal's running for president. The primaries start in about six months. He's already fundraising. Running in a race that's hardly started yet, and won't be over till next November. Once I get back, I get back to . . . not chaos exactly, but I know my feet won't touch the ground till about January 1961.'

Her own words seemed to give her pause for thought and pause for booze. She was getting steadily pissed, but it was a day to get pissed. He was beginning to accommodate the idea of a Kitty pissed. He almost felt he could join her at the bottom of the bottle.

'Good God, when you say it it sounds like something out of science fiction, doesn't it? Who ever thought we'd live to see a date like 1961? Imagine writing that on a cheque. You'd look twice at your own handwriting. So . . .I'm just putting a little distance between me and the big race. It'll be the last chance I get for more than a year if he wins the nomination. If he wins the White House, make that eight years. Tell me, Troy, when you took up with me all those years ago did you ever imagine in your wildest dream that I'd be America's First Lady?'

Of course he hadn't. Neither had she. She'd been a chatty, cheeky police sergeant, making her own small piece of history as the first woman ever to run a London nick. He was a rather raw detective sergeant, outranked by Kitty in every sense but the literal. It had all changed with her sudden marriage to Cormack. She had been Britain's first GI bride, some three years and more before the term had been minted.

'Have you told the family?'

'No. They wouldn't understand. America's just Hollywood and GI Joes to them. They probably think the presidency's hereditary. Right now they take the mickey out of my accent. They think that's really funny. As though I could or should have gone on being the Cockney sparrow. Once I'd explained about Cal's ambitions they'd be inordinately pleased and boasting to the neighbours about how well Kitty's done in America, without the first grasp of what America is. Honestly, Troy, I could do without that. I think I need time to think.'

'Do you know what America is?'

'As ever, straight to the heart of the matter in a single sentence. You are your father's son. And the answer is, I'm not sure what America is, but I know I spend a damn sight more time thinking about that than my husband does.'

'And?'

'And more booze if you want my thesis.'

Troy topped up her glass, decided to join her and topped up his own. The Kitty Stilton he had known would never have uttered a word like 'thesis'.

'America is . . .' Then she stopped. Swigged vodka and held out her glass again. Troy would never keep up with her at this pace. 'America is *I Love Lucy*, *Leave It To Beaver*, the World Series and . . . and . . . nothing – that's what America is. A culture – a popular culture masquerading as a nation state. So there.'

Pissed or sober this woman was definitely not Kitty Stilton. This wasn't like a chat with Kitty: this was like an argument with his dad, who had unlegged many a donkey on many a subject. In turn this realisation only made his bafflement, the inevitable questions, the more pathetic.

'I've seen *I Love Lucy*, but what's *Leave It To Beaver* and what's the World Series?'

'Kids' programme. Every kid in America watches it, I should think. World Series is baseball – all the major national sides and maybe even one or two from Canada.'

'Sort of like the FA Cup?'

'Bigger, more obsessive – you even get women reciting ball-game statistics to you. Fanatic followers. High drama. On a scale you'd never get here. But . . . *I Love Lucy, Leave It To Beaver* and the *World Series* are the three things that bind America together and they're all on television. That's the level at which America exists – television. I couldn't argue that it exists as a single nation on any other level – and, of course, America doesn't know this. War's different, of course. I got to America six months before they entered the war. It . . . rallied them . . . It fostered the illusion that they might be one nation, but they're not. Fostered the illusion that they're the world's great melting-pot, but they're not. Did you know Cal was part German? Fluent in it since childhood. As I've heard him tell people more times than I'd ever care to count, "German is handed down with the family Bible." My boys speak passable German. My husband is both typical and atypical. Typically any American who can trace his family to the old country – any old country – does so and never ceases to remind you that they are Irish, Moravian, Lithuanian . . . whatever. But . . . Cal is a hybrid, and that's rarer than you might imagine. The tribes, there is no better word for them, the white tribes, practise endogamy by and large . . .'

Troy had to think what endogamy was but the context helped. He wondered when in the hurly-burly of raising children she had found the time to educate herself, but she had.

'. . . and hence we have the strange phenomenon of the ethnic vote. The separate nations that really make up America when the illusions are blown away. Tell me, Troy, can you imagine your brother worrying about the Jewish vote or the Irish vote? Can you imagine the Jews or the Irish voting as a block with one mind? Can you imagine any English politician even thinking in those terms? That's what Cal will spend the next year doing – wooing, conning, cajoling. Kissing babies, wearing a yarmulka, sporting a shamrock, lying through his teeth. God knows, if the Negroes could vote he'd be wooing them too. And I'll be there with him. At his side, the loyal wife, mother of his sons. And Troy, my glass is empty.'

Troy had lost count of the number of refills he had given Kitty by the time she persuaded him to lift the lid on the piano. They'd boozed away an evening into a night. She had a remarkable capacity to stay lucid while pissed, but he felt pretty certain she was approaching her limit.

'Did you ever see *The Best Years of Our Lives*? You know, Myrna Loy and Fredric March.'

'Yes.'

'That scene where Hoagy Carmichael plays "Lazy River", so soft and slow, his hands hardly moving. Made it look effortless.'

'Hoagy Carmichael made everything look effortless. "Lazy River", "Lazy Bones" – he wrote them both.'

'Play it for me. Soft and slow.'

Troy played the song, as close as he could remember to the version Carmichael had played in the film. Kitty drooped, wilted like a flower, and laid her head on his shoulder.

'Do you think there is a lazy river – somewhere – anywhere?'

'Depends,' Troy said. 'On what you want from it. I have pretty much what I want out at Mimram – pig in its pen, vegetables green and growing in the kitchen garden, all the Art Tatum records money can buy. There's even a river Mimram at the bottom of the garden. If I fished I'd hang out a sign that said "Gone fishin'" whenever I felt like it.'

'But you're still a copper.'

'Call it balance. I've never thought of quitting – though I'm pretty certain Stan has come close to firing me more than a few times – and lately everyone else seems to want me to quit but . . . there's that ole rockin' chair waiting just to get me . . . but there's something in the job I need. Never known what.'

'Well . . . you never needed the money, did you?'

'And, these days, neither do you, Mrs President.'

'I don't want to be First Lady, Troy. I want my lazy river. If I ever find it I'll become lazy bones . . . sleep in the noonday sun . . . never make another dime . . . and hang out that sign for real – "gone fishin'".'

Troy changed songs. He could scarcely sing a note, but Louis Armstrong had a highly imitable voice. Troy threw in a few scat noises as deep as he could go and bababoomed his way through it. Kitty wept. When she had stopped, blown a good honk into her hanky, she said, 'You know, I can't stand the thought of another day as a political accessory. That's all a politician's wife is, about as important as a bloody handbag or a matching set of shoes and gloves. I make him look better than he is on his own – I make him . . . electable. God knows, there's never been a bachelor in the White House. But I really don't want that any more. Any of it. I don't give a toss. I just don't want it. I don't want to have to do it or be it.'

'What do you want?'

'I want you to take me to bed.'

Kitty Stilton just took; Kate Cormack asked.

§ 26

Kitty had none of the self-consciousness of the middle-aged woman, but then, she'd had none of the self-consciousness of the young woman twenty years ago. Modesty was always, by definition, false modesty, of which she had none. No 'Don't look at my stretchmarks' or 'Don't look at my spare tyre.' She had neither: she'd looked after herself. At almost forty-nine she was tall, lean and firm with a better tan than she'd ever have had to show if she'd spent her life in England. At almost forty-four Troy was skinny and pale, a book of scars on which she passed no comment. This was a gentler Kitty. The need was obvious, the haste absent. It was a slower, more gentle lovemaking than he'd ever known with her. And she was setting the pace. He would not have initiated the sexual rage of their younger days, but he would not have objected either. A little rage might have convinced him of his own capacity. He liked slow and easy. He'd rather liked rage too.

Afterwards. Kitty sprawled and musing. Stringing her sentences together slow and breathy. 'You remember the film?'

'Which film?'

'*The Best Years of Our Lives*. The one you were . . .'

'Right.'

'The scene where Fredric March finally gets back to his apartment in whatever one-horse town it is . . .'

'Of course, they never do tell you exactly where. There's that marvellous shot from the bomb-aimer's window as the plane comes in low over Kansas or Iowa or wherever, lasts for ages, and you see the midwest, flat and almost endless, rolling away beneath the plane. I think it's meant to give you a sense of it being Anytown, USA.'

'Have you finished? Because I hadn't. Myrna Loy is in the kitchen. March comes in the front door and shushes the kids, but Myrna Loy . . . I guess she kind of hears the silence. But she doesn't turn around straight away. There's a tangible moment of anticipation. You almost hear her breathing. Then . . . well, then . . . you know. That's not unlike Cal's return home. I mean, I didn't think he was dead or anything. In fact, I knew damn well he wasn't. But it was scary. In 1943 he'd got himself transferred out of Intelligence to a front-line regiment. He could have spent the whole damn war at a desk in Washington, but he wouldn't do it. Said it would make him sick to see other guys fighting the war while he polished a chair with his trousers. Said he'd had enough of spooks and spookery, scuttlebutt and lies. So he did the honest and stupid thing –heputhis life on theline.'

'So did Rod. Had a desk job working with Ike at Overlord HQ. Once the D-Day plans were fixed he asked to fly again.'

'Did they let him?'

'Yes. Led squadrons of Tempests over France. Made Wing Commander.'

'Cal was a full colonel by 1945. That February the Americans

– I should say *we*, the Americans – landed on Iwo Jima. That was the only time I really thought he might have bought it. About a thousand dead GIs for every square mile. He was there, as much in the thick of it as a full colonel could be. But in the end it was promotion saved him. By the end of the war he was a one-star general.'

'That's like what? A brigadier?'

'Yep. And he was one of the youngest. And he came home in 1946, and it really was like that Myrna Loy moment. Just to touch him. Knowing he was safe wasn't enough. I had to touch him. Young Walt was born nine months later to the day. Then in '47 he puts in his papers and says he's running for the Senate. His grandfather's old seat. And I said, "I thought you'd had enough of scuttlebutt and lies" . . . but he couldn't see the comparison. He won the seat easily enough. Catch Cormack's grandson and a war hero to boot. How could he lose? Even had enough of the adman in him to open the campaign in uniform, with all those medal ribbons across his chest. Soon switched to a suit. That's Cal. Wasn't a soldier any more so he couldn't pretend he was. I said yes to a soldier. For all but the first five years I've been married to a politician. Even that was tolerable. But now I'm married to a candidate. And if all goes well for him, *the* candidate. It's like being married to a suit.'

They'd just made love. Twice. She had mused away the afterglow talking of her husband. It was as well not to mind. Later, as Kolankiewicz had warned him, Troy's insomnia returned. She slept, he blazed as though floodlit in the darkness. He tried an American version of counting sheep, working out the names of all those presidents who had been bachelors, not trusting Kitty's knowledge of history any more than he'd trust her knowledge of quantum physics. Sleep through ephemera. Jefferson had been a widower – one of his daughters had been First Lady . . . which said nothing of the Second Lady, the black mistress, or of their children, born into slavery . . . and Buchanan, had he been a bachelor? Who remembered the first thing about Buchanan? He was about as important as Neville Chamberlain for much the same reasons. Woodrow Wilson had been a widower too, but remarried . . . Perhaps the only contender was Grover Cleveland,

who had married during one of his disparate terms of office .
. . but which one? However, this altered nothing. Underlying
Kitty's assertion was the inescapable truth that there'd never been
a divorced president. In a land that stamped 'In God We Trust'
on its coins, biblical rectitude was never far away and could be
invoked by the most godless of critics. The infidelities of Ike
and the curious marriage that had been Franklin and Eleanor
Roosevelt's notwithstanding, Kitty could unseat Cal at the first
hurdle. He wouldn't win a primary, let alone the nomination,
without a loyal wife by his side.

§ 27

He was the worst gumshoe Troy had ever seen. 'Encountered'
might have been a better word. Troy had not seen him, not face
to face and not clearly, but he knew he was being followed.
Reflections in shop fronts, a stout man who feigned interest in
window displays, turning too quickly on his heel, far too careful
to look in Troy's direction. Troy had spotted him yesterday, which
probably meant the man had been tailing him for three or four
days – Troy being far from alert, but his tail almost as bad.

He decided to pick the moment and the place. They were at
Seven Dials now. Troy dawdled: it would be too easy to lose him
now, and he didn't want that. He led off down Mercer Street,
turned left into Shelton Street and left again up Neal Street. One
more left turn and the gumshoe would surely get the message. Troy
turned right into Short's Gardens, right again into Endell Street
and into the first greasy caff he came to. Three in the afternoon
was the right moment, the place was empty – and hence the place
was the right place. He ordered two cups of tea and took a table in
the middle of the room, facing the window. Gumshoe pretended
great interest in the menu tacked to the A board on the pavement.
Troy summoned the waitress, slipped her half a crown and asked
her to invite the man inside.

He couldn't hear a word, but the shape of the gumshoe's lips said, 'What?' The waitress pointed back to Troy. For the first time Troy and Gumshoe looked directly at one another. Troy beckoned. Gumshoe looked from him to the waitress and back again. Pushed his trilby hat up his forehead, sighed and stepped into the caff.

'I ordered for both of us,' said Troy.

Gumshoe looked at the traditional mess of scum that was a London cuppa. 'I'm kind of a coffee man, but what the heck?'

An unmistakable New York accent. He stuck his hat on the table and sat down. A man of roughly Troy's age. Much the worse for wear – stout, balding and red-nosed. Pugilistic, but pleasant. A blue-eyed smile, like the ones Troy so rarely saw on Onions these days.

'What gave me away?' He sipped at the tea. Pulled a face and reached for the silver-topped sugar pourer.

'The hat doesn't help. Weather's too warm for a hat. Hats are hardly fashionable in England any more.'

Gumshoe swept the offending object on to a spare chair. 'Jeez, and I thought I blended in like I was part of the wallpaper. Back home I'd wear a straw skimmer this time of year. Half the men in Manhattan still do.'

'And your feet.'

'Not much I can do about them.'

'You have copper's feet.'

'So I should. Nineteen years in the NYPD. I guess we should introduce ourselves. Joey Rork.' He held out his hand for Troy to shake. 'I'm a private dick now.'

'I'm Frederick Troy. And I'm very much a public dick. I'm Chief Superintendent of the Murder Squad at Scotland Yard. But you knew that, didn't you?'

'Not at first. I found out yesterday you were a cop. And I'd no idea you were quite such a ranking cop.'

'Really?' Troy said. 'Then why have you been trailing me?'

Rork looked around. Caught the waitress's eye. 'Say, can a man still get lunch at three in the afternoon?'

'No, love. But I could do you egg an' chips and some bread an' butter.'

'Sounds fine.' He turned to Troy. 'And you?'

Troy shook his head. The thought of egg and chips made him

queasy.

When the waitress had gone Rork slurped at his tea. Troy did not prompt him.

'In two words,' Rork said, stringing the moment out. 'In two words . . . Mrs Cormack.'

'Calvin Cormack hired you to follow Katherine?'

'No,' said Rork. 'I sincerely hope the Senator doesn't know. The committee of Democrats to Elect Calvin Cormack hired me. It's quite a mouthful – they usually just call themselves the Deeks.'

'The Deeks?' Troy said, scarcely keeping the tone of incredulity out of his voice.

The waitress slapped a plate in front of Rork, a good half-loaf of skimpily buttered bread. Rork swallowed the first slice in the great maw of his mouth without seeming to chew.

'Sure. Senator Cormack is a contender.'

'"He coulda been somebody, Charlie," ' Troy said.

Rork almost choked on his second slice. 'Don't tell me, don't tell me . . . Marlon Brando in *On the Waterfront*, right? Him and Karl Malden.'

'Rod Steiger.'

'Steiger? Right. Anyways, it's for real. There is a . . . shall I say a substantial slice of the Democrat Party that prefers the Senator to Hubert Humphrey, to Jack Kennedy, and God knows anyone's better than Lyndon Johnson. A Texan in the White House. Can you imagine that?'

'Perhaps next year is the Republicans' year. Perhaps Mr Nixon is also a contender.'

'The Veep? Huh? You want to waste thirty minutes one day, sit down and list for yourself the names of all the Vice-Presidents of the United States. It's a list of losers.'

'Harry S Truman?'

'So . . . there's always gonna be exceptions.'

'Teddy Roosevelt?'

'Jeez. I'm beginning to be sorry I spoke. Let me kill this line of conversation once and for all. Veeps get to be pres if the Pres gets blown away. No one is going to assassinate Ike. I like Ike. You like Ike. Everybody likes Ike. There is no way Richard M. Nixon is ever gonna be President.'

'And Cal is?'

'Cal? Sounds like you know him?'

'Knew him.'

'When?'

'During the war.'

'But he was in the Pacific. Enough medals to build a bridge.'

'And before that, before you lot were in the war, he was in England. How did you think he met Katherine?'

'I didn't know, I guess. Nobody told me.'

And Troy guessed that it was a slow-witted gumshoe who hadn't been able to work this out for himself.

The waitress served Rork his egg an' chips. He stared at it, knife in one hand, slice of bread in the other.

'Now you put the chips on the bread and make a sandwich.'

'You do? Great.'

'Preferably with this.' Troy held up a gummy-necked bottle of tomato ketchup.

'Catsup? Great.' Rork beamed across the top of his red-running chip butty. A man who had come late in life to one of the great delights of gluttony. Troy refrained from teaching him how to stir the yolk of his egg with a chip, as it looked affected when done by anyone past puberty.

'Sho . . . you and the Shenator's wife go back a waysh.'

'Yes.'

'Wish kind of bringsh me to the point.'

'You've been sent to prevent any scandal that might endanger Cal's chance of getting the nomination.'

'You're way ahead of me.'

You bet.

'However, you ain't the problem. In fact, if you and the Senator's wife are playing hide the salami, then I admire your discretion.'

Troy had to think about this, but when he did work out what 'hide the salami' meant he could only wince inwardly at such a disgusting turn of phrase. 'I'm not the problem?'

'Nope.'

'Then who is?'

Rork pulled last Sunday's *Observer* from his pocket, folded open to the showbiz page. He tapped a large box advertisement with his forefinger. 'Dis palooka.'

It was an ad for the London Hippodrome, a theatre in the Charing Cross Road, only yards from Troy's house and only half a mile or so from where they were sitting. For the next month its stage would be filled and, doubtless, its stalls packed by the presence of one Vince Christy, a smoke-voiced American crooner who owed a lot to Frank Sinatra but had been sharp enough to learn a thing or two from Johnnie Ray. He wasn't as big as Sinatra, and never would be, but he'd outlasted Ray, survived the Elvis revolution, and had a reputation as a singer nowhere near as newsworthy as his role as one of Sinatra's Ratpack.

'Tell me,' Troy said.

Rork was well into his trough. Face stuffed full of what he undoubtedly called French fries. 'You know much about Vince?'

'No. I know he's in the Ratpack. And I don't think he's married to June Christy.'

'He ain't. And he can't sing half as well as her. Fact – his name ain't even Christy, it's Cristofero da Vinci.'

'Any relation?'

'To Leonardo? Nah. When he was a teenager in Hoboken he was a house painter – painted my mom's apartment on West 47th once – so bad she wouldn't pay him. So I figure not. But he's Italian. That's what matters. Italian, connected and proud of it.'

'Proud enough to change his name?'

'That's showbiz. That's America. Take me, for example. Rork, R-OR-K. A hundred and more years ago the name was O'Rourke. I don't know what happened to all those missing letters. America just does that. Your ancestor gets off a boat, finds himself facing an Immigration and Natz guy who can't spell pretzel, and the next thing you know Suleiman Yuriakamsohn from Lodz is Jack Solomon from Brooklyn. Believe me, that happened to my sister's father-in-law. Word for word. Then, maybe a generation later, a little fame beckons and a guy whose old man got through with his name in one piece feels he has to sound like he's an Anglo. You know who Angelo Siciliano is? Course you don't. 'Cos everybody knows him as Charles Atlas. It's just showbiz. It don't mean nothin'. Changing his name don't

110

make Vince less than Italian, don't make him less than Sicilian. If you catch my drift.'

Troy caught it. And said nothing. His father had changed the family name too. Troy was more 'Anglo' than Troitsky. Troy had no feelings about it one way or the other.

'So,' Rork was saying, 'Vince is connected. Not a made man you unnerstan but . . . connected. There are people who say he owes a few career breaks to those connections. You remember that war film from a few years back, *Hell Is a Crowded Place*? Vince gets pulled from the quicksand by William Holden?'

'The one set on a Pacific island? Christy, Holden and that tall chap – wooden actor, can't remember his name.'

'Ronald Reagan, used to be a sports commentator, "Dutch" Reagan. Shoulda stuck to it. Anyways, Ole Vince beat off some serious competition for that part. Actors who could act the pants off him – Dana Andrews wanted it, I heard, but Vince got it and he didn't have to sing a note. So, you see, Vince has influence, so when he and Mrs Cormack became, like, an unofficial item . . .'

Rork did not finish the sentence. Plied his elbow to finishing his chips instead.

'When?' said Troy.

''Bout two years ago. The Senator's wife took to spending a lot of time on the West Coast. After all, the kids are in private schools, her husband is up to his keyster in paperwork . . . A woman gets lonely.'

Bored more like, Troy thought. Bored would be much more like Kitty. She'd changed less than he had imagined in all those years away. Cal was still a cuckold.

'So she took up with Vince?'

'Vince fell for her hook, line and sinker. Nobody's sure how long it lasted, and everybody got lucky. The only paper to run with it was a Los Angeles scandal sheet, a kind of *Who Boffs Who*, a one-man gossip operation. The Party sent round some heavies and gently persuaded the guys to drop it. Week or so later some of Vince's *compadres* went to see him and broke both his arms. Guy runs a laundry now.'

'So you're not here because Katherine's actually having an affair. You're here to stop her taking up with an old flame.'

'Something like that. Once we got word that they'd be in England at the same time, it seemed like something should be watched. So I'm watching. And instead I find you.'

'But I'm discreet?'

'Believe me, if my hat hadn't just gone out of fashion I'd take it off to you.'

'So, what's your problem?'

'Vince knows she's here. This tour of his is a very last-minute thing. He's come to London for Katherine Cormack. I think he thinks no one will be watching, or maybe that no one will care. Think about it, who gives a plug nickel about the reputation of Senator Cormack over here? Who's even heard of him? I figure the average Londoner has heard of Ike and Adlai and that's about it. You and I could stand on any street corner in this town with photos of Nixon or Kennedy and most people wouldn't know 'em from Charlie Chaplin.'

'If Katherine and Christy get back together, and if our press picks up on it, and all it would take would be one Slickey of a gossip columnist, you realise they can't be leant on?'

'I was kind of hoping to get to them before that stage. I was kind of hoping that you might slip me the goods ahead of the press finding out.'

'Mr Rork, whatever makes you think I'd do that?'

'The old *quid pro quo*. You let me know if Vince comes sniffing, I don't tell no one about you and Mrs Cormack.'

'That sounds ominously like blackmail.'

'Nah . . . it's like you guys always say, you scratch my back I'll scratch yours.'

'I'll think about it,' said Troy.

Rork had finished his plateful. Sat clutching his last slice of bread.

'Usually,' Troy told him, 'one wipes the plate with it.'

'One does?'

'*De rigueur*,' said Troy.

'Jeez. And there was I thinking of all that lovely gloop going to waste and it would be the height of bad manners to mop it all up.'

'Only amongst the middle classes. The rest of us don't give a damn.'

Rork polished the china, sat back and grinned. 'So, Topcop, whaddya say?'

Troy thought about it, watched the contentment of repletion spread like a roseate glow across the man's face, watched him pop the first button on his flies, heard him belch politely into his clenched fist. This man was too stupid to get involved with, but he could see no merit for himself or Kitty in being the focus of a scandal. 'You know where I live. I think you'd better tell me where you're staying.'

'Cheap hotel in Gower Street, the Cromarty. My expense account don't run to Claridge's.'

'Well, I hope it runs to egg and chips and two teas,' said Troy. He got uptoleave.

Rork twisted his bulk in his chair to say to Troy's retreating back, 'You gonna keep in touch or what?' but Troy had gone.

§ 28

Troy dug last Sunday's *Observer* out of the rubbish and found the advertisement for Christy's concerts. He wasn't due to open for another week – unless he was completely winging it that meant he was here now, resting and rehearsing. He folded it open and dropped it on the coffee-table hoping it would look casual. It didn't. He twisted it this way and that and gave up. She'd spot it or she wouldn't. She'd comment or she wouldn't. He wasn't going to raise the name of Vince Christy with Kitty. He owed Cal nothing – Rork and the Democrats absolutely nothing. If she wanted to fuck Cal out of the presidency Troy would not care – but it came to him as he sat and tune-pootled at the piano, weaving 'My Old Flame' into 'The Man I Love' and wondering somewhat slightly at the nature of his own unconscious, that Kitty didn't care either, that she had stated her wishes the first night she had tumbled him into bed. Cal wanted the White House; she didn't. He began to wonder if she had set this up to stop him. He did not doubt that Gumshoe was right. A sex scandal would sink

113

Cal, even at second hand. Middle America would have no regard, no sympathy for his own innocence and probity: Cal would be damned by his wife's actions. A sexual liaison between the putative First Lady and a Mafioso crooner would rock America. God help their delicate sensibilities if they ever found out the truth about Senator Kennedy. When Troy had known Jack before the war he would, as the cliché had it, fuck anything with a pulse.

Troy was still at the piano when Kitty got in. He'd given his unconscious free rein and had moved to 'How Long Has This Been Going On?', by way of 'Why Don't You Do Right?' and 'Sentimental Journey'. It was almost dark. Kitty kicked off her shoes, stood behind him, hands upon his shoulders, slipping to his chest, her face buried in his hair, a hug so fierce he broke rhythm and stopped.

'Don't stop. Play one more, just one more.'

Troy began a slowed down, bass-heavy version of 'Makin' Whoopee', the pace of his playing running counter to the nature of the song. Such slow, languid whoopee.

'Makin' whoopee. Such a good idea.' Kitty took him by the hand and led him up the stairs. Undressed him then herself, pushed him back on the bed.

'Do you know,' she said, 'that I once had the pleasure of makin' whoopee in Macon, Georgia?'

'That's an awful joke,' he replied.

'True, though.'

It was too late in the day for his eyes to keep focus. The Kitty who rose and fell and thrashed on top of him was a woman-blur. He wished he could see her face. The touch, the scratch, the sweat rolling off her and on to him. But he wished he could see her face. He came into her, a wet rush that soaked his belly, and Kitty landed on his chest, breasts flattening on him, his face smothered by her hair. One last whisper of 'whoopee' in his ear before she fell fast asleep.

He felt the pleasure of her rage.

And suddenly he had, in his mind's eye, a clear image of Gumshoe, at one end of the alley and then the other, looking at his watch, noting the time Kitty arrived, noting the time she came and waiting for her to leave, and he hated it. It seemed like violation.

§ 29

The eyes-wide, head-thumping inner glare of insomnia woke him just before dawn. More than half-light seeping in through his bedroom window. Now he could see. Like a Battle of Britain pilot on carrot juice. Kitty had thrown off the covers in the summer heat. He could see the curve of her hip, the soft round mound of her arse. Tempting. Close enough to touch. She would surely wake? But when the telephone rang at the bedside she did not even stir. Jack. It had to be Wildeve.

'I hope this is one of your sleepless nights, Freddie.'

'I'm alert. In fact I'm full of lert.'

'Can you see all right?'

'Yes. It usually begins the day well and starts to wear out after lunch. Now's a very good time.'

'Good. Get dressed. I'll pick you up in ten minutes. There's a body I want you to see.'

Ten minutes later Troy stood in St Martin's Lane, waiting, unwashed and unshaven, almost certain he could still smell Kitty's perfume lingering on him. The street was empty of traffic. Jack roared up from Trafalgar Square in his big black Wolseley.

'Are you sure you're up for this?'

'Do I look that bad?' Troy asked.

Jack sniffed the air. 'You smell better than you look. And my infallible totty-indexing system tells me that isn't Miss Foxx's perfume. Why women always seem to want you when you're only firing on two cylinders has always baffled me.'

'Vulnerability,' Troy said. 'Now, where are we going?'

'Hertfordshire. Pretty well to Harpenden. They're building a new – what d'ye call 'em? – out there.'

'*Autobahn?*'

'Nope.'

'Freeway?'

'Nope.'

115

'Motorway – that's it. Motorway. The new London to Birmingham road.'

'Motorway it is. There's a bit of elevated highway – flyover, I believe is the jargon – just outside Harpenden.'

§ 30

Arc lights made the earth-moving equipment seem like monsters from childhood nightmares. A local bobby led Wildeve and Troy between metal-toothed giants, around concrete columns, through a roofless pagan cathedral to the heart of the new technology: a scraped-clear circle of compacted clay by a wooden hut. By the time they got there Troy felt as though he'd arrived at a place of primitive sacrifice. Instead of Isaac and Abraham, they had a site foreman in a hard hat, a police sergeant in uniform, and a small figure kneeling next to a dark mass of tarpaulin, shirtsleeves rolled up, Homburg pushed back on his head. Kolankiewicz.

He turned as they approached. 'You should be in bed,' he said bluntly to Troy. 'This bugger drag you out at crack of dawn just to look at a stiff?'

'I'm happy to do it. I'm at my best in the mornings.'

'I known you twenty-five years. You're always crap in the mornings.'

'Well, there's nothing like a bang on the head to change the habit of a lifetime. Now, can we get on?'

Kolankiewicz stood up, hands caked in mud and cement and human gore. 'It's not a pretty one.'

'Show me.'

Kolankiewicz whipped back the tarpaulin. It was Bosch-like – so many bodies were – large bits of flesh and bone set in concrete, hacked out and hacked up. Kolankiewicz had made an attempt to reassemble the body. Looking past the distortions created by the lumps of concrete, Troy could discern the outline of a human form. This was the body of a tall man, age indeterminable to Troy, who had had the misfortune to be decapitated and hacked limb

116

from limb. There appeared to be no sign of the head.

'How long?'

'Impossible to say with any accuracy, but allowing for the good weather we've had recently and the state of decomposition, say thirty-two hours. Maybe forty-eight.'

Troy turned to the site foreman. 'What can you tell us?'

The man tilted his hard hat up a little. Looked down at the corpse, drew breath and looked straight back at Troy. It was as though he found bodies on a daily basis. 'We clad the supports with wooden shuttering. You can't fill 'em all at once or it takes too long to set and you get cracks. Takes four days to fill a support as big as this. Yesterday morning we poured concrete. But the boards split and we had to redo it tonight. When we knocked out the last day's work we found this.'

'In the top layer?'

'Right. Top layer.'

'That means the body was dumped yesterday?'

'Had to be or it would have been further down and we'd never have spotted it. Site was empty last night.'

'A night-watchman perhaps?'

'Keeps the insurers happy. Most night-watchmen nod off before midnight. I've even known buggers get hired as watchmen who were deaf as bleedin' doorposts.'

Troy and Kolankiewicz knelt down. Wildeve conspicuously kept his distance.

'OK. Follow the bouncing ball. First no head.'

'I had noticed.'

'No hands.'

'They don't want him identified.'

'They don't call you smarty arse for nothing. But what I want you to see are the cuts and breaks. Look at the femur. The incision, if you can call it that, begins about half-way between the greater trochanter and the lateral epicondyle. It then careers raggedly-jaggedly to emerge an inch and a half lower on the inner side.'

'So?'

'Whoever did this knew nothing about anatomy.'

'Do they ever?'

'Some murderers, as well you know, have a precision that

matches mine and a cunning that matches yours. This bloke is an amateur. He killed and then disposed of the body with whatever was handy. In this case I rather think some kind of mechanical saw.'

'A chainsaw?'

'If that is indeed the term, yes, a chainsaw.'

'Good God. I hope he was dead when they did this to him.'

'He was. Now . . .' Kolankiewicz picked up his geologist's hammer and chipped away at the cement casing on what Troy took to be a section of the humerus.

'See. Same again. A quick, ragged cut at the deltoid tubercle. A neat butcher would joint the corpse – literally, by incisions at the joints. Anything else is messy, blood and bone fragments everywhere. If you ever find out where they did this, there'll be more evidence than they could ever wash out or sweep up.'

'Well, there are certain advantages to the chainsaw if you don't mind mess. It's quick. But it's not for the squeamish.'

On cue they both turned to look at Wildeve. He was listening, and looking and not getting too close. He hadn't spoken in a while.

'Are you all right?' said Troy.

'Fine,' Wildeve lied. 'Just thinking.'

They turned back to the corpse. Kolankiewicz took up his hammer again and picked up a blob of cement about the size of a cricket ball. It cracked open like a walnut. He hacked away at the interior, picked up tweezers and teased the skin of a small, fleshy object away from the sides.

'Greaseproof paper in my bag. Quick.'

Troy held out a strip and Kolankiewicz gently placed a severed penis on it.

'Amazing,' said Troy.

'How so?'

'It puts us into a different league. You chop off a bloke's head and hands, and there is motive and purpose. Without them we stand next to no chance of identifying the body. Chopping this off serves no purpose. It's . . . gratuitous.'

'Barbaric would be my word.'

They stood again.

Wildeve moved closer. 'What's up?'

Troy acted on instinct. Put his hand over the penis. Spoke on instinct. 'What were you thinking, Jack?'

'That it might be Bernie Champion.'

'It's not.'

'How can you be sure?'

'How long's Bernie been missing? Ten days? A fortnight?'

'He need not necessarily have been dead all that time – if you're going by the rate of decomposition.'

'That's a factor, but it's not the clincher. Bernie Champion was Jewish. None of King Alf's lieutenants were goy. House rule. Look at the cock.'

Troy held out the offended object on its strip of greaseproof paper. Mangled manhood. A two-inch squib, severed intact from the body – intact to the tip of its puckered akroposthion.

Wildeve went white. Looked at the fading moon and pinched the bridge of his nose. It was thirty seconds before he spoke. 'Sorry. I was being dumb. I don't suppose there's such a thing as an uncircumcised Jew, is there?'

'Not in Alf Marx's gang, and not in Bernie Champion's generation. I got invited to a couple of Brith Milahs in my time in Stepney. They're loaded with symbolism. A boy is not quite a Jew until it's done. I rather think the first test for joining Alf's mob was to drop your trousers.'

'Makes my blood run cold,' said Jack.

In the presence of a body that had been totally dismembered, limb from limb, limb from torso, head from neck, cock from balls, this struck Troy as unnecessarily squeamish. But, then, Jack was famous for puking at the scene of crime. It was a minor blessing he hadn't yet. But the day was young.

'Oh,' Kolankiewicz said, with an air of remembering something he had forgotten to mention, 'there is one more thing you should know now.'

'And?' said Troy.

'I examined the backside before you got here. The rectum is full of semen.'

Wildeve leaned over and vomited.

§ 31

Troy could not resist. It spelled temptation, it spelled stupid, and he did it just the same. He had to see for himself. Part of him, the larger part of him, was relieved when the box office at the Hippodrome told him they were sold out for the next two weeks: Vince Christy's music did nothing for him. He would kill an hour or so in the pub, then wait by the stage door in an alley off Cranbourn Street, itself but a stone's throw from Leicester Square.

What surprised him was the age span of Christy's fans. He found himself at the back of a throng of thirty or forty women who were anything from fifteen to fifty. Not that that seemed a large number – Tommy Steele and the new teen heart-throb Cliff Richard had been mobbed at personal appearances, and forty-odd didn't make a mob – but they screamed in what Troy could only think of as a sexual frenzy, the way women had at Sinatra in the late 1940s. If this ever became the norm, if Elvis ever got out of the army and played England . . .

He turned over a dustbin and stood on it to get a better view. Christy must be just inside the stage door, or they were screaming at no one. He saw a stout man with thinning hair crushed among the women. He turned, as though feeling Troy's eyes upon him. It was Gumshoe. Gumshoe without his hat. Troy would hate to be Gumshoe right now, he thought. One step too far and they'd trample him. Troy got a good look at Christy as he ducked out of the stage door and into a white Rolls-Royce – the famously wavy hair, the famously orange suntan, a beaming, pearly smile as he threw signed photographs into the air and used the scrum he'd created to dive into the car with a leggy blonde in tow, her face hidden by dark glasses and a headscarf. Troy would like to be her even less – they'd rip her to pieces if they could. As the Rolls pulled away, a dozen of the younger women pursued it, banging on the doors and windows. At the end of the alley it turned left into Leicester Square, half the crowd was gone, and suddenly Troy could hear the murmur that remained. A sad, tearful sound of joy half glimpsed, of pleasure half denied. A girl of seventeen or so was kissing Christy's photograph, and saying, 'My lovely,' to herself, over and over again. Some of the women were slumped on the ground where they'd dived to grab a photograph. It looked like the closing scene of *Hamlet*, after all the betrayal, after all the slaughter. He'd no wish to cast himself as Fortinbras. Too late the hero. It was . . . repellent.

Troy walked out into the square. A cab was parked a few yards down, towards the Empire, its back door open. The cabman waved at him. Troy ignored him. He cut through the alleys to St Martin's Lane and emerged by the Salisbury, opposite Goodwin's Court. The same cab was parked there, back door open. The cabman waved again. 'Sorry to trouble you, guv'ner. The fare wants a word.'

Troy looked into the darkness of the cab.

A small woman, dressed in black.

'Freddie?'

His sister Masha.

'Oh, Freddie.'

'What's the matter?'

He held out a hand. Masha took it and pulled herself to her feet, stepped out of the cab and wrapped herself round him. He didn't think she'd done this since they were children.

'You'd better come in for a bit,' he said. 'I'll put the kettle on . . . or something.'

A polite cough from the cabman.

'How much?' said Troy.

'Twenty-seven an' six, guv'ner.'

'*What?*'

'We was stood up by the 'Ippodrome an age with the meter running.'

Troy fished in his pocket, found a pound note and a ten-bob note. The cabman trousered the lot, said, 'You're a toff, sir.' And drove off.

Troy found himself supporting a sobbing Masha. Like it or not, the night was going to cast him, *deus ex machina*, as the late-arriving hero.

'What is it?'

'The bastard.'

'Which bastard? There've been so many in your life.'

'Vince.'

'*What?*'

'We went to the Dorchester. Wouldn't even see us. Sasha just said "Well, fuckim, then." But I couldn't do that. I had to see for myself.'

'I didn't know you—'

'His last tour, nineteen forty-nine. The winter he played the Palladium. Sasha and I . . . well, you know. We had him. Had him all winter. A lovely, juicy, Italian-American sandwich. Lots of lovely garlic and basil and mozzarella and Cole Porter all wrapped up in me and my sister. Now he won't even speak to me.'

'As you said. A bastard.'

'Did you get a look at his bit of totty?'

'Yes. Blonde. Tall – well, taller than you. That's about all I could tell you.'

'So that's it. Blondes are in. And dusky beauties pushing fifty are on the scrap-heap. Bastard.'

'Come inside. I'll put the kettle on.'

'Do stop saying that, Freddie. It's so bloody English.'

He made a pot of tea that neither of them drank. It sat on its little tray with its china teacups, just to remind them they were almost-English.

He sat opposite Masha while she dried her eyes and told him a tale of unequalled heartbreak.

'Lawrence has left me.'

'What?'

'He's gone off to live at Albany. Some old crony from his army days has lent him a flat. He's having an affair.'

The words 'pot' and 'kettle' competed for space in Troy's mind.

'He's having an affair with Anna Pakenham.'

'I see.'

'Do you, Freddie?'

'You're not blaming me?'

'No, I'm not. You introduced them, but it's hardly your fault if my husband decides to go off and fuck her, is it? There's only one person to blame for that.'

'Does Lawrence know about . . . ?'

'About all my affairs? Yes. I've never rubbed his nose in it, but

I've never made a secret of it either. I shouldn't think for one second he knows the half of it, but to know even a fraction would be enough. And do you know what really hurts?'

Troy could not even begin to guess.

'She's younger than me. Isn't she?'

'I suppose she is.'

'Suppose bollocks you know damn well the woman isn't even forty!'

'I think she's thirty-nine.'

'And I'm forty-nine!'

Masha dabbed at her eyes with her hanky, fought back a sob. 'That's why it was so important to me to see Vince, to – to have him again. I was thirty-nine that winter he and I and Sasha – but now I'm forty-nine, I'll be fifty next spring. At thirty-nine I was perfectly acceptable. Now I'm an old bag!'

'You've kept your looks. You don't look anywhere near fifty.'

She didn't, but it struck Troy as a minor miracle. This was a woman who had danced naked on the rim of hell for thirty-five years.

'That's very sweet of you, Freddie. But the fact of the matter is I've been turned down for younger women twice in one week. My life is in pieces. My children don't want to know me. I can't even begin to think how I'll tell them if Lawrence opts for divorce. Dammit, Freddie, I'm fifty years old and there's no one in my life. No one. A loyal, decent man has left me for one of your cast-offs – it *is* over between you and her, isn't it?'

'Yes,' Troy lied. When was it ever over?

'And a shit of a man I shouldn't let near me with a bargepole, who I only want because I want to be wanted, treats me like a rag he's wiped his thingie on and thrown away. Jesus Christ! I keep asking myself, what have I done with my life? What have I done to deserve this? To have it all come down to this. What have I done?'

She sobbed now without restraint, slid off the chair to her knees and puddled on the floor. Troy gently lifted her up, and sat her on his lap, much as she used to do with him when he was nine or ten and she was fifteen and he'd grazed or cut or bruised himself.

It was like watching a ship approach on the horizon. Troy could see. And seeing it so clearly did not offer any way out. It had that same sense of inevitability. Heading for them inexorably and, however indistinct, never less than obvious. Masha slumped on him, wept into his chest. A woman several times larger than life now seeming smaller than she was, curling up like a child, her feet not touching the floor. Then her head lifted and Troy saw the wind hit the sails, felt the rigging stretch taut, and saw her face approach his, a close and blinding blur. She kissed him, he kissed her back – foundered on the barren skerry of her want.

Masha fumbled. Clumsy as a teenager. His shirt tore, buttons pinging off like bullets; her knickers snagged on her heels and she ripped them off with one hand without bothering to look. She fell back on the floor, he banged an elbow and pulled back, wincing. Masha locked both hands behind his neck and drew him down.

'Please,' she said. 'I have to have someone right now. Please.'

She wriggled and scrambled until she had her skirt round her waist, his trousers pushed below his arse, his cock in her hand ready and far too willing.

He found he had literary expectations of incest. An arsenal of clunky metaphors mostly to do with looking-glasses and cameras, all telling him what he was supposed to feel in the midst of the outrageous. But it didn't feel outrageous. It felt like the culmination of a long seduction his sisters had begun on him before he was ten. They'd dressed and undressed in front of him, bathed in front of him, fucked all his friends, bored him with the details of every love affair they'd ever had. All, from the vantage-point of being flattened on her breasts and joined humping at the groin, seeming like a mixture of flirtation and proxy-sex. He wasn't outraged at himself or her, simply because it felt as though they'd done this all their childhood days. And what was childhood but a journey without maps? What was the adult life but the piecing together of the jigsaw of childhood into a map, into the illusion of coherence? It felt natural. It felt like . . . like what? Like vengeance.

Part of his mind was asking when the searing light of common sense might return. As it usually did, one split second after the betrayal that was orgasm and ejaculation? But it didn't. Once he had recovered an ounce of energy he took her by the hand and pulled her to her feet. She cast off the rest of her clothes, with not a hint of coyness, stepped out of her high heels, stood naked in the light of a forty-watt reading lamp while he kicked off his. Then they went upstairs and fucked again.

The cricket sat upon his shoulder. He flicked it off with a finger.

§ 32

It was still dark. Not quite dawn. Masha was standing, pulling her hair out of her eyes with one hand, vaguely looking for something with only moonlight to search by. 'My clothes?'

'Downstairs. Where we left them.'

She was not hiding. At least, not from him. Not yet. She stood, five foot two in bare feet, stark naked, half in shadow and half out, looking back at him and said, 'Downstairs?'

'Downstairs. On the floor.'

'On the floor?'

'We did it on the floor. We came upstairs when you said your back ached.'

'Did we?'

She went down to gather up her clothes. Any minute now he expected to hear the door slam. With that, reality would surely return. But she came back upstairs, laid her clothes across the chair and got back into bed. Side by side, looking straight ahead not at him.

'I really hate having to wear yesterday's knickers. It makes staying over anywhere such a drag. At least I've spared myself that. They're ripped to shreds. Sasha always carries an extra pair in her handbag, but I've never really known if that's her idea of forward planning or an advert.'

'Let's not mention Sasha,' he said.

'She wouldn't understand.'

'I doubt many people would.'

'No – I mean she wouldn't understand being left out.'

'Jesus Christ.'

There was a pause as Masha lay on her back and arranged her hands, the heels of each upon a breast, fingers pointing heavenward, tips touching like the buttresses in a church roof, thinking. 'You know, Freddie, I don't think we should ever tell anyone. Not anyone. Not ever.' Then she said, 'Would you just hold me? That's all. Just hold me.'

He wrapped an arm round her. Ah, well, he thought, there were worse things in life than fucking your sister. Weren't there?

§ 33

Troy lay awake watching the dawn light bounce off the wall of the building opposite his window. Masha was sleeping now, her breathing regular as a metronome. He caught the phone at its first ring.

Jack. Again.

'There's been another. Much closer to home. Adam and Eve Court.'

'Where?'

'It's an alley behind a pub in Wells Street. Leads from Eastcastle Street to Oxford Street. Shall I pick you up?'

'No. I'll walk over. I'll be there in about a quarter of an hour.'

It was so familiar. And a shock to think he had not been abroad in the city at this time of day in ages. It was London bleached out, its day only just begun. Winos around Soho Square, growling at him incomprehensibly, a crazed monologuist, poised flamingo-like on one leg in Great Chapel Street, pointing a finger at Troy and calling him a 'sinner', to no denial from Troy, prostitutes in Berwick Street smiling at him, a beat copper in Poland Street who recognised him and saluted, and then the crush of police cars and detectives in Oxford Street at the narrow entrance to the unlikely named Adam and Eve Court. Once he saw it he knew it. He'd just never known it had such a momentous name.

They let him pass with murmured good-mornings, yawning and sighing. For a second Troy wondered if he smelt of sex, then realised these men had probably been up all night and reeked of beer and fags themselves. Jack's car was parked face on at the top of the alley, headlights on dip to light up the court better than the day could manage at that hour. Jack was nowhere to be seen.

Kolankiewicz said, 'For once I cannot blame him. This one is messy.'

He lifted a rubber sheet. Rearranged by someone with a passing knowledge of human anatomy, these bloody joints of meat might pass as a facsimile of something that had once been a living, breathing human being. This one had not been dead as long as the other: it was wet with blood and guts. The smell of it smothered beer and fags. Smothered sex. Smothered everything except the stench of vomit when Wildeve returned. 'Sorry, chaps. I'll be fine now. Have you got anywhere?'

Troy said nothing, Kolankiewicz said, 'It looks much the same. Male. About twenty. Big. Put Humpty back together and I'd say about five eleven or six foot. Big in the chest and arms, plenty of muscle, not much under fifteen stones. And just like the last, no clothes, no head, no hands . . . and no cock that we've found. And taken apart with a mechanical saw.'

Kolankiewicz draped the rubber sheet over the remains.

'Semen?' Troy asked, talking to Kolankiewicz but watching Wildeve.

'Yes.'

'And where was thebody?'

'In dustbins, with the night's rubbish from the pub. Binmen found it about an hour ago,' said Jack.

'Then it is different from the last. They tried to conceal the last.'

Kolankiewicz said, 'Is it not concealment of a sort?'

Troy said. 'No. I think we were meant to find this one.'

And Jack said, 'I agree. They're making no effort to hide it. In fact, they're taking the piss. They're holding up two fingers to us, and yelling, "Catch us if you can." '

They left Kolankiewicz to it. Driving back towards the Tottenham Court Road, Troy said, 'Taking the piss? Isn't that what you said about Brock getting blown up?'

'Don't remember,' Jack replied.

When Troy got home Masha had gone.

Troy was pootling – he could term it no better – through a version of Erroll Garner's version of 'I'll Remember April'. The left hand still baffled, slam-dunking down so solidly he couldn't believe it wasn't a clenched fist. The telephone rang.

'Hiya, Topcop.'

'How did you get this number, Mr Rork?' Rork said, 'I knew you had me down for some kind of dummy . . .'

Correct.

'. . . but I'm not such a shmuck I can't work an angle and get hold of an unlisted number.'

'The embassy?'

'Ask me no questions Topcop . . .'

Still a shmuck.

'. . . and I'll tell you—'

'Cut the crap, as you Americans are so fond of saying, and tell me what you want.'

'What I want is to take you out to lunch and do you a favour.'

'You mean you want to pick my brains?'

'Jeez . . . Did a bear eat your nuts in the night? Ease up, Mr Troy.'

'OK. Where are you?'

'I'm in the pub opposite the end of your alley. I figured we could go back to the diner and have egg 'n' chips again.'

'No,' said Troy. 'I've a better idea. A much better idea.'

Out in St Martin's Lane Troy managed to beckon to Rork and flag down a cab with a single gesture.

'Where to, guv?'

'Do you know a good eel-and-mash?'

'Watney Market, guv. Pete Wallis's Eel Pie.'

'No,' said Troy, for reasons he could not fathom. 'Not Watney Market. What's the name of the one in Whitechapel? The Mile End Road.'

'If there's one there's 'alf a dozen.'

'Frank . . . Frank. . .?'

'Frank Tritten's. Youmean ole Tritt-Trott's.'

'Why so?' asked Rork, settling back in the cab.

'A culinary delight.'

'Such as?'

'Let me surprise you. The journey should take about twenty minutes. You can tell me what's on your mind.'

'Nah. Let's have a working lunch. I prefer to do business over lunch.'

'Have you been busy? I know you went to see Christy. I saw you there.'

'And I saw you, Mr Troy. But it's who else I saw that figures. All in good time. I shall – what's the word? – relish the adventure. We goin' east right? I've never seen the East End. During the war I used to listen to Ed Murrow. All those planes, all those bombs. All those plucky Cockneys. Got to admire those guys.'

'That,' said Troy, 'was a long time ago.'

Rork gazed out of the window. Every so often he'd point to the obvious and ask, 'St Paul's, right?', 'Tower of London, right?', or variations on that theme.

The cab pulled up in front of Frank Tritten's Fish and Mash in the Mile End Road, halfway between Whitechapel and Stepney Green Underground stations. Troy paid off the driver. Rork stared at the sign over the window.

'Is this, like, the native cuisine?'

'Yes,' said Troy. 'That's exactly what it is.'

They took seats. A wooden booth – a table as solid as a butcher's slab, a gleam of moisture across its swirling veins – a steamy smell of fish in the air. Rork sloughed off his jacket and rolled up his sleeves with the look of a practised trencherman before he'd even glanced at the menu.

'Anything that's *de rigger*?'

'Well, I don't think one should look at the ladies while they eat,' said Troy.

They had arrived as a group of four old ladies were finishing their eels. It looked to Troy to be a weekly outing, a ritual they had probably begun as young women at the turn of the century. They were dressed as only old women could be, in the fanciful hats and long skirts of the Edwardian era. Perched on the edge of modernity, for ever lost in a sunnier, bleached-out age buried under two world wars. Gumshoe could not resist and turned to look just as the old ladies, one after another, whipped out their false teeth, spat them into their handkerchiefs and sucked, toothless and gummy, on bones of eel, cheeks collapsing like tents in a blizzard.

'I guess not, but I meant more what's *de rigger* on the menu. What's unmissable. Now – what would you recommend?'

'The eels,' said Troy. 'I can definitely recommend the jellied eels.'

'You been to this neck o' the woods before?'

'My first beat as a uniformed copper, 1936.'

'Mine was South Bronx. Same year.'

'Or a plate of whelks. . .'

'Y'know I'm kinda peckish. Great word that – peckish. Sounds like something Charles Dickens made up.'

'You're thinking of Pecksniff. In *Nicholas Nickleby* or *Martin Chuzzlewit.*'

'Could be . . . whatever . . . but it sounds just like what it means. Peck*ish*. I'm peck*ish*, so maybe I'll have both.' He turned to the waitress – ordered 'like big helpings' with three rounds of bread and butter. 'An' you?' he said to Troy.

'Oh, I'm still recuperating. You know. Invalid food. Just a bowl of vegetable soup and a cup of tea.'

Troy was going to enjoy this. He'd never met anyone not born to it who could get through a bowl of jellied eels or a plate of whelks. Most non-Londoners were put off simply by the appearance. Most wouldn't even taste them. He'd been hoodwinked into trying them his first day in Stepney by his old mentor Sergeant Bonham. A sergeant and two old coppers giggling into their tea while an upper-crust rookie choked on one of the most disgusting textures ever to foul his palate. Salt and rubber. Never again.

'Like you said, Topcop, I been busy.' Rork pulled a small folder of photographs from his jacket pocket.

'Which implies that Mrs Cormack has been busy.'

'Yep. But not as predicted. See for yourself.'

He fanned out the photographs across the marble. Troy took out his new reading-glasses, an inevitable and he hoped less than permanent consequence of his injuries, fought off self-consciousness and sifted through the pile. Some simply showed

Kitty shopping in either Bond Street or somewhere very like it. Running through her husband's millions. None showed her with Vince Christy. One had Kitty and Troy emerging from Goodwin's Court into Bedfordbury, at which point Gumshoe seemed to have given up on them, for the majority showed her with one man. Getting out of a cab, emerging from the Quo Vadis, entering the Gay Hussar, on the steps of Claridge's, flagging a cab outside the Embassy club, embracing in the street, a stolen kiss by London lamplight . . .

'You see my point?'

'Impossible not to.'

'You know this palooka?'

'Yes.'

'And?'

The waitress bought Troy the time he craved. Slapped a fishy feast in front of Rork and one small bowl of synthetic-looking vegetable soup in front of Troy. Rork delayed the inevitable. Swallowed a slice of bread almost whole, belched delicately into his fist and, as he reached for his fork, said, 'So?'

Troy hesitated. Waiting for the first quiver of revulsion on Gumshoe's face. Gumshoe bit down, Gumshoe munched and Gumshoe smiled.

'Not bad. Not bad at all. Tell me, Topcop, you ever eat gefilte fish? Me, I'll eat anything. Gefilte fish, chop suey, shish kebab. Anything. Only thing I can't abide is pretzels – cardboard with salt on. My ex-wife says I have a stomach like a basement boiler. But, like I was saying, you try gefilte fish and food holds no terrors for you. Sits on the belly like lead shot. This, now, this is good. Do they have places like this in Soho? I could eat like this every day.'

Gumshoe one – Troy nil, thought Troy.

'You know what it needs?' Rork was saying, whirling around in search of a waitress. 'Just a dash of horseradish. Not the white, the red. The red horseradish would suit to perfection.'

Troy accepted defeat politely. 'If you want gefilte fish, try Bloom's about a hundred yards down the street. Now, you were saying?'

'Oh, yeah . . . mmmm . . . man, this is. . .'

If Rork had had false teeth he, too, would have been spitting them into his hanky the better to suck on the bones.

'Just get on with it. I can survive without a running commentary.'

'Sure. Whatever. This guy. This guy she sees all the time. That is, when she ain't seeing you. You know him?'

'Yes. I know him.'

'Un-huh?'

'Daniel Ryan. About Kate's age. They grew up together. Not half a mile from where we're sitting now.'

'Like, old flames?'

'Yes.'

'Like you?'

'No. Not like me.'

'Suit yourself. What can you tell me about him?'

Troy wondered if this was perspicacity or chance phrasing – that Rork had not simply asked, 'What do you know about him?'

'He's no "palooka", as you put it. He's one of our most successful boxing promoters. Perhaps not a national figure, but certainly a London face.'

'Boxing?'

'Been in it since before the war. Ambitious, honest. Would love to stage the world heavyweight fight here. Unless I'm mistaken he was in America earlier this year to talk to Floyd Paterson's people about a possible bout.'

'With whom?'

'I don't follow the sport, Mr Rork.'

'Boxing? Boxing? Ambitious?'

'Yes.'

'Honest?'

'Yes.'

'Y'know, I don't think there's such a thing as an honest fight promoter. In the fight game everybody's for sale and everybody's bought.'

'Not Danny Ryan.'

'You saying it don't happen here? That fighters don't get bought? That fighters don't throw fights they could win? The punchy bums like Primo Carnera don't get to the top by fights staged for easy wins? I know boxing, Mr Troy. I seen Marciano defend his title. I seen Jake LaMotta fight more times'n I can count. I'm a New Yorker. LaMotta's a New Yorker. New York is Fight-town. I polished a seat with my ass at Madison Square Garden a hundred times. Take it from me, it's a bent business. You say it don't happen here? I say nuts.'

'No – I'm not saying that at all. That sort of thing happens. Of course it does. I'm simply saying that Danny Ryan is known as one of the straightest people in the business.'

'Is that saying much? The best of a very bad bunch?'

'Maybe not.'

'Is he married?'

'Widower, I believe.'

'Anything else could fuel a scandal?'

'I think you'll find the scandal is all on Kate's side.'

Rork pushed his bowl aside and started on the whelks. Whatever pleasure he derived from them was masked by the look of professional concern. 'No, no, it's not. Your word won't be enough. I can't go back to the Deeks and say the Senator's wife is boffing a boxing promoter. The first word they'll utter will be "Mafia". Boxing is dirty, that's all they know and all they'll see. If this breaks and the press get it it would be as bad as an affair with a professional hit man or a Nazi on the run. Bad news, Topcop, very bad news.'

'You know your country. I don't. In fact I haven't been there for thirty years. But if you're right, I don't see what you can do about it.'

'Do? Do? We have to tell her, that's what. We have to warn her off this guy.'

'We?'

'OK. You got me there. I mean you.'

'And what do you want me to tell Kate?'

'Just to stay away from—'

'And how do I know this, Mr Rork? How do I know Kate is screwing Danny Ryan? Because you told me? Because you produced your sordid little snapshots? If I do that, your cover's blown. Kate knows she's being followed. What do you think she'll do? Mutter "*mea culpa*" and give him up? Or is it possible she'll call up the Deeks and fire a broadside into their intrusion into her privacy?'

Rork munched on his whelks for a moment. Jammed another slice of bread into his mouth. 'I guesh not. I guesh maybe I hadn't thought that part through.'

'Damn right you hadn't. There's no way I can tell her. You'd just better pray that she stays lucky and that you're the only one who catches Kate and Danny Ryan in the same frame. No one will be watching Danny Ryan. The press are all over Vince Christy. Look at it this way. You already got lucky.'

Rork pulled a second envelope of photographs out of his pocket. 'Maybe you're right. Cos Vince has been a very busy boy.'

He fanned out the photos. Christy and his rented Rolls-Royce at the stage door, the screaming fans, the lucky few who got picked.

Troy had to admit that whatever magnetism the man had worked like a charm. He sifted through a bevy of English beauties. All conforming to a type – Vince clearly had a thing about slim, tall blondes. A film of moisture stuck the last photograph to the one above. Troy prised them apart. Vince and a girl entering the Dorchester. Another leggy blonde girl. But the girl was a woman. And the woman was Foxx.

§ 35

Troy was in more than half a mind to call on George Bonham. It was a short walk to Cressy Houses and he hadn't seen the old man since he didn't know when. But then 'he didn't know when' was so easily pinpointed. George had nurtured him as a fledgling copper and never failed to show up at whichever hospital he'd been in at whichever crisis in his life as *wunderkind* of the Yard. Of course, Troy had seen George only weeks ago – he just wasn't wholly sure he remembered it. And then he remembered, instant and total recall, meeting the man at Edna Stilton's funeral, the conversation he had had with him, down to the last word – and even more he wondered at the tidal nature of his memory. He put Gumshoe in a taxi. Rork rolled down the window and said,

'*Mañana*.' He'd accepted Troy's word. Troy wasn't going to tell Kate Cormack a damn thing.

'Mr Troy, sir?'

Troy turned round. A young man in his early twenties stood facing him. A bony five foot nine, a mouthful of gleaming, smiling teeth and the uniform of a Hendon police cadet. All boots and buttons.

'You don't remember me, do you, sir?'

How Troy hated to hear those words. One more reminder of the number of things, of faces, of people he didn't remember. But the youth's implied opposite was right: there was something terribly familiar about him.

'Robertson, sir. You knew me as Shrimp. But me real name's Samuel.'

Troy's memory produced, rabbit-from-hat, an image of a boy of eight or nine years, small for his age, standing between Anna and the Polish Beast at his bedside in the London Hospital. The summer of 1944 revisited. Just a couple of days after D-Day. Him post-op from the bullet Diana Brack had put into him, the boy gruesome and shameless in his curiosity – 'The Tart in the Tub Case', as the press had so cruelly dubbed it – and the boy's urgency, 'It was the posh bird shot you, wasn't it?' and his own monosyllabic reply. And how grateful he'd been that the boy had not asked who had shot the posh bird, who had killed Diana Brack.

'You've . . . you've joined us?'

'Pass out next month, sir.'

The sweet flush of pride passing over the young man's face.

'You're what now, Mr Robertson?'

'Call me Shrimp, sir, everyone still does.'

'Twenty-five?'

'Twenty-three, sir. I was just a nipper when I searched that bombsite for you. I was nearly nine. All the other kids was bigger'n me, even them wot was younger'n me. I applied to join the force when I was eighteen. But I was too little. I've wanted to be a copper ever since that day you hired all us scallywags to search for you. It was me found the cartridge case, if you remember. Cost you an extra 'alf a dollar that did. But, like I said, at eighteen I

135

was too little, so the call-up got me instead. National Service, two years of square-bashin' an' bullshit – 'scuse my French. But I grew two and a half inches in the army. Must have stretched me a bit, too, I reckon. And I couldn't settle well into Civvy Street again, couldn't see meself cuttin' 'air like me old man, or drivin' a bus like me uncle Ernie, so I gave it a couple of years and reapplied. They took me. It's all down to you, Mr Troy, I'd never've thought of becoming a copper if it wasn't for you . . . and then when I saw you comin' out of the caff I just had to say . . . like . . . well . . . thank you.'

It was a stunning little speech. The weight of responsibility fell on Troy like cold porridge on to linoleum. 'Actually, Shrimp, I'm on my way to see Sergeant Bonham – he's retired now. You remember Mr Bonham, I'm sure.'

'O' course, sir. Old Bigfoot, we used to call him. If I had a tanner for every clip round the ear'ole I got from Mr Bonham . . .'

'I wonder if you'd care to come along and risk another clip round the ear'ole?'

'Don't mind if I do, sir.'

The Shrimp fell into step with Troy as they crossed the Mile End Road and headed for Stepney Green. Troy saw him glance at the walking-stick, but he asked no questions. Why would he? thought Troy. It had made the papers: it would be the talk of Hendon College. How often do chief superintendents of the Yard get blown away on the streets of London?

Bonham answered the door in his floral pinafore – a six foot seven friendly giant armed only with a sink plunger.

'It's the tea leaves,' he said. 'They block up the sink. I'd tip 'em down the karzey but they stain the porcelain and bleach'll never shift it. Ethel used to moan at me for doin' that.'

Ethel had been dead for the best part of twenty years and still Bonham spoke of her as though she'd nagged him about it only yesterday.

'And 'oo's the newboots, then?'

'Good afternoon, George,' Troy said.

'Arternoon, Freddie.'

Bonham swung back the door and ushered them into the cramped living room of the flat. Neither Troy nor the Shrimp had answered his question and he regarded the boy quizzically. 'I never forget a face, you know.'

'I'm sure you don't, Mr Bonham.'

'Give us a clue.'

'When did you last get your hair cut?'

Bonham snapped the fingers of his left hand. 'Robertson. Young Robertson. Wilf Robertson's boy. I 'ad me barnet done only last week. Yerdad neversaid.'

'There are some things me dad wouldn't boast about, Mr Bonham. Me bein' a copper bein' one of them. He thinks no one will ever tell him anything again. And what's a barber's life without gossip?'

Bonham thought this truism the funniest thing he'd ever heard and disappeared into the kitchen, chuckling to himself. Troy heard the soft pop of the gas ring go on. Warming up for the English tea ceremony. Robertson looked around the room. Ten by eight, if that. A cupboard by the standards of Troy's home life. Troy followed his gaze. The glass display case that had once held Ethel Bonham's plaster dogs and china trinkets was now stuffed full of dog-eared whodunits, the hideous wood-cased chiming clock that had been George's retirement gift from the Met, the framed photographs of the Bonhams' long-since-grown-up children.

'George raised three kids here,' Troy said softly.

'I know, sir. I grew up in a flat just like it. Me an' three sisters. You wouldn't believe the freedom of bein' in digs in Mill Hill. All the space in the wardrobe, me own room, and better still me own bed.'

It was another world to Troy, and he could see that Robertson knew it as he said it. 'Have you thought about your first posting?' he asked.

'I've *thought* about it, sir,' the Shrimp replied, with precision.

Bonham bustled in with a tray of cups and saucers, muttered, 'sugar,' to himself and bustled out again.

'It's a tricky one,' the Shrimp added.

'Wot is?' said Bonham as he returned. 'Sit down, sit down, the pair o'ye. No point in cluttering the place up.'

He sat on the edge of the armchair next to the unlit gas fire, noticed his pinny and yanked it over his head. 'You might have told me.'

'I thought it suited you,' Troy said. 'Mr Robertson and I were just discussing his first posting.'

'Wot's so tricky about that? There'll be a job for you here. Paddy Milligan's still the divisional detective inspector. Mr Milligan's a pal of me an' Mr Troy. A word from either of us and you'll be in. In where you belong. On your own manor.'

Robertson accepted the proffered tea and sat with it perched precariously on one knee. He looked at Troy and then addressed himself to Bonham. Bonham slurped tea and failed to see the expression on the boy's face. 'It's that that's tricky, Mr Bonham.'

Bonham didn't get it.

'I know Stepney Green. I know it too well, Mr Bonham.'

Bonham set down his cup and saucer. 'But where else would you go?'

'I'm thinking about that right now.'

'Where else would you go? You're a Stepney lad, a Cockney sparrer. Where else would you go?'

'It's . . .' The boy looked directly at Troy.

Troy took refuge behind a sip of tea. He'd had too many conversations like this with Bonham when he was younger.

'It's a matter of loyalties, Mr Bonham.'

'Loyalties?'

'Loyalties.'

'Good,' said Bonham. 'A man should have loyalties. To his own borough. To the force. To his fellow officers . . .'

'To his childhood mates.'

'Them too.'

'That's the problem, Mr Bonham. Not all my childhood mates are on the same side.'

'Eh?'

'Mr Robertson is saying,' Troy intervened, 'that some of his childhood friends are criminals.'

Bonham looked flustered, as though on the edge of anger so rarely expressed. 'But we don't have loyalty to villains!'

'Don't we, George?' Troy asked.

'Freddie. I expect that in that arsy-versy toff world you come from the old school tie might stretch a long way. But round 'ere the old school is Redman's Road Infants. I went there, young Shrimp went there. And we don't 'ave no old school tie. The first loyalty is to the force. If your old pal's a villain you owe him bugger all. Cos if he's villain he ain't a pal no more.'

Bonham was thumping the arm of the chair with each word, bringing up a cloud of dust with every blow. He was right. It was another world. When Troy thought of his old pal Charlie and the things old Charlie had done for which he would never be caught or tried or sentenced . . . Men like Charlie belonged in jail. And Troy had been one of those who had declined to send him there. Just a little he envied the simplicity of George's moral scheme, the absence of *ambergooities* – the ease of absolutes. He could not share them. Neither, it seemed, could the Shrimp.

Troy and the Shrimp parted company at the corner of Jubilee Street and Adelina Grove.

'You'll be all right, Mr Troy?'

'Of course. I'll either hop on the Underground at Whitechapel—'

'Hop, Mr Troy?'

'Stumble, Mr Robertson, and if I do I shall give up the effort and flag a cab. And you?'

The Shrimp pointed off down Jubilee Street. 'South, sir. My eldest sister's place in Watney Street.'

'I patrolled that as a beat copper when I was your age,' said Troy. 'I think I can say it was the toughest street I ever had to walk.'

'You should see it now, sir. Tough doesn't begin to describe it.'

'And your sister?'

'Got her name down for a council flat. She'll be relieved to get out. She skivvies, Jim skives, and the little 'uns grow up in a house and a street that should have been bulldozed years ago.'

'And you?'

'Me, sir?'

'Think about George Bonham's offer. If you do decide to come back to Stepney we'd both of us put in a word with the DDI.'

Troy gave Robertson his card, the one with his home number and no rank – Frederick Troy, Goodwin's Court, wc1. Robertson thanked him, shook his hand more vigorously than Troy thought necessary, and set off down Jubilee Street with not a hint of copper's plod in his step. As he passed the Stiltons' house Kitty's sister Vera appeared in the doorway shaking her dusters – her pinafore matched Bonham's to the petal. She spoke to the Shrimp, turned and looked straight at Troy without recognising him. It was the first victory for memory Troy had scored that day. Others' failings cheered him to the point of unrepentant *schadenfreude*.

§ 36

'You've no right to ask me that. No right at all.'

Troy sighed so audibly that Foxx was sure to have heard it at her end of the phone. 'I'd no idea you were going to be quite so hostile.'

'Troy, I am not hostile. You made your bed. Lie in it. And lying in it means not asking me questions about any man I might be seeing now.'

'Might? You *are* seeing Vince Christy. That is a fact!'

'I never thought you'd stoop to spying on me.'

'I'm not.'

'Then who is?' She yelled the last line at him as a blast of searing rhetoric. It required no answer in her mind.

He had one all the same. 'A private detective from New York.'

'What?'

'A former NYPD officer.'

'What?'

'An ex-New York cop.'

'What the bloody hell does an ex-New York cop want with me?'

Troy could almost hear the clunk as the penny dropped. He dropped his voice to a tone he thought placatory. 'He's bent. I've been trying to tell you that for the last five minutes.'

There was a long silence.

'Supposing this ex-cop is wrong.'

'I don't so suppose.'

'Then humour me, you bastard. Try to see it my way!'

'And . . .'

'And it's very handy for you, isn't it? Gives you the perfect

140

excuse to warn me off Vince. You and I break up and suddenly out of nowhere an ex-cop appears to give you the perfect reason to nag me about—'

'I'm not nagging you. I'm warning you.'

'Oh, Troy, fuck off.'

'He's not just bent, he's ma—'

All he heard was the dial tone rattling in his ear.

Foxx was making her own bed as surely as he had made his. He was not about to let her lie in it.

Less than a minute passed before the telephone rang. She was going to hear him out. But it was Jack.

'Just thought you'd like to know. We found the cock from the Adam and Eve body.'

'Where?'

'In a plain brown envelope, addressed to me at the Yard.'

'Bloody hell.'

'You know you reminded me what I'd said about taking the piss?'

'Yes – but I was wrong. It was Onions.'

'No matter. It's exactly what they're doing. Taking the piss. Puts me in mind of that letter Neville Heath wrote to the Yard in '47.'

'Forty-six.'

'Whatever. He wrote to old Bill Barratt with a pack of lies. But it was saying the same thing. "You can't catch me." Then he went right out and butchered another woman. "You can't catch me."'

'But we did. And justice was done. And he hanged.'

'So he did.'

§ 37

When the phone rang three days later, in the middle of the morning, it was Paddy Milligan, divisional detective inspector at Stepney. Troy and Milligan had been friends for two or three years only, and he was the kind of man Troy felt it would be easy to lose touch with. 'A bit of a loner' was the way Paddy was often described, and despite the fact that it might easily have applied to Troy himself, he thought it an obstacle to the job Milligan did.

'It's been a while.' Troy stated the obvious.

'Been back home. Liverpool.'

Milligan paused. Troy heard him breathe in as though embarking on a topic his instincts told him to avoid.

'It's my dad. He's got the cancer in his lungs. Truth is, Freddie, I don't think the old man'll last long.'

Troy and Milligan were about the same age. How old would the man's father be?

Milligan read his mind.

'He's sixty-nine. No great age.'

'Cigarettes?' Troy asked.

'Mustard gas,' said Milligan, and Troy felt utterly stupid that he had not seen at once that in giving him his father's age he had fixed the old man as a Great War veteran.

'It's taken up a fair bit of my time, I can tell you. I'm all he's got. I've used up all me holiday time, and a fair whack of compassionate. However, that's not why I'm calling. There's a young chap name of Robertson just coming through Hendon College, wants to work out of my nick. George says the two of you know him.'

'Well, George has known him all his life. I wouldn't be amazed if he'd been there with the midwife. I think we can both endorse the boy. He has good local knowledge, and he's not just rushed into being a copper because of some childhood notion of glamour. We turned him down a few years back. He's done his National Service and he still wants to be a copper. I call him a boy, he must be twenty-three or four. He's had time to find his way first. I think that's admirable.'

'Suits me,' said Milligan. 'I'll stamp his papers and get him down here. An extra bloke would be good right now.'

'You mean you'll still have to go back to Liverpool?'

Another breathy pause. Milligan was not a man easy with his own emotions. 'Were you there when your old man died, Freddie?'

'I was, as a matter of fact. He had me and my brother read aloud to him in the last few days. I was there when he spoke his last words.'

'Then I'll say no more. I have to be there. If the job came first, if he died while I was down south, I'd never forgive meself.'

§ 38

For ages now Troy had resisted running Foxx to earth. But if she wouldn't talk to him on the telephone, what choice did he have? He'd walked across Soho, almost to Regent Street, across the bottom of Berwick Market, along Broadwick Street and zigzagged the west Soho maze into Kingly Street. 'Street' was an overstatement. It was a long alley. One car wide. Running parallel to Regent Street on one side and Carnaby Street on the other. Unlike its neighbours, it was dark and sunless, dwarfed by the backs of the department stores in Regent Street. It was rag trade without the rags, the tailors preferring the lighter shop fronts of Carnaby Street. When Foxx had come into a small fortune three years ago, Troy had been mildly surprised at her practicality. There had been no spree. She had bought a long lease on the shop, and set up her own business importing and selling the clothes and accessories she liked. In this one crowded shop in Kingly Street you could buy 'Americana', and he was not at all sure whether that was a real word or one he'd made up, that was obtainable nowhere else in London – blue jeans Foxx insisted were called Levis, leather jackets like Marlon Brando wore in *The Wild One*, sunglasses like the ones James Dean wore in he forgot what film. It was, he readily conceded, a good idea. Perhaps a little ahead of its time, but a good idea. What he'd never been sure of was the street. It seemed the wrong street. Nonetheless, her business had prospered, and they had lived together as a couple of wholly independent means. Her money was her money. And apart from her flights to the United States two or three times a year to stock up the shop, they had not been apart until now.

There was a neon sign, a blue flicker in the shop window, 'Grapes and Wrath' (Troy had always liked the wit of this: most would have settled for the corniness of 'Stars and Stripes'), and in the room above the dim orange glow of a reading lamp behind the curtain. Next to the trade bell for the shop was a new bell marked simply 'Flat'. He pressed it several times, but there was not a sound from above nor the slightest movement of the curtain. He stood for ten minutes, telling himself every time he looked at his watch that he would go in thirty seconds, but stood an hour or more. Then he walked to the top of the street, as far as the London Palladium, then he walked back to the bottom, as far as Beak Street. When he had done this a couple of times he noticed a beat bobby watching him and realised that he, too, would regard this as slightly suspicious behaviour in anyone he did not know. But the bobby did know him, saluted, asked after his health and moved on. It was nearly midnight. He was tired. He stepped out into Regent Street, flagged a cab and went home.

When Troy got in he found a large man asleep on the sitting-room sofa. The arm had been let down at either end and still the man hung off it. Head over one end and feet over the other. Feet, in all accuracy, was foot. One foot stuck out from under a blanket, at the other end a ginger head snored whisky snores, and in the middle of the carpet stood the other foot, attached to a tin leg. Also attached to the tin leg was a note:

```
Strange woman in your bed.
Yrs
Angus
James
Montrose
Tobermory
Pakenham.
PS you appear to be out of Scotch.
```

What, thought Troy, was the mad bugger doing here? It seemed logical that Angus might not want to go home to his wife, Anna, but why here? Why me?

Not putting the light on he groped his way upstairs and from bathroom to bedroom. As he slipped into bed Kitty woke and wrapped an arm around him. 'You saw the guy on the couch?'

'I could hardly miss him. He's six foot four. Did you have to let him in?'

'He seemed lonely. Said he was a friend.'

'He is. After a fashion. Couldn't you have packed him off to your room at Claridge's?'

'Like I said, he seemed lonely.'

Troy weighed this one up. Angus never looked lonely. Angus always looked like what he was: a crackpot. War hero, decorated war hero, survivor of Colditz *et cetera* – but a crackpot. No, if loneliness was an issue it was far more likely to be hers than his, and loneliness was not what Troy would have called it.

'Youdidn't?'

'I might have.'

'Jesus Christ, Kitty!'

'What harm does it do? You weren't here. You didn't have to watch.'

'In my bed?'

''S OK. I changed the sheets.'

'But. . .'

'But what?'

'He's only got one leg.'

'That's OK too. He can still get the one leg over.'

'Whatwould you do if you met a man with no legs?'

'Inventiveness would come to my rescue. Where there's a will and all that malarkey.'

'I don't bloody believe this!'

'Troy, could we go to sleep now? You're making my brain ache.'

§ 39

In the morning Troy woke to find Kitty had slipped out. The banging and rattling coming from the kitchen could not be her, accompanied as it was by an off-key baritone rendition of 'Danny Boy'.

Troy dressed quickly and went downstairs to see what the madman was up to. He was rambling and scrambling. Philosophy and eggs with brown-bread toast. Troy accepted breakfast and ate while Angus fluffed up more eggs for himself.

'Glad you were in. I've been meaning to come round for a –'

'You mean,' said Troy, 'that you're glad I was out.'

'– bit of a chat. And don't go bearing grudges. Do I pout and go sullen when I catch you in bed with the wife?'

'You have never caught me in bed with Anna. And the last time you even suspected I might be you threatened to take off your tin leg and thrash me with it.'

'Ah . . . I was younger then.' Angus dropped two slices of bread into the toaster.

'It was only a couple of years ago.'

Angus stirred his eggs with a wooden spoon. 'It's the last couple of weeks that concern me now. I have had, for want of a better word, a revelation.'

Angus found a neat pause in cooking and leaned over the table like a preacher with a lectern.

Oh God, thought Troy.

'You will agree, old son, that we are middle-aged?'

Troy said nothing.

'And that middle age itself requires a survival strategy?'

'Eh?'

'The necessity is a plain one – to reinvent the self. To change from theman I amtothe manI would be.'

'And what would you be?'

The toaster pinged. Angus turned, caught the two slices deftly in mid-air, slapped them on to a plate, scooped up his scramble and, in what seemed to Troy to be a bit of flashy kitchen choreography, pivoted on his good leg, and sat down opposite Troy with his breakfast steaming up his nose. Only the clunk as his tin leg collided with the table spoilt the effect.

Angus winced. 'You won't believe how much that hurts.'

'You were saying . . .'

'Indeed I was . . . I've given it a lot of thought. One must see to the heart of the age in which one lives. Changing oneself is merely—'

'Angus. You cannot change yourself.'

'No?'

'You can change. But you can't change yourself. You can't will it.'

'I do hope you're wrong there. I was going to say that changing oneself is just the prelude to changing society. And to do that you must know where your society is, where its heart is.'

'OK. So what do you mean to do?'

'Simple, really. Weighed it up. Looked at it from all angles. Pros, cons, you know the score. As I see it, either I join a skiffle band or I stand for Parliament. Since I can't – as you may have gathered – keep a tune for more than about five seconds and as I do not own a tea chest or a washboard . . .'

'You want to be an MP!'

'Quite. Which is why I needed to see you. I was wondering if you might have a bit of a chat with your brother. No point in beating about the bush, is there? Could be an election any minute. Rod could be Home Secretary any day now. Got to get meself a safe seat.'

'Angus, are you even a member of the Labour Party?'

'Details, Troy, mere details.'

'I think you'll find Rod will not agree. And the answer's no. You want Rod to pull strings for you, call him yourself.'

When would people stop using Troy as an earpiece to get to his brother?

'Have you considered standing as an independent?'

'Buggers never stand a chance. Party system runs the whole shebang.'

'That rather depends on where you stand. Why do you think Rod stood for Hertfordshire? Because he was local. Local connections can still count for a lot. An English public-school accent notwithstanding, weren't you brought up in Scotland?'

'As a matter of fact, I'm from the Western Isles. My old dad cut quite a figure there before the war. I take your point. There'd be a bit of kudos in standing where I'd be known as old Hector's son, but it's an urban constituency I want. The belly of the beast.'

There was no way Angus was ever going to get the belly of the beast. There was no way Troy would ever mention this loony request to Rod. He got up to push the plunger on the cafetie're. The action seemed to break the spell of Angus's obsession, and he changed the subject. 'About the wife.'

'What about your wife?'

'This new bloke of hers.'

Troy feigned innocence. 'Anna has a new bloke?'

'Good God, Troy, do the two of you never talk?'

'About men? Hardly at all.'

'Well, I thought she might have mentioned this one. It's your brother-in-law, that git Lawrence Stafford from the *Sunday Post*.'

So – he knew after all.

An hour or so later the two of them stood on the doorstep. Troy had been edging him towards the door ever since breakfast. Angus took one step into the yard, and said, 'Just a jiffy. I owe you this.' He rolled up his trouser leg. The sun glinted on the tin as he flipped open a door in the leg to reveal a full bottle of Scotch, held in place by an ingenious system of straps and flanges. He unhooked it and handed it to Troy.

'Got the old boy in Colditz village to make me the cubby hole when I lost the leg in '42. Used to hide trowels and hammers in there during the war, goons never found 'em, and for a whole month I had the camp wireless tucked away in there, with the leg acting as an aerial. It's probably one of life's rarer experiences to feel the buttocks vibrate to the rhythm of the BBC Home Service. Nowadays I have better uses for it. This is the business. None of your blended muck. A good single malt from Skye. Talisker. Goes down like nectar. Try to save some for me.'

He legged off, swinging his tin prosthesis like a cricket bat. Out, side, forward, down, clank. At the end of the alley Troy caught sight of a figure beating a hasty retreat. It looked to him remarkably like Gumshoe.

§ 40

It was three days before he heard from Gumshoe again.

'I was wondering if I could buy you lunch.'

'OK,' said Troy.

'But this time I get to pick the joint.'

'That's OK too. Where did you have in mind?'

'You heard of a street called Strand?'

'Mr Rork, there are Malay bandits in the eastern jungle, there are Bushmen in the Kalahari, there are pygmies in the darkest reaches of the Belgian Congo who've heard of the Strand.'

'Oh – so it's kind of like Fifth Avenue?'

'Kind of.'

'Okey-doh. Meet me at a joint called Simpson's. I hear it's the best burger bar in town.'

The maı^tre d' greeted Troy by name. Troy hardly ever ate at Simpson's, but it had been a haunt of his father's – and it was the memory of the old man they were greeting rather than the living son. Troy did not have to ask for Gumshoe. He had bagged a corner booth to the right of the great fireplace. He was facing the room, waving at Troy, and wearing that little-short-of-salivating look that Troy had known overtake aged members of the aristocracy to the detriment of heart, liver and life. Many a toff, Troy thought, would doubtless choose not to die unless he could take it with him – although it was the doctrine of the Anglican faith that you *could* take it with you– but if he had to die at all he would prefer to die in Simpson's, fork in hand, ready to meet his Maker on a gastronomic high.

'Swell, huh?'

'You could say that,' Troy replied. 'Or if you had a talent for half-way decent prose you could say it was a Temple to Food. At least, I think that's what P. G. Wodehouse called it.'

'Wodehouse?'

'The writer.'

'Oh, yeah . . . H. G. Wodehouse, like *War of the Worlds*?'

'That was Wells.'

'Right. Orson Welles. Y' know, I was in New York when he did it on the radio. All those Martians landing in New Jersey. Scared the bejasus out of the whole city. Now – to business. What would you recommend?'

'Well, you won't get whelks or eels.'

'Everything in its place,' said Gumshoe. 'And I was thinking of something more in the beef line.'

'In the beef line? OK. Flag down the carver and see if he has any beef Wellington.'

'Why's it called that?'

'After the Duke, I would imagine. Can't say I've ever given it much thought.'

'Right. Duke Ellington. Very American. He's from Washington, y' know. Saw him play Carnegie Hall, Christmas of '47. Johnny Hodges did this great sax medley – "Junior Hop" . . .'

Troy raised a hand and flagged the carver.

'. . . "Jeep's Blues". . .'

The carver, so flagged, wheeled his carnivore's cart to their table.

'. . . "The Mood to Be Wooed". . .'

Troy stopped the flow of reminiscence –

'. . . nobody is as mellow as Hodges, not even Ben Webster . . .'

– and pointed out the beef (W)Ellington.

Gumshoe looked from the beef to the waiter and back again. Troy thought he might be in danger of drooling. Perhaps suggesting one thing was a mistake. Why not let him order the whole smoking carvery?

'What's the white stuff on the outside?'

'Pastry, sir.'

'So it's like . . . cow pie?'

The waiter looked to Troy in something close to despair.

'Only Desperate Dan eats cow pie.'

'Who's he?'

'A cowboy of sorts – shaves with a blow-lamp, lives off cow pie, always leaves the horns on the side of the plate. Bad manners not to, after all. He's very popular with children over here.'

'So it is American? Great. Beef Ellington it is. And for my guest?'

Troy ordered a few slices of rare roast. Wondered how much more of Gumshoe's chit-chat he could take.

But Gumshoe headed him off at the pass. Slapped down another packet of snapshots. 'Now, tell me, Topcop. Do you still say Daniel Ryan is kosher?'

Troy said nothing.

'Take a look.'

Troy slid the first few photographs on to the tablecloth. Angus

– leaving Troy's house in Goodwin's Court.

'She's seen him since, you know,' Gumshoe said, with more man-toman than Troy found tolerable.

Angus leaving Claridge's.

'I mean, what does she see in a gimp?'

Troy said nothing.

'And he looks kinda crazy, doncha think?'

'No,' Troy lied. 'And I thought we were talking about Ryan?'

He fanned out the rest of the pack. Daniel Ryan in what looked like a London nightclub. Some with a bunch of men he did not know. One with Kitty. And one with a very familiar face – that self-publicising arrogant shit Lord Steele, husband of the ubiquitous Sylvia – formerly Ted Steele, MP for Nottingham, now a Labour apparatchik in the Lords, one of the first of the new-fangled life peers. It was a minor miracle Gumshoe had not known who he was – or did the man read no English newspapers? Ted was something of a joke to brother Rod. On his elevation he had put to the College of Arms the idea that he would take the title 'Lord Sheffield Steele.' This they had duly forwarded to the appropriate Lords committee. 'But, Ted, it's advertising. You can't use a title to advertise a product! Besides you're not even a Sheffield MP.' Someone on the committee had recounted the conversation to Rod who had helpfully suggested the title of 'Lord Fork and Spoon' – it was marginally shorter, they made 'em in Sheffield and it was steel. In the end Ted had copped out and just turned his own surname into a title. To Troy and Rod he would always be 'Lord Spoon'.

'Your point?'

'The company he keeps.'

Troy tapped the photo. 'Ted Spoon . . . sorry, I mean Steele. Ted Steele. Member of the Lords. Filthy rich, and a total twat, but that's hardly a crime.'

'Look at the first one of Mr Ryan.'

Troy looked again, and failed to recognise anyone in the convivial gathering but Ryan himself.

'You know these guys?'

'No.'

'They're Citizen Ryan's kid brothers.'

'They may well be. As I recall, Danny comes from a large family. I've never made it my business to keep *au fait* with the family tree.'

Gumshoe's lip curled like Elvis's – part smile, part sneer.

'You say he ain't bent. OK. I might just buy that. But these two – his kid brothers – either they're bent or I didn't spend seventeen years in the NYPD, I don't have flat feet, I don't have haemorrhoids . . . Take it from me, Topcop, these guys are crooks.'

'What kind of crooks?'

'How in hell should I know? That's up to you guys. Or has the East End become a no-go area for the London bobby?'

It was a stinging comment. This flatfoot buffoon had turned the tables on him. If the Ryan brothers were bent somebody ought to know. Somebody should be *au fait*. But it was hardly Troy's domain – these men might be petty criminals. The Metropolitan Police Force had its divisions for that sort of thing.

'You know this place?'

'No.'

'They call it the Empress Club.'

'I still don't know it.'

'One of those side streets off Bond Street. Now, correct me if I'm wrong but that's what you'd call a classy neighbourhood, right?'

'It's what you'd call Mayfair.'

'These two palookas own it.'

'And?'

'And? And that's a hell of a lot of moolah, that's what.'

'I doubt Danny's hard up. Perhaps he bankrolled his brothers.'

'I thought of that too. But if he's that philanthropic how come these guys had day jobs in a garage underneath railway arches in Shadwell until the spring? I asked around. They were monkeys in greasy overalls until a matter of months ago. They still put in appearances at their garage from time to time. And how come they take hundreds home in cash from their club every night and help themselves from the till like it was their personal piggy-bank? Troy, take it from me, something stinks. Somebody is folding the greenbacks away. Money is changing hands like it was juggling class. These two are rotten. I can feel it in my piss. And if they are, the odds are big brother Danny is too. And even if he ain't it's too close to Mrs Cormack for my comfort.'

Troy looked again. The brothers looked to be twins. They also looked to be the best part of twenty years younger than Danny. Two big brash young men in shiny suits and an excess of Brylcreem. He didn't know them. They could be any pair of on-the-make young tearaways of the post-war world. It seemed like only yesterday, although it was probably five years, that the city was awash in young men armed with cut-throat razors, dressed in the outlandish red and purple suits, the bungy-soled brothel creepers of the New Edwardian look. They'd been known as Teddy Boys, or Teds. It was Troy's night for Teds. Perhaps this was what they'd evolved into. These vaguely menacing, cocksure young faces.

'Now, we come back to the same question. Are you gonna tell her or am I?'

'Is Kate a regular at the Empress?' He fanned quickly through the rest of the shots. 'You would appear to have only three, no, four shots of her out of about thirty.'

'Troy, just answer the fucking question.'

'It is in both our interests to see that Mrs Cormack does not become embroiled in a scandal.'

'Was that a "yes"?'

'That was an "I want to see for myself".'

'You mean you're gonna go down the Empress and spy on these guys in person and hope that the Senator's wife doesn't spot you in the crowd?'

'Sort of.'

'Jesus Christ.'

'OK, smartarse. How did you do it?'

'Me – I'm not quite as conspicuous as you, for starters.'

'Of course not,' Troy lied.

'For twosers, Mrs Cormack wouldn't know me from Adam.'

'Can't argue there.'

'And threesies, I got this from a buddy in the CIA.' Rork took a tiny camera out of his pocket.

'High-res film, no need for a flash. You can snap a guy and he'd never know.'

'You know,' said Troy. 'I thought the trick was to have it

concealed in your bow-tie.'

'I ain't wearin' a bow-tie.'

'Quite.'

'Are you pullin' my pretzel?'

Oh, God, thought Troy. Oh, God. Rork was about as inconspicuous as an elephant and, worse, he was an elephant who went around pointing a camera at people thinking no one would notice. That was the chilling thing about Gumshoe. You thought him a fool, then he surprised you, trounced you almost, and then he said something so dumb you thought him a fool all over again.

§ 41

It took Troy a couple of days to find the nark he wanted. Most of the narks he'd had in his younger days knew the East End and little else. After his move to the Yard they had tended to be Soho-centred. What he needed now was someone a little more geographically and socially mobile. Someone who might occasionally venture into Mayfair.

Shortly after the end of the war he had inherited a nark. Chief Inspector Walsh, the only officer in the Special Branch who would even give Troy the time of day, had offered him an oddity known as Fish Wally. The Branch had little further use for him, but it seemed a shame not to deploy his ears and eyes. By a coincidence Fish Wally had been recruited to the hidden profession by none other than Kitty's father, the late Chief Inspector Stilton. However, the relationship Troy and Wally had formed was based on cash not sentiment. Over the years Troy had reached the conclusion that Wally did his cash business with quite a few people. In the last ten years Wally had been transformed from a walking ragbag in a tatty greatcoat and three-day stubble to a man who could only be described as dapper. An Aquascutum blue cashmere overcoat – it would have to be a blistering summer day before Wally would venture out without it; today was a blistering day and still he wore it – an array of Harvie and Hudson, both white and striped, shirts, shoes handmade to a last of his foot at Lobb's – and gloves, gloves that hid his frostbitten lobster-claw hands. The gloves were always white and always put Troy in mind of a Disney character. Mickey Mouse and Goofy always wore white gloves. Like Mickey Mouse and Goofy, Wally never took them off. Wally ate wearing his gloves just as he was about to now. In the same greasy caff in which Troy had confronted Gumshoe for the first time. Wally turned a few heads among the working men in overalls sitting down to steak and kidney pie and chips, but he had a dignity as starched as his shirts. 'How discerning of you, Troy. I have ever been partial to the plain fare served in this establishment by Mother Riley.'

Mother Riley was standing over them, a bosom as big as Texas, clutching her order pad. She uttered what Troy wouldn't: 'I never understand a bleedin' word 'e says. Usual, is it, Wol? The kidney puddin'? And for you, Chief Superintendent?'

More heads turned. Two young men got up and left without ordering.

'Egg and chips, no bread and butter.'

Troy paused before asking Wally anything, knowing full well that Mother Riley's next move would be to yell the order down the dumbwaiter at deafening volume.

When she'd finished, it was Wally who spoke. 'What is it you want that you think we can discuss in public?'

'The Empress Club. What is it and why have I never heard of it?'

'You probably knew it before the war. It began life as the El Hassan in the twenties – then it was something else I do not recall. Whatever it was it was called it until about 1945, when it became The Swingtime, and that's what it stayed until about two months ago.'

'Why the change?'

'Change of ownership.'

'The Ryan twins?'

'So I gather, but of them I know next to nothing. The club was owned by someone you may well know – Bobby Collington.'

'The bandleader?'

'The same. The King of English Swing, as he called himself.'

Troy had never been to The Swingtime, but he'd heard

Collington's records. They always struck him as a milk-pudding version of the real thing – the real thing being probably the old Tommy Dorsey band – and definitely not to his taste, at least not to his taste while Duke Ellington was still around. He said as much to Wally while Mother Riley slapped the meal in front of them.

Wally gazed down at his steaming plate silently for several seconds, his knife and fork untouched. 'You know,' he said, looking up at last, 'how certain things habitually remind you of the rituals of childhood?'

Troy nodded.

'With every meal served by another hand, and this does not happen when I cook for myself, but these days I so rarely do . . . with every meal I hear my father's voice saying grace, urging his sons and daughters to a gratitude they scarcely felt or understood. The Germans shot my father. Most of my brothers and sisters too. My Catholicism lapsed into atheism overnight. Yet still my mind recites the ritual words of thanks, and does so in his voice. I have the gratitude now, I have lost the god. How curiously we are constructed. Do you ever think of your father, Troy?'

'Every day,' said Troy tersely. 'Where were we?'

'You were telling me you had no taste for old Bobby Collington's music. You will like the new sound of his club even less. Bobby is, I believe, a partner of the Ryans, whether he likes it or not, and the club purveys the latest jazz, which I believe is called Trad and is the height of fashion.'

Trad, Troy thought, was rubbish. The New Orleans sound of King Oliver and Kid Ory turned into a hammy seaside pastiche – all boaters and stripy waistcoats – that scarce deserved the name of music.

'What do you mean "whether he likes it or not"?'

'You would not be asking me about the Empress if you did not have your suspicions. Do you really think they bought their stake in the club? I think Bobby got strong-armed. These days he hangs around looking nervous and wishing he had retired to a bungalow in Frinton-on-Sea.

Or so I am told. I have not, you will appreciate, been to see.'

'Could you find out more?'

'I can always find out more. I could even talk to old Bobby, but as to what he will say . . .' Wally let the sentence run down, forked in a good helping of kidney and mash, the godless satisfaction of gratitude lighting up his eyes.

'Do you mean to look for yourself ?' he asked.

'I was thinking of going tonight.'

'It's members only, but I should think a discreetly placed bribe would do the trick.'

§ 42

Troy arrived after ten thirty, thinking this would be in the interval between sets, to find they hadn't even started. The trick was played and a tenner did it. A six-foot, sixteen-stone plug-ugly bouncer, who cheated on his employers and saw Troy for what he was at first glance. He wondered how long it would take before the word suffused the whole club. 'Old Bill's in tonight.'

'Anywhere?' said the talking suit by the velvet ropes.

'Side booth, quiet and shady.'

It was an old-fashioned look – not tarted up but not shabby either. The clean, yet elaborate lines of art deco. The red and sandy colours the original designers of the El Hassan had meant to suggest Morocco or Egypt. As though the accretions of the last twenty-odd years had been peeled away. As though new management had taken over the club, ripped out half a ton of plasterboard and found a pre-war nightclub intact beneath. Troy had the vaguest memory of the place. He rather thought he'd been there some time in the 1930s when it had been known as The New Yorker or The Manhattan or something equally silly, long after it had been the El Hassan. He'd been there in '36 or '37 at the height of the Depression – and as that word flashed through his mind the real name of the club sprang fully fledged to memory. It had been sillier still – The Roaring Twenties, after the Bogart and Cagney film. He had not been twice. They had still played twenties music, the frenetic, tasteless pretence of the carefree . .

157

. so out of place in an age that had cares by the million. It was a sound raucously echoing in an empty hall long after the party had ended. Perhaps 1959 was exactly the moment to reopen the club in its original form. In a mere quarter of a century we had gone from never having it to never having it so good. There might be many in Britain who had not noticed they had never had it so good, but the Prime Minister had assured us it was so. It seemed to Troy to be touch and go. (Or was it stop and go?) Make the most of it while it lasts. Given the fickle, almost neo-embryonic nature of English culture at the moment it was perfectly possible that in six months a job lot of labourers would be ushered in with a hundred sheets of pegboard to whack up and this glimpse of a lost era would be lost once more.

From his side booth he had a good view of the centre tables and the better-lit booths nearer the band. He was looking around when the lights dimmed and the band took to the stage. A crooner's voice said, 'One, two, three, four', the stage lights went up and a nine piece band in blazers striped like deckchairs struck up an ear-bendingly awful version of 'Chattanooga Choo Choo'. They followed this with a sousaphone-led rendition of 'Bye Bye Blackbird' that the crooner crooned through a tin megaphone. Troy wondered how long the set would last. Could he get through it without euthanasia? Yet . . . yet . . . the audience clapped enthusiastically after every number – some even whistled and yelled. What, thought Troy, as people seemed to say to him so often nowadays, is the country coming to? Many numbers on, they ended the set with the ritual slaughter of 'Lazy River'. In so short a time he had come to think of it as Kitty's song – it was more than slaughter, it was murder.

When the house lights went up again, he caught sight of Kitty, clapping politely at the death of her song. And when she stopped clapping, she leaned over to Danny Ryan and whispered something in his ear. She was not looking his way. There was only one light at his table, illuminating the cocktails menu at head height. Troy reached for his hanky and twisted the hot bulb in its socket. If Kitty looked now, it was unlikely she'd see anything but an outline.

As he looked around he saw another canoodling couple two

booths further back from Kitty. Foxx, head on the shoulder of Vince Christy. A waitress stood before him and blocked his view.

'Nothing, thank you.'

'You gotta order summink. 'Ouse rules. Two quid minimum.'

'Water, then.'

'Water don't cost two quid, water don't cost tuppence.'

'Bring me a glass of water and I'll pay two quid for it. Just move.'

In the time it took to get rid of her, the empty booth behind Foxx and Christy had received two occupants. Troy began to wonder if there was a surprise the evening would not spring on him. Ted Steele, Lord Spoon as Troy knew him, and quite possibly the last face Troy expected to see in a Trad Jazz club. Tom Driberg, a maverick back-bencher from the Labour Party, and old friend of Troy's since the war, an even older friend of his father's and someone the very mention of whose name could provoke Rod to rage or laughter. Troy had the merest sliver of sympathy for Rod's point of view – if you wanted your party elected to power, an unrepentant, indiscreet queer on the benches didn't help much. Troy had had no idea Spoon and Driberg were friends. Acquaintances inevitably – Spoon sat on the Labour front bench in the Lords – but friends? Unlikely. An odd couple, even physically. Tom Driberg had never been particularly handsome, even as a young man, and in middle age seemed to have developed a striking resemblance to a sleepy dog, but somehow managed to look effortlessly upper crust (although what upper crust or elegant *with* effort might look like Troy had never been able to work out). Lord Steele was in good shape, far from seedy at fifty or so, tall, good-looking in that greying sort of way, and ever so faintly continental in appearance, in much the same way Troy's brother Rod was – and almost always to be found, as he was now, puffing at a Gitane. It was only the second or third time Troy had seen the man in the flesh, rather than in one of his customary husband-as-accessory poses in the newspapers. Troy wondered about the transparent vulgarity of the man, the way he lent himself to his wife's headlining antics, and he wondered, too, about the Sheffield Steele story. Was it apocryphal? He didn't know the man, yet he'd taken the piss out of him for years – he'd been a joke to Troy and

Rod – but that was them, when they wanted to take the piss they did it. And they were forever making up nicknames for politicians. Troy had dubbed Harold Wilson 'Mittiavelli', Rod had christened Nye Bevan 'Humpty'. Steele had been 'Spoon' for about a year now. Might there be more to Steele than Spoon?

In the interval the club was filling up for the second set. It must be getting on for midnight and still they came. The Empress Club, he realised, was that fashionable sort of place one went to with the defining phrase 'We're going on somewhere' – the place you went to after the theatre or the restaurant, only to roll home around dawn. Almost on the stroke of midnight two figures appeared and stood in front of the velvet ropes, surveying the floor below them with a look Troy could only describe as proprietorial. The Ryan twins. And what Rork, who was, thankfully, nowhere to be seen, had failed to capture in his snapshots was the sheer swagger of the men, or rather more than swagger – even the Teddy Boys had had swagger, and this was so much more. This was, in the vocabulary of the unimaginative, 'presence'. Troy preferred the local argot 'clout' – these men had clout. He played a mental game he often played. He looked into the looming hulks of these men for the trace of the two little boys they must once have been, and it seemed to him they had been born fully-fledged into this cocky brutality. As they stepped on to the floor, a man in his sixties, whom Troy recognised as Bobby Collington, appeared, spoke a few words, received a patronising mock slap to his face and vanished again. Fish Wally's description had been precise: Collington had the look of a man who dearly wished he was anywhere but where he was. But Troy would not have called it nervous – he would have called it fear. Then the Ryans moved from table to booth, booth to table, glad-handing like royalty and beaming with pleasure. It seemed to Troy that they moved through the throng like the prow of a ship slicing through water – the whole room rippled to the wave they made. He knew now why they had changed the name of the club: it was their mistress and their empire.

At Spoon's booth they sat down and talked, just as the waitress reappeared with Troy's glass of London tap and a bill for two quid. Troy paid her, turned over the bill and scribbled on it.

'I want you to give this to that gentleman over there.'

'What *gentleman*?' she sneered.

'The one looking like a sad bloodhound, talking to the Ryans.'

'Boss don't like bein' disturbed by punters.'

Troy had three quid in change from his 'cocktail'. He pressed it into her hand and said, 'Take a chance. After all, how bad is their bark?'

She pulled a face at this but took the cash and the note all the same. Troy watched as Driberg read the note and looked around. Troy risked waving from the shadows, saw Tom mouth, 'Excuse me,' and get up.

'Last place I expected to find London's greatest aficionado of Art Tatum. Hardly your cup of tea, Troy.'

'I could say much the same to you. But my excuse has to be better than yours. I'm working.'

'Ah – police business. I see. Our hosts?'

'Who else?'

'Rough types, Freddie. That's all. Rough types who've done rather well for themselves.'

Troy shook his head, leaned in a little closer to Driberg. 'No, Tom. Wide boys running a racket. Walk away from it.'

'Really? What sort of a racket?'

'I'm not sure and if I were I wouldn't tell you, but take my word for it – if those two aren't already the subject of a Scotland Yard investigation, they soon will be. Walk away from it.'

'Bit melodramatic, don't you think?'

'Tom. Just take a hint. And count yourself lucky you're getting it. I won't be doing any favours for Spoon.'

The changes were subtle – the pause, the barely audible intake of breath and the faintly quizzical tone Driberg had used so far was replaced by something more gleefully earnest. 'How neatly ends meet. I was wondering if there was a favour you might do for me.'

'I think you'll find I just did.'

'I meant one I was about to raise before you beckoned.'

Oh, God.

'OK. Let's hear it. But if it's anything to do with your peculiar way of spending your evenings . . .'

'Sex has no part of it. It's the new sex.'

161

'The new sex?'

'Politics.'

Oh, God.

'Then you'd better share a cab with me. I'm not having this conversation here.'

'But I'll miss the band.'

'Do you really care?' said Troy.

They left the booth. Troy took a last look at the sexual motley. Kitty laughing at something Danny Ryan had said, running a finger tantalisingly down his broken boxer's nose, not even remotely aware of Troy's presence, the other hand sliding up and down Danny's arm between the elbow and the shoulder. Affectionate. Possessive. Foxx smouldering – that overworked Hollywood-movie-mag Ava Gardner/ Julie London word – as she looked across Christy and straight at Troy. It was for the best. If any of them had to spot him it was better by far it be Foxx rather than Kitty.

Out in the street. Twelve thirty at night and still as hot as noon.

Another piece of the rondo fell into place. A last, unpredictable piece. As Troy and Driberg were leaving, Anna and Masha's husband, Lawrence, were coming in.

'Oops,' said Lawrence, with a grin on his lips. 'Bloody awful timing. How've you been, Freddie?'

That was what men of Lawrence's class did when they thought they'd been caught out. Grinned like schoolboys, and rebutted all unspoken accusations with a guiltless heartiness. Anna just looked away and Troy heard her semi-silent, half-whispered, 'Oh, fuck.'

He took Lawrence by the arm and left Driberg to find a cab.

'Pure coincidence, Freddie, honestly,' Lawrence went on.

Troy stopped him. 'Shut up. I couldn't give a damn. Just don't take Anna in there. Take her somewhere else. I don't care. I've no axe to grind. Just not in there.'

Troy and Lawrence had known each other for twenty years. Troy had a better relationship with Lawrence then he had with his own brother. Lawrence was looking intently at him, trying to read him. 'Freddie. Do I detect a tone of professional interest?'

'Yes.'

'Getting ready to raid them?'

'Lawrence, for Christ's sake . . . I'm not in the fucking Vice Squad.'

'Then what's going on? If there's a story here, I expect to be the first to know.'

'I can't tell you. But when I can you will be the first to know. Your paper can have an exclusive. But not now. Just find a better dive. There must be nightclubs more fashionable than this.'

'This place is supposed to be the *next* most fashionable club in town.
Up and coming. Just thought I'd take a look. Apart from that I don't know the first thing about it.'

'You won't like the music. And you'll like the management even less.'

'Ah. Is that a clue?'

Driberg tapped Troy on the shoulder. 'We're off.'

Troy looked at Lawrence waiting for his clues. Looked at Anna – wholly lacking the bravura self-confidence that was Kitty, or the *sangfroid* that Foxx had mustered. Anna was red in the face, embarrassed as hell. He'd just ruined her evening and he knew it.

'I'll call you,' he said, speaking to Lawrence, looking at Anna. 'I'll call you.'

§ 43

As the cab wound its way through the maze of narrow streets towards Regent Street, and back into Soho, Driberg stated his case, looking out of the window more than he looked at Troy, in a pretence of diffidence. 'Bound to be an election soon,' he said.

'I know,' said Troy. 'People keep telling me that.'

'And I was wondering . . .'

'There's something you want me to ask my brother?'

'Quite. You took the words out of my mouth.'

'After all he's going to be Home Secretary any day now.'

'Quite.' Driberg seemed oblivious to Troy's sarcasm.

'And you were wondering . . .'

'Quite. I was wondering. I mean to say . . . well, let me put it this way. I can't be a back-bencher for ever, now, can I?'

That, thought Troy, was perfectly possible.

'So, I was wondering. Does Gaitskell have a job in mind for me?'

Troy bit his tongue.

'It would be insufferable to be overlooked again. Do you think perhaps Rod could sort of . . . you know . . . sound him out on my behalf?'

Of all the favours Troy's friends and acquaintances had sought to solicit from him on the matter of his brother's impending rise to power, this had to be the daftest. But it was the only one Troy felt even remotely inclined to grant. 'I may be able to help you, Tom, I may not. But shall we finish the night's business first?'

'Be my guest. What's on your policeman's mind?'

'I would not have thought you and Spoon likely friends,' said Troy.

'Ah, well, buggers can't be choosers.'

'But he's married!'

'So am I. And Spoon's on his second wife by the bye. First divorced him when he came clean about his tilt. Gentlemen's agreement. Private detective, an obliging whore, a daytrip to Brighton – all very kosher. You'd never have known he was queer from the divorce proceedings. New wife is equally a gent's bargain. He told her up front. She fig-leafs him, and in return Ted indulges her vulgar displays of ostentatious wealth. You know, personally, I think Ted is inwardly wincing whenever Sylvia poses for one of those endless photos we get plastered across the papers. And I think the gold-miner's helmet and the white boiler-suit for the trip to Brinsley colliery were something approaching the limits of good taste. The silver pickaxe with rhinestones in the handle might have been a tad too vulgar, you never know. But . . . he bought her the gold-plated Daimler. It never was gold-plated of course, 'cept for the handles. The first lot really were gold plate, but when they got nicked Ted replaced them with something that looked gold and simply kept up the story of a gold-plated Daimler. Come to think of it, that's almost a Hollywood film title. Wasn't there one a few years back called *The Gold-Plated Cadillac*?'

'You're saying he's queer?'

'I just did. Do try to keep up, Troy. Queer as a four-pound note and with a penchant for rough trade. In fact, a complete pushover for any strapping young chap with a northern accent. Nothing seems to get Ted going a like a bit of the 'ee-bah-gums'. But then . . . the finer things in life are so easy to recognise. Once the veil has been lifted, that is.'

Driberg turned from looking out of the window to looking at Troy as he uttered this last sentence. As a rule Driberg's queer propensities caused Troy no problem. Moral, legal or otherwise. He had long subscribed to the English dictum that, whatever the law said, the queer's responsibility was the same as anyone else's. Not to do it in the street and frighten the horses. But he felt the merest shudder of revulsion as Driberg hinted that he didn't know what he was missing. He changed the subject. 'You're in luck, Tom.'

'I am?'

'Rod and I are having a drink with Gaitskell tomorrow night.'

§ 44

Troy had been home less than an hour, and was lying down listening to his Brubeck LP again. It made up for the torture his ears had suffered at the Empress Club. He loved the insistence of 'Blue Rondo A La Turk', a driving piano riff – that was the word, wasn't it, 'riff'? Some piece of old Constantinople that had reached California by way of Vienna – and the only contribution from the drums seemed to be brushed cymbals. 'Take Five' on the other hand seemed to reverse the pattern, the piano providing rhythm, Joe Morello on drums all but supplying the melody. It was close to hypnotic.

The door burst open. Foxx slammed it behind her. 'What in the name of heaven gives you the right to spy on me?'

Troy didn't move. He said softly, 'It was bad luck you being there. I was spying, but not on you.'

'Liar!'

'You should keep better company.'

'Bastard!'

Something went flying from the shelves by the door as she lashed out at the first things to hand. The light was dim, but he could see her well enough. She was less angry than she made out – tears of rage were tears still, and breaking something, anything, was enough to slow her down.

'I don't mean Christy. I mean the Ryan twins.'

'Who?'

'The owners of that club you were in.'

Foxx knelt down next to the sofa and thumped him on the chest, but with no force behind it.

'You sod, Troy, you total utter fucking sod.'

A blow for every other word. He felt nothing, as though the paws of a cat had walked across his chest. Then she drooped, her hair trailing across him, her tears soaking through his shirt. Troy ran his fingers through her hair. She didn't stop him. She sobbed for what seemed to Troy like an age, then said, 'Are you telling me the truth?'

'When have I ever lied to you?'

She raised her head off his chest, now she could laugh and cry at the same time. 'How long have you got? Lie to me, of course you lie to me. You always do.'

'Not now. There's something odd about the Ryans and that club. If your new lover wants to show you a good time, steer him in some other direction.'

'You're not going to tell me I should leave him and come back to you?'

'No,' he said. 'We'll take that as read. Where is he, by the way? Stuck in a taxi in St Martin's?'

'Back at the Dorchester.'

'Are you going there?'

'Don't know.'

'It's late.'

'I know.'

'You could stay here.'

'Maybe.'

166

'It's one of those warm summer nights you always loved. In fact, it's a heatwave. Can't remember when it last rained. We could sleep with the window open. We could put Delius on the gramophone. One of those nice scratchy seventy-eights you like. None of that stereo nonsense. "Summer Night On The River". Old Tommy Beecham. You used to be dotty over that. Then we could listen to London shut down.'

'I s'pose we could. I quite like the stuff you've got on now.'

'It's Brubeck . . . and I have fresh oranges and eggs. We could have breakfast in bed.'

'P'raps.'.

Foxx flopped on to his chest again, and let out the mother of all sighs. They did not move.

'Of course,' she said, into his ribcage, 'it wouldn't mean I'm coming back to you. It would be just for now – just because it's too late to go home.'

'Of course,' Troy lied. They did not move.

§ 45

Later. Hours later. Foxx sleeping, Troy waking, he found a new form of counting sheep springing unbidden to his thoughts. The idling mind pieced together his own 'Blue Rondo'. Cue Dave Brubeck on piano, with one cymbal from Joe Morello. Right now, he thought, current mistress Kitty, also known as Kate, was in bed with her old lover the broken-nosed boxing promoter Danny Ryan. Or, if the night had changed course, she was in bed with Anna's husband Angus, the lunatic, one-legged accountant. Cue Gene Wright on bass. Ex-girlfriend Anna was in bed with his brother-in-law, Lawrence, editor of the *Sunday Post*. The smoky crooner Vince Christy, current lover of the woman sleeping at Troy's side, Shirley known as Foxx, former lover of the current mistress, Kitty, also known as Kate, now sleeping with the broken-nosed boxing promoter or the lunatic, one-legged accountant, was cold turkey at the Dorchester or had mustered new groupies.

Cue Paul Desmond, alto sax. And he hadn't a clue where or with whom his sister Masha, wife of the errant Lawrence, editor of the *Sunday Post*,former lover of the smoky crooner at the Dorchester, was. But he was trying not to think of Masha. And Masha was surely trying not to think of him. After all, he hadn't heard from her since . . . Cue Morello on drums.

§ 46

A casual passer-by who chances this evening to be gazing in through the window of Kettner's, the fashionable London restaurant in Romilly Street, or the less casual passer-by, weaving his way to his table and taking in the crack as he did so, might possibly notice three very different specimens of the genus Englishman, all similarly attired in the garb of their class, two old Harrovians and a Wykehamist, somewhat the worse for the copotation of alcohol. The first, a short, slightly stout man in his fifties, whose hair rises up in curly wisps – a long, almost pointed nose much beloved of caricaturists. This is the leader of Her Majesty's Loyal Opposition, the Right Honourable Hugh Gaitskell MP, a man said to be one of England's great wits. Given that the next general election cannot be much more than a couple of months away, he is de facto,the PrimeMinister-in-Waiting. The second, a tall, sort of foreign-looking bloke, also in his fifties, thick, dark hair turning rapidly to salt and pepper, who is, should the passer-by be quite so nosy, found to be wearing odd socks – a lifelong bad habit of which his wife of twenty-five years has been quite unable to cure him. This is the Right Honourable Sir Rodyon Troy Bt, MP, DSO (and bar) DFC, the Shadow Home Secretary and a man said by his younger brother to 'exude a terrible decency'. The third and last, a short, dark, demonic-looking elf of a man, aged about forty, with eyes like polished jet, a walking-stick propped against the side of his chair, his socks matching. This is Chief Superintendent Frederick Troy, 'of the Yard', as he is wont to remind us – a man without a Rt Hon or a medal to his name, a man described by his elder brother as 'the most devious little shit in history'.

And they are all giggling like schoolboys who have found the cherry brandy.

'*He's got to be joking,*' *Gaitskell is saying, and not for the first time.*

'*Does Driberg joke?*' *Rod asks.*

'*Most of the time,*' *Troy replied.* '*But not this time.*'

'*What the bloody hell does he expect me to do? Put one of England's most notorious buggers in the cabinet?*'

'*Wouldn't be the first,*' *Troy says, and the other two giggle like idiots, each silently drawing up a list of highly placed pederasts who have been of great service to their country by day and up dark alleys by night.*

'*It's rich,*' *says Gaitskell.* '*Rich.*'

'*You've got to admire his nerve,*' *Rod says.*

'*Or,*' *Troy adds,* '*his lack of self-knowledge.*'

'*Oh,*' *says Gaitskell.* '*I think Tom knows himself very well. After all, what's the first criterion of self-knowledge – of knowing what you are? It's got to be knowing what you like.*'

'*And so fewofusdo,*' *says Troy.*

For reasons Troy cannot perceive, this sends his brother off into a spluttering fit that showers the table in a champagne rain.

'*Did you hear the one about Tom at Buckingham Palace?*' *Gaitskell says.* '*No,*' *Rod says, and Gaitskell and Troy look at him astounded.* '*You should get out more, brer,*' *Troy says, and it is Gaitskell's turn to shower them in champagne.* '*Shall you tell him, Hugh, or shall I?*' *Gaitskell waves him on, speechless with mirth.* '*I'm not sure exactly when this was, but Tom had dined with George VI at the Palace, so I suppose it wouldn't be long after the war. On the way out he spots a guard on duty outside his box, busbied, upright, rifle, the lot – and the old urge seizes him. Knowing they are not permitted to move or speak while on duty Tom goes down on his hands and knees, unzips the chap's flies and blows him. Right there, in the open air at the gates of Buck House.*'

'*I say again, you've got to admire his nerve.*' *Rod pauses to refill his glass and let the heaving chests of his potential audience subside. Then he says,* '*Did you hear about Tom and Nye Bevan?*' *Gaitskell and Troy look at him astounded. Later – nearer midnight – the Troy brothers have poured the Leader of the Opposition into a cab and pointed him north towards home. They are in Troy's house, trying with little success to make coffee. Neither of them can get the match to the flame for shaking with laughter. Rod sputters, the match blows out for the third or fourth time and Troy turns off the gas and says, 'Forget it.'*

'Forget it? Forget it? Can't go home like this. She'll fucking slaughter me. Gotta sober up.'

'Forget it. Let's give Driberg the good news instead.' Rod is all but rolling on the floor. Troy fears he might explode, but reaches for the phone anyway.

'Tom? Tom?'

'Troy? You make me sound like the piper's son. Do you know what time it is?'

'Haven't the fogging fuckiest. Just got in from a drink with Gaitskell. He's offering you a job next time round.'

Rod screeches. Troy shushes him.

'What was that? Somebody with you?'

'Just my brother. Listen, listen . . .'

'I am.'

'The job, the job.'

'Yeeees?'

'Arse. . .'

'Eh?'

'Arsh. . .'

'Arsh?'

'Arshbishop of Canterbury.'

Rod howls. Troy cannot but join in. There is silence from the other end of the line. Then . . . 'You pair of shits. You pair of drunken shits.'

And Driberg hangs up.

Troy puts down the phone. His brother is crying tears of joy. The phone rings. Troy reaches for it and says, 'Tom, Tom, Your Grace.'

And the voice says, 'No, it's me, Jack. There's been another body found. Whole this time. Can you get down to Limehouse?'

The jolt of sobriety ripped through him just as though he'd walked into a door. And normal service was resumed.

§ 47

Jack sent a car for Troy. A unmarked suped-up Wolseley 6/90 with a uniformed WPC at the wheel.

'Where are we going?' Troy asked.

'Regent's Canal Dock, sir.'

A Glaswegian accent. Troy looked at the face. Ringlets of red hair bursting out beneath her peaked cap. Just a little, she reminded him of the Kitty of twenty years ago. He didn't know the woman. 'You're new?' he asked.

'Mary McDiarmuid, sir.'

'You're Wildeve's driver?'

'As a matter of fact, sir, I'm your driver. I was assigned to you the day Mr Brocklehurst died. I guess you never got round to reading the paperwork.'

Without doubt she meant the day Brock was blown up, not the day he died. Troy could see no point in setting her right. 'Quite,' he said.

He climbed into the back. The first lurch forward almost made him puke, brought home to him how pissed he was. He took refuge in sleep. Woke as the Wolseley swung off the Commercial Road into the dockyard.

It was a moonlit night. Barges bobbing on the basin. Another Wolseley, undisguised, 'Police' blazoned across the doors, lights glaring out across the water. Shrimp Robertson guarding it like a sentry. Two uniformed coppers dodging across the tops of the barges.

Troy knew he couldn't do that. Even on a good day without a skinful of booze he couldn't do that. He felt a hand on his shoulder. 'Freddie? The body's over here.'

Troy turned to face Jack.

'Good bloody grief. You look awful.'

'I'll be fine,' Troy lied.

'No, I should never have called you out.'

'Whole, you said?'

'Eh?'

'The body. You said it was intact.'

'More or less. Not like the others at all.'

'Let me see.'

'Do you really want to see?'

'Yep.'

Wildeve led him round to the front of the car. The body lay under a blanket between the lights and the water. Wildeve nodded, and one of the coppers whipped the blanket away. A fat, sodden corpse, bloated with gas after a few days in the water, the pale and pasty face of death. Troy turned away and vomited.

After a few seconds, when the heaving had stopped and all he could taste was bile, he felt Jack's hand on his shoulder again. 'Sorry, Freddie. I shouldn't have—'

'It's OK.'

'It's usually me who pukes, after all.'

'It's OK. It's the booze.'

'The booze?'

'Champagne with Rod.'

'Ah.'

'And.'

'And?'

'I know the man.'

'You do?'

'Rork. Joey Rork. Known him a couple of weeks.'

There was a pause Jack seemed reluctant to fill. Troy took his arm and levered himself up off the wing of the car. 'Let's look again.'

Rork had died from a single shot to the head – eyes open, looking at his killer. Only when Troy reached the hands did he realise what Rork had suffered. Where his knuckles had been there was a glutinous mess of flesh and bone. But he was past puking now. He was halfway to sobriety.

'Drill,' he heard Mary McDiarmuid say.

'Really?' Jack's voice, with a hint of astonishment.

Troy stood up, wished he'd remembered to bring his walking stick.

'They drilled out his knuckles with one of those electric drill thingies.'

'Jesus Christ! Why?'

Mary McDiarmuid looked at Troy as though telling him they

were dealing with an innocent – but Jack could be like that, seeing the worst man could inflict on man as a matter of duty day after day and yet still baffled by it.

'Well,' said Troy, 'it's a pretty surefire way to get someone to tell you what you want to know.'

Jack looked down at the body, then back at Troy. 'Was he the sort of chap to tell them?'

'I don't think he had anything to tell them,' said Troy. 'And if he'd talked they'd have shot him after one knuckle or two. Most men would crack after one knuckle. They wouldn't have bothered with all ten.'

This was the moment at which Jack usually puked. He didn't. He put out an arm and caught Troy as he wobbled.

'You'd better get me to a nick and take my statement,' Troy said, soft as a whisper.

'Statement, my arse. I'm taking you for a cup of strong coffee.'

§ 48

George Bonham might not have been the last man in England to sleep in a nightshirt – but he was the last whom Troy knew. He answered the door without a flicker of surprise, even though Jack's hammering had clearly roused him from his slumbers.

'Coffee, George. Black and sweet,' Jack said.

'You look awful,' Bonham said, looking at Troy.

'I know. People are kind enough to keep telling me.'

'White as a wossname . . . sheet.'

Wildeve and Mary McDiarmuid lowered Troy on to the sofa. Robertson stood in the corner, clutching his helmet, looking stranded. Jack waved him down into a corner chair.

'Where's your inspector?' Troy asked.

'Beg pardon, sir?'

'Where's Inspector Milligan? We're on his patch. I would have thought . . .'

He followed the Shrimp's gaze to Wildeve.

'Paddy's had his problems,' Jack said. 'He's in Liverpool on a compassionate. His dad. He's dying.'

'Dying?'

'Lung cancer.'

'Of course. He told me. I'm almost certain he told me.' Troy sighed. 'But . . . but . . . he should be here. We can't do this without him.'

'He'll be back. And George is right. You do look bloody awful. This can wait. It can wait till morning. Let's get you home as soon as we've got something warm inside you.'

'There are things you should know.'

'Wait for the coffee, Freddie. You haven't enough breath to blow out acandle.'

Bonham stuck a mug of sickly sweet instant coffee into Troy's hands, wrapping his fingers around it as though he thought it would slip from his grip.

Troy sipped and tried to pretend he thought it pleasant or beneficial. 'Joey Rork,' he said. 'Or did I tell you that? Whatever. Joey Rork. A private eye from the States. Ex-NYPD. And I rather think he was out of his depth.'

Jack prompted: 'In what way?'

'I had dinner with him about three days ago. He'd been following Danny Ryan. Been doing that for a while. At dinner he produced a stack of photographs – he did that every time we met, but this time it was obvious he was getting very close to Danny. No long lenses. He was in the same room.'

'Danny Ryan?' Jack cut in. 'Is this something to do with boxing?'

'I doubt that. In fact I think Danny Ryan might be incidental. Rork wasn't wild about my assurances that Danny was straight, but it was Ryan's brothers that got his copper's hackles up. He was absolutely convinced they were up to something.'

'Who are these brothers? I've never heard of them.'

'Neither had I – I kept telling Rork. I used to know Ryan before the war, and I've followed his career in the papers just like anyone else – and I've seen him in person perhaps a couple of times since, but as for any brothers, they were news to me. I don't know them.'

There was a cough of polite attention-seeking from the other side of the room. Jack, George, Mary McDiarmuid and Troy all turned to look at the Shrimp – reddening slightly and wary of the position he was in.

'Spititout, Mr Robertson,'Jacksaid.

'You do know them, Mr Troy.'

'I do?'

'They was with me and Tub Flanagan and all them other kids that day you paid us all to search the bombsite where Alma Terrace used to be.'

'That was—'

'Nineteen forty-four, sir.'

'I was about to say it was ages ago. Of course I don't know them. I can't even remember what they looked like.'

'But they remembered you, Mr Troy. You was their hero. Right up to the end of the war that gang they used to have with old Tub was known as Troy's Marauders. I was in it meself. I oughta know.'

Jesus Christ.

'I was a hero meself for a while, 'cos I found the cellar where the body was. But I was too small to hold me own against the twins, but they—'

'Enough! I don't want to hear this.'

Bonham muttered a *sotto voce* 'I told you so', and vanished into the kitchen.

Troy leaned back, stared at the ceiling and said, 'Shit, shit, shit.'

Jack spoke softly: 'Freddie, it's time you went home.'

'No, I should make a statement.'

'You should be in bed.'

'What's the point? I'll be wide awake in four hours, buzzing like a sodding bee.'

'Bed,' said Mary McDiarmuid, with more authority than Jack had mustered, and Troy let himself be hoicked up by one arm and steered to the door. 'George,' he said, turning back to Jack.

'Later,' Jack said. 'Later.'

Mary McDiarmuid drove like Fangio. He was back on his own doorstep in less than twenty minutes.

'Do you want me to come in, sir?'

'No. I'll be fine. Now, tell me, are you permanently assigned to me?'

'In so far as you're expected back, yes, sir. In the meantime I'm floating a bit too freely. I get whatever comes up.'

'That can be remedied. But when we're alone it's Troy. Forget the rank. Save it for when Onions is about.'

He was fiddling with the door key and failing. She took it off him, turned the lock, shoved the door open and stuck the key back in his hand with a 'Whatever you say, boss.'

Inside, he kicked off his shoes, sloughed his jacket on to the floor. He hadn't the strength to pick it up. It could wait till morning. It could all wait till morning. He couldn't remember when he'd felt so tired. He hauled himself up the stairs to the bathroom, scrubbed away the taste of champagne and vomit with his toothbrush, spat peppermint toothpaste at the basin – and as he did so caught a trace of something else on the air. Lately he'd known his nose to play tricks, not as many as his eyes, but he had found himself smelling the most unlikely things – rubber, salt and vinegar, cardamom. Now it was a scent. Something familiar but unplaceable. The upper frequencies of Dior? With the toothbrush still sticking out of the side of his mouth, he pushed open his bedroom door, and saw the round bump of Kitty's backside in his bed. He could not fault her timing. At once appropriate and awful.

§ 49

His prediction was wrong. He did not wake at six, simply because he had not slept. Kitty had not stirred. He had lain motionless for most of what was left of the night, while his mind and memory had roared.

He had liked Gumshoe. He had not realised this until he had been confronted with his corpse. He had found that while part of his mind examined the wounds with a detached, professional eye, another part had looked at Rork's beetlecrusher shoes and found something inexorably sad in the sight of those huge flat feet; that same part had wondered what had become of his hat.

Gumshoe gave way to the Shrimp. The Shrimp was proving

to be a ragbag of surprises and secrets. Troy's Marauders? Good fucking grief. If it weren't so bizarre it would be funny. And George, that hushed 'I told you so'. Had he been waiting the best part of twenty years to say that? Troy found he could remember George's exact words on that bitterly cold day in the February of 1944, the restrained outrage that Troy had bribed a bunch of schoolkids to look for a dismembered body.

'It's a scandal, Freddie, a scandal. They're kids. They should be in school. If the mums find out . . .'

And Troy had brushed George off. It was so easy. George had been at the back of the queue when God gave out smarts – the nicest man on earth, not the brightest. And then he'd said, 'You know, Freddie, there are times I think there's nothing like a spell at the Yard for putting iron in the soul.'

With hindsight, that near-perfect science, Troy thought it the most acute sentence George had ever uttered. Was that what twenty years at the Yard had done to him? Put iron in his soul? Wasn't that what Trubshawe had hinted at after Sasha's outburst at the funeral? The 'ambergooities' of the Yard put iron in the soul.

He could see that posse of urban cowboys in his insomniac's mind's eye. He could see Tub Flanagan – fat boy with Elastoplast across his glasses. He could see the Shrimp, small for his age, wiry and street-smart. If Troy had been taking bets rather than whacking out tanners and half-crowns that day he'd have put money on the Shrimp to grow up to be a villain. It seemed so much more likely than that he would become smitten with the idea of becoming a copper. He could see a boy whose name he never knew juggling a smoking cocoa tin he'd turned into a winter handwarmer. But, try as he might he couldn't see a pair of twins. To listen to Bonham it had been the corruption of youth, the spike of iron. It all seemed so long ago . . . Besides, it had been 'adventures with Jack and Ralph'. Hadn't it?

§ 50

He must have nodded off. The clock on his bedside table read ten a.m. and Kitty was gone. He flung back the bedclothes and a small piece of paper fell to the floor. He picked it up and reached for his glasses.

```
Fat lot of use you were. Why didn't you
wake me when you got in? K
```

Bugger, bugger, bugger.

He felt dehydrated. More the alcohol than the midnight murder. He stumbled downstairs, sank a pint of cold water, picked up the phone and rang Claridge's. Mrs Cormack had not yet returned. He left a message asking her to call him back and ran a bath. He was dragged from it minutes later by the phone ringing.

'Freddie,' said Jack, 'if you're up and about I'm sending a car for you.'

'A car?'

'Time to take your statement. You are up to this, aren't you? I mean, I could always come to you.'

'I'm fine. Just . . .'

'Just what?'

'Just not right now.'

'Not right now? Freddie, last night you were wilting like last week's daffs and deadly keen to get it all down on paper.'

'I need time.'

'We don't have time. What we have is a body.'

'Just a few hours.'

'What's up? Tell me what's changed.'

'Nothing.'

'Freddie – I don't know why but you're lying to me. Whatever it is, get it fixed and be at the Yard by six. How long do you think I can hold Stan at bay? For Christ's sake!'

'Jack, I'm sorry. I'm not holding out on you.'

'Freddie, that's exactly what you're doing and if a witness did it to you you'd chuck him in the cells till—'

'I'll be there. I'll be there at six.'

'In the meantime I want a few basic facts. I'm not losing a day.'

'His name was Joey Rork.'

'You told me that last night!'

'He was a private eye, ex-NYPD –'

'That too!'

'– and he had a room at the Cromarty in Gower Street.'

'Now we're getting somewhere. How long had he been at the Cromarty?'

'Weeks. I couldn't honestly say how long.'

'Why was he here? How do you come to know him? He surely didn't fly over from New York just to follow Danny Ryan?'

'Jack, that's the bit I'd rather tell you at six.'

'You're asking an awful lot, you know.'

'I know, I know. Honestly.'

Jack hung up. Troy felt a little as though his junior had just read the Riot Act to him. The phone rang again.

'Bastard.'

'You were sleeping so peacefully.'

'Smarmy bastard. Where were you anyway?'

'Limehouse.'

'At that time of night?'

'I'm a copper. You were one yourself, once upon a time.'

'OK, OK. Don't rub it in. So, Sherlock, did the pleasure of some poor bugger's cold flesh lure you away from the infinitely greater pleasures of my warm flesh?'

'Pretty much.'

'I thought you were still off sick.'

'Wildeve and I have an arrangement. Kitty, we have to talk.'

'That's got to be one of my husband's favourite phrases. It usually means he has to talk and I have to listen.'

'Can you come over now?'

'No.'

'Can I come to you?'

'No.'

'Kitty, this is important. I have to see you.'

'That's how I felt last night. Fat lot of good it did me. No, Troy, my sisters and I are lunching here, then going shopping up West – good God, "up West". I shouldn't think I've used that phrase in twenty years. Just goes to show you can take the woman out of Stepney and blah-deblah-de-blah.'

'When, then?'

'Tea. You can buy me tea to make up for last night. Tea at the Café Royal. Be there at four.'

Kitty rang off. Troy was left thinking that he was cutting Jack's deadline very close and that the Stepney had long since been taken out of Kate Cormack. About a fortnight after Kate Cormack had been taken out of Stepney, he rather thought.

At noon he rang Kolankiewicz. 'What killed that bloke we fished out of the canal basin last night?'

'Nine mill. Judging from the powder residue, not point-blank range but not more than ten or twelve feet either. Nothing fancy. The most common ammunition there is nowadays. And nothing powerful. The bullet came out of the poor bastard's brain intact. If you get lucky and find the gun I can do a match.'

'Who would be stupid enough to keep the gun?'

'And . . . besides the obvious signs of torture, which I assume you flatfoots noted, there was bruising to the back of the head.'

'Such as?'

'Such as someone sapped him. And disarmed him.'

'What makes you say disarmed?'

'Shoulder holster. Left armpit. But no gun.'

Damn. They'd allowed the hysteria of the moment, the grotesque fact of a brutal death and the pointless complication of his own physical weakness to distract them. Jack or Troy or someone should have searched the body last night. Worse, Gumshoe had traipsed around London for weeks with a gun up one armpit and it had not even occurred to Troy that he was doing so.

'Anything else?'

'I'd say the man was American from his clothes and his dentistry . . .'

'He was.'

Kolankiewicz let this pass without comment. 'Not a snappy dresser, his shoulder holster was tailor-made but his clothes were all off the peg. Off the peg but clean. I'd say he'd had the suit dry-cleaned in the last week or so. Hence I think the oil stains on the trousers, around the calves and knees, might be evidence.'

'Might? What sort of oil?'

'The sort you'd put in your car.'

'Can we match that?'

'To what? You could bring me samples from every garage in England and it would match ninety-nine per cent of them. All it tells us is that he was in a garage, but even that could be significant.'

'A tailor-made holster, you say. Tailor-made for what?'

Kolankiewicz paused. Not his customary mode. 'It could be one of several models. However, I have in my possession a gun that I believe fits it perfectly.'

'Well?'

'Smith & Wesson.'

'Smith & Wesson what?'

'.357 Magnum.'

'Where on earth did you get one of those?'

Kolankiewicz strung out his sentences, the pause between each one longer than the pause before, the pitch of his voice rising slightly with every fractional utterance. 'A fact-finding visit to Washington a couple of years ago. A day or two spent with our colleagues at the FBI. A careless moment. A souvenir. Of sorts.'

'You mean you nicked it?'

'I think this is where I whistle something from *The Wizard of Oz* and try to look if not innocent then disingenuous. You, however, would be far better advised to weigh up what I said a few sentences back.'

'Eh?'

'They disarmed him, Troy. Someone is walking around London with a gun that will shoot holes in solid concrete.'

'A hand-held cannon,' Troy whispered.

'What?'

'At the end of the war you and Bob Churchill came out to Mimram. Bob trained me up on handguns – he had a Smith & Wesson then. That's what it felt like – a hand-held cannon.'

§ 51

Troy was late getting to the Café Royal. Kitty was waiting, sipping at her Earl Grey, nibbling a slice of Battenberg, surrounded by the results of a day out with her sisters – 'packages from Liberty's, packages from Harrods, headscarf for the sister, knickers for the wife . . . Close your eyes, my darling, as the gentlemen pass by . . .'

Her mood was good, the therapy of shopping – she smiled at Troy, stood up to give him a smackeroo on the lips and beckoned to a waiter. By the time he could sit down Troy felt smothered: Kitty's kisses, a sea of tissue paper unwrapped around him, and a busy young man setting tea and cake before him. There was nowhere to rest an elbow, no obvious way through the smallness of small-talk.

Kitty rattled on about her sisters, the generosity of her mood persisting without bitchiness to the point where, if he had been able to concentrate, he might have concluded that she was once again a Londoner, if only for a day, was once again the 'sparrer' from Jubilee Street, now the weight of being Mrs Cormack was off her, if only for a day – but he could stand it no longer.

'We have to talk,' he said, halfway through an account of Reenie trying on something meant for a woman half her age and size.

'There you go again. That phrase. OK. Don't listen to me. Just spit it out. Be brutal. See if I care.'

She did care. As he told her, care etched itself into every line in her face. By the end she was a simmering volcano, on whose rim he perched with precarious toehold. 'And you didn't tell me? My husband sets a private eye on me and you don't bloody tell me?'

'Not Cal. The Deeks.'

'Do you think that matters? Weeks you say, weeks with this jerk following me around, spying on me, and you don't tell me. You shit, you complete and utter shit!'

'You may be right. And if he hadn't been found murdered last night I might not be telling you now. But he has been murdered, and I cannot not tell you, and you have to make a statement.'

'What?'

'Rork came here to follow you and Vince Christy. When you

seemed to have nothing to do with—'

'Seemed! I did have nothing to do with the slimy bastard. He called me up at Claridge's and I blew him out of the water!'

'Then you have to say so. You see, Rork was following Danny Ryan, not just you.'

'And the Yard think Danny did this?'

'I don't know what they think, but you have to tell them what you know. We both do. I have to make a statement to Jack Wildeve at six today.'

'I don't know anything. I never saw or heard of this Rork fellow. All I know is my husband and my lover – if I can grace you with that term – conspired to treat me like a ten-dollar hooker in a crappy gumshoe novel. Troy, if you think I'm talking to anyone except the head of that committee of fools who want Cal for president, then think again. I'm making no statements. Not now. Not ever. And as for you . . . fuck you, Troy!'

Kitty had shattered the politesse of afternoon tea. The four o'clock susurrus had ceased. Every head in the room had turned. She stood up sharply – her cup overturned – grabbed her packages and left.

Troy watched Kitty storm out with no expectation that she'd turn back or glance at him. She did rage like no other woman he'd ever met. His sisters specialised in scorn. Foxx would hardly ever expend more energy than it took to hint at an infinite sadness nudging towards regret. Anna? Anna he couldn't quite pin down, but his wife did rolling sarcasm, her eyes glancing momentarily upwards to the indifferent heavens as if to say, 'God spare me from this jerk.' It had taken him more than a moment to realise it but the woman staring at him from across the room *was* his wife. If he'd wanted to follow Kitty, he neither could nor would now.

He crossed the floor. 'Hello,' he said simply.

Tosca looked in the direction Kitty had gone as though expecting to see scorchmarks on the carpet. 'Jeezus! Do you know who that was?'

'Of course. I'm not in the habit of dining with total strangers.'

'Sorry, that was dumb. What I really meant was, how long have you and Senator Cormack's wife been . . . y' know . . .?'

'May I join you?'

'Don't fuck me around with your English manners, Troy, just sit down and answer the fucking question.'

Troy pulled out a chair, sat down and faced his wife across a dining-table for the first time since the previous December. He'd heard not a peep from her since. 'How do you know Kitty and I are . . . "y' know"?'

'Kitty?'

'An old name. Long before she was Kate.'

'So the two of you been having y' know for a long time?'

'I haven't seen her since the war.'

'But when you did see her?'

'Yes. We were y' knowing.'

'Before or after me?'

'Before. Two or three years before. Now, don't tell me you've just breezed into London for an uncharacteristic display of jealousy?'

'Fuck off, Troy. I don't know why I came. But I can tell you this. Kate Cormack is pretty well the last person I expected to find you having y' know with. Did I ever tell you I knew her husband?'

'No,' said Troy. 'I think I can safely say that's one of the many things you never bothered to tell me.'

'We were both stationed in Zurich in '41. Just before we got into the war.'

'Odd,' said Troy. 'That's when I met him. 1941. Just before you lot decided to join us. We must have just missed one another.'

'Story of my life, Troy. Like I just missed you this afternoon.'

'You've been to the house?'

'Yep. Screwed my courage to the thingummy and knocked on the door.'

'I was only out getting a paper. You could have waited.'

Stupid remark. One of Tosca's characteristics was that she didn't wait. She was time and tide in a five-foot package.

'How long are you here?'

'No. I'm not answering that.'

'Could we meet again?'

'We're meeting now.'

'I meant . . . alone.'

'Sure. I'm at Claridge's. Come round this evening – say, seven?'

That was cutting it fine.

'OK.'

'Good—'cos we have to talk.'

'There we go,' he said. 'That phrase again.'

'What phrase?'

§ 52

Troy was early getting to the Yard. He called in at his own office. It had been weeks. Swift Eddie Clark was at his desk, his home-made coffee machine burbling away behind him as strong Blue Mountain made its way from a boiling jar to a flask, by way of a Bunsen burner and several feet of glass piping. It was, possibly, the finest cup of coffee to be had in the whole of London. When Eddie said, 'He's in with someone,' Troy accepted a cup and sat down to wait.

'Who's the extra desk for?' he asked.

'The Scottish bird, sir. Seems hell-bent on making herself at home. Rang Admin and ordered the desk herself. If she looks like she's permanent maybe she won't get posted back to the drivers' pool. She's got shorthand and typing too, sir. Always useful.'

On cue Mary McDiarmuid appeared in the doorway. 'Mr Wildeve'll be just a couple of minutes. Shall I run you home after?'

'I don't know how long I'll be.'

'That's nae problem. Me an' Edwin've got lots to be getting on with.'

She smiled at Clark. Clark managed a flicker back. He hated being called Edwin.

'What have we got?' Troy asked.

'The Ryans seem to have watertight alibis. Four blokes all willing to swear they were in an all-night pontoon game. Mr Wildeve collared them this morning. They sent for their brief. They were out by lunchtime.'

'The drills?'

'If there was one in that garage of theirs there was a hundred. Mr Kolankiewicz is testing them . . . but . . .'

185

Mary McDiarmuid did not need to finish the sentence. They both knew how futile it all was. A drill in a garage was scarcely more optimistic than the needle in the haystack.

Troy waited. Eddie and Mary McDiarmuid rustled papers and talked to each other *sotto voce*. Troy felt as if he was in a dentist's waiting room rather than his own office. Rarely had he felt more out of it.

A few minutes later, Troy heard Jack's office door open and footsteps coming down the corridor. Kitty stood in the doorway, Jack behind her.

'It's very good of you to come in, Mrs Cormack.' Jack, mouthing the platitudes of the job.

'It was no trouble,' answered Senator Cormack's wife, and as she turned to gaze stonily at Troy, Mrs Cormack was all he could see – Kitty was suddenly invisible. The woman he knew entirely absorbed by the woman he didn't.

Jack turned to Troy, his look almost as stony, and said, 'Ready when you are.'

Troy could not face typing out a statement. Kitty and Tosca between them had contrived to exhaust him. Trapped between love and death, all he wanted to do was lie down.

'Mary?'

'Yep?'

'Would you mind taking my statement?'

She picked up a notepad and followed the two of them into Jack's office. Jack glanced at Mary McDiarmuid, saw the pad and pen and nodded. He sat back in his chair, looking as weary as Troy felt. Troy doubted he had had any sleep at all.

'Right, Freddie, tell me the lot. Tell me everything.'

Troy told him. And when he had finished Jack said, 'And you thought none of this worth a mention. It didn't raise your professional hackles?'

It was an unusual experience being carpeted by his junior, but Troy's inner voice was whispering, 'You had it coming, Freddie. You brought this on yourself.'

'No.'

Jack made a cut-throat gesture to Mary McDiarmuid and she stopped writing. 'You and I break the rules. I get you out and about to look at some of the ripest murders we've had in a long time and you don't see it as a give-and-take process?'

'Jack, what did I have to give?'

'That an American was loose on the streets of London with a gun the size of a Sherman tank, for starters!'

'I didn't know about the gun, honestly. And for the life of me I can't see any link between Rork and the murders you're investigating. In fact, I thought what you thought when you phoned me up last night . . . that this was just another . . . that you'd summoned me out to look at another boy . . . I didn't think Rork was in that deep. If I'd reported to you I have no idea what it was I should have been saying.'

Troy took Jack's pause as assent. When he finally spoke it was to move the subject on if not a mile then round a corner. 'And Mr Robertson surprised us all.'

'Quite.'

'Then I think it's time we had a word with Mr Robertson.'

Troy found refuge in the 'we'. However angry Jack was about the mess with which Troy had presented him, he was still talking as though they were a team.

'Off the record?' Troy asked.

'Why would I do that?'

'He's a kid, Jack. He's been in the job a matter of days. He's fresh out of Hendon. It would be grotesquely unfair to put anything on his record at this stage that we aren't totally sure of.'

'OK. Where, then? And it has to be soon. Whatever it is that's buzzing in young Robertson's head I want to hear it.'

'How about my house tomorrow morning?'

'How about your house in an hour and a half?'

Troy did not argue. Jack would not have understood.

While Mary McDiarmuid fetched a car, Troy drifted along to Onions's office. His secretary, Madge, had gone home. Both inner and outer doors were open. Onions was at his desk, slaving at paperwork under a reading lamp, rapidly scanning pages and scribbling his initials. As Troy came in he looked up once, the green shade casting a dragon-skin across his face. 'I've heard,' he said simply. 'You're in the shit again. Don't even think of askin' me to let you back early. Just bugger off.'

'But—'

'Bugger off!'

§ 53

The cast was slow to assemble. Mary McDiarmuid insisted on driving Troy home and stayed to eat dinner with him. He could find no way to tell her to go. He desperately wanted to phone Tosca. He couldn't do that with Mary there. He could go upstairs and phone on the bedroom extension, but he'd still be conscious of Mary. Instead he cooked for her: a vaguely Italian chicken and mushroom in white wine sauce that caused her to raise an eyebrow. 'If you're this good a cook, boss, I'm surprised you're still single.'

'I'm married,' he said bluntly. 'Don't ask.'

Eddie turned up alone. Troy was uncertain whether his being there at all was his own idea or Jack's, but Jack arrived ten minutes later and seemed not in the slightest surprised to find Eddie sipping tea on a straight-back chair in the corner, as ever trying to look like part of the furniture. And lastly, came Shrimp Robertson and George Bonham.

It had turned into an evening of warm summer drizzle, moisture simply hanging rather than falling to coat everything in soft focus. The droplets glistened on the Shrimp's uniform, clinging to the blue-black tunic, shining like diamond on his silver buttons. He took off his helmet and clutched it, not in the way coppers do, who have long since given up wondering what to do with it, but clutching it with pride. The Shrimp wore his whole uniform with pride, even down to the boots, so shiny you could see your face in them – but that was often true of former National Servicemen. If little else they knew how to shine shoes. Troy could not remember that pride. He had fought his father to be allowed to become a copper in the first place, and the old man had quickly resigned himself to it as a comic novelty. But Troy doubted he had ever felt the pride Robertson felt. He had hated being in uniform, and going 'plain' had come as a relief. Whatever happened now, he hoped it did not take the shine off the boy's pride in the job.

'I 'ope you don't mind, Mr Wildeve, sir, but Mr Bonham and me we go back a long way. In fact I've known Mr Bonham all me life. Mr Bonham can speak for me.'

'You're not on trial, Mr Robertson, but George is welcome all the same. This isn't about anything you've done . . . It's about . . . local knowledge. You're the one with the local knowledge and before you it was George.'

It was, Troy thought, a surprisingly tactful speech. All the same, George and the Shrimp sat on the edges of their chairs, looking completely unsure of the situation. Jack stood, Mary McDiarmuid sat on a stool by the fireplace, and Troy found himself with the *chaise-longue* to himself. All in all the room felt too full, too many people crammed in, as though the inevitability would be some sort of rupture.

'The Ryans?' Jack began simply. 'Tell us all about the Ryans.'

Shrimp looked at George; George looked at Jack. 'If you want the lot, the kit an' caboodle, you'd better let me start,' he said.

'Fine.'

'I knew their father, old Mickey Ryan. I say old, he was younger'n me. But that's the way he was. He came back from the war in 1918 old – just worn out, old and half bonkers. He'd two kids, both born just before the war, Danny and Mickey junior. But Mickey junior and the wife got took in that bad 'flu epidemic in '17. Mickey came back to Blighty to find Danny being looked after by his grandparents. He took Danny home with him, went back to his job at Billingsgate. Hated it, as far as I could see. Hated life. Sometime in the twenties he remarried. There were four kids. Martin in about '24, Alice in about '29, she died before she was one, and then the twins in '35, Patrick and Lorcan. The followin' year his second wife dies, and the same year, that summer of 1936, Mickey takes a trip out to Walton-on-the-Naze, takes off all his clothes and walks out into the North Sea. No one ever saw hide nor hair of 'im again. That leaves just Danny. He'd be in his early twenties by then, I s'pose, and he takes the twins. Danny's a bloke with a heart of gold, and he's the nearest thing those twins ever got to a dad. But he volunteers in 1940. And Martin, their other brother, dies on the beach at Normandy. So when the war's over Danny comes back to find a pair of scallywags who've been passed from one aunt to another for the best part of six years.'

'That's where I come in,' said the Shrimp. 'I known the Ryans all me life. Born in the same hospital, grew up in the same streets. They're only eleven months older than me. It's just like Mr Bonham says, we were all little sods – war on, half the dads away fightin' . . . bound to happen. Often as not we just skived off school and gave all the lip we could to the grown-ups. We'd skived off school the day Mr Troy met us in '44. But we could be worse than that. We nicked things. What kid didn't? My dad thrashed me for that. We smashed things. What kid didn't? My dad thrashed me for that too. But Paddy and Lorc went further than any of us. They could be cruel. I mean vicious. They thought it was hilarious to bait some poor dog, catch and skin it. I saw 'em carve up a Jack Russell once. Belonged to some poor old woman down Jubilee Street. Only thing she had in the world, but they caught the little blighter and they butchered him. It made us all just a bit wary of 'em. You couldn't predict what they'd do next. Mind – they weren't stupid. One or two of my old mates would do things so daft they were askin' to get caught. And they did time in Borstal for it. Not the Ryans. They knew not to get nicked, and they knew how to put the blame on somebody else. I say me dad thrashed me a few times – sometimes it was for things they'd done. That sort of drove a wedge between us. By the time I left school I wasn't havin' much to do with 'em. When it came time for National Service I was prayin' not to get sent to the same camp as them. But I did. I went through basic with them. And you know what? They kept their noses clean. They was model soldiers up front, "Yes, sir, no, sir, three bags full, sir." And behind the scenes they was nickin' everythin' that wasn't nailed down. They peddled NAAFI stuff all over West Germany.'

Troy looked at Eddie to see if this struck a chord. Clark had run a nice little business in NAAFI coffee beans in Berlin just after the war. Eddie looked blank, not a flicker of identification. Jack stood with his back to the fireplace, saying not a word. George picked up the thread.

'After the war Danny went into boxing. He'd been Light-

Heavyweight champion in the army. You know the rest. Pretty soon he was managing anyone who was anyone. He tried to get the twins to take an interest, thought it might just sort of level 'em off. But they didn't want to know.'

'And when they finished in the army,' the Shrimp picked up, 'Danny sets 'em up in that garage under the railway arches in Shadwell and tells 'em that's it. They make a go of it, or they don't, but they needn't bother comin' runnin' to 'im for 'andouts cos there weren't going to be any. Last two or three years that's wot they done. They run a garage, they traded cars and it looked like they was keepin' their noses clean all over again. But they weren't. Least, I reckon they weren't.'

'How can you be sure?' Jack speaking was like a ripple running through the air. He oozed scepticism.

'I know the Ryans, sir. But I s'pose what you mean is what do I know that they actually did? First whiff I got of it was earlier this year. I was still out at Hendon. There's a chippie in the Mile End Road called Foster's. It's common knowledge that half the businesses in the Mile End Road paid protection to Alf Marx's mob. Everybody knows it but nobody squeals. Then, February I think it was, when old Alf was still on remand, pre-trial like, my sister tells me this story of two young blokes that try to muscle in. They went round Foster's and told old Joe he should pay them from now on. So, as you'd expect, Joe Foster gives 'em grief, tells 'em how he pays money to Alf Marx to keep toerags like them away from his shop. You know what they did? Joe had this old ginger tom, been there for years it had. They picked the poor bugger up and flung 'im in the deep-fat fryer. That's when Joe caved in and that's when I knew it was the Ryans. Cos that's just the sort of stunt they'd have pulled when I was a kid. But there's more. You remember last March some poor sod was found out in Eppin' Forest nailed to a tree like Jesus on the cross?'

Troy and Jack looked at each other. They'd never solved that one.

'They did that too. I know cos I saw 'em do that to a Labrador when I was about twelve. Foster's chippie, that bloke in the forest . . . that's when I think the Ryans started their takeover. Cos while Alf Marx ran things nobody would have dared.'

'Let me get this straight,' Jack said. 'You're saying these Ryans, who are what, twenty-four or twenty-five, have taken over Alf Marx's rackets?'

The Shrimp stopped, looked at Jack and then at Troy, aware for the first time of the import of what he had said. 'Yes,' he said. 'I suppose I am saying that.'

'And you've been how long at Stepney?'

'Just a couple of weeks, sir. But that's not the point. Point is, I know the Ryans. I know what they're capable of.'

'And you didn't think to tell us until now?'

The Shrimp stopped again, he and Troy looking straight at each other.

'Would any of us have believed Mr Robertson?' Troy said. 'I'd've asked him where his hard evidence was. I might even have been dismissive of his childhood assessment of the Ryans. And there is, as we know, the matter of loyalties and loyalties compromised. It would have been easy for Mr Robertson not to come back to Stepney. He could have gone to any nick in the country. He need not have set foot on his own patch. But since he did, and since he knows what he knows . . . why should a young copper risk his career for what was no more than gossip?'

'Was?' said Jack. 'You mean it isn't now? Freddie, there's enough sleight-of-hand in your last statement to baffle Houdini. It's local knowledge, it's gossip, it's not to be repeated and then it is? And if it's true, why haven't we spotted them? We're the good guys. Not only that we're meant to have an efficient, if *ad hoc*, system for gathering information. How can two Irish yobbos knock an entire Jewish gang off the map and we don't know about it until now?'

'Jack, who in any nick is responsible for keeping an ear to the streets?'

Troy turned to the Shrimp. 'Remind me, Mr Robertson, who's your detective sergeant?'

'Mazzer, sir. Al Mazzer.'

'What's that?' said Jack. 'Italian?'

'No,' said Troy. 'I rather think it's Jewish.'

'That's right, sir. I reckon Mr Mazzer is Jewish.'

'Jewish,' George chipped in, 'and bent.'

The Shrimp was quick to protest, 'I never said that, Mr

192

Bonham.'

'He's gotta be, hasn't he? Stuff like this going down and the DS doesn't bloody know? When I ran that nick we'd've known. We'd have had all the tittle-tattle off the street and we'd have known what was bollocks and what wasn't. We'd've known. If this Mazzer's not bent . . .'

Jack said, 'You know him, George?'

'I've seen him about. Flash bastard. Brought in from Leytonstone two or three years back.'

'And?'

'And what?'

'Do you know for a fact that he's bent?'

'No – but I'll lay you a penny to a quid.'

Robertson looked at Troy desperate for a way in.

Troy said, 'Let's hear from Mr Robertson. He works with Mazzer after all.'

'Well?' said Jack.

'Mr Bonham's right, sir. Al Mazzer is a bit flash. And the talk in the nick is . . . well, y' know.'

Troy thought Jack would explode. A slow ascent, but a steady one. He'd known Jack too long ever to be surprised by him completely. But knowing just when Jack would decide to go by the book and when he would leap in where only fools and Troys would ordinarily tread was impossible. He'd known Jack bend and break the law to back him up, and he'd known him rat him out to Onions when time and circumstance dictated.

'That's it? That's all the two of you have to point the finger at a fellow officer? He's a bit flash? He's a bit bloody flash? Well, it's not good enough. I can't go to the commissioner with what amounts to no more than the gut feelings of a wet-behind-the-ears recruit and, forgive this, George, a man who's been retired for five years. He'll blast me off the bloody mountain. Now, there is something amiss in the borough of Stepney. That much is obvious. But you cannot expect me to take what the two of you are saying seriously when it amounts to no more than gossip. And I'll say now that I'm appalled by all three of you. Where, where for Christ's sake, is your judgement? Freddie – you've been ill. Can't blame you for that, but has it rotted your brain?

I cannot waste time listening to your crackpot theories. We do not go around pointing the finger at our fellow officers without the slightest shred of evidence. And if we took heed of every daft rumour we heard, you and I would both have been drummed out of the force years ago. What we have is a system, a system that the three of you now seem to be trying to circumvent. There ought to be a sign on the desk of every divisional detective inspector saying, "The buck stops here." If there's anyone to blame it's got to be the man in charge. Now, when is Inspector Milligan due back?'

'Tomorrow,' said the Shrimp.

Jack's voice soared. Eddie and Mary McDiarmuid looked blank and baffled. The Shrimp had turned white; Bonham was red with embarrassment or restrained rage.

'Tomorrow I shall fry Milligan's ears in chip fat. If the Ryans have muscled in on the Marxes, he's the one who should have known, and he'd better have a bloody good explanation! I've got bodies piling up like the St Valentine's Day massacre and I want answers! In the meantime, I want nothing of what was said here leaked. If so much as a word of this gets out I shall come down on the lot of you like a ton of bricks!'

Jack left without another word.

Troy took advantage of the *chaise-longue*, and quietly stretched out: Jack had worn him out. He'd seen dozens of Jack's rages over the years, but this one had the unique quality, if that was the word, of coming when he, not Troy, was running the show.

A few moments passed in silence. Then Bonham got up with a quiet 'I'll be off then,' and opened the front door.

The Shrimp looked blasted, muttered his 'goodnight,' and they left together.

Mary McDiarmuid moved to a position from which she could look clearly at Troy and said, 'I'm the new girl here. Would you mind telling me what all that was about?'

Troy sighed at the effort, but the words were ready and able. 'Jack feels cornered.'

'Cornered?'

'I've presented him with a *fait accompli* and he doesn't like it. But he'll come round, maybe not tomorrow or the day after, but

194

he'll come round.'

It was Eddie's turn to express bewilderment.

'What *fait accompli*?'

Troy thought about this. Clark was the most trustworthy man he had ever known. Not that he was honest, straight as a die *et cetera* —far from it. But he was bent in all the ways Troy himself was bent. For much of the time so was Jack, but when he wasn't he wasn't.

'Who do you think blew up Brock? Who do you think put me in hospital? Who do you think snatched Bernie Champion? We've been looking at Brock's murder from the wrong angle from the start. We assumed it was vengeance. That Brock had been blown up as tit-for-tat for sending Alf Marx down. Nothing of the sort. The Ryans hit Brock just to show Alf's gang they could. To scare the living daylights out of them. And they took Bernie to get control of the territory. What we just heard from George and young Robertson is the first thing I've heard in weeks that explains what happened to me.'

'And Joey Rork?'

'Rork just blundered into it. He followed the Ryans thinking he would learn something about Danny. They killed him. Rork wasn't a complete fool either. He spotted them for what they were. Two tearaways on the up. He didn't think they were just ringing cars. He thought they were making serious money.'

'They're not much more than kids. How could they just take over? Us not knowing about it till now is one thing, but how?'

'How many of Alf's mob went down with him?'

'Six or seven?' said Eddie.

'Eight,' said Troy. 'The gang was left in tatters.'

Eddie thought about this. When Eddie thought about things, Troy knew, he was, often as not, faking to give the appearance of due consideration to what had been on the tip of his tongue anyway. 'Do you remember, sir, what you said at Mr Brocklehurst's party when Alf Marx went down?'

'No.'

'I was standing next to you, sir, you were talking to Mr Wildeve but I heard you all the same. You said, "Nature abhors a vacuum." '

'I did?'

'Yes, sir. Let's hope Mr Wildeve remembers too.'

§ 54

Troy reached for the telephone and called Claridge's. Only when Reception answered did he realise he didn't know what name to ask for. 'Miss Tosca?' But there was no Miss Tosca staying there. 'Mrs Troy?' It seemed so unlikely. Mrs Troy it was, but she had checked out half an hour ago.

He lay back on the *chaise-longue*, the phone sitting on his chest like an obelisk. It might ring. He'd wait. He might by force of will be able to conjure her up like a will-o'-the-wisp.

About ten minutes later he heard the door open. He hadn't bothered to lock it after he'd finally ushered Eddie out with 'It's ten o'clock. Bugger off home.' All the same, the strength of his will was a surprise.

He saw a pair of spiky heels step into the arc lit by the reading lamp behind his head, tilted a little and saw the hem of a rain-spattered trenchcoat. The trenchcoat pooled around her ankles, he looked all the way up and saw . . . Kitty, a vision of a creamy-white summer dress, so translucent he could see through it . . . a collage of light and shade, curve and hollow. She flicked the hem at him, brushing it gently across his face. 'If you say you haven't got the energy, you 're dogmeat.'

She plucked the phone off his chest, and lay down in its place, nose to his nose, lips to his lips . . . lips to his ear.

'Phoning someone, were you?'

'Claridge's,' he said simply, marvelling how neatly the truth became a lie.

§ 55

In the middle of the night the phone rang.

Not Jack?

Not another dismembered body?

Surely?

It was Tosca. At the sound of her croaky hello, Troy turned to see if Kitty had woken. She hadn't.

'Where are you?'

'Heathrow. My plane leaves in less than an hour.'

'Leaves for where?'

'Not gonna tell you that. We don't have the time. I just wanted you to know you blew it.'

§ 56

Troy and Milligan met in the Chandos about half an hour before closing time. It was the first time Troy had been into the pub since the night Brock had been killed. The blast had forced the place to smarten up a bit. It had lost its front windows and, in replacing them, much of the pre-war feel of the place had gone – peeled off with the wallpaper, thrown out with the chairs and tables. No bad thing, thought Troy – it had given it a look of its own time, brought a bit of old London into the 1950s. Kicking and screaming might well be the cliché – if that could in any measure qualify the effect of a bomb. It had been Brock who kicked and screamed as his skin turned to cinder on his flesh.

'I'm sorry to drag you out, Freddie, but there are things I need to tell you.'

Troy noted that Milligan wasn't saying 'talk about', he was saying 'tell'. He looked awful. Another man's dying had put years on him. At best Paddy was the sort of bloke who looked in need of a shave or half asleep, but those were the illusions of appearance not the man. But now the bags under his eyes, the lines scored in each cheek were real. His dad was killing him. 'I can't go on. I've got to put in me papers. This thing with my old man is tearing me apart. I can't be in two places at once. So I've decided. I'm puttin' in me papers.'

It was eerie. Paddy was using exactly the same words Brock had used, in the same pub, at the same time of night. If it weren't for the refit, it might even have been the same table – they were sitting in the same spot.

'You don't have to do that, you know.'

Milligan was weeping silently, two small rivulets coursing down his cheeks. Troy reached out a hand, but before he could touch him the man had whipped out his handkerchief and honked. A rough seizure of self-control that didn't quite work.

'There's compassionate leave,' Troy said softly.

'How much do you think I've had in the last four months? I've exceeded any reasonable limit they might have. My nick's going to hell in a handcart. Jack said as much this afternoon.'

'You've seen Jack?'

'Came over to Stepney. I'm not sure I'd ever say Jack was a mate, but we've been through a couple of scrapes together – you know, you were there yourself – but today I felt like one of the dogs. He was – he was on the edge of rage all the bloody time. I could feel it. He didn't let rip. But he let me know in no uncertain terms what he thought of me.'

Troy said, 'It's not Jack's decision, fortunately. It's Onions's. And Jack's been like that a lot lately. We've all seen it. He's too many unsolved murders on his hands. At least five at the moment – if you count Bernie Champion.'

Troy had thought a bit of professional interest might make Milligan perk up at this, but he ignored it.

'He closed the door to my office and asked me straight out, did I think Al Mazzer was bent?'

There was no way out now. No amount of sympathy could grant leeway to spare his feelings. 'Is he?' Troy said simply.

Milligan reddened, visibly. Tightened his fist round the double whisky he had not yet touched. 'I'll tell you what I told Jack. No. Absolutely fuckin' not! Do you think I'd accept a bent copper in my nick? Do you think that because a bloke's a bit flash, dresses well, he's automatically on the take? No, Freddie, no!'

Paddy's glass shattered in his hand. A jet of blood and Scotch shot out across the table. Troy looked up. The whole room was staring at them now. Troy stared back until the heads turned away and the bar-room buzz began again. He passed a clean handkerchief to Paddy, watched as he staunched the cuts to his hand, wiped at his cheeks, red with rage, wet with grief.

'We had to ask,' Troy whispered.

Milligan whispered back, 'I know, I know. Somebody tipped you off, nobody's sayin' who . . .' Again tears welled in his eyes, he bent his head and his voice rumbled in his throat. 'I'm sorry, Freddie. I really am. I'd better go.'

Troy placed a hand on his arm and gently held him. 'There's still something to be done.'

Milligan raised his head, a mask of pain and misery. 'What?'

'I can talk to Onions. Onions can talk to the chief constable in Lancashire, the ACC in Liverpool. We can get you a transfer.'

'There's nothing. I asked. If I asked once I asked a dozen times.'

'Manchester, then? Warrington? Preston?'

Milligan drew deep breaths, calmed himself before answering. 'Truth to tell, I didn't look that far afield. All I could see was being there. Me being there, in the 'Pool. With me dad in the 'Pool.'

'But you could,' Troy proceeded slowly, 'handle things from Warrington or Manchester or . . .'

'I suppose so. It's just that all I could think of was . . .'

'Then let me handle it. I'll talk to Onions. I'll get you the transfer.'

'Can you really do that, Freddie?'

'Of course,' Troy lied. 'But there's one other thing I need to know.'

'Right.'

'The Ryan twins. Did Jack ask you about them?'

'Yep. And I told him. We've had those two marked since they got out of the army. They're villains right enough, but small-time. They live in Watney Street – half of Watney Street is crooked. I reckon they ring cars and fence a bit of stuff. They've got a garage under the arches in Shadwell. I've raided them a couple of times. Never been able to catch 'em. But it's only a matter of time.'

'So, they're not the East End's new Mr Big?'

'Freddie, it's good of you to try and cheer me up, and funny as that is I really don't feel like laughin' right now.'

§ 57

Onions was not in a good mood. 'Why is Milligan pestering you? Doesn't he know you're off sick?'

'He's not pestering me. We had a couple of drinks in the pub and it all came out,' Troy lied. 'Stan, trust me. Do this for me.'

'Hasn't he had any leave?'

'I believe he's had lots of leave, but the fact remains he needs more.'

'OK, OK. If I agree to this, though God knows why I should, then there are consequences and there are questions.'

'Of course.'

'Who's number two at Stepney and is he capable of running a nick until we get someone in or promote some lucky sod?'

'He's called Al Mazzer, and the answer's no. He can't be allowed to run a nick and he shouldn't be promoted.'

'You know the bloke?'

'Never met him.'

'Then whatever it is you're not tellin' me I think you'd better tell now.'

Troy told him. Jack would just have to live with it. He could almost see Onions's fuse catch light.

'What? What? On the word of a constable who's still wet behind the ears?'

'Yes.'

'Freddie, I do not take lightly to my coppers being called crooked. I want hard evidence before I act on stuff like that.'

'I believe Robertson.'

'Freddie, you've never met the man. I'm not pointing the finger at a copper on the word of a green recruit.'

'Then you and Jack think as one. You are in the majority. But all I'm asking is that you do nothing. I'm not saying haul him in, kick him out. I'm saying leave him exactly where he is.'

Silence.

'You can do that, Stan. Can't you?'

'I can. But that still leaves us without a DDI for Stepney.'

'An outsider. Someone who's never worked in London before.'

'Who?'

'Let me sleep on it.'

§ 58

In '56 Troy had investigated a case in the north of England. A furniture salesman from a one-horse town in the middle of Derbyshire had vanished, and the wife had appealed to Troy. Unfortunately Troy had found not a live if straying husband but a dead frogman, and he'd found him underneath a Russian battleship in Portsmouth harbour. The ramifications of this had rumbled on for weeks. It had been a diplomatic incident. Out of it came two visits to Belper, Derbyshire. One had resulted in his relationship with Foxx, the other in a debt of gratitude to a young policeman, who had defied his bosses to help Troy. Troy had kept in touch with Detective Sergeant Ray Godbehere. Sooner or later, he knew, there would be a way to repay the debt.

'It's been a while, Mr Troy,' Godbehere said. 'I almost thought you'd forgotten me.'

'No, a few months, surely.'

'No, sir, it's more than a year since you last rang.'

'And have there been changes?'

'What? In this nick?'

'Yes.'

'Mr Warriss is due to retire next year. I don't believe he intends to recommend me for the promotion in his stead, if that's what you mean.'

'Your accent. Are you a local man?'

'Not exactly. I'm from Sheffield.'

'Any particular prejudice against London?'

'Lead me to it.'

'Fine. Leave it with me and I'll get back to you later today.'

'Mr Troy, not so fast. You can't just dangle this in front of me without a clue as to what it is.'

'You're the new divisional detective inspector of Stepney. I'll get your file plonked in front of the commissioner later today, and when he rubber-stamps it I'll call you back.'

'And I'm supposed to concentrate on me job in the meantime? Bloody hell.'

'No, Mr Godbehere, you're supposed to pack.'

§ 59

Forty-eight hours passed.

Onions called with a terse 'You'd better be right about this bloke.'

Jack called with a terser 'Cunt.'

§ 60

Troy could not face another meeting in the Chandos. It had, in so short a time, achieved too symbolic a value. He would always associate it with the physical dissolution of Brock, and the spiritual dissolution of Milligan. When Godbehere called he suggested instead the pub nearest his own house – the theatreland watering hole, the Salisbury in St Martin's Lane, a plush, mirrored, gilded boozer in the high Victorian style.

He watched Godbehere at the bar, wondering if at thirty he'd had that same young, determined look about him. He knew he had, he just found it so hard to remember. It was like an age of innocence, and that, too, was in the nature of an illusion. He'd never been innocent, as Kolankiewicz reminded him once or twice a year when the vodka had washed away the last vestiges of the old man's caution.

Godbehere slapped down a ginger beer in front of Troy and a large vodka for himself.

'Are you settled in?'

'I've digs across the river in Southwark. I never think it pays to live on the manor. I've a room in a house practically on top of Borough Tube station.'

'Underground,' Troy said. 'Only tourists call it the Tube.'

'I think there are one or two at Leman Street nick who think I might be a tourist.'

'Have they made you welcome?'

'The air of resentment is so thick you could stuff it in your pipe and smoke it. But that'd be true of any nick you could post me to. It won't last. I'm in charge and they know it. Mr Wildeve came round in person on the first day. I felt anointed. If he doesn't want me there he's not letting on.'

'I don't think Jack knows what he wants.'

'Can I be frank, sir?'

'Of course, and drop the "sir".'

'Then,' Godbehere went on, 'I don't think that matters. You're calling the shots. It's what you think that matters. And you do know what you think or I wouldn't be sitting here. I'd be stuck in Derbyshire still wondering if I'd make it past sergeant.'

'Quite.'

'You got me down to the Smoke for a purpose. I'm curious to know what.'

'What has Jack told you?'

'He was blunt. Very blunt. Told me he thinks my predecessor fucked up in spades. Filled me in on the problem with the Ryans. Made it clear I'd got my work cut out, and told me to have no hesitation, "none whatsoever," I think he said, in calling in the Yard when I saw fit.'

'And your detective sergeant?'

'Mr Mazzer? He told me to watch Mr Mazzer. Wouldn't go any further than that. Warned me he'd been passed over for promotion and there was bound to be friction.'

'It's more than that,' said Troy. 'Mazzer's bent. Jack is being exceptionally cautious in not warning you of that. That, after all, is why you're here. Report to Jack what you see fit, but report everything to me. I don't want Mazzer watched, I want him cut out. I want him marginalised until I know what he's up to. And I want him to know as little as possible of your investigation into the Ryans. Tomorrow you'll get a call from a chap called George Bonham. He was station sergeant at Leman Street for years. Meet him at his flat. Tell no one what you're doing. He'll put you in touch with every East End nark he knows. You're to build up a dossier. I want to know everyone who works for the Ryans, every job that can reasonably be put down to them, all their assets, every piece of property they own, every bank account they have, everyone who's ever so much as taken a tanner from them.'

'You think Mr Mazzer's taken the odd tanner?'

'I'd like to say I know it in my bones. But I can't. It's a hunch. Not a guess or a longshot. A hunch. And I've gambled a lot persuading the commissioner to act on my hunch. Have you raised the issue of the Ryans with Mazzer?'

'Oh, aye, I raised it all right.'

'And?'

'He told me they were "fly" – that was his word "fly", "fly and harmless".'

§ 61

Bruno is tied to a dining chair with gaffer tape. His wife Glenda is also taped to a chair. The difference is that they've taped across her mouth too. Bruno can see the flare of her nostrils above the strip of black plastic and the wide-eyed stare of panic in her eyes. She is grunting.

Ryan presses the barrel of his revolver into Bruno's forehead. 'I'm gonna ask you one more time, Bruno—'

'Fuck you!'

Ryan pulls back the gun and cracks him above the ear with it.

'Naughty, naughty. Now. Here me out, old son. I'm gonna ask you one more time. You tell me where my money is or your missus gets it.'

'You wouldn't d—'

Ryan swings round neatly, levels the gun and shoots Glenda Felucci in the face. Bone and brains splatter out across the wallpaper, a fountain of blood a foot high spurts from the back of her head, the chair goes over backwards and Bruno finds himself looking up the skirt of his dead wife. A grotesque and trivial indecency.

Ryan puts the gun back on Bruno's forehead, but all Bruno can say is 'Waa, waa, waa, waa.'

'Oh, fuckin' 'ell. Oh, fuckin' 'ell. Bruno! Bruno!'

Ryan slaps him, but all Bruno can say is, 'Waa, waa, waa, waa.'

'Oh, fuckin' 'ell. Just tape the bugger up, will you?'

'Shouldn't we kill him too?'

'If we kill 'em both, you plonker, we'll never get our money back, now, will we? Just tape up that clanging manhole. I can't bear to listen to 'im.'

It's forty minutes before the police arrive. The first man in throws up at the sight of Glenda Felucci. The second pulls down her skirt and tears the strip of gaffertape off Bruno's mouth.

Bruno whispers, 'Ryan.'

For several hours it is all he says.

3

The Life of You

§ 62

August burnt. A searing sun in a cloudless sky. It was a favourite month of Troy's. The persistence of childhood. His birthday fell in the last week of August, leaving three whole weeks of anticipation. Even now, when he scarcely bothered to acknowledge birthdays, to see August on the calendar created that same sense of waiting for something. August burnt. He sat on the shady side of the court, read an American novel Kitty had abandoned on his bedside table – *Henderson the Rain King*, by Saul Bellow. It appeared to be the tale of a man who was partly inspired, partly crazy and completely frustrated. It was not Kitty's kind of book. It was his kind of book. And he read in the papers of droughts in East Anglia, of peatland fires in Derbyshire, of the extended national tour to the Royals and Empires of provincial Britain by one Vince Christy, of the impending state visit of President Eisenhower – and of the murder of Glenda Felucci in an Essex village and the almost immediate arrest of two unnamed suspects.

And he called Kolankiewicz. 'What kind of gun killed Bruno's wife?'

'A .357. Can we either of us be surprised at that?'

And he waited for the call from Jack that never came. August burnt. August was a month of waiting.

§ 63

Stanley Onions professed a taste for whisky amounting to discernment. Troy knew him better than he knew himself. Onions's idea of whisky was a cheap blended from an off-licence that he would flood with tap water. Troy cared little for spirits at the best of times and would drink them only to 'join' whoever had pulled the cork or twisted the cap. He had done this a lot with Kitty of late. He could see himself doing it this evening. Onions bulked on his doorstep. Blue suit, black boots, short back and sides, bullet-headed, bull-brained and bear-bodied, a battered brown briefcase under one arm, a bottle of whisky clutched in his hand – the commissioner of the Metropolitan Police Force disguised as an ordinary copper. The last thing he was. Apart from the odd days when protocol forced him into blue serge and shiny buttons, this outfit, and variations on a theme, were all he ever wore – and it was still a disguise. Onions was an *extra*-ordinary copper.

'You goin' to let me in or do I have to stand here all night?'

'Sorry, I was miles away.'

'You were staring like you'd never seen me before.'

No, thought Troy, like I've seen you almost every day for twenty years.

Onions held up the bottle. A treat for the two of them. 'Get a couple of glasses and a jug, lad. I'm gasping.'

This was a lie. If Stan had been 'gasping' he'd have put on a brown mac and a cloth cap and sunk a couple of pints in a West End pub, safe in the knowledge that the sharpest reporter in Fleet Street was unlikely to recognise him. Just another displaced Lancashire lad. If he turned up with whisky, he was up to something.

Troy came back from the kitchen. A drowned Scotch for Stan, on a rock for himself.

'Don't know how you can drink it like that. Ice with everything. American nonsense. Cheers.'

As far as Troy was concerned, one ice cube thinned out whisky all it needed to be thinned. He didn't mention that while Stan was swilling a mixture of London tap and corner-shop blended he had helped himself to a shot of Angus's single-malt seven-year-old Skye Talisker. 'Cheers,' he said.

The sofa screamed as Onions flopped his bulk down on to it.

'How are you keepin'?'

Well, thought Troy, begin with the obvious. 'My vision's

blurred. Sometimes, particularly if I've slept well, it's close to normal in the mornings. But I don't sleep well. I end up exhausted and catnapping during the day. My appetite's erratic. One day I'm Jack Spratt, and next I'm his wife. And my balance is still a bit off, but I don't really need a stick to walk any more. It's just belt and braces. My memory's fine now, my blood pressure is normal and I have a resting pulse at a healthy fifty-five. My libido's through the roof . . .'

'Lib-what?'

'Forget it. Oh, and I've got these for reading.' He plucked a pair of glasses off the mantelpiece. Stuck them on the end of his nose. Onions looked overwhelmed by the torrent of words. 'Corrects my eyes enough to read. The optician says I won't need them once my brain recovers from the knock and gets its wires uncrossed.'

'I'd hang on to them if I were you. Forty-three? You'll need reading glasses by the time you're fifty. I did.'

'How cheery. I feel so much better for you sharing that snippet with me.'

Onions let this go. 'So . . .' he said. 'The upshot of that Nobel Prize acceptance speech is that you're not too bad?'

'Fair to middlin', as you might put it yourself.'

'Be a damn sight quicker if you'd just said that.'

'I'd rather not be imprecise while you're looking for excuses to retire me.'

Onions held out his glass for a refill. 'Which kind of brings me to the point,' he said.

'The answer's still no.'

'Oh, that's not what I've come about. That's over and done with. I can't force you so that's that.'

'Fine. So, what's what?'

'It's that girlfriend o'yours.'

'Foxx?'

'No. The posh one. Used to work for the Pole.'

'Anna.'

'Right. Your doctor. She's on at me to find you summat to do. Says you'll recover quicker with some sort of . . . whatdeyecallit? Stimulus.'

Troy had had no idea that Anna had talked to Onions since

211

he left hospital. He rather admired her persistence. Still more he admired her loyalty, strain it though he would. 'You could,' he said, 'simply let me back on the job.'

Onions swilled Scotch. 'No,' he said. 'That I can't do, not without the Yard's surgeon passes you a1, but . . .'

'Stan. In 1944 you kept me off work for nearly six months regardless of what the Yard's surgeon said, just because you—'

'No, I bloody well didn't. I know you think it was plain vindictive on my part, but you're wrong. You were sicker than you knew and, if the truth be told, I let you back too early and you needed surgery.'

Troy could hardly deny this.

'And by your own admission you're not right. Your 'ead's not right.'

'I could hardly lie about that. Stan, if I walk you to St Martin's Lane to flag down a cab there's a one in eight chance you'll see me wobble.'

'You know, this could be the first conversation I've ever had with you without thinkin', the bastard's either lyin' to me or he's not lettin' on about summat.'

Clearly Jack had made no mention of after-midnight visits to corpses dotted around the roadworks of the Home Counties or stuck up back alleys in the West End.

'So, what are you offering?'

'Just this. I'm swamped. In partickler I'm swamped without you. So this I'll say . . . the next big murder comes along . . .'

If corpses jointed like pork or dumped in concrete didn't constitute the 'next big murder' Troy wondered what monstrous scale of crime Onions had in mind.

'. . . you can help the Yard solicitor prepare the prosecution. No roarin' around in your Bentley, no nickin' villains. Just the procedural stuff. The paperwork. And not at your desk. Here, in the comfort of your own home.'

Silently Troy cursed him for this. He sounded like an advert for bottled beer. The comfort of his own home? Paperwork? Scotland Yard solicitors? Police procedural? What could be more clichéd? What could be deadlier to the soul than police procedural? What could be less interesting? What could be more boring?

212

Then Onions opened his briefcase and slapped in front of Troy a buff-coloured file labelled simply 'Felucci'.

'Say nowt! Say nowt or I'll put it back in me bag, tek me bottle of Glen Wellie and bugger off home. Say nowt. Just listen. Jack's got the Ryan twins in custody. Been three days now and he's got bugger all out of 'em. Tomorrow at noon we'll be served a writ of *habeas corpus*. He'll be told to charge 'em or let 'em go. Now, I know they did it, Jack knows they did it, I should think by now you know they did it. But he hasn't charged 'em yet. I've not let him. Mind, he's fit to charge 'em because he couldn't charge 'em with the murder of that American he found floating in the canal. But that's not good enough. That's frustration driving the lad. If we charge 'em now it has to stick. What I have done is this – I had Swift Eddie transcribe and type up everything before I left this evening, every report, every last damn jotted detail. I want you to read it. Just as well you can't sleep cos I want it read overnight. I want you in the Yard at nine sharp tomorrow morning, and I want you and me and young Wildeve to meet with the duty solicitor and come to a decision.'

'Can I speak now?'

'Be my guest.'

'Who is the duty solicitor?'

'Sir Owen Rhys.'

'Does Owen know you've asked me for a second opinion, because that's exactly what you're doing?'

'Know? He asked for it himself. Between you and me and the shithouse door, Owen's found Jack a pain in the arse over this. He thinks it'll be better coming from you.'

'What would be better coming from me?'

'Whatever it is that has to come. We charge 'em, we don't charge 'em. Either way I want a decision by noon.'

'What is Owen saying?'

'No, Freddie, no. You read the file. You make your own mind up and get into that meeting with Owen. You'll have about three-quarters of an hour before Jack and I join you, and if the bugger jumps the gun I'll bust him back to sergeant.'

§ 64

Troy sat up half the night with the file Eddie had typed up. It was a trip to Cloud Cuckoo Land, a falling down the well. It was the most absurd thing ever to come his way with the name of 'evidence' attached to it. Tomorrow was going to be hell.

§ 65

Troy and Rhys met in Troy's office just before nine. Troy had known Sir Owen Rhys since before the war. Before the war he had looked almost typical of his profession; now he was heading rapidly towards the day when he would be the last man in London to wear a wing collar. Onions left them to it and did not show up until gone half past nine, looking as he always did, spick and span but wearing his suit like armour. By then Troy and Rhys were in total agreement. Today was going to be hell.

Ten minutes later Jack Wildeve and Ray Godbehere came in together, Godbehere looking somewhat fresher than Jack. Jack looked deathly pale, save for the redness around the eyes, clutching a cup of Swift Eddie's espresso – the synthetic buzz of nights propped up on caffeine and speed visible in the unsteadiness of his hands. His fingertips must surely tingle with the sensation of electricity. Troy had never quite been able to share Jack's fondness for amphetamines. They all used them from time to time. It was the nation's favourite pep pill. He'd even known Rod to come home from all-night sittings at the Commons with the saucer-wide look of speed in his eyes. There'd even been talk a while back that Anthony Eden had chewed them like jelly babies during the Suez crisis.

Mary McDiarmuid brought up the rear, clutching a shorthand notepad. Troy was almost certain no one had asked her to take shorthand notes, any more than they'd asked her to park her desk in Eddie's office. He was almost as certain that everyone else in the room would assume that someone or other had. She flourished her pencil, smiled at Troy, wicked green eyes glinting. He wondered if, having bluffed her way to a seat uninvited, she'd bother to take notes.

Mary was not the problem. Jack was the problem. Troy could feel the repressed rage in him. He thought they would all be lucky to get through this without an explosion of some sort. And if Jack blew, could Onions be far behind?

'This is hard,' Rhys began. 'Hard. But I cannot see that a prosecution brought against these men would succeed.'

For a moment everyone in the room was looking at Jack. He was pushing the cup around the saucer, one finger on the handle in a gesture of unconvincing idleness – but, the ball so bowled, he slammed for six. 'They did it,' he said bluntly. 'I know they did it. You know they did it.'

'Quite,' Rhys replied calmly. 'But you know as well as I, Chief Inspector, that my job is to advise on the preparation of a Crown Prosecution. And I cannot advise on proceeding with a case that is most likely – and I say again, most likely – to be thrown out.'

'Sir Owen, with all due respect . . .'

'With all due respect', particularly when uttered by a man like Jack, was a phrase to set Troy's alarm bells ringing. Jack had little or no respect for anything. It was something the two of them had in common.

'. . . do you have any idea who the victims were in this?'

It didn't require an answer. Rhys was not the sort of man who would have answered.

'Bruno Felucci is probably the biggest fence south of the Trent. He has no record, he has no convictions for anything more significant than speeding in a built-up area. All the same he is known. To me, to Freddie, to the commissioner, and doubtless by now to Mr Godbehere. It doesn't take a John Osborne to piece together the drama of that night out in Essex. The Ryan brothers had something they'd stolen. They'd placed it in Felucci's hands to be fenced. They'd waited for their money. And when they got fed up waiting they went out to Bruno's and did what most men wouldn't have dared do to him. They tied up him and his wife and said, "Give us our money or we'll shoot your wife." If they'd known Bruno better they might not have dared. If Bruno had known them better he might not have called their bluff. That, plainly and simply, is what happened. Felucci can declare till he's blue in the face that he is a legitimate businessman on whom two thugs simply burst in for no apparent reason, and the press can steer clear of libel and print such nonsense, but that is what happened. I have no doubt about it and neither has anyone else in this room. I have witnesses who saw them leaving the house – their alibi is tissue-thin – and if I get long enough I'm damn sure I can find the weapon because I think they're too enamoured of it to throw it away. If we do not charge them now they'll walk.'

Jack knocked back his Eddie special in a single gulp. Looked from Rhys to Troy and back to Rhys.

Rhys passed the bat to Troy. 'Chief Superintendent Troy has examined the dossier overnight, I believe. I wonder, what could you tell us, Mr Troy?'

It was better this way, Troy knew. Better by far that he be the one to light the blue touch-paper than Rhys.

'As I understand it, Jack, Felucci hasn't identified either of the Ryans.'

Troy leafed through the dossier. 'The first officers on the scene say Felucci was muttering the word "Ryan" but also add that he seemed delirious. Your own notes from your interviews with Felucci at the hospital, in which you observe that he seemed by then to be rational, state that Felucci denied recognising his attackers and said that he could remember nothing of what he might have said after his wife was killed. The day after this you put him through two separate identification parades, and he failed to pick out either of them.'

'Freddie, I was with him. He was lying. You could almost feel the man cringe as he passed them.'

'I don't doubt it . . . but bear with me. You have also a postman on his way to the sorting office at around five a.m., in the company of a London Transport District Line driver on his way to the depot at Upminster. They see a man – not two men, but one – outside Felucci's house getting into what they both agree was a Ford Prefect, creamcoloured and tatty. They even have a partial

216

on the plate, PGF – a Surrey designation, I think. So far, so good. Yet when put through an identification parade—'

'Freddie, they identified them!'

'To be precise, Jack, they each identified only one Ryan . . .'

Troy paused for a second, glanced at the file hoping Jack would fill the gap with some recognition of the approaching absurdity. He didn't.

'. . . but not the same Ryan.'

'Freddie, they're twins, for Christ's sake. Identical twins!'

To Troy, who had grown up with twins, twins were only identical to the unobservant. This was not the moment to say so. 'Then it's all the more remarkable that they didn't identify them both.' Remarkable? It was bonkers.

'It's enough to go into court with.'

'And it's little enough for the defending counsel to seriously query who they thought they were identifying. It is less than positive ID, and any halfway decent barrister will demolish it in a matter of minutes. It's an absurdity the like of which I cannot recall. If they wanted to play clever-dicks each Ryan could turn round and say it was the other.'

'That isn't what they're saying.'

'I know – what they're saying is that they were elsewhere.'

The fuse was burning steadily now. Jack was juggling incredulity and anger. 'Say it, Freddie. Just say it. I want to hear you make their alibi sound credible. It can't be done, but all the same I'd like to hear you try.'

Troy went on undeterred, read out the preposterous statement in a matter-of-fact voice. 'Patrick and Lorcan Ryan say they were in bed at home with Alice Marx, wife of Alf Marx, currently serving fifteen years for armed robbery.'

Jack opened both hands to the room. 'QED!' His hands returned to the table, the index finger of his right hand thumping down with every phrase. Onions and Rhys were not looking at him. Mary McDiarmuid had given up the pretence that she was there to take notes and stared at Jack. Troy watched Jack; Godbehere watched Troy.

'Alice Marx walked into the Yard yesterday morning with a cockand-bull story they have clearly got her to make up. When I asked them where they were they refused, repeatedly, to answer. One of them eventually said, "With a lady I cannot name," as though it were a matter of good manners. As though I were interviewing some adulterer caught in a cheap hotel in Brighton rather than a couple of killers. Alice Marx came in at a prearranged time. They planned it that way. A last-minute alibi just as their brief goes for his writ. The pretence strung out for the best part of three days that they were protecting the honour of a lady. The notion of the wife of London's Mr Big, its Jewish Mr Big, sleeping with acoupleof Irish yobbos twenty yearsher junior . . . Have you .ever heard anything so implausible?'

Jack's gaze roamed around the room, seeking an assent he wasn't going to get.

'All the same,' Troy said, 'you couldn't budge her. And I cannot see that counsel will either.'

'Freddie. It's lies, it's all lies.'

'I know. They did it. I've no doubt that they did it. I know. But I've also known Alice Marx since I was a beat bobby – take it from me, you put her in the witness box and she'll stand there like the Rock of Gibraltar. I don't know how they've got her to lie for them, but they have. And now she's made her statement she'll stick to it.'

Jack surrendered what little remained of his patience. One hand counted off points on the finger of the other. 'I have two witnesses. I have an alibi that is as shot full of holes as a pair of old socks—'

'You have no forensic corroboration. No blood, no car, no weapon.'

The fingers counted off again: 'They burnt everything they were wearing. They run a garage, so the car is in a thousand pieces by now, spread over every scrapyard in London. They have the gun stashed. To come up with corroboration I need time.'

Onions spoke for the first time since greeting them all, slicing methodically through Jack's rage.

'Time,' he said softly, 'is what you don't have. We've been served a writ of *habeas corpus*. We've less than two hours.'

'You mean you're going to let them walk?'

Onions looked at his wristwatch. 'Not a minute before I have to but, yes, at noon they walk.'

218

Jack rose from his chair. Both hands momentarily locked into his hair, as though he would yank it out in a second. Only now could Troy see how dishevelled he was. The suit looked as though he'd slept in it, but Troy could only guess when Jack had last slept. He doubted he'd slept in three nights. 'I do not believe this!'

Rhys cut in. It seemed like an age since he'd last spoken. 'Chief Inspector, I think a case in which guilt or innocence hinges on the ability of eyewitnesses to identify and distinguish between identical twins might be without precedent. You got lucky in having two eyewitnesses, unlucky in that they did not agree. Unlucky they saw only one man at the scene of the crime. If they'd seen both, things might well be different. Or if they'd identified the same brother you might have the ghost of a chance. With them identifying different brothers—'

'But they're idiots. Complete idiots.'

'No, Mr Wildeve, they're our witnesses. If they're idiots, they're our idiots.'

'I simply do not believe this. I do not fucking believe this. You're going to let them walk because two idiots cannot agree, two complete fucking idiots? I do not fucking believe this!'

Onions got up and said tersely, 'My office. Now.'

And Troy was grateful that the old man had not exploded. Jack was pushing him to the limit. He'd done it many times himself. It would be good to know when Onions would explode, but impossible to guess. He was cutting Jack some slack. Troy wondered if Jack was cool enough to recognise this and back down now.

Rhys had got up and was pretending to find the view from Troy's office window interesting. Mary McDiarmuid sat with her pencil between her teeth. Godbehere was still looking at Troy.

Jack turned to Troy, the waving hands flopping at his side as though drained of all energy. He, too, was looking straight at Troy.

'Shit,' was all he said. And 'Shit,' again.

He turned his back on them and followed Onions.

Mary McDiarmuid flashed a fake smile at Troy over the pencil. The next to get up was Godbehere.

'Spititout,' said Troy.

'I was just wondering, Mr Troy.'

'Yes?'

'What have you got me into?'

Troy turned to Mary McDiarmuid. 'Where are you holding them? The cells?'

'Interview room four.'

'The one with the mirror?'

She nodded.

'Good. I'd like to take a look at them before we turn them loose.'

§ 66

The Ryans sat opposite one another, either end of a fag-burnt wooden table into which dozens of bored suspects had scratched their initials with anything from blunt pencils to cufflinks over the years. They were past that. They didn't even look bored: they grinned and giggled like schoolboys, as they played the most elementary of non-sequitur word games.

'Parsnip.'

'Toad.'

'Twat.'

This brought on near hysterics.

'Yugoslavia.'

'Bournville.'

Another fit of giggles rendered them both speechless. Troy had seen his sisters do this. It was not the unlikeliness or absurdity of sequence and juxtaposition that mattered, it was how close the random words came to what the other was actually thinking. If one were to believe Hollywood, and *The Corsican Brothers*, twins were not just telepathic: they felt each other's feelings as well as thinking each other's thoughts. Troy thought this was bollocks, but his sisters would never quite abandon the notion that a common identity meant common thought. If they each felt what the other felt, then that was more than likely because they did everything together. So, it seemed, did the Ryans. And the constant company of the second self did for them what it had done for Troy's sisters. It had made them into overreachers. Arrogant egotists who thought rules were for fools. Men born to transgress.

'Catford.'

'Winklepickers.'

'Dogshit.'

'Coppers.'

Then both heads turned as though choreographed by Busby Berkeley, both bodies rose from their chairs, four legs propelled them to the mirror. They pressed the palms of their hands and their noses to the glass like the postcard kid outside the sweetshop, flattening flesh, like dead meat hit with a hammer.

'Coppers,' they said, breathing mist on to the glass. 'Dogshit, coppers, dogshit.'

And they laughed so hard they could hardly stand. Troy could not but admire the synchronicity.

He became aware that Jack was standing next to them. He had no telepathy with Jack.

'First time you've seen them since the war?' Jack said softly.

'No – I got a look at them at the Empress.'

'Of course. What are you thinking?'

'I'm thinking in cliché– a cliché of our class, I'm afraid, but a true one none the less. You can take the man out of Shadwell, but not Shadwell out of the man.'

'They still live in Shadwell.'

'They may live there, but they're taking over the West End. They have clean fingernails, decent haircuts, Savile Row suits, handmade shoes and, for all I know, you, me and they all patronise the same shirtmaker. They've got it, they're flaunting it, and it disguises nothing of what they really are. They still drink tea from the saucer.'

'Are we snobs now, Freddie?'

'If you recall, Jack, most of the Yard refers to us as the "Tearaway Toffs". Fine. Be a toff for two minutes. Look beneath the bespoke suit. It's the veneer on their animal hide. I'm amazed that there are people who cannot see it. I'm amazed that there are people who see charm and egalitarianism in this. Perhaps that's what we're doing, preaching about egalitarianism and the new meritocracy, and failing to see that the two are contradictory. Meanwhile this rough beast slouches towards Mayfair. The Empress will just be the beginning if we don't stop them.'

'Quite,' said Jack, much as Troy might have done himself, then, 'Don't you think it's time we stopped fighting one another.'

'Way past,' Troy replied.

'Then perhaps the first thing is that you get yourself off the sick list and back to work. Having you on the outside pissing in has been a pain in the arse. You've just cured a massive headache for Stan. Surely now is the right time to ask the old man.'

'He won't do it. Last time he told me to bugger off. He'll be more polite about it now, all the same, the basic message won't change. But I'm working on it.'

'How?'

'Stan's going to get shit for this. There'll be pressure on him. God knows who these two have bought. Possibly even political pressure. Thinking like a toff again, that's the one thing class and upbringing have not equipped Stan to handle. He needs me. He just doesn't know it yet.'

'Are you sure?'

'Oh, there'll be pressure, all right. I can guarantee it.'

'And this pair of laughing jackasses?'

Jack put a finger on the glass, where one or other of them had left a trail of spittle. The Ryans were cavorting about the room, yelling, 'Coppers' and 'Dogshit' at one another as though they'd just discovered a Zen mantra or a football chant. It was music hall at its worst. They slipped their expensive jackets back off their shoulders, tucked up their bespoke trousers legs and duckwalked like Max Wall. Showmen with a captive audience.

'I mean to say,' Jack went on, 'they're going to have a free hand until we can catch them at something else. They'll be kicking sand in our faces just like this until we do. Stan's just told me to ease off them. No surveillance until further notice. I think you're right. He's getting pressure. Their brief's already screaming about victimisation.'

'Did Stan say anything about Mazzer?'

'No.'

222

'Then we'll follow Mazzer. That is, if you now agree we don't have much choice?'

'I can't see what Mazzer can have had to do with the murder of Glenda Felucci but, yes, I concede the point. Mazzer is all we've got now. I just wish it were more.'

'Set Eddie on to him. He looks less like a copper than anyone else on the force.'

'Eddie's working on the review.'

'What review?'

'Stan's manpower review. Eddie's got the job of assessing how many blokes we can strip from the divisions and draft into Notting Hill if it starts to boil over like it did last year. The last thing Stan wants is more race riots.'

'How long?'

'It's due in in about ten days. We could always urge Eddie to bashit out in five.'

'Fine. That gives me time to do what I have to do. There are a couple of people I need to talk to.'

§ 67

Troy's Bentley pulled up in a leafy avenue in Hampstead Garden Suburb. Once he had told Mary McDiarmuid to wait and the sound of the engine had rattled down to nothing he stood and listened. This wasn't London, this was someplace else. The sound of a blackbird, a child in the distance laughing, the gentle mathematics of a Bach well-tempered prelude drifting through an open window. This wasn't London.

He checked the address he'd copied down from her statement. Alice Marx had bought herself a corner house on Palmerston Grove – the unquaintly named Rutherford Court. Don't mix science and politics, as Troy's father had once told him. An L-shaped house, with the front door set squarely in the long stroke of the L, a new-looking fence separating the short stroke for privacy – privacy in a street where your neighbours were not cheek-by-jowl, where lace curtains did not twitch, and housewives did not stand in the doorways giving out the gossip. This wasn't London. This wasn't Hampstead, this wasn't a garden and it wasn't a suburb. This was what Ally Marx had chosen to escape London. Troy had often wondered why Kolankiewicz had chosen to live here. He'd never explained, but it had something to do with the man's sense of security. His end to running. The same might apply to Ally Marx.

Troy yanked on the bell-pull.

'My God. My God. Where did you spring from? It must be – what? Ten years?'

Alice Marx was probably about the same age as Troy. She hadn't worn well. A good dye job dealt with the grey hair, but nothing would erase the sharp creases round her mouth where she'd spent a lifetime doing just what she was doing now, pulling on a cigarette, pursing her lips and letting the smoke roll down her nose. She was a good shape, Mrs Marx, a slender figure in silk blouse and cotton slacks, but her face could only be described as the ruin of a former beauty. She didn't seem to give a damn.

'More like fifteen, Ally.'

'Sergeant Troy, Sergeant Troy, George Bonham's little boy.'

Troy could hear the rhyme, a taunting schoolboy metre. He was pretty certain she couldn't.

'It's Chief Superintendent now, Ally.'

'I always knew you'd make good. Alf always said you'd run the soddin' Yard one day.'

'You going to invite me in?'

'Of course. I don't need to ask why you've come, do I?'

She turned on her heel. Left him to close the door. He followed her into a big sitting room. A model of neatness, not a cushion out of place, the magazines fanned out across a heavy glass coffee-table, a paperback copy of *Peyton Place* splayed on the arm of a plush, apricot-coloured armchair, and an ashtray on stilts with a whiz button to make unsightly fag ash vanish in a flash.

Alice turned to face him. 'You wanna talk, right?'

'Yes.'

'Then take off your jacket and roll up your shirt.'

'Eh?'

'You wanna talk to me, you do as I say. I'm not talking to you 'cept off the record. So I wanna know up front that you're not making any records. Roll up yer shirt.'

'Alice. I don't think we have that kind of technology.'

'Shirt or walk, Troy. Your choice.'

Troy removed his jacket, feeling as though he were in front of the school matron, and hocked his shirt up above his nipples.

'Oy-vey!' she said, softly parodic. 'Troy, you've taken a battering in your time.'

Troy said nothing. Turned his back to her so that she could see that he did not have whatever device she thought he might.

'OK. So you're clean. Come in the kitchen and I'll make us some coffee.'

She set the kettle to boil. Scooped an inch of ground coffee into the bottom of a cafetie`re and chattered about her decorators and her builders and the trouble she'd had getting the house as she wanted it. 'It's not being able to work with your own. That's what it is. I got a lovely bathroom now. The doin's . . . but half the tradesmen in North London are idiots. And can you get a Jewish plumber? Can you my fanny. There's no such soddin' thing as a Jewish plumber.'

Troy had a momentary vision of marble tops and gold taps. Perhaps a lavatory seat in a seahorse pattern. A pale green bath. The innate snobbery of his upbringing sitting calmly with the radicalism of his family's politics, thinking nothing of his inward sneer at the lack of taste so manifested.

At last she stuck a cup and saucer in front of him on what he knew was termed a 'breakfast bar'. She pulled up a stool. He perched opposite her, thinking this was the most uncomfortable posture to eat any meal and that if it was designed for breakfast he'd far rather take it standing up as his father had done, pacing round his study, bowl of salty porridge in hand, belting out ideas to the boy Troy faster than Troy could catch them.

'Ginger nut?' she said.

'Love one,' said Troy.

She rolled the packet towards him. As he bit into one she said, 'Dunk if you want. Alf always did. I could never get him to stop. Couldn't get him to drink the real stuff either, but you're used to it, aren't you? Can't see you drinking Maxwell House.'

It was the first time Alf 's name had come up. He wondered where the mention of her husband would lead her, but all she said was 'When you're ready.'

There could only be one question. 'Why?'

'Why?'

A slow stirring of her coffee, her eyes not meeting his. Then the upward tilt of the head, eyes locking on to his like radar.

'Millie,' she said simply.

'Millie?'

'I've known Millie Champion all my life. She was Millie Levine when we was kids. A couple of years younger'n me. A skinny scrap of a girl with legs like beanpoles, and two trails of snot hangin' off her nose like icicles. We nicknamed her Raggety. I imagine there are still blokes in Bethnal Green who think her name's Raggety. Millie's the little sister I never had. Bernie? A pain in the arse. I never thought she should marry a putz like Bernie. But what could I say? I'd married Alf. I hadn't a stiletto heel to stand on. But, like I said, we grew up together. We stuck together. She cried on my shoulder when Bernie disappeared.'

Troy wondered if there might be mention of Alice crying on Millie's shoulder when Alf got banged up for fifteen years. There wasn't. She paused to sip coffee and picked up her thread with no mention of Alf.

'So. When those Irish sacks of shit went to her and said she'd never see Bernie alive again if I didn't come up with an alibi for them she didn't have to plead with me. I said yes straight away. I don't see what else I coulda done.'

'Bernie's dead. You know that, don't you?'

'You found the body?'

'Not yet.'

'And maybe you never will. But you're right. Of course Bernie's dead. But what kind of a friend would I be if I kept telling her that? I just said I'd do it. I alibied the bastards.'

'When?'

'Two days before they went out to Bruno Felucci's. They knew what the odds were. Chances were they'd end up shooting somebody. I just never thought it would be Glenda. In fact, I'd no idea what I was covering them for until I read it in the papers.'

'A blanket alibi for that night?'

'If you like.'

'Did they get in touch with you personally?'

'Worse than that. I met with them up West in a hotel. Just to get our stories straight and to come up with enough to withstand cross-examination if it ever came to that.'

'Such as?'

'Such as we all stripped off. I had to be able to point to a mole or a scar or whatever it was. I told 'em up front. Any funny business and I'd scratch their eyes out. But there weren't no funny business. That was what was so odd. It was business. That and nothing more. And do you know what sticks in the mind? No offence, you being a goy and all, but the ugliest sight in the world has got to be an uncircumcised prick. And I had to get a gander at two of 'em. Never seen one before. And there I was lookin' at a matchin' set. Like two choppers in babies' bonnets. And I went round their place, so I could clock the colour of the wallpaper and which side the light was on and all that nonsense. Then it was all down to time and chance. If they pulled off whatever it was I'd not hear from them. I was to read the papers, and if I saw anything I could expect a phone call and I was to get hold of my brief. We was thorough. We must a'been. Or you lot wouldn't have let 'em walk, would you?'

'We'll get them.'

'You'd better.'

'You wouldn't consider withdrawing your evidence?'

'Fuck off, Troy. I've told you. I've Millie to think of. While she's got the hope . . . besides, it was more than just me, wasn't it?'

'What makes you say that?'

'A feeling. Well . . . more than a feeling. I got told to go to the Yard and make a statement. So I got me brief and I did it. But if I was all they had to get their lyin' arses off the hook you'd have had me back at the Yard half a dozen times with my brief interrupting you every two seconds, now, wouldn't you? No, Troy. I reckon you had a piss-poor case. You've come to me cos you want confirmation of what you already know. The Ryans blew away Glenda Felucci – you just can't prove it.'

'I will. Sooner or later.'

227

'Don't waste your time, Troy. Do London a favour. Take that scum off the streets. Blow them away, if you have to.'

Troy got up from the stool, an ache in his back telling him God never meant man to sit on one in the first place. Alice slipped ahead of him to the door and held it open for him. Watched as he leaned on his stick in the doorway. He could see her expression melt.

He stood in the garden waiting for whatever it was that was taking its time to surface in her.

'I'm not completely hard, you know. I did hear you got caught in that explosion what killed that copper what sent Alf down.'

'His name was John Brocklehurst.'

'I know what it's like.'

Troy did not ask what 'it' was.

'It was nothin' to do with us. You do know that, don't you? There's not one of Alf's boys would have done a thing like that.'

Troy said nothing.

'Could you like, you know . . . send my . . . you know . . . condolences to his wife?'

'John was a widower, Alice. He had no wife. Just two sons who'll never see their father again. On the other hand . . . with any luck you'll see Alf once a month for the next twelve to fifteen years and then you'll get him back. Older, wiser and knowing how to sew mailbags. That is, if he doesn't divorce you for the adultery you've just put your name to.'

'He knows I didn't do that. Besides, I'd divorce the bastard myself if I had grounds.'

Troy looked at the sky. A clear blue summer's day. Heard again the song of the blackbird. Bach had given way to Delius, a whisper of *Brigg Fair*. A melody designed to induce soporific happiness, evoking the haze of a summer's morning, the sound of a skylark, and a hint of anticipation. As English a sound as music and the BBC Third Programme had to offer. A perfect moment to put the boot in.

'Try desertion,' he said, heading for the gate.

'Is it desertion?'

'Well . . . he's not here, is he?'

'Hardly his fault, is it? That'll get me laughed out of court.'

She was almost shouting now as Troy opened the gate.

'Then it's mental cruelty, Alice. Run it by your brief. Tell him how it pushed you to the brink being married to a professional thief, how his life of deception and the revelations at his trial were more than you could bear. Tell him how you nearly lost your mind.'

Nothing in her expression told him she was aware of either the irony or the satire in what he'd said. His last sight of her was her sucking on another fag and mulling the idea over. He'd probably just wrecked what remained of Alf Marx's marriage. It was worth a smile.

§ 68

Troy arranged to meet his brother-in-law, Lawrence, the same evening. Lawrence had suggested Troy come to his borrowed rooms at Albany rather than to Fleet Street. Troy had not asked whether Anna would be there. Lawrence had both tact and bravura. Ordinarily one could rely on the former, but Lawrence was not leading an ordinary life. At fifty-something, he was a first-time adulterer. He might just want to brazen it out.

Troy passed Anna in the ropewalk. Another of her flowery summer dresses, not one he'd seen before – some sort of purple daisy pattern – and a shawl for the onset of evening.

'I've been given half a crown and told to go to the pictures. I gather you two have things to discuss that chaps can only discuss *en chap* as 'twere?'

'How have you been?'

'Nothing doing, Troy. If I say I'm sad you'll gloat. If I say I'm happy you'll find some scornful one-liner. Let's talk about the only thing that matters. How are you? You're looking pretty good, by the bye.'

'Is that a professional opinion?'

'Strictly doctor to patient.'

'My eyesight's improved no end. I'm not even sure I need the stick any more.'

He tapped one leg gently with the walking stick, in much the way Angus would tap his tin leg to show it rattled.

'Then if you don't need it, don't use it. Has it occurred to you how much of what you're going through might be simply psychological?'

'No,' he replied honestly.

'The stick is a prop, Troy. And I mean that in the melodramatic sense. Throw it away.'

Anna walked on. He had not taken three steps when she called to him. 'Troy, it wasn't you sent Angus haring off to Scotland, was it?'

Lawrence flung the door open, looking every inch a Troy. Braces dangling, tie at half-mast, a bottle of wine in one hand. 'You're early. You didn't, er . . . did you?'

'We had a bit of a chat, yes.'

'And now we have our bit of a chat, eh? It's work, isn't it? I assumed it was work when you telephoned.'

Lawrence flung himself down in an overstuffed armchair, and yanked the cork out of the bottle. Troy looked around. He'd not been inside Albany in years. It was still intimidating. Everything on the grand, too grand, scale. Everything ordered, in its place. He couldn't believe it suited Lawrence. Not quite the Spartan quarters of the army officer who was its regular occupant, but simplicity and system in a setting of gilded, bachelor indulgence. What Lawrence was used to was a ramshackle house in Highgate, strewn with books and papers and kids' toys.

'What's up?'

'Nothing. I used to know the chap lived in the flat below.'

'I don't think they call them flats, Freddie. They're gentlemen's sets or some such nonsense.'

'Killed himself about ten years ago.'

'We've both us had a bellyful of suicide lately, so why don't we change the subject? In fact, let's get to the subject.'

Troy sat down opposite Lawrence and accepted a large glass of claret. 'Those chaps who run the Empress. I promised you a story.'

'So you did.'

'We've talked to them about two murders in the last few weeks. Pulled them for the most recent. Let them go today under *habeas corpus*.'

'Pity. I'm damn sure they did it.'

'You know about them?'

'Don't be naïve, Freddie. After our little chat outside the Empress I opened a file on the Ryans. I've picked up every bit of chit-chat there is on the street, I've greased the palms of more oily narks than I could count. I'll admit it's a piss-poor thin file at the moment, but the truth is obvious – the Ryans run the East End nowadays, don't they? Or are Scotland Yard the last people to discover this?'

'I rather think that may be true. We've been pissing in the dark.'

'But on the other hand. . .I've had nothing about them being pulled. I mean nothing definite. I had assumed they were the two hauled in for the Felucci business, but no one has confirmed that. Your people resorted to the "unnamed suspects" line, as I recall.'

'Nor will anyone confirm it. Their brief's running circles round Stan, claiming intimidation or harassment or whatever. We won't be charging them and we won't be naming them.'

'So what's my "scoop" . . . if I may use such an inadequate term?'

'I want you to leak your file to every other newspaper in London. I want you to use Fleet Street's old-boy network and get what the Ryans are up to in every paper in the land. Every paper except yours.'

Lawrence took this remarkably well. Drained his glass, filled it again, stared at his socks, then stared at Troy.

'Why would I want to do that? We're streets ahead of the competition on the Ryan story. You can't just ask me to give it away.'

'If you let the competition make the running, suggestion, innuendo, gossip, everything but the names, they can whip up a storm. Then when the time comes I will name them and you'll be the one to break the story.'

'You'll name them? But you can't say when?'

'No, I can't.'

'Supposing they sue?'

'We'll have to be prepared for that. But if I catch them first . . .'

'Catch them? I thought you were still off sick?'

'I was coming to that.'

§ 69

It was a pleasure to watch it unfold.

Troy sat, two mornings later, in the sunshine of Goodwin's Court with all that day's papers in front of him.

The *News Chronicle*,the *Daily Mail*,the *Daily Sketch*,the *Daily Herald*, *The Times* and the *Manchester Guardian* all played a variation on a theme. How London was rife with rumours to the effect that two young thugs had taken over the East End, had taken possession of an unnamed London club, and had evaded the best efforts of Scotland Yard to catch or prosecute them. They steered clear of the libel law by offering only nebulous hints as to who these men might be. It wasn't headlining stuff, it was gossip and hence back-page gossip-column material, but it would be a blind man who missed it.

At lunchtime Onions phoned. 'Have you seen the papers?'

'Just the *Guardian*,' Troy lied.

'It's in most of 'em. Not the *Express*,or the *Post* but most of 'em. I know, I had Swift Eddie read the lot.'

That might have told Stan something. The Troys owned the *Post*. It was the weekday version of the much larger *Sunday Post* that Lawrence edited.

'D'ye reckon the lad leaked it?'

The lad was Jack. Occasionally Troy wondered what age Jack would have to reach before he'd be anything else to Stan. 'No, I don't. Jack would have named them, wouldn't he? Considering the rage he was in, he wasn't going to be coy about it. If he'd told the press he'd have named them. And the press would have printed it, wouldn't they?'

Onions thought about this. Onions did not come from an era in which the criminal looked to his libel lawyer. 'I suppose you're right. Doesn't make it any easier, though. We've had that shit of a brief on the phone half the morning. Talked about a smear campaign, and how those two Irish gobshites would be in touch with their MP and all that malarkey.'

'Ignore him.'

'I can't ignore him. It's way past that stage. I tell you, it's come

to a pretty pass when villains can get their brief to ring up the
Yard and boast about their political clout.'

§ 70

The following day the *Daily Express*, the *London Evening News*, the
Evening Standard, the *Star* and the *Daily Telegraph* joined the fray.

It was Saturday afternoon when Lawrence called Troy.

'There has been a development. I am invited to dinner by Rod
at Church Row this evening.'

'In what way is that a development?'

'I am invited to meet Maurice White. And I am invited to
meet Ted Steele – Lord Spoon, as you and Rod are wont to call
him. The last time I saw Lord Spoon was in the Empress, deep in
conversation with the Ryan twins.'

'You went in? I thought I told you not to?'

'Grow up, Freddie. Now, do you feel like gatecrashing your
brother's dinner party?'

'If I do that neither Rod nor Spoon will say what it is they have
to say. But I'll be there all the same. And I'll be listening.'

'Listening? Where?'

§ 71

As a child Troy had learnt by the age of five that he could ride
from the cellar to the kitchen to the dining room inside the
dumb waiter, hauled through the entrails of the house by his
elder brother. It was not a favour he could ever repay. Rod was
always too big to haul anywhere. By the age of eight he had
discovered that being packed off to bed while the grown-ups
entertained – Rod at fifteen now counting as a grown-up – had
its compensations. When the ladies retired the cook usually took

to her chair and slept for half an hour in front of the range. A boy well placed with his body scrunched into the dumb waiter could hear all that the gentlemen had to say over the cigars and brandy. In this fashion Troy had been made privy to the thoughts of Lloyd George in 1926, and some ten years and countless eavesdroppings later, to the thoughts of Joachim von Ribbentrop, the new Reich ambassador to St James's – or, as his father had called him, 'that fucking Nazi'.

It was a matter of chance. When the terms of his father's will dictated that the Church Row house in Hampstead be given to Rod, no one had argued. It was big enough for them all. What did it matter whose name was on the deeds? By then Troy had his terraced cottage in Goodwin's Court, Masha and Lawrence had their house in Highgate, and Sasha's money had bought Hugh what Hugh thought suited his position in society, a house in Lord North Street, so handy for the House of Lords. All the same, Troy had never quite got round to surrendering the keys his father had given him on his sixteenth birthday in 1931.Since Rod had taken up residence he had always rung the bell, and tried not to take his hospitality for granted – something Rod did all the time with Troy's house in Mimram.

On the Saturday evening, Troy used the key for the first time in fifteen years and let himself in quietly. There would be no cook to outwit, just Rod's wife Cid.

He approached the dining-room door. There was a crack in one of the upper panels, just about level with the eyes of an eight-year-old.

He peeked in. They were on pudding. And the only woman present was Cid. Troy doubted they would have had whatever conversation Lawrence had been summoned for with Cid in the room. She had ways of discouraging men from talking shop. When she left – 'retired' was scarcely the word to use in this day and age – they'd get to whatever it was. Troy went down to the kitchen and gently slid up the hatch on the dumb-waiter.

As he turned round he found himself face to face with his sister-inlaw, mouth open ready to scream. He clapped a hand over her mouth and waited as she clocked who he was.

'You lunatic, Freddie. You nearly scared me half to death. What are you doing down here in the dark? Come to think of it, what are you doing here at all?'

'I came,' he whispered, 'for the cigars and brandy.'

'Oh. You mean the conspiracy? I might have known.'

'Is it a conspiracy?'

'What else would you call it? No wives invited and dinner-table conversation that would bore the bum off a rhino. Of course it's a conspiracy. Rod is up to something. I don't know what and I don't want to know what. But you do, don't you?'

''Fraid so.'

'Well, I'm not staying up for it. Whatever it is, please don't let Rod make a bigger fool of himself than is necessary. I'm off to bed.'

Troy was far too big to sit inside the dumb-waiter any more. He pulled up a chair and stuck his head into the shaft. He could hear perfectly – all that was required was to overcome the sensation that he was on the guillotine waiting for the chop. Rod had only to choose this moment to send a cold terrine back down . . . He wondered how the ice would be broken and by whom.

He even heard the scratch of a match as one of them lit up a cigar. Probably Maurice White, he thought. And it was Maurice who spoke first.

'It's very good of you to agree to meet us at short notice, Lawrence.'

'I'd be a poor excuse for a hack if I couldn't smell a story, Maurice.'

'It's not so much a story,' Rod said. 'It's a . . .'

Troy knew his brother would never get to the end of that sentence. He always fluffed his lines when he was feeling guilty about something.

Maurice bailed him out. 'I'm not sure it's a story either. I'd prefer to think of it as a party matter. After all, we're all members of the Labour Party. Aren't we?'

Nobody said yes to the obvious.

'And it's less about creating a story than correcting one.'

'Really? I can hardly begin to guess what you mean, Maurice.'

Rod found his voice again. 'It's a long story . . .'

'Which one? The one we're correcting or the one I'm creating?'

Rod doggedly ignored this.

'We, that is the Party, mean to come into office with a committed programme of urban renewal. That's hardly surprising. It's been in every manifesto since the war and it'll be in the next one.'

'Why does that not sound like success?'

Rod ignored this too. It was the kind of remark that usually had him saying things like 'I'll knock your block off.'

'A few weeks ago Maurice approached me with a project for redeveloping a site in the East End.'

'You mean a bombsite?'

'No,' Maurice chipped in. 'We mean the redevelopment of slums.'

'Knocking houses down? When London has its biggest housing shortage since 1940?'

'Knocking 'em down, Lawrence, and rebuilding 'em.'

'I see . . . and where is this site?'

'Watney Market. My manor. I was born there.'

'And you want the next government, the next Labour government, to rubber-stamp this?'

Rod again: 'It'll be more than that. It'll be a sort of partnership.'

'A partnership? Between a Labour government and venture capital?'

Troy could almost feel Rod gagging on his Calvados.

'Doesn't sound exactly socialist to me, Rod.'

'It's not incompatible either. Think of it as a Public–Private Partnership.'

'I'll try, but it sounds to me like an acronym in the making, and a recipe for a scam.'

Ted Spoon spoke for the first time. 'It's detail, Lawrence, merely detail. We wish to be the contractors for this project. There's no reason why we cannot build decent homes for working people. We are self-made men who simply want to put something back into the community. As a Fleet Street editor you are familiar with the work and lives of both Maurice and myself, if only for the purposes of writing our obituaries at some distant date.'

'I wrote yours myself last summer, Ted. We try to plan ahead.'

Whether he meant to or not, Lawrence had broken the tension. Ted Spoon laughed out loud and Maurice and Rod joined in. As the laughter died down, Troy heard the clink of the brandy bottle doing the rounds. Rod's sense of relief was almost palpable.

Someone complimented Rod on the brandy, *sotto voce*. Someone coughed loudly, and Spoon picked up where he'd left off, but with a lighter tone in his voice. 'We're both working-class boys made good, Lawrence. We've given away millions. Simple charity. Almost effortless. Sign a cheque and salve your conscience. It's almost too easy. This . . . this is a project that takes us back to our roots. It's a real chance to do something for a whole community.'

'I see. And you want me to write something about this?'

'I would be only too happy if you did, but no. Maurice was right when he said this is less the creating of a story than the correcting of one.'

'I'm sorry,' Lawrence lied, like Troy. 'I don't quite follow.'

Maurice took over. 'You can hardly have missed the rumours about gangland villainy. It's been in all the papers.'

'All the papers except yours,' said Rod, and Troy wondered about the curious path of genes: that his own father could have produced an eldest son capable of such stupidity, of such gaffe-making, foot-in-gob stupidity.

Lawrence said nothing, forcing Maurice to spell it out.

'All those rumours concern two brothers called Lorcan and Patrick Ryan. They're Danny Ryan's younger brothers. They run several businesses out of Watney Market, and the rumour about them owning a nightclub up West is also true. Danny's done very well since the war and so have his brothers. They're partners in this project too.'

'All of them? Danny too?'

'No, not Danny.'

'I see. And what is it you want me to do?'

'We want you to print the truth.'

'I always print the truth.'

Spoon again: 'We came to you because you alone of the Fleet Street editors have chosen not to repeat these groundless rumours.'

'Groundless? Perhaps. But if you ask me to refute I will inevitably have to repeat in order to refute. I cannot deny what I do not know to be false.'

'Trust me,' Maurice ventured. 'It's all lies.'

'You know, Maurice, when someone says, "Trust me," my journalist's hackles rise.'

'Lawrence, all the stories are bollocks. I know these people. I grew up among them. It's a case of give a dog a bad name. You come from a place like Watney Market and trouble comes looking for you the minute you set foot out of the door. You don't need to be bad: bad is the condition of living. I have a juvenile record meself, but I made good. And I can tell you now, the Ryan twins have no worse a record than I do. We've all been there. What I've seen in the papers in the last few weeks is a refusal to let working-class kids grow up and clean up. I don't wholly blame the press for that. I blame the police, who seem to want to pin everything that goes down in East London on them. The truth is, there's something in our society that cannot bear to see a kid from the slums make good, something that will always rake up their background and use it against them. That's why we're Labour. All of us, you, me, Rod and Ted. Because we don't believe a man is damned by his beginnings. We believe in making good, we believe in equality and we believe in meritocracy. We take the Ryans on their merits. In a project like this we need local knowledge. Men who can speak for the community. Without the Ryans we've got a project, that I can't deny, but without them it doesn't connect to the lives of the people in that community. If we don't get that local involvement then we might as well be a company from America or Germany just steaming in, knocking down and building up. Bricks and mortar, sure, but the life wouldn't be there. We need these men. We need men like these men. Put simply, they're being slandered.'

'No, Maurice, they're not. Not until someone names them.'

'OK – all but slandered, a gnat's bollock away from slandered. But they're good blokes, we need 'em. There has to be some way to set the record straight.'

It was a stunning speech. Rod would have been jealous of Maurice on the hustings. Troy could not see his brother-in-law falling for it for one second.

'Rough diamonds, eh, Maurice?'

'If you like. I'd call 'em a new breed of entrepreneur. But rough diamond sounds kosher enough for me.'

'Maurice, I'm a working-class kid. Don't let the accent and the tie fool you. Listen to my surname. Stafford was Steafaoin when my dad was fresh off the boat in 1899. I was the sort of kid who could pass exams. I got a scholarship to Merchant Taylor's, and then a scholarship to Oxford. An education that my family could no more have paid for than they could have bought the moon. I've no more ignored or forgotten my origins than you have and, like you, I've the odd blot on my record as a child. Things I did that I deeply regret and that I'll be embarrassed to see in my own obituary if the buggers I work with are ever so crass as to show it to me. But the past is a foreign country. No one spreads rumours about me being involved in rackets. And to ask me to accept that the level of rumour that now engulfs London is simply the result of some sort of class prejudice or police conspiracy against two upright citizens is beyond belief. I don't know what you think I can do for you. But it isn't creating or correcting a story, it's killing a story. A story is either an abortion or a living, breathing, kicking, screaming thing with a life of its own. I don't know how you kill it. And there's nothing you can say would ever make me want to try.'

Troy knew an exit line when he heard one. The meeting was surely over. Lawrence had just fired the final broadside. Time to make himself known. He raced upstairs and sat on the bottom step of the next flight trying to give the impression that he'd been there for some time. When the dining-room door opened, Rod emerged followed by Lawrence. He was clearly about to utter some sort of apology to Lawrence when he noticed Troy. 'How long have you been there?'

'Long enough,' said Troy.

'Are you going into town, Freddie?' Lawrence said. 'We could share a cab.'

They ducked out sharply. Neither of them turned round, but Troy knew that Rod was standing on the doorstep staring at them all the way to the end of the road.

Lawrence flagged a cab. 'Your place or mine?'

'I think it's time we went to your office. Two cups of coffee and a typewriter, and tell them to hold the morning edition.'

'Fleet Street,' Lawrence said to the cabbie.

When they'd moved off Lawrence said nothing for a while. As

239

they came within sight of King's Cross he said, 'Is that what you wanted?'

'Wanted?' said Troy. 'It's certainly not what I expected. Although Rod's capacity to behave like an ass should surprise neither of us.'

This seemed to hit the mark. There was thinly held rage in Lawrence's next remark: 'What did those stupid buggers expect me to do? They call in the editor of a national newspaper to ask him to kill a story that's already the talk of the town? And I have to sit there and listen to Rod defend the reputations of a couple of crooks? What the hell was he thinking?'

'I think you could say he wasn't thinking. That's the problem. Rod is a believer. The number of things in which he is willing to believe, either temporarily or as a matter of lifelong commitment, are legion. One of which is that, by and large, people tell him the truth.'

'Since you put it that way . . . I still find it hard to believe you're related. And I've known the two of you for twenty-five years.'

§ 72

Troy talked. Lawrence typed. Troy was envious of the electric typewriter. At the Yard only Onions's secretary had anything so modern. Most coppers, Swift Eddie excepted, typed badly with two fingers. Lawrence could type quicker than Troy could think.

Every so often a girl with a ponytail and a flared skirt would bring them coffee. At ten to two on the Sunday morning she brought no coffee but tapped on the glass face of her wristwatch.

'She thinks we're cutting it fine,' Lawrence said. 'That's OK. I think I've finished.'

The Sunday Post

I speak as an outsider, as many of my critics would surely remind me, were I not so pre-emptive, but rarely in my years in London have I been witness to such a tidal surge in rumour, to the manufacture of stories seemingly without detail or substance. I am put in mind of the ingenious fabrications of Titus Oates – no, not that one, the other one – but the elaborate lies of an individual, however much believed, cannot fairly be compared to what appears to be a collective body of opinion that has set itself to the half-telling of a tale. And therein lies the problem. Why is this tale of which we have all read in the last week only half told?

To avoid confusion, permit me to essay a short summary of the rumour that appears to have seized Fleet Street. There is a new power in the criminal underworld. Following the conviction of one Alfred Marx, whose deeds my papers have reported at length elsewhere, a new, younger breed of thug has taken control of the East End of London. Not content with this, they are said to have taken over by force one of Mayfair's more fashionable nightclubs, and to have entertained there members of both Houses of Parliament. Furthermore, the interest of the police in these men has led to no charges – yet the rumours persist that these men are responsible for two, and possibly three murders in recent weeks. I doubt any of you would argue with my summary, terse though it is.

My point, however, is not simply to repeat the rumour and list the allegations. It is to ask questions. Where, if not with Scotland Yard itself, do these rumours originate? If these men are responsible, why have they not been charged? If they are not responsible, why have the gentlemen of Fleet Street been made privy to what I can only describe as an ullage of information and disinformation? There is something wrong with both our press and police force if the relationship has turned into an unproductive symbiosis. It surely runs counter to the public interest.

Hence I say to Scotland Yard – charge these men or stop

feeding the grinding wheels of rumour.

Hence I say to my colleagues in Fleet Street, name these men and take the consequences or stop doing the bidding of an inefficient ally who, having failed in the course of natural justice, is seeking the mere appearance of justice by other means.

And, since it has ever been this paper's policy not to ask of others what it would not readily give itself, the men in question are Patrick and Lorcan Ryan of Watney Market in Shadwell. The club they are said to own is the Empress, in Mayfair, and the company they keep includes such luminaries as Edward, Lord Steele and Mr Maurice White.

Troy hesitated over the last name. Lawrence had stopped typing and was waiting, fingers poised to hear if there was going to be more. Troy wasn't naming Driberg. Lawrence was refraining from reminding him of this. Troy was not going to name Driberg. Perhaps he owed him that favour. And there remained the problem of the signature. It seemed just a tad too much to expect Lawrence to put his name to this, even though he undoubtedly would if asked. Troy certainly couldn't sign it himself. And he had dictated it, consciously or not, in the style, the particular style, of one journalist. No, there was only one name that would do. He leaned over Lawrence and typed with two fingers . . .

Alexei Troy

'Are you sure?' said Lawrence.

'It's what my father would have done. What he would have said.'

'Really? I'm not sure Alex would have known a word like "symbiosis". I had to think how to spell it myself.'

'If he'd known the Russian for it, then he would also have known the English.'

Lawrence tore the page from the roller and glanced quickly down it with the eye of an accomplished speed-reader. 'Rod'll play hell.'

'Let him.'

242

'You know, I've never published a piece under the name of a man who's been dead for fifteen years before.'

Troy said nothing.

'But . . . we'll do it. If they sue they sue.'

'We can afford it. Besides, we haven't libelled either Spoon or Maurice. They won't like it but it's hardly libel. They do keep the company of the Ryans. You and I have both seen Spoon with them. And I doubt there'll be any shortage of witnesses to their relationship with Maurice. The only people who can possibly sue are the Ryans. Even then I'm not sure it's libellous. We're not saying they're crooks. We're printing what might be called common knowledge.'

'*Au contraire* – I think it's uncommon knowledge. And I'd hate to be the one to go into court and claim gossip and tittle-tattle as prior publication.'

Troy said nothing.

'And, of course, all my so-called colleagues in Fleet Street will tell me I stitched them up.'

'Sorry.'

'Don't be. It's dog eat dog and they know it.'

§ 73

Troy had just yanked his copy of the *Post* from the letter-box. He had set down his first cup of coffee of the day and had flipped forward to see his father's name in print once more. It worked. It worked magnificently. It filled half a column on the left-hand side of page twelve, and it made his skin rise up in goose pimples. He had brought the past to life when he set his hand to signing that name, and put a shiver up his own spine. The telephone rang. It was Rod. Of course it was Rod. But in his present mood he would not have been much surprised to hear his father's voice.

'You shit. You conniving little shit!'

'What makes you think it was me?'

'Lawrence would never have used the old man's name! You

shit, you—'

Troy hung up on him.

Ten minutes later he had reread his first piece of journalism since his own stint on the *Post* in 1934 and found he had no regrets. The phone rang again. It was Onions.

'How are you?'

'OK.'

'Good. Get yourself over the Yard. The MO wants to see you.'

'On a Sunday?'

'I want you back on the force before the day's over. Get to the MO and get yourself signed off.'

'Supposing he—'

'He'll do what he's bloody well told.'

'Fine,' said Troy, expecting Stan to ring off. But he didn't. Troy could hear the lurking sentence.

'You couldn't have stopped him?'

'Stan, even if I'd known what Lawrence was up to I would have had no way of stopping him. He doesn't work for me. He doesn't work for Rod.'

'I work for the bloody Home Secretary. He's been kicking my arse all morning. Just get signed off and get back.'

Then he did ring off.

A small voice in Troy's head said, 'Game and set.' Nothing would make him invoke the hubris of 'match'.

He was shaving when the phone rang yet again.

Rod said, 'Just tell me what you know. I can't pretend Ted Spoon is a friend, but he's a colleague. Like it or not.'

'It's quite simple. Mo and Spoon are putting money into development for profit. Watney Street is ripe for the picking. In fact, if they get all the necessary permissions, there is not only a gold-plated business opportunity, there is the possibility of government funds to assist in their fleecing of the East End. They'll bulldoze the houses, stick the families in high rises and say bollocks to the notion of community. Your so-called public-private partnership just allows them to fleece the taxpayer twice over. Or were you kidding yourself your hand-outs to Mo and Spoon somehow wouldn't end up in their pockets? It's too rich to walk away from, or let anyone deter them. Hence they need you. You could be in government any day now – I seem to hear that phrase with an awful regularity. Hence they will deal with gangsters . . . The Ryans are gangsters, they run Watney Street, so Mo and Spoon are paying off the Ryans, in money and protection. Protection works both ways. The Ryans deal in East End protection – "Pay us or we will become the people from whom you need protection." Mo and Spoon offer the other protection. "Get into bed with us and we will deliver cover for you. We have the ear of Rod Troy, we have the ear of Lawrence Stafford." Haven't you worked this out, or has the political prospect of putting one over on the Tories and finally getting the East End into shape blinded you?'

'Jesus Christ.'

'When Maurice White calls someone a rough diamond he means the man is armed and dangerous. The plain fact of the matter is that Mo and Spoon are courting a couple of murderers. And they know it. I don't know what cock-and-bull story Maurice came to you with, but you've behaved like an ass, a first-rate, bone-headed, gullible ass. He flattered your messianic sensibility, the overweening notion you've had all your life that you can set the world to rights. All Lawrence and I did was clear the board so you can see who the players are. Anyone who wants to do business with the Ryans can no longer pretend there isn't an issue. The bluff Mo tried to pull on you last night won't ever work again. You know what Maurice White is? I'll tell you. Kitty's little brother summed him up nicely at old Edna's funeral. He said, "Mo's the man who sold the world." I could not put it better.'

'Jesus Christ.'

Rod went silent. All Troy could hear was his breathing. The thought that perhaps he had hit too far below the belt approached his consciousness and crept away again. At last Rod said, 'And Ted Spoon. What is he?'

'I don't know – yet.'

§ 74

Sarcasm was nothing. Troy could handle sarcasm.

'I can't tell you how honoured I am, Chief Superintendent, that you have consented to consult a doctor for the living instead of the Polish ghoul you are wont to favour with your custom. Forgive me if I feel for a pulse. It's a habit of mine.'

Troy wondered how Sir Ronald Middleton MD, chief medical officer to Scotland Yard, would look with a black eye, and said nothing.

'I've been told to put you back on the force, as I've no doubt you know. But that doesn't mean I'm not going to give you the works.'

Middleton held Troy by the wrist and gazed down at a large pocket watch with a sweeping second hand. Then he let the wrist drop and neatly swung the watch back into the pocket of his waistcoat like the music-hall comic Jimmy Edwards. Clearly he'd practised this for hours.

'Fifty-six,' he said.

'Healthy,' said Troy.

'A wee bit on the low side. You should be feeling stress right now, natural stress at being in someone else's hands. A slightly elevated heart-rate would be normal.'

He had one of those pinpoint torch things in his hands now and was shining it first into Troy's eyes and then into his ears.

'But you're not normal, are you, Mr Troy? You're odd. You're the clever dick who thinks the rules were made for someone else. Shirt off.'

Middleton tapped on Troy's naked chest. Listened through the cold end of his stethoscope. Fingered an old scar on his ribcage. 'Potato peeler, wasn't it?' The bastard was smiling now. 'Or did you think there were secrets at Scotland Yard?'

Troy was definitely going to thump this sod.

'Drop your trousers.'

'Is this really necessary?'

'Drop 'em, Mr Troy. And when I say cough try your best to oblige me.'

When it was all over and Middleton had exacted a pound of flesh in ritual humiliation, Troy was tying his tie, and Middleton was jotting notes into a file and talking without looking at him.

'There's good news and bad news.'

'And?'

'Well, the good is that I can pass you back to active service without having to tell the commissioner that it's against my better judgement and advice. You're fit, Mr Troy. Surprisingly fit.'

'So what's the bad news?'

Middleton looked up. The cat that had got at the cream. 'You've been that way for a while. I'd estimate you've been a1 for at least a couple of weeks. If you'd come to see me then instead of wasting your time with Dr Death, you'd have been back on the force a while ago.'

'But . . . I haven't felt well.'

'Purely psychological, Mr Troy. All you needed was the prospect of work to make your mind shape up as your body has done. That, after all, is the trouble with the dead – they have bodies, they no longer have minds.'

Middleton slid his glasses way down his nose and looked at Troy over the top. He held out a stamped form. 'Just let the commissioner have this. Good day to you, Mr Troy.'

§ 75

On automatic pilot, the following morning, Troy slipped his glasses into his top pocket and was reaching for the walking-stick by the hallstand when it hit him – perfect balance, 20/20 vision, a steady hand that stretched out for the walking-stick without so much as a hint of a tremor. Middleton had been right. All he'd needed was to be told. Anna had been right. If she ever listened to him again, he'd tell her as much.

Swift Eddie Clark and Mary McDiarmuid were waiting for him when he got into work. A cup of hot black coffee and a smile.

'Lose the uniform,' Troy said to Mary.

'What?'

'You're a detective. Civvies from now on. No point in looking as though you're on crossing duty.'

Troy stood behind his desk. Looked around. There was blank white paper on his blotting pad, ink in his inkwell, a neat array of ballpoint pens, a glass ashtray full of paperclips, an empty out-tray, a single handwritten note in the in-tray: 'I've sent a copy of my report to your GP. Good luck, Mr Troy – Ronald Middleton.'

Troy decided to take it in the spirit in which it had surely been intended. It was congratulation and warning in a single sentence. The old man's way of saying, 'Don't overdo it.' Normal service had been resumed. It was as close to bliss as man ever came.

He sat down, lord of most of what he surveyed, palms flat on the worn leather of his desktop. They were staring at him. Standing like Harbottle and Albert.

'Well?'

Mary McDiarmuid and Eddie exchanged glances.

Mary McDiarmuid said, 'Orders, boss?'

Orders? He'd almost forgotten how to give orders. 'What are you working on?'

'Mr Wildeve has me cross-referencing missing persons with the files on those two cut-up boys. Do you want to see it?'

'Not yet. What I want is everything on the Ryans, the Feluccis and Joey Rork.'

'I've got those,' said Swift Eddie. 'Mr Wildeve sent them over last night.' Less than a minute later he dumped a pile of brown folders on Troy's desk.

'I'm still working on the commissioner's manpower review.'

'How long? I need you now. In fact, I need you to put on your old mac and do some footwork.'

'Me mac? In this weather?'

'It was a metaphor.'

'Footwork?'

Given his preferences not only would Swift Eddie never leave his desk, he'd have a camp-bed, a Primus stove and sleep in his office.

'A nice stroll around Stepney.'

Eddie looked deeply disappointed with his lot. Assumed an

248

air of oppression and misery. It was his front, his way of getting people to make demands on others instead of on him. Troy had seen it a thousand times. He stared Eddie down in a matter of seconds.

'I'll be shut of it tomorrow.'

'OK. Just tell me when.'

Troy began to sift through the pile. There was so little, he thought, so little of any substance. It was a poor showing after weeks of investigation. There was almost nothing in any of the files he didn't know already. But for the last item in Rork's file.

Troy picked up a blue page. The note clipped to it read 'Brought in by F. Jones prop. Cromarty Hotel 4th August.' That was more than a fortnight after Gumshoe had died. It was an aerogramme, an innocent-looking – Troy thought it had been chosen for just this effect – missive. A large sheet of sky-blue paper, almost tissue-thin, folded over five times and gummed along the three outer edges. It was postmarked Washington DC, 15 July, and it had neither a date nor a return address on the letterhead. It looked to have been typed on a portable by a man not accustomed to typing or Tippex.

Dear Joe,

It may be a while before you get this. I'm not ~~epredd~~ expressing it or anyhting conspicuous and, needless to say, if you ever get anyone asking you how you came by it you're on your own. Sorry kid. That's just the way it is.

This is what I could find out and pretty much how things roll out. The lovely Kate is rummaging around in the top drawer yet again. But - she would wouldn't she?

First - Tom Driberg. He's a member of their parliament, but I guess you know that. An MP since the war. Typical ~~Engilsm~~ Englishman. Public school. Oxford - all the right moves in all the right places. In short we have nothing you couldn't have learnt from Who's Who. A maverick pain in the ass is all we know. All the right moves, but not all the right noises. Not favoured by the present ~~leaderhsi~~ leadership. And not the likely lover for Katie - for 'typical Englishman' read querr.

Daniel Ryan. Nothing. There isn'ta file of any kind.

Frederick Troy. Nothing per se . . . but there's a closed file on his old man that reads like Dashiel Hammet meets Buldog Drummond.

Alexei Troy, born Troitsky, in Russia in Godknows-when, died 1943. They - and ~~remme~~ remember this pre-dates the CIA by yard and a half so it's mostly what Hoover and the Feds thought was worth passing on - had all the suspcions and none of the proof. Red or White or candy-stripe like a goddam barber pole? Whatever. The guy left Russia in 1905, got to England in 1910, built up a newspaper and publishing empire - sizeable interersts here too - second only to Beaverbrook. Only time the file showed a glimmer was in 1941 when he broke the story of the German ~~inavs~~ invasion of Russia before it actualy happened. Took some reading between the lines but it's clear that he knew. No conclsuion drawn, you didn't have to be a stargazer to see that one coming. His other son is a top man in the opposition. Looks to be in the next cabinet the way things are going - war hero (worked with Ike in 1944 and is still friendly), champion of the poor, all that stuff. The guy you ask about is a copper right? He's just noted as 'and son' on a visit to NY in the twenties. But if he's a ~~Lodn~~ London bobby he's got to be straight, right? Right. But . . . I was in London during the Berlin Crisis in '48. And I kind of think this guy is the same Frederick Troy who busted Johnnie Baumgarner. In which case that we don't have file with his name on it is kind of remrakble. The way I heard it, and every other agent in ~~Lodn~~ London for that matter, was that this Troy pointed a gun at Johnnie's head and dared him to reach for his. Like he'd have killed Johnnie without a second thought? Quien sabe? Whatever - just watch your step.

Lord Edward Steele. Take a drink, Joe. Sit yourself down. You'll be here a while. The file was half an inch thick. Born (we think) Erdrich Strelnitz, Strelnik(c otional)z or Strelnikov in either Czech Bohemia or Hungary circa 1908/1910. Could be Jewish, but he's denied that often enough. Nothing more known before 1946 when he arrived in England from France, speaking ~~perfrect~~ perfect English and toting enough money to start his own business. The Brits give him a passport at once, no questions asked, from which Langley deduces that he was working for them throuhghout the war. The sort of thing tha could easily be checked, but nobody has. Would also explain the money - some sort of scam appropriating Resistance funds supplied by the Brits, maybe a bit of ~~judiscu~~ judicious looting - who knows? Starts cheap restaurants, like soup kitchens, moves into catering

as a whole and insofar as the British
have any food faster than fish and chips
(you tried that yet?) he was the king
of fast food by 1950. Givn the state
of their food rations in those days, a
smart move. Fortune estimated at several
million, and that's pounds not dollars.
Now he's into everything, construction,
investmnt, you name it. MP for Nottingham
(as in Sherriff of) 1951-55 (yyou have t
ask yiuself did he get bored?). Knighted
1955, a lordship or whatever they call
it New Year's honours last year. Now -
he was the choice of the Labour Party.
Unlike the Driberg guy he really is in
favour.

So far, so god. But here's the stingeroo.
He's on our payroll. Has been since '48.
No real idea what he does but he does
it. Anyway your guess will be the same
as mine - he finks on the Brits. After
all sombody has to, they tell us sweet
fuck all at the best of times. Langley
think he'son the take from the Israelis
as well, and seem not much bothered by
this even though they may not be the
only ones keeping Lord Ed in the manner
to which. He is very well connected. He
visited Ike at the White House in '53,
and got introduced to the Veep too. That
one seems to have blossomed. He and Dick
Nixon have met half a dozen times since
'53. He has stayed with Pat and Dick and
the fucking spaniel in Florida and Pat
and Dick (not the spaniel) have stayed
with Lord Ed at his stately type home
in England. I doubt that Dicky knows
the connection to Langley - it would be

unlike Ike to tell his Veep so much as a
~~sukk~~ syllable more than he has to - but
that hardly matters. Thing is, Nixon is
a creep, has a finger in every pie, he
has more angles than a ~~romb~~ rhomboid (or
do I mean a trapezoid? fuck me i spelled
that right!) and is paid off by more
crooks and mobsters than you could cram
into Joliet with a team of meatpackers.
By the company hekeeps. . .?

If the lovely Kate Cormack is getting
herself mixed up with Steele and guys
like Steels then I can see the Deeks
crapping themselves. Jesus, Joey, that
woman is . . . what do the Brits say? .
. . a wagonload of monkeys. Two racoons
in a burlap sack if you see what I mean.
Personally I have every intention of
voting for Senator Cormack (anyone's
better than Dicky), but we could end up
with a First Lady who is a major ~~embara~~
~~embarrasm~~ . . . fukit!!! - embarrassment.
'First Lady Fucks Brit Spook' - not a
headline you'd want to read. Bring back
Dolly Madison.

Watch yourself old buddy . . . whoever
this Limey pal of yours is who said Lord
Ed was a 'total twat' is wrong, dead
wrong . . . now burn this.
'Your Old Pal Pete'

Troy knew the reference. There was a Ring Lardner story in which
a man spread mischief and slander by writing to total strangers
and signing off 'Your Old Pal Pete'. Or was it Al? Maybe it wasn't
Lardner, maybe it was Twain corrupting Hadleyburg? Either way
it was obvious Pete was not his real name and it was pointless
even to try and find out – he wouldn't know where to begin. All
that mattered was that Gumshoe had had a friend in Washington

who could dish the dirt. He did not know whether to be flattered or surprised that Rork had included him in the enquiry. There'd been no mention of Angus. Perhaps Angus was so obviously, so crankily harmless.

Troy yelled for Swift Eddie.

'Why wasn't I shown this?'

Eddie sat down opposite Troy, took the sheet of paper from his hand, read it in a single take and passed it back.

'I thought we had a deal, Eddie?'

'Indeed, sir. But Mr Wildeve was concerned not to bother you with things that lead nowhere.'

'Lead nowhere?'

'His exact words, sir.'

'Really?'

'Do youthink it leads anywhere?' said Eddie, in a tone that implied he knew damn well it didn't.

Troy said nothing.

'Mr Wildeve also said, sir, that it was your wont to go ferreting around in spook stuff into which he and I would eventually get dragged and he was, and I quote, "on me tod", he decided to let you find out in your own time.'

'Dragged in?'

'We all kid ourselves about one thing or another, sir.'

'It's not that it doesn't lead anywhere, Eddie, of course it doesn't. But it's another card in the hand, isn't it? Having the dope on Lord Spoon might come in rather handy.'

'Mr Wildeve said that too, sir. I think it's what bothered him most. What do you intend to do with the info now, if youdon't mind me asking, sir?'

'I'll think of something.'

He folded the aerogramme back into its compact form and shoved it in a pocket. It was too precious to leave in a desk drawer. It wasn't so much a card in the hand as an ace in the hole.

Predictably Onions had every nagging phone call redirected to Troy's office. Every half-hour or so Mary McDiarmuid would ring him with the *Mail* or the *Standard* – for whom Troy had a standard line. The press did not dictate the investigations of the Metropolitan Police Force. If they had evidence they should bring it forward now or risk a charge of obstructing the course of justice. If they did not have evidence and wished to publish items on the Ryan twins, then that was between them, the Ryans and the laws of libel. This shut no one up, occasionally produced laughter, and, from a reporter on his family's *Evening Herald*, produced a knowing snigger.

But there were also the politicians. The bigwigs had had their say to Onions. It was the also-sat, the back-bench green-leather arse-polishers who now phoned Troy. Most East London MPs sought some form of reassurance, banging on about 'descent of the area into lawlessness', 'mob rule', 'the bobby on the beat' and so on. Troy resorted to the meaningless brush-off as practised by the royals, 'Something will be done.' Then a Conservative MP, Sir Albert Stokes: Marylebone South, telephoned. Troy was thinking that he'd seen enough knights lately to last a lifetime and was wondering what this might have to do with Sir Albert when it dawned on him. The Empress club was in his constituency. He heard Troy's platitudes with good grace and, just when Troy thought he was about to ring off, said, 'You're not related to the other Troy, are you?'

'What other Troy?' said Troy.

Then Les Gidney called. Les was the Labour MP for Stepney. Watney Street, the Ryans' home and garage were all in his constituency. He was, *de facto*, the MP to whom the Ryans should complain if their boast to Onions had meant anything. Troy wasn't at all sure they had – not that that meant they wouldn't. Troy knew Les slightly. Another 1945 man, elected straight from khaki. A plain, working-class bloke, not at all easy with the likes of Rod and Gaitskell and their public-school socialism, but, Troy thought, one of the good guys.

'I'll get them, Les.'

'I don't doubt it. But it is baffling.'

'What is?'

'It's a sort of circle game. Wheels within wheels, that sort of thing. It's only a few weeks back that Mo White was wanting me to meet them to talk about what he called "development opportunities around Watney Market". And then just a few days ago Rod suggested I come to a meeting with him and Mo and Ted Steele. I said no to both.'

'The Ryans' reputation preceded them?'

'No, Freddie. Not all. Truth to tell I'd never even heard of them. That alone is worrying. And, needless to say, I've heard *from* them rather too much lately. If it were left to them I'd spend the rest of my time in Parliament writing outraged letters to the commissioner. But, no, I turned down both meetings because I know Mo White, known him all my life. And I trust him about as far as I could chuck him.'

'Les, Stepney has a new detective inspector.'

'I heard. Has this anything to do with anything? I knew Paddy Milligan. I thought he was all right.'

'He is. Family troubles. He wanted a transfer back to Lancashire. The new chap's called Ray Godbehere. Why don't you introduce yourself? See he meets the people a new DDI should meet?'

When Mary McDiarmuid announced a Dick Goldblatt, Troy called a halt to it. 'Isn't he the Tory for Golders Green?'

'I think it's Neasden, boss. And I rather think that's Goldfarb. This chap said Goldblatt.'

'What's the difference? Get a number and tell him I'll call him back.'

'Will you?'

'No.'

§ 77

He liked the feeling. An old feeling rendered anew. Made fresh. To get home after a day's work. To find the evening still light, to have a cup of tea whilst listening to the news on the Home Service, and then to sit in the yard with a glass of wine and the evening paper and watch dusk creep over London. He could do this any day and, indeed, had done so most days this summer, but without the solid sense of a day's work behind him it wasn't the same. He liked the feeling that he might have earned it.

Troy was ready. He had heard enough of the day's news – once Parliament no longer sat, the press, wireless and television were held to be in what was called the 'silly season'. Licensed trivia. Lots of statistics about cricket and the weather. It seemed to begin just after Wimbledon fortnight and the term struck Troy as arsy-versy. Politics was a very long, very silly season. He had the folding chair tucked under one arm, a glass of Chaˆteau Bouvard-Pecuchet '46 in one hand and the other outstretched to the latch, when someone knocked at the door. Bugger.

A stout bloke in his late forties, overdressed for the weather and gleaming with sweat, stood in the yard. He had an attaché case dangling at the end of one arm, and looked as though his day had been a hard one. Troy was not about to make it softer.

'Mr Troy? I'm Representative Dick Goldblatt.'

Representative of what? Troy thought better of asking. 'I'm sorry, I never buy on the doorstep. I've all the brushes I need and I've never really wanted a subscription to the *Reader's Digest*.'

The stout bloke drew himself up, took the sagginess out of his posture, the better to stand on dignity. He was taller than he'd seemed. Troy hoped he wasn't a Jehovah's Witness.

'I'm Representative Dick Goldblatt of the 103rd District of New York.'

'You mean you're a Congressman?'

'I thought I just said that.'

'There can only be two reasons you're here, then.'

'Try me.'

'Kate Cormack?'

257

'Yowza. And the other?'

'Joey Rork?'

'Strike two, Mr Troy. Now, are we going to stand on your doorstep all night or do you feel like offering me a glass of whatever it is you're drinking and giving me a few minutes of your time?'

'Do come in,' said Troy. 'I was wondering why no one had turned up to claim the body.'

Goldblatt followed Troy into the house, accepted a glass of claret. Troy watched the hostility begin to melt in him.

'Y' know, there are plenty of guys would've cold-cocked you for that wisecrack about brushes.'

'Who said it was a joke?'

Goldblatt's face split into an amiable grin. He swigged at his wine, smacked his lips, pronounced it 'great', and settled himself on the sofa.

'Let's get serious,' he said, still smiling.

Troy pulled out a chair from the dining-table and sat down to face him. Goldblatt flipped open his case and pulled out a folded copy of the *Sunday Post*.

'A friend at our embassy read this over the phone to me. I was on a plane three hours later. It mentions two murders. And a possible third. I get to thinking Joey was one of those. Am I right?'

Troy nodded.

'And these Ryan brothers. They're related to the Danny Ryan Joey reckoned Mrs Cormack is boffing?'

Troy nodded.

'And the two are connected. These hoodlums taking over is somehow . . .' Goldblatt's hand circled in the air conveying his disbelief better than his words '. . . connected to Joey's investigation and to Mrs Cormack's, ah . . .' the hands waved again, this time in imprecision '. . . affair?'

'No,' said Troy. 'I think that's a very unfortunate coincidence. Joey got it into his head that if the brothers were bent so was Danny. And that compromised Kate. I couldn't get him to see that there was no connection.'

'And this article. I assume you've read it. This article asserts that you have these Ryans in the frame, they're suspects, but suspects you cannot touch. You guys used to be the premier detective agency in the world.

When I was a boy you guys were the stuff of legend. I grew up reading Sherlock Holmes. Now you can't catch a couple of hoodlums? So the question is, what the hell is going on at Scotland Yard?'

'First, your memory deceives you. In Sherlock Holmes we were the bumbling idiots to his smartarse private detective. Second, we are investigating Joey's murder. I know they did it. I will catch them. You need have no worries about Scotland Yard.'

Goldblatt slapped the paper down on the coffee table. The editorial face-up.

Before he could speak Troy said, 'Look at the signature, Mr Goldblatt.'

Goldblatt turned the paper, fumbled in his inside pocket and pulled out reading glasses. 'Alexei Troy. A relative?'

'My father. He died fifteen years ago.'

'I don't get it.'

'I wrote that article, Mr Goldblatt.'

'I still don't get it.'

'Then I can't make it clearer.'

'Try me.'

'No. You've had your say. It's my turn. Who sent you? The Deeks?'

'I'm chairman of the Deeks. I have responsibilities.'

'To get Calvin elected.'

'I was thinking more of the responsibilities I have to Joey's family.'

This was not a turn Troy had anticipated. Rork just didn't look married. He'd given no thought to the prospect that he might be. 'Joey was married?'

'Twice. And divorced twice. A kid from each marriage. Joe junior just graduated from Columbia. Billy's still in high school. Wants to be a cop like his old man.'

'So you're taking the body?'

'I guess I am. I have a lot of explaining to do back home.'

'And you'll see to the needs of his family?'

'That's under discussion.'

259

'Mr Goldblatt, I will look after the dead. I'll give Joey justice. He was a better detective than I thought. I misjudged him. But if he'd not been good at his job he'd never have got so close and he might still be alive. I'll look after the dead. However much money you have raised to buy the next election for Senator Cormack, I suggest you set some aside for Joey Rork's children. Do we have a deal?'

Goldblatt gave the matter a moment's thought. 'We do. But there's one thing more you could do for me.'

Troy was suspicious of this and said nothing.

'Mr Troy, you could send Kate Cormack home.'

Still Troy said nothing.

'I read all Joey's reports. I know about you and Mrs Cormack. I have no problem with it. The Deeks have no problem with it. America will have no problem with it. It seems to me that you have enough discretion to see that America will have no problem with it. But you've known her a long time. Could be she'll listen to you. Mr Troy, please send her home before you wrap this case, before it becomes so deep she's mired in it. I'm not thinking of the presidency, I'm not thinking of the election, I'm not even thinking of Calvin. I'm thinking of her kids. I'm thinking of her. You're worried about Joey Rork's kids. That's good. We both should be. But we should both be worried about the Cormack kids too. Please send her home.'

It was a moving little speech. Enough to earn Goldblatt the respect of a man who, until now, had been quite willing to despise him simply because of his occupation. Troy wished he could respond in spirit, but the truth got in the way.

'Mr Goldblatt, Kate Cormack doesn't listen to anybody.'

§ 78

Three days later Onions appeared in Troy's office first thing in the morning. Fine, thought Troy. If he feels he has to check up on me. Fine.

'Things have cooled off a bit,' he said, lighting up a Woodbine and perching next to the gas fire as though it were mid-December and not the hottest summer for umpteen years.

'Cooled off' meant he wasn't getting the outraged phonecalls. Troy decided to tell him the truth. Hot or cool.

'The Ryans are suing the *Sunday Post*.'

'Jesus Christ.' Onions inhaled and stared after the ash he had flicked into the hearth. 'What is the world coming to?'

One day, maybe, Troy would tell him.

Half an hour later, Troy and Mary McDiarmuid gathered to hear Eddie Clark report on two days' foot-slogging around Stepney.

'First off, sir, he doesn't know you're on to him. He may hate the fact that the Yard brought Mr Godbehere in over his head, but he seems to think it's the shit end of an ordinary stick. He's showed no suspicion and no caution. I rather think I could have dressed up as a chicken and followed him. He just doesn't pay attention. Not that he doesn't show basic caution. He does. And that brings me to the first point. He leaves the office, and he leaves his flat in Stratford, to use public phone-boxes. He doesn't want to be overheard and he doesn't want to be traced. But it's a routine. He does it on the assumption that no one would ever follow. It's habit and he's lazy about it. He favours two boxes. One in the Whitechapel Road, by the Underground station, and a second in Stratford Broadway. I don't know who he calls. But he's used both on each of the last two days. It would be easy to tap them.'

Troy said, 'Let's take who he's calling as read. We won't get the tap, so I'm not going to bother asking for it.'

'On Wednesday he visited the Stratford branch of the Westminster Bank. I had Internal Records check up on how his pay cheques are cashed. They always clear through the Westminster. So far, so good. But yesterday, he nipped out just before closing time to call in at the Islington branch of the District. He was just cashing a cheque. He came straight out still counting his money and got back into his car. Assuming he was going back to the nick, I opted to go into the bank rather than follow him. They were iffy but I flashed me warrant card and the manager gave in. The account is in his real name. No disguises. Except that he never told them he was a copper. They had him down as something in the rag trade – a furrier. He opened it three years ago. March of '56. I checked that against his personnel file. It was eight weeks after he was transferred from Leytonstone. He has £112 in a current account and £3,285 and a few shillings in a deposit. What you'd call a nice little earner. And in case the airy heights of top brass have given you any illusions, he's a sergeant, I'm a sergeant. It's more than three times what I earn in a year. In contrast the current account at the Westminster has fifty-eight quid in it. 'Bout what I've got in mine, I should think.'

Mary McDiarmuid said, 'We've got him.'

'Not so fast,' said Troy. 'We don't know whether he has a dear old granny who's making over a fortune to him in small chunks. We don't know whether he plays the horses.'

'He does play the horses, as it happens. I found a betting slip in his coat pocket. Lovely Lady in the 2.30 at Redcar yesterday. Came in last. I had two bob each way on Ramona. Came in second. It pays to study a bit of form. I wouldn't have backed Lovely Lady if all the other horses had had only three legs. So, I think we can safely say he's not making a killing at the bookie's. Which,' said Eddie, 'brings me to his assets. He's single. No girlfriend that I've spotted, but there's the weekend to come. The flat is rented. One bedroom, one living, kitchen and bath. Perfectly affordable on a sergeant's pay. I slipped the lock while he was out. Nothing you wouldn't expect in the home of a bloke with no kids. Radiogram and a fridge. And while plenty of people have neither I'd say both were affordable on what he earns. The car's a Ford Zodiac. Personally I've always thought it a wide-boy's car. A monster with bench seats. You know what that means, don't you sir? It's a bit flash, but then that's what young Robertson called him, as I recall. A bit flash. Mazzer's car has a sticker in the rear window with the supplier's address on it. I went round there. He traded in his old one, and bought the new one on the hire purchase. Nothing odd about that. Affordable. Again. So I started to think, what's the point in being on the take and having three grand in the bank if you can't spend it? So when he hung up his jacket for a caff lunch yesterday, I hung up mine too, and I got a close look at his. That's when I found the betting slip. The suit was a nice bit of clobber with a Carnaby Street label inside. I went round to the tailor. He has an account. Not exactly Savile Row, but none of your fifty-bob tailors. They're discrete suits but they're classy. They don't look like Burton's and I bet they don't feel like them. And on a sergeant's pay I couldn't afford one. The tailor says he's made four a year for him since 1956.'

Troy did not know how many suits he owned. But he rather thought the average Englishman owned one and one only. And since he never wanted to dry-clean a suit in the first place, owning only the one suit was not a problem for the average Englishman. Twelve suits was preposterous.

'All in all I begin to think that "flash" was more precise than we thought. It wasn't just a run-of-the-mill insult. It conveys what the coppers he works with have noticed about him, but haven't quite registered. If you see what I mean. I think he's too smart to spend conspicuously. In fact, I think he's saving it all up for the day when he's no longer a copper. In the meantime, he's got the one weakness. And if no one has looked at the cut of his suit and the quality of his cloth, and the frequency with which it changes, then it could be he handles it rather well.'

Troy said, 'The second bank account is stupid. If it didn't attract our attention, there's still the Inland Revenue. It would have been smarter to stuff it under the mattress.'

'There was nothing under the mattress. I looked. Nor in the top of cistern in the lavvy. I didn't have time to prise the gas fire off and look up the chimney. But I could go back with a spanner.'

Mary McDiarmuid ignored this and said, 'What Edwin's come up with is enough for a10 to open an internal investigation, surely?'

'Itis. ButIdon't want a10 anywhere near it. I just want to be sure.'

'I thought you were sure?'

'I am sure. I just want to be sure sure. Certain.'

'But he's the Ryans' man?'

'I've acted on that notion all along.'

Mary McDiarmuid said, 'Do you not think, boss, that the Ryans moved pretty damn quick to get someone on the inside so soon?'

'Not a bad point, sir,' Eddie chipped in. 'Mazzer's had that second bank account for years. For all we know he's working for somebody else not the Ryans.'

Troy felt stupid. He'd walked up to the obvious, circled it and missed it.

'Mary, get the car brought round. We have a call to make.'

§ 79

Once more Mary McDiarmuid drove Troy out to Hampstead Garden Suburb. A tatty grey Trojan van was parked outside Alice Marx's house; the side gate was propped open. A large black man was pushing a wheelbarrow full of rich black topsoil towards the house and a second pushed a barrowload of horse dung. Troy looked down the side of the house to the back garden. Alice had clearly discovered something the East End could not offer. A hundred-foot back garden and the joys of gardening. He followed the second man. At the back of the house Alice stood chatting to the first, an unlit cigarette in her right hand, gesturing towards the flower-beds. As the second man approached she noticed Troy and Troy got a clear look at her. She was neither dressed nor made-up for gardening, the clothes too neat and too new, the face too bold – not that Troy could think of a shade of lipstick that went with hollyhocks, hostas and horse-muck.

'Forgotten how to use the phone?' Alice snapped at him.

'This won't take more than a couple of minutes.'

'You've called at a really naff time.'

'OK. One minute.'

Ally held out the cigarette to the first man. Around his waist he wore a workman's leather belt, all pouches and pockets, secateurs, knives, a trowel, a short-handled fork, all the handy tools of a handyman.

'Match me, Sidney,' she said, and Sidney pulled a cigarette lighter from one of the pouches and held the flame to the tobacco. He somehow contrived to make every muscle, every bi-and tricep, ripple along his arm to bulge through the short sleeve of his T-shirt. Ally looked at Troy across the end of her fag, a wicked glint in her flinty eyes. 'Out front. We'll talk out front.'

She brushed past Troy, propped herself against the side of the van in a laconic, contrived pose, blew smoke and said, 'Well?'

'I have a favour to ask.'

She spluttered over her fag. Troy thought she was choking and soon realised that this was what passed for laughter.

'What makes you think I'll do you any favours?'

'Nothing. Nothing at all. But I have to ask.'

'Then I'll surprise you. I owe you one. Ask away.'

'You owe *me*?'

'I got meself a brief. Not one of Alf 's, one on me own. You were right about mental cruelty. I can divorce the bastard. I *am* divorcing the bastard. So whatever it is, Troy, spit it out and take yer chances with yer auntie Ally.'

Troy paused to let this sink in, to be certain in his own mind that there was more to this than mockery.

'I need to know if Alf and Bernie had a bent copper on their payroll.'

Ally inhaled deeply and exhaled at length. 'Y' know, that's an awful lot to ask. If I say yes, then really, when it comes down to it, I'm grassing someone up, aren't I?'

'Ally, I don't even think in those terms. A bent copper is a bent copper.'

'And to Alf it's a useful voice on the inside.'

'You're through with Alf.'

One last pause, one last billowing cloud of Player's Full Strength, and she said, 'Yes. Alf had – or should I say has? – a copper working for him.'

'Do you know his name?'

'No. But he shouldn't be hard to find. Can you imagine Alf or Bernie trusting anyone who wasn't Jewish? And how many Jewish coppers do you think there are in London? How many Jewish coppers do you think there are in *East* London? Now – is that it or was there something else? Cos if we're done I have a nice six-foot shvartzer to do.'

'Do?'

'Oh, I mean to have Sidney. Or maybe Jayjay. Or maybe both. Like you said, I'm through with Alf. Do you know I was a virgin when I married him? And I've been faithful to the sod all my married life. It'll be like losing my virginity all over again.'

'Ally, you're the most unlikely-looking virgin I've ever seen.'

'And if it weren't for the fact that neither you nor I are into pervy peekaboos I'd say, "Just watch me, Troy, just fuckin' watch me."'

She dropped the cigarette, ground it into the paving with the toe of her golden slingback shoe – the perfect footwear for gardening and seduction – and stepped past Troy with a final 'And next time, phone first!'

When Mary McDiarmuid rounded the corner, he slipped in beside her.

'Do you know now?' she said.

'Yes. Mazzer worked for Alf Marx. The Ryans took him over. Money, threats, it doesn't matter which. They turned him and then he fingered Alf's lieutenant Bernie Champion for them. We should have spotted this ages ago. Bernie would never have let himself be taken. Someone had to set him up. It was Mazzer. I'd put money on it.'

'Do we pull him?'

'Not yet. I need Mr Mazzer where he is.'

'Where to, then? The Yard or home?'

'Neither. Take me to Hampstead. I think it's time I had a bit of a chat with my brother.'

§ 80

Rod opened the door with 'Decided to knock this time, have you?'

And Troy replied, 'I'm here on the same subject. If you want this conversation on the doorstep, that's fine by me.'

Rod swung the door wide and stomped off, as much as a man in carpet slippers can stomp – all the way to the back of the house, into their father's old study, where he had the desk covered with a scattering of parliamentary papers. It was the summer recess. This was Rod being diligent but wearing mufti – the baggy trousers were corduroy, the shirt was an old one destined for his wife's duster bag, frayed at the cuffs and collar, and, as ever, the socks did not match. One black, one red.

'Will this be quick, Freddie? As you can see I'm up to my neck.'

Troy took the aerogramme from his inside pocket, shoved it at Rod and sat down to wait. Rod put on his reading-glasses, read the first few lines standing, then, without looking, shoved a mess of papers aside, made room on his desk, sat and read the rest with his head down.

Troy stared past him, out into the garden. In his youth there had been a quince against the back wall. It wasn't there now; perhaps it had died. Perhaps his sister-in-law, Cid, had ripped it out. It was hers to rip, and she had none of the excessive sense of conserving the past merely because it was past that infected both Troy and Rod, that led to the old man's fountain pen still being parked on the edge of the desk, next to the inkwell, where he'd left it one day in 1943.

On cue, the thought summoned the woman, and his sister-in-law came in, saying, 'I thought I heard your voice. Are you staying for lunch?'

'No, he can't stay, Cid. He's busy,' said Rod, without looking up.

'Are you?' she said to Troy.

Troy said nothing.

She turned to Rod, said, 'You can be so childish sometimes.' And left.

When he'd finished, Rod laid the letter flat, walked to the window, in a move he had surely blocked out in his mind, took off his reading-glasses, polished them on his hanky, gazed a minute at the brick wall where the quince used to be, thought the same thought Troy had thought, and said over his shoulder, 'What is it you expect me to say? That I didn't know? That Spoon has made a fool of all of us? That Kate Cormack is making a fool of you?'

Troy ignored the last remark. 'No. Nothing of the sort. If you tell me you didn't know I won't believe you. Of course you knew, you're not in the least bit surprised.'

Rod faced him now, the ham actor advancing upstage. 'Freddie, the only surprising thing is that *you* know.'

'Fine – but I do have a question. Knowing what you know, why do you accept it? What value can there be in having a spook you know about?'

Rod blinked rapidly and rubbed at one eye with his fist. 'Are we talking in confidence?'

'I'm on duty, Rod.'

'You have a professional interest in Spoon?'

'You know damn well I have. I told you that the last time we spoke.'

'And you still expect a straight answer?'

'Rod, as you are ever reminding me, I'm the devious one, not you.'

It was too easy a reassurance – it wasn't a reassurance at all: it was a back-handed flattery, but when Rod took his seat again and stuck his glasses into his breast pocket, Troy knew he was going to tell him anyway.

'OK. It wouldn't be all that hard to figure out, after all. And if the penny drops you'll come crowing to me as though you'd just caught Jack the Ripper. But what I have to say will be of no professional interest to you whatsoever. What is worth knowing you already know. Spoon works for the CIA. I've known for about eighteen months. And I've no intention of telling you how I found out, so don't ask.'

'Who else knows?'

'There's three of us now. You, me and Hugh Gaitskell. One too many, but there you are.'

'And Hugh is tolerating a spy in his shadow cabinet. I say again, why?'

'Freddie, what happened last winter?'

'It snowed. Buddy Holly died. Worse still, he got knocked off the number-one spot by Russ Conway, and I was tempted to smash the wireless.'

Rod sighed. 'On the geopolitical front.'

Troy had to think about this. The boot was on the other foot. This was usually the sort of thing he put to Rod. Rod was painfully spelling out to him something he hadn't guessed. It was an oddly strange feeling. The Prime Minister had been to Russia, wearing a silly hat and plus-fours, the French had gone mad and elected General de Gaulle president . . . and an odd-looking bloke with a bushy beard had . . .

'Cuba?'

'Give the boy a coconut. Yes, Freddie, Cuba. Cuba, Fidel Castro and a left-wing revolution on the American doorstep.'

'I think you'll find the word is backyard, rather than doorstep. And do we know Castro is left-wing? I would have said that's a hard one to call. It's a bit early for the Americans to be screaming Commie. He's nationalised a few things, he's stopped them treating Cuba like the world's biggest corporate brothel. I have difficulty assigning a political label to that. It's nationalism, and it's moral. Is it really Communist?'

'I doubt that Ike draws the fine distinctions you do. But what I do know is that as much as anyone as cool as Ike – and I've known him nearly twenty years – as much as anyone as cool as Ike can be paranoid, he is paranoid about Cuba and Commies in his own backyard. The damage done to the Americans' confidence in us by the likes of Klaus Fuchs, Burgess, Maclean – all those sort of chaps – is all but unimaginable. Try to see a value in Spoon. Spoon is the Americans' man in our midst. We are a left-wing party about to take power, about to take control of the nation that up to now has been their staunchest ally. They are going to need some reassurance.'

'Why? Does Ike suffer from the delusion that Fuchs or Burgess or Maclean were supporters of the Labour Party? The party of the average working bloke? That the average working bloke is a KGB spy? Rod, I knew Guy Burgess. Working bloke he was not. I doubt he ever did a day's work in his life.'

'The English class system will mean fuck all to Ike. I would not even begin to explain to him why all our spies are toffs. The fact that Guy Burgess was not born to the cloth cap and the brown boots will be too subtle for any American. Crude as it is, it remains, and please don't argue the toss, that we are the party of the Left and hence suspect. Every Labour government there's ever been has been suspect – the Red is always under the bed. There will always be people willing to believe we are hand in glove with the Soviet Union, always people willing to believe stuff like the Zinoviev letter. The first whiff of nationalisation and there are people in Washington who'll be pointing the finger at us and screaming Commie. Dick Nixon, to name but one, has built a career on Commie-baiting. Spoon and Nixon, as your source makes perfectly clear, are like that.' Rod held up the crossed fingers of his right hand.

'So Spoon is what? Your feed back to Washington?'

'Better than that – a direct conduit back to the Americans, and via Nixon to the heartland of their paranoia. He'll be privy to what goes on, he can rat on us all he likes. In fact we'll be mightily pissed off if he doesn't, because he'll never learn anything about us that cannot be favourably received in Washington. Spoon will know what we want him to know. No more, no less. Of course, we can't stop him speculating . . . but we'll see he gets all the information he needs. And if by some twisted logic the American people see fit to elect Nixon president next year . . .'

Rod waved a hand in the air, wafting away the sentence into the obvious. Troy thought about it. It was worth a little thought. It was little short of brilliant. 'You didn't think this up.'

'What makes you say that?'

'It's too clever by half.'

'I shall ignore the insult – but basically you're right. Hugh came up with this one.'

Troy pondered 'this one'. Better than brilliant, it was wonderfully devious. So much so he wished he'd thought of it himself.

'You're overlooking one thing.'

'Which is?'

'Spoon is still bent. Nothing to do with being a spook. Nothing to do with all those dodgy deals you're endorsing in the East End. The man is bent *per se*.'

'Bent how?'

'Can't tell you that.'

Rod folded the aerogramme and handed it back to Troy. 'Thank you, Freddie. This has, as ever, been a one-sided exchange. But before I tell you to fuck off, did nothing else about this letter strike you?'

'Such as?'

'The remarkable similarity between the account of Spoon's early life and that of our father.'

'Rod, I find that an odious comparison.'

'It's there in black and white. Read it again.'

Troy put the letter back in his pocket unread.

'What are you going to do now? About Spoon, I mean.'

'Nothing until I have evidence.'

'And if you find evidence?'

'I'll return the favour. You'll be the first to know. But I'll tell you now. Don't bank on having him as your tame songbird in the next cabinet.'

'A hint, Freddie, just a hint, a bit of a *quid pro quo*?'

'No, Rod. No hints. I'll either get the evidence or I won't.'

§ 81

Back in the Bentley, heading south down Haverstock Hill, Mary McDiarmuid said, 'Home?'

Troy said, 'Stepney.' Then, 'The butcher's bodies.'

'Yes, boss?'

'Let's try a new approach. Let's come at it backwards.'

'Eh?'

'Let's presume an identity and try to prove it.'

'I'm listening.'

'Young and male we know, sexually assaulted we know – let's drop the notion of the sex as part of the subsequent violence, let's draw a line between the two acts, buggery and murder, and presume no direct connection between the two and hence let us presume consent to the sexual act and let us sidestep the conclusion that the killer was also the bugger. Let's presume three things, working class, northern accent . . . and homosexual.'

'Well, that would whittle down the list. Could I ask why those three criteria?'

'Ted Spoon's bent. The marriage is a fig-leaf. His penchant is for rough trade – specifically for young northern lads. Let's proceed on the assumption that whatever he is doing for the Ryans by way of business deals, they are doing something simpler, far older and far simpler, for him.'

'Procuring?'

'I can't think what else to call it. Procuring – then murder.'

'Do you think Spoon knows these boys end up murdered?'

'I'm damn sure he doesn't. But I want to be there when he finds out.'

'But . . . why kill them?'

'For the same reason they killed Brock. To show us they can. It was something Jack said when we found the second body. "They're taking the piss," he said. They'd tried to hide the first. They made no attempt with the second. They used it to hold two fingers up to us. It was a message and it said, "Can't catch me." And it said it to the Metropolitan Police force. Took me a while to work that one out. But it took them a while too. Otherwise they'd have flaunted the first corpse.'

'Aha.'

'Why do I find no element of surprise in your "aha"?'

Mary McDiarmuid said nothing, a concentrated pause.

'Well?'

'I read the file on one of your old cases.'

'Which old case.'

'The Diana Brack murders.'

It had been an age since anyone had uttered that name to Troy.

'And?'

'Well, there are similarities.'

'Similarities?'

'Do you not think they're copying the crime?'

'Copying?'

'In 1944 Diana Brack and her accomplice cut up a corpse and tried to dispose of it.'

'I know.'

'A dog found one arm.'

'The left, as it happens. Do try to be precise.'

Mary McDiarmuid ignored this. 'You found the rest . . .'

'I know that too.'

'. . . with the help of a gang of kids, two of whom, according to Constable Robertson, were the Ryan twins. You heard him – you were a hero to that bunch. I say they're cutting up corpses in imitation – of a bizarre kind.'

She had her eyes on the road, but they flickered to look at him as he studied her words in silence for the best part of a mile.

'When did you figure this out?'

'I've been thinking about it for a while.'

'And when were you going to tell me?'

'I thought I just did. But there's more. I heard you asking Edwin why you'd not been shown something on Joey Rork this morning. The airmail letter? Am I right?'

'Yes.'

'It's not the only thing Mr Wildeve didn't tell you. The prick in the post . . .'

'No, he told me about that.'

'What he didn't tell you is that it wasn't addressed to him – it was addressed to you.'

'Jesus Christ.'

'They're not just taking the piss or copying an old crime. They're not holding up two fingers to the whole of the Metropolitan Police force. It's you. They're aiming the lot straight at you.'

For a while they drove in silence, this time of Mary McDiarmuid's making. Crossing Spitalfields, Troy could all but hear the cogs in her mind crunching over. 'Tell me,' he said.

'We're proceeding on the assumption that the Ryans are responsible for Mr Brocklehurst, those two young men. Joey Rork *and* . . . Bernie Champion?'

'Yes.'

'Then why haven't we found Bernie Champion? We've found everybody else. Why aren't they flaunting that?'

'Because they need the illusion that he's still alive to put the screws on his wife and Ally Marx.'

'So they've got Bernie very well stashed. Somewhere we wouldn't think of looking?'

Not a bad point, thought Troy. Worth some thought. He'd think about it.

§ 82

As Troy was coming into Leman Street police station a man in his early thirties was coming out. He passed Troy without a word, and stood with his back to him, fiddling with the keys to his two-tone – did they come any other way? – Ford Zodiac parked at the kerb. It was, thought Troy, a little surprising that Mr Mazzer did not know him by sight, but just as surprising that he should be able to spot Mazzer merely by Swift Eddie's description of his suit and his manner. He reminded Troy of a small boy jingling the coins in his pocket. Not that Mazzer was doing any such thing, but something about him amounted to the same effect: a combination of caution and boastfulness. He wasn't saying 'Look what I've got,' but he was letting you know it all the same. Eddie was right – in his own words, 'The suit set him back a bob or two, none of your fifty-shilling tailors' – but what he hadn't mentioned was the grooming. Al Mazzer hadn't got that haircut down the Mile End Road from Shrimp Robertson's father, or any ex-army barber whose talents extended to short-back-and-sides and no further. Troy could not think from where he got the phrase, but it was appropriate. Mr Mazzer looked like the sort of bloke who would pay for a shoeshine and tip well in restaurants – and these days so few would do either.

Mazzer wound down the window, placed a hand on the door, thinking. Troy could see the manicure now – no bitten or nicotined fingernails. Perhaps that was the secret of wealth you could never flaunt: you spent it on the small things of life, the little things that made all the difference but would be hardly noticeable. Then Mazzer turned the engine over and looked in the rear-view mirror. He must have caught sight of Troy's Bentley parked twenty or so feet behind him. He looked at Troy now, and for the first time he seemed to recognise him. Troy turned and walked into the police station.

'You just missed Mazzer,' Godbehere said.

'No,' said Troy. 'I don't think I did.'

§ 83

They compared notes. Godbehere had compiled a list of all known 'Ryan associates' – a euphemism for a gang.

'George Bonham was great,' Godbehere said. 'Makes you wonder why we retire people at that age. And that MP you put me on to, Les Gidney. He introduced me to half a dozen local councillors, including two blokes off the planning committee. I've a good idea of what the Ryans own, and what they paid for it. They've been spending like two Irish sailors on shore leave. They have property all over the manor, but better still they've been buying up most of Watney Market. The market itself and the side-streets belong mainly to two insurance companies who've owned them since about 1890. The Essex and Herts Assurance and the London-Liverpool Commercial. They've let the houses rot, basically. Done the minimum maintenance to comply with the law, and God knows that isn't much, and collected minimum rent. Even with the housing shortage they've proved a poor investment, and the Ryans are buying one or two a week for a matter of a few hundred apiece. Last month they picked up the whole of Cridlan Street for twelve thousand pounds.'

'What? All of it?'

'All twenty-three remaining houses. The whole damn lot. Mind, Cridlan Street didn't belong to either of those insurance companies. The owners put it up for auction.'

'And they were?'

'Would you believe the Church of England?'

Troy had no difficulty believing this.

Godbehere continued, 'Gidney thinks they're playing a waiting game, waiting for a compulsory purchase order. The council buys the houses at a whacking great profit – and all without the bother of having to evict tenants.'

'It's better than that. They get permission to develop the site, become part of a consortium to rebuild, and the consortium pays the Ryans a huge kickback. And the government tops it all with a fat handout under the name of urban renewal and a national housing programme.'

'Hell's bells,' said Godbehere. 'It's the perfect con. They'll be rich twice over. But that brings me to the bad news. You'll need more resources than I've got to find out where they keep their money. I've tracked down a few bank accounts – after all, they need some to look legit. But where the money from the rackets gets laundered before it's fed back to something legit . . . I don't know.'

'That's OK. I'm concentrating more on where they get it than where it goes. Now,' said Troy, 'the gang.'

Godbehere handed Troy a badly typed sheet of names. Most of them meant nothing to Troy. If this was East End villainy it was a generation and more that had grown up since Troy walked the beat. But half a dozen names looked familiar.

'Are you thinking what I'm thinking?' Troy asked.

'I am, sir. A lot of Jewish names.'

'The remnants of Alf Marx's gang, getting by the only way they know. Serving their new masters.'

Troy pulled out his list.

'I got this from John Brocklehurst's files. A good portion of Alf 's gang went down with him. I crossed those names out. I'd guess there were a dozen or so left on the street when he went down. The Ryans seem to have recruited seven, if your narks have it right.'

Godbehere took the list and set them side by side on the desk.

'Stan Cohen.'

'Not one I ever met,' said Troy.

'Arthur Cantor.'

'In his day one of the best petermen in London. Lately I think he's done not much more than run errands for Alf and Bernie Champion.'

'Saggy Stein.'

'Drove the car on Alf 's bank jobs. Spent most of the forties in Parkhurst.'

'LouLevy.'

'A thug. If Alf wanted legs broken or arms twisted, Lou was the man.'

'Dave Silver.'

'Never heard of him.'

'Mal Gelb.'

'Nor him.'

'Moses Kettleman.'

'Ah . . . Mott Kettle. Petty thief, pickpocket, bookie's runner and police informer. My first collar in 1936. I caught Mott brazenly stealing women's underwear from a stall in Whitechapel market. He got three months. Then in 1938 I caught him for receiving and the judge put him away for two years. By the time he got out the war was on, he was nearly forty, the army wouldn't call him up at that age and he didn't volunteer. He did what a lot of skivers did – he worked the black market, worked it stupidly and poorly and took getting nicked as an occupational hazard. It's not that Mott was at the back of the queue when God gave out brains, he was probably just looking the other way.'

'You think he's the weak link?'

'I think they're all the weak link. Pull the lot.'

This, clearly, was close to the last thing Godbehere had expected to hear Troy say. 'If you don't mind me asking, sir, why?'

'Because the Ryans will expect it. If we've done this properly, they now know I'm here. They know you've been building up a file and they'll expect action. Mr Mazzer will surely have told them that.'

'But I've shut Mazzer out – just like you told me to do.'

'Quite. But he'd be a very poor excuse for a detective if he hasn't been able to come up with a version of what's happening. Fragmented, maybe, with a lot of guesswork filling in. Nothing like being cut out to make a copper nosy, after all. And if he hasn't tipped the Ryans off then I've overestimated them all.'

Godbehere nodded as though finally seeing the whole picture for the first time. 'You do realise they'll turn up with their briefs?'

'Some will, some won't. And if the Ryans feel like spending money on a lawyer for the likes of Mott Kettle, then I'll eat my hat. Pull them in, and ask them about their whereabouts on the nights Joey Rork and Glenda Felucci died. Ask them till they curl at the edges with boredom. And let's put on a show. Lots of police cars, lots of uniforms, a few sirens. Let's make ourselves visible.'

'Do you think they'll know anything?'

'No. In fact, I'm damn certain they won't. As I said, Mr Godbehere, we're putting on a show.'

§ 84

Mott reminded Troy of the first time he had ever met Fish Wally. The sheer intensity of neglect and plain grubbiness. Wally had improved beyond recognition. All he'd required was an income remotely commensurate with his taste. Mott had got worse. He'd greeted Troy with 'How long is it now, Mr Troy?'

And Troy rather thought it had been seven or eight years since he'd last encountered Mott. Now he was fifty-six or -seven. Thin, in that undernourished way that still characterised Wally and which Troy was fairly certain he'd never shake off, but thinner than thin – he was scrawny. A scrawniness emphasised by the fact that his suits always seemed to be hand-me-downs. This particular hand-me-down had been made for a man much stouter than Mott and hung on him with all the elegance of a barrage balloon snagged on a telegraph-pole. He looked tubercular. Grey of skin, red of eye and sporting a manicure that would have had Mazzer throwing up in the gutter. Buckets of lemon juice, mountains of pumice would never shift the nicotine from his fingers. It had gone way beyond the tips. It crept down his fingers to the second joint, looking like blackleg on a potato haulm. The suit was a wartime relic, the wide-trousered, tight-waited fashion of the early forties, nipped at the back of the jacket with a strap – tastelessly brown, faintly enlivened by a pencil-line red stripe, worn shiny at the knees and elbows, and piss-rotten at the crotch.

He greeted Troy like a long-lost friend, rising from his chair, one hand clutching a cigarette, one outstretched as though he would shake hands given half a chance. Not knowing why he had been pulled, the sight of a man who had put him away twice was close to familiarity.

'As I live and breathe – Mr Troy. How long's it been now, Mr Troy?'

'Sit down, Mott.'

'What is it – fifteen years? Twenty? I've followed yer career, y' know. Local boy made good an' all that. You've done really well for yerself. I said that the first time you nicked me. I said, "That young copper's going to go far." S'welp me I did. I said to the lads, "That young man'll be in a top job one day." A top job. I did. Honest I did. A top job. And now . . . 'ere you are. A Scotland Yard detective an' all. I said you'd go far. I did. I did. A top job.'

It seemed to Troy that Mott would go on all night like this. He held up a hand as though he were on point duty in traffic. Anything to stop the babble of nonsense. 'You've not brought your brief. You're entitled to have a solicitor present.'

'Mr Troy, I ain't done nuffink. What would I want with a lawyer?' The mouth split into a broad smile, a cave of stained teeth. The hands spread in a disarming gesture, fag ash scattering across the table. 'Besides, you ain't cautioned me yet.' Mott smiled the wider. One point scored in the midst of his babble.

'Anything you say . . . and blah-de-blah . . . Let's take the caution as read, shall we?'

'Why are you cautioning me? I ain't done nuffink.'

'Where were you on the night of July the seventeenth?'

Mott still smiled. 'Blowed if I know.'

'Or August the fifth?'

And smiled again. He was enjoying the game. 'I'd have to ask me social seccerterry.'

'How long have you been working for the Ryans?'

The smile vanished. Mott resorted to a fit of coughing to disguise the reality of his reaction. The name 'Ryan' alone might have been enough to turn that sallow hide pale.

Troy waited for him to finish hoiking, straighten up and put another cigarette to his lips.

'Never 'eard of 'em.'

The match shook in his hand. Troy gripped Mott's hand in his and guided the flame to the tip, squeezing hard as he did so. Mott twisted his head to get closer to the flame, accepting pain as a fair price for his shot of nicotine.

'I'm sorry, Mott. I must be going deaf. I thought you just said you'd never heard of them.' Troy let him go.

One swift, greedy drag, and another fit of coughing. 'Well. I've 'eard of 'em. O' course I 'ave. Everybody's 'eard of 'em. But that's it. I don't know nuffink. I ain't done nuffink. I just . . . 'eard of 'em. That's all.'

'New kids on the block, eh?'

'Yeah . . . that's it . . . new kids.'

'New kids who bumped off John Brocklehurst, Joey Rork and Glenda Felucci, and made Bernie Champion vanish into thin air.'

Mott inhaled deeply and blew out a long cloud of smoke. 'We was all shocked by what happened to Mr Brocklehurst. It weren't right. And poor Glenda. I knew 'er when she was a little girl. That weren't right neither. I never 'eard of that other bloke. But Bernie . . . Bernie's just taking a break.'

'Bernie's dead, Mott.'

'No . . . 'e ain't, Mr Troy. 'E'll be back any day now. I reckon 'e's away on a spot of business. 'E'll be back any day now, you mark my words.'

'Bernie was set up by a member of your team, set up and bumped off by the Ryans. The Ryans then came to you lot, the dregs at the bottom of Alf and Bernie's pickle barrel, and told you they were taking over. You've spent the summer working for the new kids, only they're not kids. Now – where were you the night Bernie vanished?'

'It was a Thursday the last time I saw Bernie. An' I always play snooker on Thursdays.'

'And you've witnesses to this?'

'Every Thursday since 1945. Sid Stott's pool room by Stepney Green station. Ask anybody.'

'So who was with Bernie that night? Who drove for him, who was meant to be guarding him?'

'I never drove for 'im, Mr Troy. Why would Bernie want me drivin' for 'im when he had Louand Saggy? Two o' the best . . .'

The brick dropped so clunkily on to the table that even Mott heard it and stopped.

'So it was Louand Saggy who set Bernie up?'

'I don't know nuffink.'

'You stood by and let two of your mates sell out the man who'd looked after you since you got out of the nick nearly twenty years ago. You stepped aside and you let a pair of tearaway kids blow him away.'

'I don't know nuffink.'

Troy got up to leave, Mott yelling at his back, 'I don't know nuffink! What could I know? Bernie ain't dead, Bernie'll be back!'

Troy left Mott alone with Shrimp Robertson, and went in search of Godbehere. Godbehere was just emerging from an interview with Lou Levy. 'He's the only one who brought his brief. I feel like I'm playing in the yes-no interlude in there. I'll get gonged off any minute.'

'I think I know why Lou might be the only one who wanted a brief. He's probably the one who helped Mazzer set up Bernie for the Ryans.'

'I don't think he'll confess to that in a month of Sundays.'

'Nor do I. String it out as long as you can – until about half an hour before the pubs close if possible. I want them in a pub tonight, bewailing their lot and shooting their mouths off.'

'I've been with them just over an hour and we're already at the point where his brief is saying, "My client has already answered that question, Mr Godbehere." I'm running out of new ways to phrase the same question.'

'Try for ten o'clock at least – and then turn them loose. Everyone but Mott. Let Mott spend a night in the cells.'

§ 85

Troy caught the Underground back to Charing Cross and walked along the Embankment to Scotland Yard.

Mary McDiarmuid was still at work in his outer office. A pile of files a foot high on her desk – a dozen or more spread out across the floor, and Mary on her knees hunched over them.

'I think I've got something,' she said, turning to look wry-necked at Troy.

'So soon?'

'Once you lay down criteria, so much else just falls away. Doesn't make the conclusion the right one, but it does throw up possibilities that fit the initial assumption.'

She was learning fast. That was an Eddie Clark sentence. The precise phrasing of the consummate philosopher con-artist, offering no hostages to logic or fortune. A retreat always open to

281

an implicit 'I told you so.' Troy knelt beside her – a movement that would have sent him reeling with giddiness a fortnight ago.

'There's two that really stand out. Him . . .' Mary slapped the flat of her hand on an open file. '. . . and him.'

She reached across the floor and pulled a file nearer to them. 'Naill Devanney. Aged twenty. Been missing since last Christmas. Labourer on a council road crew in Warrington. His mother reported him missing the day after Boxing Day. He has the physique to be either of these. And you'll see . . .' She held up the photo to Troy. 'Quite the pretty boy. I could fancy him m'self.'

'But,' said Troy, 'queer?'

'Boss, nobody, however worried about their son, is going to walk into a nick anywhere in Britain and say the boy is queer. What Mrs Devanney actually said was that he was always getting picked on at work, and that he'd been beaten up a couple of times outside pubs. I'd put money on Niall being a poof. I'd put money on him knowing he was different, holding back most of his life and only acknowledging it when his mates started calling him a nancy-boy and making his life into hell.'

'Bad as that, eh?'

'I'm from Glasgow. Take it from me. Most working-class men feel threatened by queers, or anyone they suspect might be.'

'And the other.'

'John Mackie from Skelmersdale.'

'Where's that?'

'Lancashire, sort of between Liverpool and Bolton. John was nineteen. Vanished in February. Not a labourer. A clerk at the Co-op accounts department. But he belonged to a gym and went in for bodybuilding. His parents went to the police together after he'd been gone five days. There's nothing so definite to make me think he was queer, except their reluctance to talk about their son's character, friends, hobbies – you name it . . . To judge by their answers to the local police they hardly knew the lad. Either they're not telling what they know or he led a double life. Either way I can feel my thumbs pricking.'

'Quite,' said Troy. 'I think it's time we called in a favour from Mr Milligan.'

'Mr Milligan?'

'He was transferred to Warrington.'

Paddy heard Troy out, offered to call a friend at Skelmersdale and to drive round to the Devanney household in person. But there was a but. 'Knocking on someone's door and saying, "That lad you reported missing may well be dead. And, oh, by the way was he a shirtlifter?" isn't exactly guaranteed to get results. Not on Merseyside anyway.'

'I'll leave that to your tact, Paddy.'

'Give me about an hour,' he said.

As Troy rung off, Mary McDiarmuid was standing in front of him clutching a note. 'The strangest character rang up. Sort of bloke who'd use three words where one would do. Name of Fish Wally. Wants to meet you. St Stephen's, as soon as you can.'

§ 86

It was warm in the upstairs room at St Stephen's Tavern. Warm and empty. It was the watering-hole of MPs – this being the summer recess, there was not one to be seen. Just the odd peer and the odder policeman, stranded like crabs in rock-pools at low tide. Empty, and warm enough for Wally to have forsaken his overcoat. But for the Mickey Mouse gloves he looked rather like a barrister, with his black jacket and striped trousers. He sat at a centre table, sipping neat vodka. When he saw Troy enter he raised the glass and indicated more of the same. Troy changed a fiver at the bar and set a glass apiece in front of Wally. He would have liked an ice cube in his, but he did not feel like hearing Wally's lecture on how to drink vodka.

'I am sorry to drag you out, but this is as safe as anywhere. I have news, of sorts. I caught up with old Bobby Collington. A day or so after we last met he decided to retire. Something proved too much for the old man. I tracked him out to a seaside boarding-house.'

'Frinton?'

'Herne Bay. Where he lives under the tender care of a Mrs

Cravat, whilst looking in every estate agent's for a suitable bungalow. The man is clearly through with London. Indeed, to invoke Dr Johnson, I thought he might be through with life. He was reluctant to see me, but I oiled his wheels. In fact, you owe me for a first-class return fare and a bottle of single malt. But . . . he eased up and he talked. The Ryans came into his office – I do not know precisely when, but it must have been around the time we last met – high on the thrill. Bobby thought they were drunk at first, but it dawned on him that it was the intoxication of action. After all, he and I and you saw so much of that during the war. The garrulousness of it all. The constant, compulsive rehashing of a moment. As potent as any drug, you will agree. They told him how they had, and I quote, "bumped off a copper's nark".'

'They did,' said Troy. 'Or, at least, I can see how they might think he was a copper's nark.'

'Understandably Bobby panicked. He told them he wanted out and offered to sell them his remaining share of the club for twenty thousand pounds. He took five. Within forty-eight hours he had let his flat in Marylebone, and set off for Kent with a suitcase and a portable gramophone. He says he will never go back to London. Nor, alas, will he ever repeat anything of what he told me. I don't know what use it would be in court anyway, but I rather think Bobby would die before he'd testify against the Ryans. They have him well and truly scared.'

'I need a witness, Wally.'

'Collington is not your man. I begin to wonder who is. This pair seem to scare the living daylights out of everyone they meet. You need a very brave man, a very foolish man . . . or else you should be praying they do something utterly stupid.'

'I'm working on that,' said Troy.

He bought Wally another vodka, left two fivers under the glass, saw the gloved hand make them disappear like a music-hall conjuror, and went back to the Yard.

§ 87

'Nothing doing,' said Milligan. 'The couple in Skelmersdale wouldn't let my mate over the threshold. They slammed the door in his face as soon as he asked the question. I had better luck. I got past the front door – but Devanney practically chucked me out of the house once he realised what I wanted. His wife was more willing. I could see she wanted to talk. But for the old man she might have done. But your guess was right. The rage had motive. Kept banging on about "no son of mine" and all that malarkey. The boy's a poof all right. In fact, I don't think he ran away, I rather think the old man threw him out.'

'Does the old man work?'

'Foreman in a cable and wire works.'

'And the wife?'

'Oh, no. "A man's not a man who can't keep his wife" . . .'

'And all that malarkey. Fine. Go round there in the morning and have another go at her. If I'm not at the Yard I'll be in Stepney.'

§ 88

The last call of the day was overdue, and unexpected. It disturbed Troy to think that out of sight was ever out of mind.

'Where've you been?' Kitty said.

Concern or small-talk? He replayed her voice in his mind's ear looking for signs. 'I'm back at work,' he replied, racking his brains to remember when he had last seen her. 'And you?'

'Scotland. London got so damned Singapore, didn't it? Danny whisked me away to a breezy castle on a Scottish loch for a couple of weeks. You know what a loch is?'

'A large static body of—'

'Don't be so literal. It's a lazy river. That's what a loch is, a really lazy river.'

'So you finally found it?'

'I wouldn't say that exactly.'

'Which one was it?'

'God knows. Ickle or Muckle. I wouldn't have a clue. It might even have been the one with the monster in it, for all I know. Just west of Glasgow and east of the sun – and it was bliss. For a while it was bliss.'

'I've been east,' he said, wondering if she'd take the bait.

'East,' she said. 'East? You mean Stepney?'

'Yes.'

He counted the beats as she paused.

'You're going after Danny's brothers, aren't you?'

What did it matter if he told her? As he had said to Godbehere, they knew he was there. He wanted them to know he was there. What did it matter if they found out by a second route, a roundabout route, that he was on to them? If Mary McDiarmuid was right and the Ryans had him in their sights, what did it matter if they knew he had them in his? They would expect nothing else.

'Did you think I wouldn't?'

'No . . . of course not. You're a copper. It's just . . . it's just that it's got nothing to do with Danny.'

'I know.'

'You mean that?'

'Yes.'

'Good. Because I'm keeping out of it. I'm not going to get involved and I'm not going to let Danny get involved.'

§ 89

Insomnia was nagging at him again. That light tearing of the flesh. That random searing of the mind. That tumbling cascade of faces. Foxx as he had last seen her in the midst of her confusion. His sister standing lost and baffled in his room, wondering where her clothes were. The long stare his wife had given him across the room in the Café Royal – the wide-open, nut-brown eyes. Then every image blurred and resolved down to one. Diana Brack, hand outstretched, fingertips touching his, leaving him – all those years ago on the dance-floor of the Berkeley, leaving him. And then, when everything turned to black . . . Kitty's voice, the cadences in her questions.

Last . . . the repetitious nature of Mary McDiarmuid's questions. Less now the product of insomnia than the cause. 'Somewhere we wouldn't think of looking?' Somewhere we wouldn't think of looking? Where would we not . . . ?

Around four a.m. he reached for the telephone and called Bonham. 'When did Bernie Champion disappear?'

'Wot?'

'Bernie Champion. He vanished, what, two months ago?'

Troy could hear Bonham struggling from sleep to waking, but he'd hardly struggle with dates. He'd already reached the age when the most interesting thing in any newspaper was the obituary column.

'More like three, nearer thirteen weeks.'

'And when did Edna Stilton die?'

'Same week.'

'And the funeral was the week after?'

'We was there, Freddie. If you can't remember that—'

'And the old boy who came hobbling up to us to tell us his wife's grave had been vandalised?'

'Arthur. Arthur Foulds.'

'And have there been other, similar attacks since?'

'No. I'd've heard. After all I go to a soddin' funeral there at least once a fortnight. Or it seems as though I do.'

§ 90

'Alice, it's Troy.'

'God almighty, Troy, do you know what time it is?'

'You did say to phone first.'

'I know, but not at this bleedin' time. You'll wake me shvartzers.'

'Ally, there's a car on the way for you.'

'To take me where?'

'St George's churchyard.'

'What? The one in Shadwell? If you think I'm gettin' up at five o'clock in the mornin' to traipse back to the bleedin' East End you can—'

'Ally, I could have called you or I could have called Millie Champion.'

'What have you found?'

'Nothing yet, but I want you there when I do. You'll want to be there when I do.'

§ 91

The coroner was probably no happier about Troy's morning call than Alice Marx, but he made less fuss. Troy had a police motorcyclist collect the exhumation order, and asked George Bonham to bring a spade and a shovel off his allotment. The only person he didn't have to knock up was the verger of St George-in-the-East. He wondered about the protocol of telling Arthur Foulds they were about to dig up his wife's grave, and thought better of it. If he was right, they'd not even hit the lid of her coffin. The exhumation order was a legal cover note for the police arse and nothing more.

He had roused Mott Kettle himself, but it was obvious Mott had not slept, and from the fug that washed over Troy when he opened the cell door it was just as obvious he'd smoked the night away. All he said was, 'Don't I get breakfast first?'

'Only if you're prepared to lose it later.'

At the graveside they waited. Troy, Godbehere, Bonham, Mazzer, Shrimp Robertson and Mott Kettle. Waited until Troy's Bentley pulled up at the Cable Street gate, and Ally Marx got out. Headscarf and dark glasses, slacks and a flowing silk coat. Every inch the film star. Except that, Troy was certain, Elizabeth Taylor would not have had the kingsize cigarette hanging off her bottom lip. 'All you boys waiting for me. I don't know what to say. But I reckon "Ready when you are" should about fit the bill,' she said.

They all looked at Bonham. Bonham handed the spade to Mazzer and the shovel to Robertson. Troy hadn't suggested this, but it was a touch he relished. Let Mr Mazzer be the one to get London clay on his Carnaby Street suit. Old Arthur had restored his wife's grave. The polyanthi were blossomless now, but stood in ranks like toy soldiers on some miniature Waterloo making up the British square – and not a weed in sight. Whoever had messed with the grave three months ago had left it alone since. Now the police were the vandals. But Troy knew it hadn't been vandals in the first place.

'Did it have to be so early?' Ally whispered to Troy.

'Any later and we'd have an audience.'

Robertson carefully set Arthur Foulds's plants to one side and leaned on the shovel while Mazzer dug. It took him less than two minutes to hit something.

'It's soft,' he said.

'Then go carefully.'

Bernie Champion had always been a dapper man. Not tasteful exactly, but neat. The first thing Troy recognised were the silver buttons on his blazer. The thug whose pose was to look like a retired RAF officer – blazer, grey cavalry twill trousers, brown suede shoes. He never had looked like a thug: he'd looked more like a professional cad who hung around the seaside resorts of the south coast preying on rich, susceptible widows.

Several weeks underground hadn't done wonders for his appearance. But for the clothes Troy would have been uncertain as to whose rotting remains they had exposed. But Ally Marx knew him. The fag was dropped, the handkerchief withdrawn from a sleeve and pressed first to her mouth and then to her eyes. And Mott Kettle knew. The ashen look on his face was not the general, disturbed face of a man shown a corpse, it was the blood-drained face of a man finally confronting what he had denied for so long.

Troy walked to the edge of the grave, knelt down, scraped a bit more earth off the decaying face, and beckoned Mott closer. 'Look,' he said.

'I don't need to look no more. I can see from here. I don't know him. How could anyone know him?'

Alice Marx screamed, 'It's Bernie, you fucking idiot! It's Bernie! Tell him it's Bernie, Mott, or are you going to be a complete fool all your fucking life?'

Mott muttered, 'I don't know him, Al, honest I don't.'

She grabbed Mott by one arm, twisted it and shoved him at the grave. He tripped over the spade, fell full length into the dug earth. Troy took a step backward and caught him only inches before his face would have crashed headlong into what remained of the corpse's.

'Take a good look, you fucking moron,' Ally yelled. 'It's Bernie. It's Bernie! What have those Irish pricks got over you that you can't see it?'

Mott recoiled as though he'd been burnt, scrabbling around on the grave until Bonham extended the bear's paw and yanked him to his feet.

'It's Bernie, you stupid little putz. It's Bernie!'

Before anyone could stop her Ally reached down to the corpse with both hands, tore open the flies to show a blue, purple, black and swollen circumcised penis.

'Now do you believe me? Or do you think they make a habit of burying kikes in a place like this?'

§ 92

Mott drank black coffee and smoked his tenth cigarette of the morning. Hacked into his fist for the hundredth time, the sound of sputum stuck in his throat, a redness with the effort that almost brought tears to his eyes.

'It could be anybody.'

Troy was scarcely listening any more.

'I mean . . . it could be anybody. Ally always did have a way with words. I mean there's plenty o' Jews in London. Why does this dead Jew have to be Bernie? For all we know Bernie's done a runner with a bit o' totty. He was always a ladies' man was Bernie. That's probably it. He's holed up in Bournemouth or Eastbourne with some tart. That'd be old Bernie, wouldn't it, Mr Troy? It could be anybody. I mean anybody. Don't have to be Bernie. Stands to reason. It don't have to be. Could be anybody.'

'Wearing Bernie's clothes, with Bernie's cheque book in his pocket? Of course.'

'Planted, Mr Troy. Planted to make you think it's Bernie.'

'Mott, nobody planted anything. They hid him in the last place anyone would look. You're familiar with the old adage "can't see the wood for the trees"? That's what the Ryans did. Hid him where we would not see him for looking. Once we found him, if we found him, what did it matter that it was Bernie? Nobody planted anything. They set him up, they topped him, then they dug a hole and shoved him in it. They could have done it to any one of you. Then they came to you lot, you miserable bunch of yes-men, and told you they were taking over and anyone who didn't like it would be taking a hike to the bottom of the Thames. And you, Mott, you just rolled over and said, "Walk on me", didn't you?'

Mott flicked the ash from his fag on to the knee of his trousers and rubbed it in. The ashtray was only a foot away from his hand and still seemed too far for the effort. 'Mr Troy, what is it you want me to say?'

Silently Troy weighed up the man who faced him across the table. Kettleman looked even more pathetic than he had yesterday. A scruffy ragbag of clothes posing as a man. A scarecrow made of straw that somehow lived and breathed his foul breath over Troy. A life hardly worth the living. 'Nothing,' he said. 'You can't say anything because you don't know anything. You never did.'

'I spent most o' last night telling you that.'

'And I believe you, Mott.'

'Then I can go now, right?'

'Right. You can go. I'll need about five minutes. You finish your cigarette.'

Next door Alice Marx was bashing away at an old Met-issue Smith-Corona and scattering as much fag ash as Mott. Shrimp Robertson sat across from her.

'He's supposed to type it for you,' Troy said.

'The boy types with two fingers. I'd be here all day if I had to wait for him. I can touch-type. Or did you think I'd never done a day's work in me life?'

Troy let Robertson go.

Ally stopped typing, tore her statement and its carbon from the roller. 'I never wanted to do this. I told you that. You're a bastard. But Bernie's dead now. No two ways about it. There's nothing left to lose. I suppose,' Ally said, 'that you're gonna tell me there was no other way to do this?'

'There wasn't.'

'Fine. I won't break yer bollocks over it. But there's gotto bea *quid pro quo*.'

'What do you want?'

'Don't send a squad car roaring round to Millie Champion's with some tosser of a copper to tell 'er 'er 'usband's dead.'

'I wasn't going to.'

'Let me do it. I don't want to do it. But I have to. If you see what I mean.'

Troy did. 'My driver will take you to Millie's. When you're through she'll take you back to your home. And I'll put a copper from Hendon on your door until this is over.'

'And that shitbag, Mott?'

§ 93

Troy released Mott Kettle, returned to Godbehere's office and sent for Mazzer. He was witnessing Ally's statement when Mazzer walked in. The sweeping, overlarge, quasi-Cyrillic sprawl of his own signature. Big enough and long enough for Mazzer to have no doubt about what he'd just done.

'Mott's at the desk picking up his possessions. Tail him. If you have to stay up all night, tail him and don't lose him.'

He put Ally's statement into a brown folder marked 'Kettleman' and dropped it into a desk drawer. Mazzer was still standing there.

'Yes?'

'Nothing, sir, nothing.'
'Keep me posted. I'll be back at the Yard most of today.'

§ 94

Onions appeared in his office again. A bad day. A day in uniform. All those oak leaves and silver trim. Troy could see the seething anger at life and fate and nothing in his eyes. Occasionally he wondered how long Stan would stick the job. The bitterness of it was overwhelming. Too late in his career to be effective, too tied up in red tape for a man like him to slice through. The pinnacle of any copper's career amounting to no more than the biggest frustration of that career. Brock had made the right move. He'd tried in his way to tell Stan as much. Brock might – no, would have been happy on his allotment. But once you'd reached the absurdity of being Sir Stanley Onions how could you ever put on your overalls and your hob-nailed boots and earth up spuds on your allotment again?

Onions lit up a Woodbine, popped the buttons on his tunic and heard Troy out in silence. 'You're getting a warrant?' he said at last.

'I don't think I am,' said Troy.

A deep drag on his cigarette. 'You've enough to pull 'em now.'

'It's too soon.'

A splutter of coughing, a fleck of tobacco picked from his tongue. 'Too soon? Too soon for what? The sooner those buggers are off the street, the sooner the toffs and the wankers are off my back. You may get the press and the back-bench timewasters, but I still have to answer to the Home Secretary and every junior minister who wants to have his two penn'orth. And I still have to read the editorials every day. "A Sea of Crime in the East End", "Scotland Yard Losing Control", "The Country Going to Hell in a Handcart". The toffs want to hang me out to dry, can't you see that?'

This required tact. If Stan was open to tact he was, and if he wasn't he wasn't. 'Stan, we've lost them once. Surely you can see that the next time we pull them it has to stick? There can be no loopholes. We have a reversal of their alibi. That will be meat and drink to their brief. He'll argue that we coerced Ally Marx into withdrawing one statement and making another. He'll say it here and he'll say it in court.'

'It's hardly going to wash with a jury, though, is it?'

'We don't have the luxury of waiting for a jury. We have to be one hundred per cent certain before we put those two in front of a jury. Alice's statement does nothing to mitigate the confusion of Jack's two eyewitnesses and what happened at the line-up. It's a bit less of a mess but it's still a mess.'

Just when he thought Onions was about to launch himself into another tirade Troy was saved by the bell. He picked up the phone and Onions silently took his cue and left.

'I did as you asked,' Milligan said. 'Mrs Devanney came clean. Young Niall got his marching orders from his dad. She tried to get between them and the old man thumped both of them for her trouble. She wept buckets this morning. She has a bit of difficulty accepting that her son's queer, but she's a realist – she isn't denying what her senses told her. Accepting that he's dead . . . that's another matter. She can't quite take that in. But – and it's a huge but – she wants to know for sure. In fact, she wants to see the body.'

'Oh, God. Did you tell her the state it was in?'

'I did. And she wept yet more buckets. But she's a tough old stick. Insists she has to see for herself. I agreed to drive her to the station tomorrow. She should be at Euston around quarter past two. If you don't mind me suggesting, I think you should have a WPC there with you. I don't know what her reaction will be when she sees the corpse.'

'Point taken. If it was a simple matter like *a* corpse I would still be concerned, but this is like a pack of human joints. I don't see how her seeing them can do any good.'

'Ask yourself this, Freddie, would your mum know you from an arm or a buttock? Can a mother somehow see the body she wiped and washed for ten years in the grown man or even the remains of the grown man?'

'I don't know,' said Troy. 'I honestly don't know.'

§ 95

As Troy was leaving his office, Mary McDiarmuid parked out front with the engine running, Eddie called him back with the single word 'Stepney.'

Troy picked up the phone, glancing at his watch as he did so. Five to two. 'Ray, this has got to be quick.'

'It is. Mazzer just reported in. He lost Mott. Nearly forty-eight hours of traipsing after him and he lost him.'

'Where?'

'On the Underground. Mott led him a dance and lost him in the change at Bank station around ten o'clock this morning. Mazzer went back to Mott's digs in Vallance Road, gave it a couple of hours and reported in.'

'Where is Mazzer now?'

'At home in Stratford. He'd been up two nights in a row.'

'Fine. Let's leave him there for the time being.'

'And Mott?'

'Mott is creating his own fate.'

'Eh?'

Troy rang off and dashed for the car.

He had been wondering how he'd know Mrs Devanney. Godbehere's description of a 'woman hammered by life and husband' didn't seem much to go on. But being late helped. The crowd was off the train and most of it had vanished into buses, tubes and taxis. She stood out on the concourse looking exactly as Godbehere had said, 'hammered'. Paddy had called her old – 'a tough old stick'. She was, in all probability, no older than Troy himself, but she looked sixty. Grey hair, a short dumpy body, varicose of leg, her best floral print summer frock, the sort that, in its leafy browns, always struck Troy as looking more like wallpaper than cloth, the fawn macintosh that the English never quite had the confidence to abandon even in summer draped across one arm, an over-large black handbag on the other, flat sensible shoes and the merest touch of make-up – no eye-shadow or mascara, but foundation and lipstick, applied with the skill of someone who hardly ever wore make-up but whose sense of occasion would not let a day like this pass off as the quotidian. How did one dress to identify a dead son? Like churchgoing on a summer Sunday?

'Mrs Devanney, I'm Frederick Troy of Scotland Yard. This is WPC McDiarmuid.'

'Pleased to meet you,' she said, flat and low and in control.

Troy sincerely hoped she would stay that way. 'It's a short drive to the Yard,' Troy said. 'I was wondering, would you care to have lunch first?'

'I'd just like . . . I'd just like . . . to see my son.'

They drove to the Yard in silence. Mrs Devanney looked out of the window with the same curious eye Rork had shown – the mark of the first-timer – but none of Rork's gung-ho enthusiasms. If she wondered what was what she never asked.

Kolankiewicz had limited facilities for the cold storage of body parts, and Troy had suggested that there was both clarity and consideration in taking the parts out of their bags and arranging them into the semblance of a man.

'What,' Kolankiewicz had asked, 'is a man without head, hands or cock? It'll still look like something out of Baron Frankenstein's workshop.'

'But we'll do it all the same,' Troy had replied.

He was pleased to see, as the shelf rolled out from the cold-store, that Kolankiewicz had draped a clean white sheet across the body. It bought them a few seconds of time. If she was having second thoughts, there was one last chance to say no.

'No. I have to look. D'ye see?'

There was pleading in her eyes. The deference the poor often felt in the face of authority, not knowing what power they had over her and little presumption to say the choices were hers and hers alone.

'Of course,' said Troy, and Kolankiewicz pulled the sheet back to the waist, exposing the jagged black line at the neck where the head had been severed, the cuts in the arms, and the stubs at the wrists where the hands should have been.

Mrs Devanney stared, paling but unflinching, looking at the body not at them as she spoke.

'Could I . . . could I see the . . . the rest please?'

Kolankiewicz rolled the sheet back past the feet.

Mrs Devanney shuffled sideways. 'Would it be possible to turn over the leg? The left one. Just on to the side.'

Kolankiewicz turned the two pieces of the left leg. It had been severed above the knee, and the skin had been peeled away by the concrete mix from which he had rescued it.

'You see them little scars, down the left side of his calf? And that one on the kneecap? Fell off his bike when he was eight. That bump on the shin is where the bone knitted. The leg never did recover proper. It was as strong as the right, but try as he might he could never build up the muscle to match it. It always looked that bit the smaller. I told him I couldn't see it, and if his own mum couldn't see it no one else would. But I was lying. Trying to make him happy. He never believed me.'

She turned her attention to the left hip. A vivid white scar. 'Jumped the back fence as soon as his leg was healed, just to show he could. Snagged himself on a nail. Bled like billy-o. Took five stitches.'

Now she looked up at Troy for the first time since Kolankiewicz had rolled back the sheet.

'Mrs Devanney, are you sure?'

'His dad said he was accident prone. But truth to tell he was just fearless. I never saw him frightened of anything or anyone. He just didn't seem to see risks, and he never complained when he took a tumble. It was all in a day's work for Niall. He was hardly ever without an Elastoplast or a scab. His dad said he wasn't long for this world. Turned out he was right, didn't it?'

'Are you sure?'

'Am I sure? You don't have children, do you, Mr Troy?'

None of them had children, but to answer was just a distraction. 'If you had, you'd know.'

Kolankiewicz pushed back the shelf.

It was time for Eddie's special brew. In Troy's outer office Mrs Devanney stood and stared at Eddie's coffee-making contraption. Eddie made tea. Troy went to his desk and took out the photograph, a grainy ten-by-eight blow-up made from the snapshot Mrs Devanney had given to the police when she'd reported her son missing. A smiling eighteen-year-old with thick black hair and good teeth. He was trying to associate the face with the body parts – a mental exercise to reassure himself that probably wouldn't work. When he looked up, Mary McDiarmuid was standing in front of him with Mrs Devanney. For a moment all he could hear was the habitual bubbling of Eddie's coffee machine, the hissing of the kettle and the sound of what seemed to be one long sigh emanating from Mrs Devanney.

'Boss?' Mary had Troy's attention now. 'Mrs Devanney brought you a photograph.'

Mrs Devanney held out another snapshot to Troy. He turned over the one he had been holding, hoping she had not seen it and took the one she proffered. It was a hand-coloured print from the 1940s. Handcolouring had had its day and gone the way of polyfoto. It brought a touch of cinema, and had never looked less than synthetic. There was Niall Devanney, aged eight, a scruffy cherub with curly hair and startling blue eyes, grinning at the camera. Technicolor tints allowed for, a child of remarkable beauty, if remarkable recklessness.

Troy looked back to the boy's mother. She had her son's eyes; he had had hers. Blue beyond blue, the kind of blue to which only Technicolor did justice, and with a faint Oriental upward slant. It seemed she was about to speak, a flickering in the lower lip. But the tears welled in her almond eyes, and in a swift, sudden turn she flung herself on Mary McDiarmuid and wept into her shoulder.

§ 96

It seemed like an age before Mary McDiarmuid was back from Euston station.

'The train was late. I could hardly leave her. I took her to a caféin the Hampstead Road. Actually got her to eat something. An Eccles cake and a cup of tea.'

'Good,' said Troy, without taking his eyes off the spread of photographs on his desk. Here a torso, there a thigh.

'She said a lot more. I'm not sure how much of it is of any use. I could've taken notes, but it didn't seem . . .'

'It wasn't. You did the right thing. She told you her life story, right?'

'Right. Do they always do that?'

Troy looked up. 'Not always, but I've known a lot that do. At this point they want the story to mean something.'

'She was desperate for it to seem to real. To me at least. If she said, "Do you see?" once, she said it a thousand times. She asked me how it had all come to this. I thought better of telling her the truth. I didn't mention the precise circumstances of Niall's death – the buggery an a' that – I just stated what I thought was obvious. He'd fallen in with the wrong crowd. Christ, what an understatement that was. I did start to wonder, is this what it's like being on the Murder Squad? The problem isn't the dead, it's the living.'

'It gets worse. Can you handle it?'

'I think so.'

'Good. Because things are going to get a *lot* worse before the night is over.'

'Eh?'

Troy waved the 'eh?' aside, much as he'd done with Godbehere. 'I want to put the file in order. Put it together in terms of the grotesque. Start with feet, work up to the head shots we have of those two boys, and remove anything that's superfluous. File all the written work separately.'

'OK. Can I ask why?'

'It's time.'

'Time?'

'Time to tackle Ted Spoon.'

'What makes you think he'll even see you? He's not the sort to let coppers past the door without prior notice. Give him any notice and he'll have his brief there, telling him not to answer a damn thing.'

Troy folded open that day's copy of *The Times*, and held it out. 'Read it aloud, Mary.'

'"President Eisenhower's visit culminates this evening in a Second World War reunion dinner, given in his honour by Sir Rodyon Troy, the shadow home secretary and a wartime colleague of the President, at his Hertfordshire home Mimram House. Field

Marshals Montgomery and Alexander will be among a guest list thought to total more than fifty. Also present will be Marshal of the RAF Lord Tedder, President Eisenhower's deputy in 1944, Harold Macmillan the Prime Minister, a former political adviser at Allied HQ, Mala Caan VC, and Lord Steele, who, in 1944, led Resistance activity behind enemy lines in Normandy . . ."'

'Enough. You can stop there.'

'No, boss. I can't. It goes on to mention the high level of security at Mimram this evening. US Secret Service, Special Branch and the Hertfordshire Constabulary.'

§ 97

The Hertfordshire Constabulary had closed off the lane leading to Mimram. At the sight of Troy's Bentley two constables simply hauled the barrier aside and saluted as he passed.

At the gates of Mimram there was a copmotley. Two plain-clothes detectives, the village bobby Constable Frank Trubshawe, two American agents and a man Troy knew and did not much like – Chief Inspector Derek Hurst of the Special Branch. It was all too apparent who was who. The Americans still sported the over-short wartime crew-cut. And in contrast to their British counterparts, they were neat in black suits that looked as though they had been cleaned and pressed. Hurst and his men had Branch written all over them, that shabby, threadbare look of suits with shiny elbows that Troy thought so typical of the brute force and no-imagination brigade.

They all looked at one another. Clearly they had not anticipated another vehicle. Troy stepped out of the car. Trubshawe looked vaguely quizzical, approached Troy and said, 'Evenin', sir. We weren't really expecting you.' And Troy was almost certain he heard Hurst mutter, 'Oh, shit.'

'I'm sure you weren't, Mr Trubshawe, but if you gentlemen would be so kind as to make way. . .'

One of the Americans pushed past Trubshawe. 'Just a minute.

Are you on the guest list? We have sixty-four guests on the list, and you're the sixty-fifth person.'

Troy held out his warrant card at arm's length. The American moved closer, mouthing the words on the card with his lips. As he reached the last syllable of 'Superintendent', Troy whipped the card away, turned to Hurst and said, 'Tell him, Mr Hurst.'

'Mr Troy is head of the Murder Squad at Scotland Yard,' said Hurst.

'So – what are you telling me? That you have a case here? Tonight?'

'Indeed I do. Now, if you'd just—'

'Bullshit! The gates are closed. Nobody else gets through. Go back to Scotland Yard and tell 'em *Mañana*. Or you'll have a diplomatic incident on your hands.'

'You have ten seconds,' said Troy. 'After that I'll leave and in forty minutes I'll be back with forty coppers and you'll be charged with obstructing the course of justice. Now, that will be a diplomatic incident.'

'You can come back with Ali Baba and the forty fuckin' thieves, it ain't gonna—'

Trubshawe was tugging at the American's sleeve. He finally got his attention and whispered to him.

'Whaddya mean, his house? I thought it belonged to that big guy with the odd socks.'

Trubshawe whispered again.

'Jesus! Why wasn't I told? I do not believe this. I do not fucking believe this. Does nobody tell me anything?'

The American looked at his colleague and said, 'OK. OK. Larry, get the radio. Tell Marco two more are comin' up. Chief Superintendent Troy and. . .?'

'WPC McDiarmuid.'

The walkie-talkie crackled. Larry turned his back on them, and the two Special Branch officers pushed open the gates.

'I hope,' the American said to Troy, 'that you think this is worth it. Because if you fuck up up there your balls and my ass will be on the same line.'

'Trust me,' said Troy.

As they headed up the drive, Mary McDiarmuid said, 'Boss, tell

301

me. Are you really going to pull Spoon in front of the President and the Prime Minister?'

'Only if he makes me.'

§ 98

It seemed to Troy that he did not recognise his own home. That he had stepped into the set of a black and white film bearing a tantalising resemblance to *L'Année Dernière à Marienbad*. People moved slowly about the blue room in evening dress, a tidal surge of shiny lapels and bow-ties. An awkward elegance, set to the soundtrack of a baritone murmur.

Mostly they were men. That made sense: most of Ike's wartime colleagues had been men. The wives were passed over for an evening, and among the few women Troy thought he knew was a woman he thought might have been a secretary to Churchill during the war – not that he could see Churchill anywhere – and Mala Caan, who had survived interrogation at the hands of the Gestapo and was one of the few ever female recipients of the VC. She was talking to Spoon, but then, if the CIA and *The Times* were to be believed, they had in common the dangerous past of having worked behind enemy lines in France. Troy was looking for Rod, when Rod found him, grabbed him by one arm and whisked him into a hushed huddle.

'What exactly do you think you're playing at? You said you wouldn't be here. Dammit, Freddie, you're not even dressed.'

'That's because I'm working.'

'What?'

'I made you a promise that when I knew what Spoon was up to you'd know. I know now, and I can tell you. It's just that you won't want to know.'

'You can't arrest him here, for God's sake.'

'I've no intention of arresting him, but he is going to talk to me. He's going to look at the evidence.'

They both glanced back into the throng.

'Sod it, he's talking to Ike and Mac now. Freddie, I appeal to you – wait. We'll be going into dinner any minute – wait until after.'

Rod was pinching now, his thumb and fingers sinking into Troy's arm. Troy took his hand and unpeeled the fingers one by one.

'Rod. Get it through your head. This isn't some financial irregularity. This isn't a bit of clandestine pederasty, although I'd bet money Spoon has engaged in both. This is multiple murder. Young men butchered like mutton and dumped on the streets of London.'

'Good God! And you think Spoon did that?'

'No, but he knows the men who did. The same men you and Maurice White argued should be left alone.'

Troy left Rod speechless, and headed for Mala Caan, Harold Macmillan, Lord Spoon and the President of the United States.

Ike was saying, 'And . . . my successor, whoever he is, may well not be able to avoid another war. Laos is containable. I doubt Vietnam is. It's not for me to commit troops to Vietnam, but others may not have that choice.'

Macmillan nodded. If Troy was feeling generous he might well have assumed that the air of doing so 'sagely' was not contrived, the bloodhound eyes, almost always tinged with sadness, staring off at nothing, past Ike, past everyone else in the room. 'You don't say?' was his less than memorable response.

'South East Asia is a quagmire in the making, waiting for us all to step in . . .'

Troy was about to step in, when Rod caught up with him, wearing his bravest face, and said, 'Ike, have you met my brother?'

Troy never had met Ike. They had stood on the pavement outside Overlord HQ in St James's Square one day in 1944, and for one brief moment looked eye to eye. But they'd never spoken. The only thing he remembered about his reaction to Ike was how small he'd seemed, almost fragile. He looked bigger now, taller than the newsreels led one to believe. Office lent stature, but surely not literally?

'Frederick Troy,' said Troy.

'Were you with us in the war, Mr Troy?'

'Indeed I was, Mr President. I was a detective at Scotland Yard. In fact, I still am.'

Spoon knew. Troy knew he knew, and when, after a few minutes of pointless pleasantry, Troy pointed off in the direction of his study, Spoon followed without question. Rod followed too, but that was fine by Troy.

Mary McDiarmuid closed the door behind them. She'd already laid out the file on Troy's desk.

Spoon's opening gambit was a cliché. 'This had better be good.'

Troy said, 'I'm so glad, Lord Steele, that you chose the easy course. I can't pretend that what happens next is private. Miss McDiarmuid and I are serving police officers and we are both on duty. But if you answer my questions I see no reason why the PM or the President should have their evening disturbed, and you can rejoin the dinner party.'

Spoon turned to Rod. 'Did you know about this?'

'No, Ted. And I still don't know.'

Mary had already sat down. Troy said, 'Shall we sit?' and extended a hand to the chair opposite, on the other side of the desk. Only Rod remained standing, leaning against the wall by the door, with his arms folded.

Troy said. 'You know I run the Murder Squad, don't you?'

'Yes.'

'I have no brief in Vice, so please accept my assurance that you are not a suspect in any case I am investigating.'

'Why would I be of any interest to the Vice Squad, Mr Troy?'

'Stop bluffing. I know you're queer. I know you have a taste for rough—'

Spoon was out of his chair and heading for the door before Troy could finish.

'Lord Steele, the house is surrounded by policemen. A coincidence, but a timely one. If you try to leave now we'll just have this conversation in public – I'll wash your dirty linen in front of people who know you and respect you.'

Spoon went back to his chair, blazing with unspoken anger, and stared at Troy.

'As I was saying. I don't care what you get up to in your private life. All I ask is that you look at some photographs and tell me if you recognise anyone.'

'I don't seem to have any choice. Do I?'

It was a nice show of bravado, and to anyone but Mary McDiarmuid and Troy it might have been convincing. When Mary set the first photograph in front of him Spoon showed no shock, only outrage and incomprehension.

'It's a foot. A severed foot. How, in God's name, do you expect me to recognise anyone from a foot?'

And one by one, piece by piece, Mary laid out the entire jigsaw of the corpse that had been recovered near Harpenden. Troy watched the blood and anger drain from Spoon's face, but it was the shock of gore and guts, it wasn't the shock of recognition, and he took it surprisingly well. Many a man would have puked.

'What's your point, Mr Troy?'

Troy looked at Mary McDiarmuid. She set down the full-face shot of Niall Devanney. Spoon reached out. For a moment Troy thought he was going to pick up the photograph, but he was gripping the edge of the desk just enough to steady himself. He was fighting for control of his expression, and he was winning. Whatever else he might be at this moment, Ted Steele wasn't going to be a pushover.

'I say again, Mr Troy, what *is* your point?'

'Earlier this year, I do not know precisely when, you had sexual relations with this man, Niall Devanney, aged twenty. The illegality of that act does not concern me. All I want to know is who introduced him to you.'

'I can't help you, Mr Troy.'

Mary McDiarmuid laid out the shots of the second corpse, one by one, but faster until they spread like a royal flush, with only the face of John Mackie missing.

Spoon was paler than Troy thought possible for a red-blooded mammal, but his voice barely quavered. Troy had seen men reduced to croaking whispers looking at shots such as these. He'd known policemen vomit at the sight. He'd seen women collapse like rag dolls. He did not look at Mary McDiarmuid.

'I can't help you,' Spoon said again.

'I don't know what name he gave you, but he was called John

Mackie. He was nineteen. And you did know him, didn't you?'

Spoon said nothing.

'And you had sexual relations with him too?'

Spoon said nothing.

'Lord Steele, were these young men procured for you by Patrick and Lorcan Ryan as a result of your visits to the Empress club?'

Spoon sat rigid, but Troy saw tears form in the corners of his eyes and begin to roll down his cheeks. It was incongruous and almost shocking. He stared at Troy with not a flicker of expression on his face, as though the tears that wet his cheeks were no more than splashes of rain from a summer shower.

'I say again, I can't help you.'

It was less than an admission, more than a denial. What it was was precise.

'The Ryan twins introduced you to these young men for sexual purposes and when they became an inconvenience to them they butchered them like pigs and dumped the bodies in pieces. We found one on a building site in Hertfordshire, the other outside a West End pub. They'd both had anal intercourse, and we have semen samples. Lord Steele, what is your blood group?'

Steele put both hands on the desk and leaned as close to Troy as he could. 'I can't help you. I say I can't help you.'

And then, so softly Troy doubted even Mary McDiarmuid heard, 'They'll kill me. And then they'll kill you,' his voice rose to a normal pitch and he said, 'Now if you'll excuse me I'd like to go to the lavatory.'

Troy showed Spoon to his bedroom, gave him a towel and pointed him in the direction of his bathroom. He heard the gurgle of running water, and then Spoon said, 'Troy, are you listening?'

Troy was.

§ 99

Rod was still in the study when Troy returned five minutes later and he was looking at his watch. 'Freddie, I really have to get back.' There was an entirely different tone in his voice. Acceptance. More than acceptance.

'If you'd care to join us . . . you know where your DJ is . . . and I'm sure Cid will have something that would fit Miss McDiarmuid . . .'

'Rod, you're waffling. Go and join your guests. I can't think of a single thing I'd want to say to Ike, and the thought of having to listen to Monty is enough to put me to sleep. I got what I came for. And I'm sorry I had to do it this way. If Spoon doesn't slit his throat in my bathroom he'll be joining you. Enjoy it – the friendships are perhaps the only thing I ever envied about your war.'

Rod smiled faintly, touched his shoulder, and left.

Mary McDiarmuid said, 'Why did you not give me the nod to show him Mackie's face?'

'We got one right. What were the odds on us getting both right? Diminishing, I'd say. If we'd got it wrong, he'd have known we were bluffing.'

'So, you're not arresting Spoon?'

'For what? He's done nothing I can or would ever want to prove.'

'Boss, he's also admitted nothing about the Ryans. Or did he do that upstairs?'

Troy shrugged. 'No matter. I know the truth now. He's tougher than I'd ever have thought, but do you really think we couldn't crack him in the witness box? Can you see him holding up to questions from a skilled QC?'

There was sleight-of-word in this. Question without statement.

'Tougher than we thought?' Mary McDiarmuid echoed. 'That I can't deny. All the same, boss, you still need a witness who'll talk now.'

The telephone on Troy's desk rang. He and Rod had had separate lines for over a year now. It had to be for him. He picked it up.

'Mr Troy? Ray Godbehere. Thank God, I've been trying everywhere. You'd better get back to Stepney. The Ryans just shot Mott Kettle in front of a dozen witnesses.'

§ 100

Godbehere got the day shift out of bed.

'That includes Mazzer,' said Troy.

But Mazzer was not answering his phone.

'Then send someone round there. We're calling in Mr Mazzer's loan.'

'What loan?'

'All the borrowed time he's been living on lately. Now, tell me what happened.'

'I've an eyewitness in the interview room, if you want it first hand.'

'Who?'

'Wilf Robertson. Barber in the Mile End Road.'

'Shrimp's father?'

'The same.'

In the interview room, a small, dapper man – no sprinkling of his customer's clippings, and the look of someone who shaved twice a day, and wielded the Brylcreem without mercy – got up and held out a hand for Troy to shake. He knew Troy. Troy did not know him.

'You was famous back in the old days, Mr Troy. You know. Towards the end of the war, an' that.'

'You must be very proud of your son,' Troy said, exercising a standard repertoire and not really caring whether he was or not.

Robertson blushed a little. Lowered his head. 'A good lad,' he said softly. 'Done me proud he has.'

Troy pulled back a chair to let them all know the pleasantries were over.

Robertson sat down; Godbehere leaned against the wall and folded his arms. 'I wonder, Mr Robertson, if you'd be so kind as to tell us one more time what you saw.'

'Course. It was like this. I got me shop down the Mile End Road. Next door to the Paviour's Arms it is. I been there since 1926, and my dad was there before me since 1895. The Paviour's our local. Once or twice a week I go in there after work. I don't stop cuttin' till late – no point in closin' at five, after all. I get the trade mostly from blokes comin' off shift after a day's work. Best hour of the day is six till seven, so often as not I work till gone eight. It was slack tonight, though. I shut at seven on the dot. Went round to the Paviour's just after openin' time. Watched the regulars come in. You know the sort. The usual half-dozen. Blokes who only go home to sleep. About quarter of an hour after me Mott comes in. I've known Mott Kettle all me life. Cut his hair since I was a lad. Always the same. Whip round after with the taper, and a packet of three for the weekend. Anyway, Mott comes in. Orders his pint. Finishes it quick, and he's just got his lips to the second when the doors open and the Ryans walk in. By now the pub's beginnin' to fill up a bit. Like there's a dozen or more of us. I've had me two penn'orth out o' Mott, and I'm chattin' down the far end of the bar to Barney Hamlin from the fishmonger's. The Ryans have, like, got this way of shuttin' up a room whenever they walk in. I seen 'em do it since they was no more than teenagers. They stood dead centre, and people sort of waved away from 'em in ripples. Like water on a pond. And Mott gets a feel of this and he turns round and greets 'em like they were his long-lost sons. Slaps his money on the counter and orders drinks for 'em. Smilin' all the time, like, and it takes a while for the penny to drop that they aren't smilin' back at him. Then one of the Ryans says, "We hear you spent a night in the nick, Mott." Mott pulls on his pint, wipes the froth from his lips, still smilin', like, and says, bold as brass, "Yeah, but they got nothin' outa me. It'll take more than a pillock like Troy to get the better of old Mott."

'Then one Ryan says, "Mott, you are such a fuckin' idiot," pulls out a gun the size of a howitzer and shoots Mott in the leg. I hit the floor. Everybody ducks. Mott goes down screamin'. Whichever Ryan it is – and truth to tell I've never been able to tell 'em apart since they was snot-nosed little brats 'angin' around my shop – whichever, he passes the gun to the other, says, "Mott, you always were a total twat," then he turns to the other and says, "Finish him," and the other one puts the gun to Mott's head and it blows apart like an overripe melon dropped on the greengrocer's floor. And then the Ryans walk out like they'd just nipped in for a packet of fags. And I go over to Mott to see if there's somethin' I can do, and there's nothin' I can do, cos poor old Mott 'e's got half his head missin', an't 'e? And the landlord calls the police, and most everybody else does a runner cos they don't want to mess with it. And me I'm lookin' at Mott, and I'm thinkin', Mott, you always was a scabrous little git, but what did you do to deserve this? And I think there's nothin' 'e could have done. Cos ole Mott was 'armless. A wrong 'un, right enough. But 'armless. Ole Mott wouldn't have 'urt a fly.'

Robertson ground to a halt, almost tearful as he spoke of Mott. Troy could not but help think that Wilf Robertson would be the only one to shed a tear for the passing of Moses Kettleman.

'You say you've never been able to tell the Ryans apart?'

'That's right. Not since they was nippers.'

'So you can't say for certain who fired the shot that killed Mott?'

'No, I can't. But they both shot him. They each took the gun and they each pulled the trigger. They each wanted to take a piece out of Mott. Does it matter which one of them?'

'No,' said Troy. 'For once I don't think it does.'

Back in his office, Godbehere said, 'All the other regulars have come forward since. It seems as though nobody thought Mott deserved to die like that. I've thirteen witnesses backing up what Mr Robertson said.

'Nobody's seen the Ryans since. Except, of course, that the phone hasn't stopped ringing with people who think they've seen them. They've been seen in Notting Hill and Clapton – within five minutes of each other. I'm trying to get everything checked out, but right now it's a matter of sifting the real calls from the panickers. But one thing's certain. London thinks they've overstepped. Nobody's hiding. Every man in that pub came back and talked to us. Every last one of them made a statement. Some less reliable than others, some with so much form you'd never want to put them anywhere near the witness box – but some, like Wilf Robertson, whom you'd count as respectable locals, honest as the day is long.'

'Quite,' said Troy. 'Robertson is enough to hang them.'

He asked for the list of properties owned by the Ryans.

'Call West End Central. I want the Empress closed and searched. What's being done about a general search?'

'I haven't bothered with the recent acquisitions – they're still inhabited after all – but we've been round to every likely place on that list, the house, the garage, the warehouses. Nothing. So far, nothing. Seventy years ago we'd have put a man at Victoria station and watched the boat-trains leaving for the Continent. But this is 1959. We've got motorways . . . there are a thousand ways out of London.'

'And we're not looking for Oscar Wilde,' said Troy.

There was a tap at the door. The desk sergeant entered. ' 'Scuse me, sir. DC Shelden's just called in from Stratford. No one's answering at Mr Mazzer's flat. Shelden thinks it's empty.'

'Tell him,' Godbehere said, 'Tell him to wait. Tell him to sit on the doorstep until Mazzer shows up. When Mazzer shows up I want him here pronto.'

The desk sergeant looked quizzically back at Godbehere. 'You mean like arrest him, sir? Arrest Mr Mazzer?'

Godbehere passed the quizzical gaze to Troy.

'No,' said Troy. 'Escort him. Don't arrest him. I don't want him unduly alarmed. Just tell him he's needed. Tell him Mott Kettle is dead and we need a report.'

§ 101

Troy called Swift Eddie at the Yard.

'Forge my signature on six chits. Pick up six handguns from the armourer.'

An hour later Troy was staring down at the case of guns Eddie had delivered. He'd never ordered weapons issue on such a scale before. He was clutching the chit carbons, bearing Eddie's uncannily accurate forgery of his own name. He looked from the guns to Eddie. They were at the edge of Wonderland and they both knew it. One step more and they would be through the looking-glass. 'We can't go after them empty-handed,' he said.

'Of course not,' said Eddie.

There were times Troy thought Eddie read minds. Perhaps this was not one of them.

'There was one other thing, sir. I bumped into—'

'Yes?'

Before Eddie could answer the door opened and Jack walked in. 'I rather think it's all hands to the pumps, don't you?' he said. 'Is one of these for me?' Jack picked up a Webley, flicked open the chamber, fed a handful of bullets into it and spun it like a character in a cowboy film. One step into Wonderland. 'We can hardly go after the buggers empty-handed, now, can we?'

And there were times Troy thought Jack read minds.

§ 102

Mary McDiarmuid drove Jack and Troy to the house in Watney Street.

'I thought Ray had already been here? And it's the last place they'll come back to,' Jack said.

'I need to see it.'

'See what?'

'See . . . them.'

'See them?'

'See them . . . as they are. . .'

'I don't quite follow you here, Freddie.'

'What we've seen so far is . . . on the level of a myth. We're chasing mythical beasts. They exist in the words of those they've encountered, they exist as their victims narrate them . . .We haven't really met them.'

'You know, they told me when I joined that you could wank for England when the thesis took you. We do not need to "meet" them, as you put it, we do not need to know them – we merely have to nick them before they kill anyone else. And *I* met them for three sodding days at the Yard. Take it from me. They're real enough.'

They stood in a living room less than ten feet square. A clichéof working-class life before the Second World War. A worn but sturdy three-piece suite in black and green leatherette – so big it made any movement across the room into an obstacle course. A beige-tile fireplace with a scorched white gas-fire in its hearth and two glazed spaniel dogs on its mantel. A brush, a poker and a shovel disguised by the figure of a brass knight-in-armour. Three plaster ducks flying up the wall. And not a speck of dust to be seen. It was a house to turn out of and turn into. A house rendered spotless by the daily cleaning woman. It was almost clinical.

'No dirt,' Troy said. 'No vice. Where there's dirt there's vice. Everyone has some vice.'

'I don't believe it,' Jack said. 'I don't believe they live here.'

But they did. In the first bedroom there was a built-in wardrobe full of bespoke suits and hand-made shoes. The second was different only in that a paperback copy of *Peyton Place* lay splayed upon the bedside table atop a copy of *Parade*, a risqué magazine that printed photographs of women without blouses or bras.

'There's your vice, Freddie. Ordinary as it comes. The most ordinary sin in the universe.'

Troy pulled open a drawer in the tallboy. Cotton underpants that had been ironed. Socks in neat little balls – socks that had been darned.

'Savile Row suits. Lobb shoes . . . and darned socks.'

'I don't get it,' Jack said. 'I don't get it. They pull jobs, they terrorise the East End, they rub shoulders with toffs and politicians. They dress from Savile Row. And . . . they kill people. And at the end of the day they come back here. To this. Why?'

'The womb?' said Troy. 'Wouldn't you relish someone who darned your socks? My brother's wife darns his socks. We could buy an empire of socks, but still he wants the reassurance of a woman's touch with the darning-needle. It's a womb. You go out in your tailor-mades and you come back to darned socks.'

'Spare me the Freudian stuff, Freddie. If it's their womb then it's one they're prepared to put under the wrecking ball if the price is right.'

'Just an idea,' said Troy. 'I've been trying to see them as the two boys Robertson tells me I once met. I don't seem to be able to manage it.'

'I don't have to. I encountered them as they are. What they might have been means nothing. Now, are we through?'

'Not quite.'

Mary McDiarmuid drove them to the Ryan twins' garage under the arches of the London, Tilbury and Southend Railway in Cable Street.

'More nostalgia?'

'Eh?'

'Don't you recognise it, Freddie? It's the same arch we were in in '44 – the one Sidney Edelmann had as a bomb-shelter.' So it was. Troy looked around. The huge steel H-beams reinforcing the roof, the three-quarter-inch armour-plating Edelmann had pinched from the docks to guarantee the safety of his small branch of the Communist Party of Great Britain. Edelmann had died the same night Troy had killed Diana Brack. It was a coincidence that the Ryans should be running their business out of this particular arch – they could have been in any one of thirty or more – but Troy was in a mood to respond to coincidence.

He could hear Edelmann in his mind's ear – 'As I live and breathe it's Mr Troy. Lads, lads, it's my old friend Constable Troy' – almost see Edelmann, hamming it up like a cross between Quasimodo and a Shakespearean clown. He'd not been here in years. He and Jack had been 'granted an interview' with Edelmann not long before his death – and a few weeks before that he'd encountered the Ryans for the first time. He could see Edelmann, he could hear Edelmann, he could smell Diana Brack – the drenching scent of *Je Reviens*. Reach out a hand and he could touch her. But he couldn't see the Ryans. Couldn't see the little boys the Ryans had once been.

'Well?' said Jack. 'Nothing,' said Troy. Nothing and everything.

§ 103

It was the most frustrating time of Troy's life. The Indian Summer caught like brushfire. A new wave of heat seared London. Jack traded him in for a detective constable, for a man with nothing to say and an obligation to listen. 'I've heard all I want to hear of Freud.'

Troy went out on calls with Godbehere.

Godbehere said, 'I've never gone out armed before.' And looked at the gun as though he'd no idea what it was or how it worked.

Troy shoved his into a jacket pocket, felt the weight pull his suit out of shape. He had forgotten to ask Eddie for holsters. Godbehere stuck his in the waistband of his trousers and looked like a man about to stick up a bank. 'It all feels wrong,' he said. 'Like we're playing at it.'

'We're not,' said Troy.

It was the most frustrating time of Troy's life. They trailed across London from St Katherine's Dock to Silver Town, from Wapping Wall to the Balls Pond Road, and saw not a glimpse of anything Troy would grace with the word 'clue'. All of London was willing to turn in the Ryans, half of London seemed to phone up to say they'd seen them, but Troy found himself in empty rooms and crowded streets, looking at the space where they might once have been, listening to the chattering voices build their narrative from men to myth – 'They was in a Mark 7 Jag, honest, it was parked right there, couldn't have been less than twenty minutes ago'; 'They walked into the Dog and Parrot, bold as brass and ordered two halves of shandy' – and feeling the gun in his pocket tug at him like a chain and anchor.

Almost a day and a half had passed like this. Jack was sprawled across a chair in Godbehere's office. Godbehere seemed to be sleeping bolt upright – snoring gently. Eddie was off somewhere trying to rustle up coffee. Mary McDiarmuid slept on the floor behind the desk, her head pillowed on Troy's rolled-up jacket.

'Freddie, it's nearly two in the morning. We've most of us been on since the day before yesterday. Ray's been up nigh on forty-eight hours. The only one who's had any sleep is that poor sod you've got camped out on Mazzer's doorstep. You've got to call it a night.'

'Not while they're out there.'

'I'm not saying call it off. I'm saying change shifts. Let us go home for a few hours and come back fresh. You're the one who's so damn keen on psychology. Look at it this way. We've answered every call, chased every lead, searched more than twenty houses, taken a hundred statements and got nowhere. It's demoralising, and it's doubly demoralising without sleep.'

Behind him Mary McDiarmuid stirred.

'Mr Wildeve's right, boss. We've given it our best shot. Let's go home. If only for a few hours.'

Troy gave in. Jack would have nagged him until daybreak if he hadn't. Mary McDiarmuid said she'd drive him home, Eddie volunteered to stay in the office, and Godbehere and Jack would drive to Southwark together.

'Eight,' said Troy. 'No later than eight. Everyone back here at eight.'

§ 104

Troy sat next to Mary McDiarmuid in the passenger seat of the Bentley. She turned the key in the ignition and nothing happened.

Troy yawned. 'It does that from time to time. For some reason, it helps to put the lights on first. God knows why.'

Mary flicked on the lights, picking out Godbehere's Wolseley, forty-odd feet in front of them.

'Now try ag—'

Troy caught sight of a black wire trailing from the petrol cap of the Wolseley. Saw Ray hunching down to turn on.

Mary McDiarmuid turned the key again. The windscreen cracked from side to side.

Troy had not seen the explosion that killed John Brocklehurst. He wasn't even sure he'd heard it. The memory of that triple bang was now no more than something from a dream. One, two, three, *boom*, you're dead. Godbehere's Wolseley left the ground in a ball of orange flame. The Bentley shot backwards, Troy and Mary McDiarmuid bouncing off the seats to bang against the windscreen. The windscreen cracked from side to side. The Wolseley came to earth, crashing down on to the pavement, wheels splayed as though the car had been flattened by a giant hand, swatted like a bug.

Troy found Jack in the doorway of the police station. He'd had enough warning and enough reflexes to shield his face, but the blast had flung him into the door. He was bleeding badly from the head. His shirt was sliced to ribbons.

Troy dragged him inside, sat with his head in his lap, tearing strips from the remains of the shirt to staunch the head wound.

'Ambulance, Mary. Ambulance.'

But Eddie was already on the phone.

Troy looked up at Mary, pale and wide-eyed, a trickle of blood seeping gently from a cut on her forehead. 'Ray?' he said.

Mary McDiarmuid shook her head.

Boom, you're dead.

§ 105

Eddie slapped a length of cable and a spark plug on the desk in front of Troy.

'Why aren't we dead?' said Troy.

'You had a full tank. Mary filled up last night. There was so much petrol in the tank of your car that there wasn't enough space or fumes to ignite when the spark plug was charged. You were lucky. It was rigged properly. A couple of pints less petrol and you'd both be dead.'

§ 106

Troy watched Jack carried into the ambulance. Saw his eyes flicker open. Wondered whether the look was recognition or bewilderment. Felt Mary McDiarmuid tugging at his sleeve. 'They found Mazzer.'

'Where?'

'Turned up at his flat. Said he'd been at his sister's in Hornchurch, sleeping off a double shift.'

Troy called Kolankiewicz at home.

Still wide awake at two in the morning. Soft and clear. 'Who else would it be but you at this time of the night?'

'Do you have anything in your bag of tricks like scopolamine?'

'How very *Boy's Own* of you, my boy. No, I don't. But doubtless I could come up with a cocktail of my own that would have much the same effect.'

'There's a squad car on its way from Hendon. Lights flashing. No speed limit. Come via my house. There's a bottle of Talisker under the sink. I may have need of it. Get here as quickly as you can.'

Kolankiewicz was there in less than an hour, coat pulled on over his pyjamas, Homburg on head, Gladstone bag in hand. The Webleys were scattered across Godbehere's desk. Someone had dutifully put them under lock and key when Troy had called an end to the shift. He'd got them out again.

'I heard,' Kolankiewicz said. 'Armageddon.' He opened his bag and put the bottle of Talisker and a .357 Magnum on the desk.

Troy did not think he had seen a Magnum since Bob Churchill had taught him how to use one nearly fifteen years ago. 'Why did you bring that?'

'I fear you may need it.'

To Troy it was as though Churchill had spoken to him from the grave. He steered a mental path round the voice, said, 'Do you not think that if the Yard had wanted me to have a gun like that they would have issued me with a gun like that?'

'Call it parity. If they came at me with one of those, I would want to have as much firepower as they do.'

'Tricky,' said Troy. Much as Churchill might have done.

Kolankiewicz spoke with a shrug in his voice, the devil's easy way with words. 'You've issued a chit for it,' he said. Then he reached over to the pile of guns and slipped one of the Webleys into his battered old Gladstone bag. 'Six chits, six guns. It'll all be above board.'

'No,' Troy said softly. 'It will simply appear to be above board.'

'Whatever,' said Kolankiewicz. 'Let us concentrate on the drug, shall we? There's no way we can ever give that the gloss of legitimacy.'

He reached into his bag again and pulled out a hypodermic syringe and a small bottle of colourless fluid. 'Now, which pig do you want me to stick?'

'Time for Mr Mazzer,' Troy said to Mary McDiarmuid.

'Fine, boss. But you should put your jacket on. You're covered in Mr Wildeve's blood.'

Troy looked down at himself. She was right. His shirt was turning brown with drying blood. Mary McDiarmuid picked up Troy's jacket off the floor, still bundled up as a pillow, shook it and handed it to him. By the time she wheeled in Mazzer, Troy still looked scarcely half respectable. The crumpled suit, the two-day growth of beard. Put together, he and Kolankiewicz looked like the two tramps waiting for Godot. Mazzer looked baffled, clean-shaven, brushed and combed, washed and neat – but baffled.

Troy held out his right hand for him to shake. 'Al.'

'Mr Troy.'

Mazzer took the hand, the beginning of a smile creeping across his face. Troy pulled on the hand, hit Mazzer as hard as he could with his left and dragged him face down on to the desk. Kolankiewicz stepped out from behind the door and whacked the syringe into Mazzer's backside. It seemed to Troy that Mazzer was about to speak, that the first shock of momentary unconsciousness from the blow to his head had passed, but the drug hit him like a soporific breaking wave and the eyelids fluttered shut.

Kolankiewicz pushed him back into a chair. 'No more than five minutes, then he should come round. At which point he'll be very cooperative. You'll have about ten minutes' clarity before he slips back, and then he'll be out for a couple of hours and wake up with a terrible thirst. But I have to ask – what makes you think he wouldn't tell you what you want to know in the first place?'

'I don't have the time,' said Troy. 'What I have is Jack in hospital and what's left of Ray Godbehere on the slab.'

Mazzer's eyes opened. He had the look of a man happily drunk. 'You hit me,' he said simply.

'Yes. I hit you. Now I want you to answer a few questions.'

'Yes.'

'Where are Patrick and Lorcan Ryan hiding?'

Mazzer inhaled deeply, held on to it as though staving off vomit. Then he said, 'Yes. Warehouse.'

'What warehouse? We searched their warehouses. We searched everything on the manor.'

'Stick to straight questions,' Kolankiewicz said. 'Less for him to understand.'

Mazzer stared, Troy saw his eyes turning glassy and vacant. Mary McDiarmuid turned the desk lamp around and shone it right in Mazzer's eyes. 'I saw it in a film,' she said. 'It might work.'

It did. Mazzer jerked suddenly and slurred out the words, 'Wrong manor. Yes.'

'Then which manor?'

'South of the river. Yes. Rotherhithe. Mandarin Wharf. Yes.'

'Where's that?'

'Yes. By the Hanover Stairs. Right on top of the Thames tunnel.'

Mary McDiarmuid was scanning the list of the Ryans' assets. 'It's not here. There's nothing south of the river.'

'There wouldn't be,' said Troy. Mazzer lolled sideways. Troy pushed him back the other way. 'What are they waiting for?'

'Boat. Boat up the river. Yes. Take them to Hamburg. Yes.'

'Jesus Christ,' said Troy. 'It's Dickensian. It's like something out of Dickens.'

'You aim too high,' Kolankiewicz said. 'It's more like Edgar Wallace.'

'Yes.Edgar.Yes . . .Edgar Wallace.Yes.'

'He's burning out,' Kolankiewicz said. 'He'll be senseless in less than a minute.'

'Can I?' asked Mary McDiarmuid.

'Be my guest,' Troy replied, turning his attention to the streetmap.

'Who are they after?' she said.

'After?'

'Who's the final target? It surely wasn't Mr Godbehere? Who were they trying to kill tonight?'

Mazzer let out a drunken giggle. 'Yes. Sergeant Troy.'

'*Sergeant* Troy?'

'Sergeant Troy, Sergeant Troy, Bigfoot Bonham's little boy.'

Troy looked up from the map. 'Jesus Christ.'

'Sergeant Troy, Sergeant Troy, Bigfoot Bonham's little boy.'

It had the repetitive taunt of Georgie Porgie, he who had made the little girls cry, and once uttered, the rapid spiral of narcotic dementia turned it into a mantra. Mazzer could not stop saying it.

Over and over again, 'Sergeant Troy, Sergeant Troy, Bigfoot Bonham's little boy.' He was still reciting it when they lugged him to the cells. But when Troy slipped back to leave the bottle of Talisker by the bunk, he was snoring like a dog.

§ 107

A portly sergeant from Rotherhithe met them at Mandarin Wharf. A portly sergeant and two constables.

'Is this all you could muster?' Troy said.

'The whole nick's gone down with food poisoning, sir. I'm the desk sergeant – Tom Kinney. I've had to shut the nick just to get the three of us here.'

Troy had only Mary McDiarmuid and Robertson. To have recalled the day shift would have taken too long. The thought of Swift Eddie with a gun was unthinkable. It was almost light. It seemed to Troy that they were all too old, too young or the wrong gender.

'Are the Ryans in there?' he asked.

'Somebody's in there. One o' my lads saw a light on the first floor. And I could swear there's a smell of fried bacon hanging around.'

Kinney pulled a large-scale map from his tunic and spread it out on the bonnet of Troy's Bentley.

'It's what used to be Gilligan and Campbell's Yarn Warehouse. They went bust during Suez, shut up shop two or three years back. The place has been up for sale ever since. Truth to tell, if it's changed hands, I didn't know about it. The blokes on the beat check it out from time to time. But it's pretty secure. We've had no reports of dossers or break-ins. After all, there's nothing in there to steal. Now, there's lots o' ways in and out. But we went right round the outside while we was waitin'. All but two are boarded up or padlocked on the outside. This one on Peck Street and this one, which opens straight on to the riverside yard and the jetty. There's nothing moored at present.'

'You weren't seen?'

'We're not complete idiots, sir. We was quiet and we was careful. After all, for all we know these villains are armed.'

'You can bank on it,' said Troy. 'In fact . . .' He hefted the case of guns on to the bonnet. '. . . so are we. Everybody take one.'

Kinney looked at the guns. The two constables looked at Kinney.

'What's the problem?'

'Well, sir . . . it's just that we've never . . .'

'With any luck, Sergeant, you won't have to.'

Kinney picked up a gun. His men followed. Kinney broke the chamber open, checked the bullets, and they followed like Boy Scouts learning woodcraft. If he'd stood on one leg and hopped they'd have bounced around like frogs.

'I want you three to go to the Peck Street door. Keep well back, keep under cover, take no risks, but let them know you're there.'

'What?' said Kinney. 'You mean like "Come out, the game's up"?'

'If you like,' said Troy. 'I'll go in by the riverside, and Mr Robertson here will take the gate.'

'And you'll just like . . . nick 'em . . . like on yer tod?'

'Yes,' said Troy.

'Bloody hell.'

§ 108

The warehouse loomed up in front of them. Seven black storeys. The grime of centuries caked on. Row upon row of iron-shuttered windows. Every shutter at a different angle, as though signalling in semaphore. A giant Advent calendar in black and rust. The first hint of eastern sunlight playing across the surface, picking out a gigantic G and a faded C. Troy thought of all the wartime films he'd seen over the last few years, it almost didn't matter which – the fighter plane coming out of the sun.

He shrugged off his jacket and threw it into the back of the car – bloody and shirtsleeved once more. Mary McDiarmuid backed the car off and Troy and Shrimp Robertson stood at the gates to the dockyard.

Troy had no time for it but the look on Robertson's face was the same one he had been wearing that night they had fished Rork's body from the canal basin. The urgency of something that might burst within him that had eventually led to his account of Troy's first – and so far only – encounter with the Ryan twins.

'Whatever it is, save it,' Troy said.

'Can't. Gotta speak.'

'Mr Robertson, we haven't got the time.'

'Gotta. Gotta ask. Sir, why am I stuck out here and you going in alone?'

Robertson's speech had rattled out with the rapidity of a machine-gun. Troy heard the cry go up from the other side of the building. The corny melodrama of 'This is the police!'

'Why? Because it's not six weeks since you were a cadet at Hendon.'

'You mean if they, like, come out shooting? Cos I bet I've had weapons training more recently than any of us.'

'You're staying here.'

'Remember the Derek Bentley case, sir? They teach it in college now. Don't approach an armed man alone.'

'You're staying here.' Troy checked the gun.

'Metropolitan Police guidelines state, sir, that . . .'

Safety off.

'This is no time to be quoting me the rule book.'

Six .357 bullets in the chamber.

'. . . that an unaccompanied officer –'

Troy stepped through the gate into the yard, but Robertson followed, undeterred.

'Go back, Mr Robertson. It can't be long now.'

'– an unaccompanied officer when in pursuance of—'

'Stop. Stop right now!'

Troy pushed Robertson, and pushed him again.

Troy pushed Robertson. The push saved both their lives.

§ 109

The Bentley was pulled up outside, at the river's edge. Mary McDiarmuid stood by the driver's door, hands thrust deep in her coat pockets.

'Are you wearing gloves?'

She took her hands from her pockets to show that she was.

Troy handed her the gun. 'Bag it and keep it clean. It's evidence. Now, the nearest police box.'

They drove a couple of hundred yards to a police box in Jamaica Road. Troy called an ambulance for Robertson, then called the Yard and asked to be put through to Onions at home.

'Wildeve's in hospital. Godbehere's dead. So are the Ryans.'

'What?'

'Wildeve's in hos—'

'I mean how?'

'I shot them.'

'You shot them?'

'Yes.'

'Jesus wept. Half an hour. OK? Half an hour. My office.'

Troy sank back into the passenger seat of his Bentley. Closed his eyes.

They had plenty of time. There was no way Stan would get from Acton to the Yard in half an hour.

'Back to the Yard. And let's try sticking to the speed limit, shall we?'

§ 110

Troy stood in the doorway of Onions's outer office. A lipsticked cigarette burned in the ashtray, the reading lamp cast its circle on a sheaf of white papers and grubby carbons, the electric typewriter hummed and rattled in conversation with itself.

He walked through into Onions's own office and sat down in the visitor's chair, facing the desk. The blinds were still drawn, only slivers of sunlight slicing in. That was fine. Darkness was fine.

Several minutes passed. He could hear telephones ringing somewhere down the corridor. Then the phone in the outer office rang, and he heard hurried footsteps, the sound of raggy lungs dragging on a cigarette and Madge Hardwick's voice: 'Yes. Yes. The commissioner's on his way. Yes. I'll tell him.'

The bell rang gently as she laid the receiver back in the cradle. Then the stifled scream as she noticed Troy. 'You daft bugger! You nearly scared me half to death. What the bloody hell do you think you're doing sitting there in the dark?'

She stepped a pace into the room and flicked on the light. Noticed Troy's shirt and trousers, stained with Wildeve's blood, stained with Shrimp Robertson's, stained with his own. A coat of many colours, all of them reddish-brown. He knew how it looked to her and he didn't care.

'I'm waiting for the commissioner,' he said simply.

'Well, you've done it now, haven't you? You've bloomin' well done it now. I always told the boss you were mad, and this time you've proved it. You've gone too far this time. Too far by half. You mad bugger. What do you think you're playing at?'

The forgetfulness of her own rhetoric let her stray too close. Troy grabbed her by one arm. 'Madge, what is it you think I've done?'

'Let go of me!'

'Tell me.'

'You killed those men, didn't you?'

'Quite. I just shot two men in cold blood. So, tell me, Madge, why push your luck?'

He let go and she ran from the office, straight into Onions, babbling, 'He threatened me! He threatened me!'

'Madge,' Onions said softly, 'what are you doing here at this time of night?'

'The manpower report. I was just—'

'Go home, Madge.'

'He threatened me. The mad bugger threatened to—'

'Go home, woman! For once in your life do as you're told!'

Madge cowered, snatched her handbag off her desk and ran.

Onions appeared in front of Troy. He, too, had pulled his suit on over his pyjamas. It gave him the faintest resemblance to a clown. He flicked off the overhead and turned on his desk lamp. 'Jesus wept. Jesus wept.'

He flopped himself down in the chair behind the desk, hands rubbing at his face. When he took them away, Troy could see the redness in the brilliant blue eyes, the inflamed, sleepless eyelids, the way-past-midnight stubble on the chin, the infinite world-weariness that Stan had become since the job took him over.

'Had she been here long?'

'A brief encounter.'

Onions smiled at this. 'They can never be brief enough, can they?'

Troy said nothing.

'How's Wildeve?'

'Better than I was.'

'You could have called me when he was hit.'

Troy said nothing. Took the reproach for what it was.

Onions said, 'Tell me. Tell me everything.'

Troy told him.

Eventually he reached, 'They came at us like cowboys in a western. Guns blazing. One with a sawn-off shotgun. One with a handgun. Robertson went down at once. I hit the deck. Told them to stop or I'd fire. They kept coming. Guns still blazing. That's when I shot them. The next thing I knew Sergeant Kinney had arrived with a couple of constables. They fixed up Robertson, put a tourniquet on his leg. I phoned you. Came straight here.'

When he'd finished Onions said, 'Does Godbehere have any family?'

'I don't know,' Troy replied, feeling the only touch of guilt he would feel that evening.

'What's the charge? Mazzer, I mean. What are you charging him with?'

'Dunno,' said Troy. 'I'll think of something.'

'Who's in command back there?'

'The sergeant I just mentioned. Name of Kinney. Out of Rotherhithe.'

'A uniform?'

'Yes. I mean, Godbehere's dead, Jack's in hospital, Mazzer's under arrest . . . I'm . . .' Troy held up a blood-soaked arm as though he was a marionette jerked upon a string.

Onions seemed to take in his whole appearance as if for the first time that night.

'Jesus Christ, what do you look like? You're covered in the stuff.'

'Most of it, most of it isn't mine.'

'We'll have to get someone. There has to be someone.'

Troy no longer cared. It wasn't his problem any more. It was just logistics. Onions seemed at last to be gathering up the ragged pyjama cord of thought.

'Jesus H. Christ. Let's get this over and done with.'

One last rubbery rub at his cheeks and jowls to shake him into life.

'First off, where's the gun now?'

'My gun? McDiarmuid has it.'

'How many shots were fired?'

'I don't know,' Troy lied.

'And young Robertson was a witness to this?'

'No, no, he wasn't, he was out cold.'

'And you had no choice, right?'

'I just said – they'd already shot Robertson.'

'Both of them?'

'I think,' Troy played an aria on a theme of truth, 'that you will find both their guns have been fired.'

'And they shot at you too?'

Troy pointed to the holes in his trousers, and the florin-sized rings of blood around them.

'Right,' said Onions. 'Right. . .So. . . there'll be an inquiry . . .

327

You realise I'll have to suspend you while it's on?'

'Of course. I wouldn't expect anything but to be . . . suspended.'

It struck Troy that it was the first time in his entire career as a copper that he had been suspended. He wondered if the same thought had occurred to Onions.

'And you'll have to get your injuries seen to. And I mean a proper doctor, not that Polish lunatic. Then, if you're up to it, type up your report and let me have it before noon. I'll stall the press till then.'

'The press?' Troy said.

'Freddie, I used to think you didn't have a naïve bone in your body. They'll be all over this. A dead copper and two dead villains. Of course they will. Or did you think you could set them on to me without them wanting a piece of you when the time came?'

One thing Troy had always admired in Onions was his unpredictability.

§ 111

Mary McDiarmuid drove him to Goodwin's Court. He almost nodded off next to her, a half-waking state in which he knew where he was and could hear the outside world, but less audibly than the cricket on his shoulder. One voice repeating, 'Not like this. Not like this.'

§ 112

When he got home, he found Kolankiewicz had already let himself in. His Gladstone bag was open on the table, a bottle of Polish vodka open next to it. Just as well. Troy could not face Anna.

In the open bag he could see the Webley Kolankiewicz had

all but confiscated from him and, next to it, wrapped in a sheet of clear Cellophane, the Magnum. He wondered at what point Mary McDiarmuid and Kolankiewicz had got together. Then he remembered, he had told her it was 'evidence', and if it was, what else would she do with it but give it to Kolankiewicz? Perhaps there was no conspiracy. Perhaps it was all a conspiracy.

'You ready for this?'

Troy snapped out of his reverie and pulled off his trousers. His right leg looked like the surface of the moon.

'This will hurt.'

'Let it,' said Troy. 'Just pour me a vodka first.'

As Kolankiewicz picked out the first piece of buckshot with a pair of tweezers Troy said, 'Did you look in on Mazzer before you left?'

'Sleeping like a baby.'

'And the whisky?'

'Three-quarters gone. If we – and it is not often I bracket myself with you, my boy – if we are lucky, he will remember nothing in the morning.'

'Quite,' said Troy wincing at the stabs of pain. 'We – if that is not the word that offends you – are going to get away with it.'

'Get away with what?'

§ 113

Troy pushed Robertson. The push saved both their lives.

Each had taken a step back from the confrontational force of it and the first blast of Patrick Ryan's shotgun had ripped between them, peppering Troy's right leg and tearing a piece out of Robertson's left. The boy fell. Troy had heard the crack of his skull on the cobblestones as he spun to earth himself. The second blast roared over his head – he landed on his right side, palm flat upon the stones, his left hand levelling the revolver on Ryan as he lurched towards him.

Ryan was running, the breech of his sawn-off shotgun open.

Running, trying to reload and run at the same time, blocking his brother's aim.

'Pat, you fuckin' berk, get down!'

Lorcan Ryan was weaving around his twin, trying for a clear shot and failing, the handgun waving far too wildly in the air.

Patrick Ryan was fumbling, couldn't get the breech of his gun shut. Troy shot him twice in the chest and blew him off his feet. He fell backwards, bent at the knees, arching into the posture of a crab – but Troy wasn't looking at Patrick Ryan any more: he was looking at Lorcan Ryan, who had finally found his aim.

It was the last thing he expected. Ryan had dropped the gun without a single shot fired, and sent it clattering down to the cobblestones. Then he had knelt and taken his brother in his arms. Bloody and tender – the death rattle scarcely risen in the dead man's throat.

Troy got slowly to his feet, his gun on Ryan, feeling behind him for Robertson. The boy groaned. Troy glanced down at him. He was still out – the bleeding was bad but it was all from his leg. Troy stepped backwards and groped for Robertson's collar, meaning to drag him to safety.

Lorcan Ryan was cradling his brother's head, much as Troy had done with Jack a couple of hours before, cradling the head, hugging it to his chest and wailing like the worst of Trojan women. A deep-throated wail, a wail drenched in the anguish of the self-pitying. The keening of a man who had been above nature, a man to whom this could not and did not happen.

Troy took a grip on Robertson and heaved.

But Ryan stopped wailing and spoke. 'You can't leave us like this.'

It was a voice remarkably free of hysteria.

He wasn't screaming.

He scarcely raised his voice.

It sounded almost calm, almost rational.

'You can't leave us like this. Not like this.'

Troy looked at Robertson. The faintest stirrings of consciousness. It would be minutes before he came out of it. Troy let him fall, took a dozen slow steps towards the Ryans, until he could see the guns clearly, until they lay at his feet almost side by side. The shotgun had fallen from the dead fingers of Patrick Ryan, breech open. Troy looked down at it – a custom-made hammerless twin, a faint RC, carved in the stock, the entwined initials of its maker, Robert Churchill – now a brutal stub of wood and steel, crudely hacked off at the stock and barrels. A dark, small voice whispered in Troy's ear, 'It's the life of you, Mr Troy, the life of you . . .' Bob Churchill, hovering over him like a guardian angel. 'What they can come at you with . . . what they can do to you . . . if . . . if . . .' Troy kicked it behind him. The revolver was Rork's, the Magnum .357. A tap of the foot and Troy sent it skidding across the cobbles until it lay within the reach of Lorcan Ryan.

Troy lowered his own gun, let it hang level with his thigh, finger on the trigger, thumb on the hammer, and said, 'Pick it up.'

For a moment he thought Ryan had not heard him. Then he had gently laid his brother's head on the cobblestones and inched around to face Troy. He put one hand over the butt of the revolver, still looking up at Troy, as if saying, 'We're level now' – watching his face.

Troy was watching his hands. Whatever glint of madness or malice flashed through Ryan's eyes, Troy did not see it. When Ryan's fingers closed on the gun, Troy blew his brains out.

Ryan's whole body rose up with the force of the shot, then crumpled like a saggy balloon, the gun pointing to heaven, and some reflex in the muscles of his hand twitched like a galvanised frog's leg on the trigger – a single bullet spent itself in the breaking sky.

Seconds later Sergeant Kinney had run up to him, red-faced and breathless.

'Bloody hell,' was all he said.

Troy had turned away, looked at the two young constables putting a tourniquet on Robertson's leg, looked at Robertson, conscious, bothered and bewildered, and walked past him.

§ 114

It was a night without sleep, a night without women. Just as well. His leg hurt like hell. And he would have hated to have to explain to any of them. It was a night spent musing, musing on images that he would scarcely have said troubled him, but which, nonetheless, he was incapable of dismissing readily from his mind.

He could see 1944 so clearly. That bitter winter's day out on the bombsite when he had recruited the kids of Stepney Green into an *ad hoc* and, as Bonham had insisted, highly immoral posse – a motley of gabardine mackintoshes, an array of ill-fitting hand-me-downs, outsize jackets tied up with string, brown boots, pudding-basin haircuts, bruised and scabrous kneecaps – eight willing heroes, who saw themselves as Tex Ritter or Gene Autry, galloping to his rescue. All they asked was to be bribed and he had bribed them. He'd never forgotten Shrimp, who had bargained with him over possession of the cartridge case, or Tub, who had found the body in the first place . . . or Carrots, who had juggled a smouldering cocoa tin from hand to hand, and he could remember names like Spud and Plonk and Plug, but until today, if he rolled his mental projector down that row of children, half of the faces would have eluded memory. Now he could see them all – for the first time in fifteen years he could see the two boys who'd stood sixth and seventh, next to the carrot-headed boy with the cocoa tin, a bit bigger than the others, two smirking, nudging twins, who'd seemed throughout to be sharing a private joke, slapping each other, and always on the verge of giggling themselves silly. Robertson had seemed the hard one – withholding information until the last minute, talking to Troy only in private and demanding an outrageous half-crown for what he had to say. The twins had seemed for all the world to be no more than a couple of scallywags who'd seized any excuse for a day off school. Neither of them had even spoken to Troy.

But in his mind's eye – which he knew to be an unreliable organ – Troy could not make the transition from the Ryans of 1944 to the Ryans of 1959, from boys to men, any more than when he'd seen the Ryans at the Empress he had been able to imagine them as kids, from scallywags to murderous thugs, from living to dead.

The dead were never less than grotesque to Troy. It never failed to take him by surprise how immediately the human body lost all resemblance to a living thing once the life had been extinguished. No dead shape ever looked to him like anything that could have lived. The colourless wet corpse that had been Diana Brack, the dead weight, the useless lump of flesh that had been Norman Cobb. As they bled out, both the Ryan brothers had looked like giant crabs, an inhuman contortion, hunched over and twisted, like something you'd find on a beach in an adventure novel, like something you'd tap cautiously with the tip of your boot to see if it still moved . . . like something in *The Coral Island*. But this wasn't *The Coral Island*. This wasn't games with Jack and Ralph. This was . . .

Sergeant Kinney had run up to Troy, panting for breath.

'Bloody hell,' was all he could say, and bloody hell it was. Two spreading puddles of blood that joined into a creeping crimson tide, seeping out across the stones and vanishing into the cracks. Bloody hell.

As Kinney's gasps subsided, Troy became aware of the sound of the river lapping against the stone wall, the creaking arm of a wooden hoist jutting out over the Thames. Then silence. A crystal moment in the light of dawn. The two crabbed bodies in their Savile Row suits, beached upon the cobbles, rockpooled in their own gore.

'He asked for it,' Troy had said simply.

'Been asking for it for fuckin' years,' said Kinney, with no grasp of what Troy had really meant. And Troy had realised that no one would. Whatever it was, murder or mercy, he would get away with it.

Only Mary McDiarmuid had guessed the truth. He could see it in her eyes, hear it in her voice.

Troy sank back into the passenger seat of his Bentley. Closed his eyes. They had plenty of time. A slow drive to Westminster and he would have something to say to Stan. Something economic and plausible.

'Back to the Yard,' he had said to Mary McDiarmuid. 'And let's try sticking to the speed limit, shall we?'

'Are you OK?' Mary McDiarmuid had said.

'OK?'

'How do you feel, Troy?'

'Feel?'

He was not happy. Happy was not the word. He might be content. Content might be the word. He felt . . . no, *it* felt . . . it felt natural. It felt like . . . like what? Like vengeance.

Stan would not have understood . . .

The cricket perched upon his shoulder. An image as unbidden as the others. A voice saying softly over and over again, 'Not like this. You can't leave us like this. Not like this.' Troy flicked it off with a fingernail and thumb.

He slept a couple of hours between seven and nine. When he awoke the voice had gone silent. He never heard from it again.

§ 115

Kolankiewicz offered Troy the 'courtesy' of a look at his report before it went to the inquiry. Troy read it over. It was brief and to the point. The Ryans had died of gunshot wounds: Patrick of two shots to the chest, although the first had been fatal, in that it had pierced the heart, Lorcan from a single shot to the head. Kolankiewicz recorded that he had retrieved all three bullets from the brick wall of the warehouse, and that they were too damaged for identification – but since no one was contesting that Chief Superintendent Troy had shot both the Ryans, this was scarcely a problem. He also reported on the buckshot he had removed from Troy's leg, the buckshot the London Hospital had removed from Robertson's, and the buckshot found in the dockyard wall. There was, he wrote, no trace of any bullet fired by Lorcan Ryan, but without doubt the gun had been fired that night and there were powder residuals on Ryan's hands.

It was a neat sleight-of-hand, thought Troy. Kolankiewicz had avoided any mention of the bore of the bullets in question, and had dismissed as an unspoken norm the fact that three bullets had passed clean through the victims at such a velocity as to destroy themselves in the wall. Six guns had been collected from the armourer, and six returned. Troy had little doubt that the one that had killed the Ryans now lay gathering dust in some drawer in Kolankiewicz's office.

The same day Sir Orrin Mitchell, chief constable of Shropshire, made the journey to London to head the inquiry.

What, Troy thought, this inquiry needed, if truth were its concern, was a man with a mind like a corkscrew. Sir Orrin asked sensible questions, questions without edge or subtlety or deviousness. And Troy answered. He was not wholly sure at first, but by his second interview he was convinced they meant to turn no stones and wanted merely the simplest confirmation of his story.

Troy met Robertson in a corridor at the Yard. The boy walked with a stick. It was as though he and Troy had traded places.

'I'll be OK. It was just a flesh wound. They reckon I'll be back on the job in a few weeks.'

'Does it hurt?' Troy asked.

'Not much. I reckon answering questions'll hurt more.'

'Just tell the truth,' Troy lied.

And when Sir Orrin Mitchell whitewashed Troy to the nation's press, he spoke of 'a long-serving officer' and 'the line of duty' – and of a medal for the boy.

§ 116

They had Jack in the London Hospital in Whitechapel. In the same private ward Troy had been in when Diana Brack had shot him in 1944. He'd been there when the first doodlebugs had fallen. Just to see the room again triggered the memory. The window blowing in, a hundred thousand glass snowflakes showering down across the bed.

Jack was going to recover quickly. He would not go through what Troy had gone through. The first time Troy went to see him he was sitting up in bed eating heartily, surrounded by books and newspapers. The second time he was flirting with a pretty young nurse and had managed to persuade her to part with her home telephone number. The third time he told Troy he would be discharged the following day – all things permitting.

And then he said, 'When did you decide to kill them?'

It occurred to Troy to say nothing, but Jack deserved an answer. 'Dogshit,' Troy whispered, 'coppers, dogshit, coppers.'

'As long ago as that, eh? And when did you decide Mott Kettle was expendable?'

Now Troy said nothing.

§ 117

Troy got home from the hospital to find Kitty installed in his house. Her shoes had been kicked off by the door, her handbag dumped in the middle of the floor, an empty glass stood next to an open bottle of vodka on a side table, and the Erroll Garner record she'd bought him pounded out its concert to no one. He looked up the stairs. A low light on in his bedroom. He went back to the sitting room and turned off the gramophone.

'I was listening to that!'

He'd thought very little about Kitty since her last phone call, and when he had thought about her it had been to wonder if he'd ever see her again. Not in the literal sense of see, but whether they would ever pick up the haphazard relationship where they'd left it. He tried to remember the last time they'd slept together. Had it been the day he'd come clean with her in the Café Royal – sent her storming out and storming back? Was it as long ago as that? Had she spent the last few weeks exclusively with Danny Ryan? Or was Angus still a minor player in her game? Had the trip to Scotland been a mere coincidence? Or . . . why ask? The permutations of possible players in Kitty's game could be little short of infinite.

He went upstairs. She was reading by the light of the bedside lamp.

'What?' he asked, with curiosity born of habit.

She held up a slender paperback, *Death Likes It Hot* by one

336

Edgar Box. A pseudonym if ever he saw one. How did writers make up these things?

'Much more me than anything else you've got. Can't be arsed with all those gloomy Russians – all those -ikovs and -bogovs.'

It was just as well death liked it hot. It was a stinker of a night. Kitty had the windows wide open, and lay with a single sheet tucked under her arms.

Troy sat on the edge of the bed, wondering what she wanted, wondering more what he wanted. He kicked off his shoes, threw his socks into a corner and bought himself time to think with five minutes in the bathroom, but thinking did not come easily. He looked at himself in the mirror, toothbrush sticking out of the corner of his mouth, a dribble of minty toothpaste rolling down his chin, and thought of nothing. He was tired. The strain of the last few days was finally catching up with him. Deceit could be so wearing.

Kitty had put down the book, splayed across the bed.

She peeled back the sheet, first one breast and then the other. A daring gesture in a woman half her age. A daring glint in the green eyes, daring him. She wanted to fuck him. He, he concluded via a process of inertia, wanted to fuck her. Inevitably, then, they would fuck. He wanted the fuck, he wanted the sweat of sex on a muggy night, he wanted to see her pluck her damp hair from his eyes, to feel the release of flooding semen spattering the two of them and sticking them together with unholy glue.

Kitty peeled the sheet back to her thighs and kicked it away. Troy shed his clothes in silence and plunged into the oblivion that was Kitty Stilton.

Many men needed a post-coital cigarette – Troy needed food. He got up and slipped on his trousers.

'Where are you going?'

'Feeling a bit peckish. Going down to the kitchen.'

'Why put your pants on?' Kitty flung off the sheet. 'I can't sleep. Do you have anything like aspirin?'

'If I do it'll be in the kitchen. I'll bring it up.'

Troy found no aspirin and called up. Then he heard the bump of Kitty's feet on the floor, and the sound of her padding downstairs barefoot. 'Bound to be some in my handbag.'

'It's where you left it – in the middle of the floor.'

Troy sliced bread and put together a Cheddar and piccalilli sandwich, the mustard yellow goo almost luminous in the low light.

'Kitty?'

He had heard no feet ascending, no expletives as she turfed out the contents of her bag.

'Kitty?'

'Troy – you'd better come in here.'

Troy stepped into the living room. He could just make out Kitty, stock still by the fireplace, naked and bedraggled.

'Troy . . .'

Danny Ryan stepped out of the darkness of the opposite wall, into a narrow shaft of light from the kitchen. He was clutching an old Second World War German Luger and pointing it at Kitty. Kitty had neither raised her hands nor attempted to cover herself.

'Troy . . .' she said again, faint as a whisper.

Troy stepped between Kitty and Danny.

Danny was shaking, the barrel of the gun waving like barley in a summer breeze, his finger unsteady on the trigger. He was in one of his neat black suits – it looked as though he'd slept in it, but the man himself didn't look as though he'd slept in days. There was a grey stubble on his chin, and a red-eyed tint of madness.

'You shouldn't oughta done it, Troy.'

'Put the gun down and go home, Danny.'

'They was kids. Not much more than kids. You slaughtered them like they was pigs.'

'They were pigs.'

Behind him Kitty said, 'For Christ's sake, Troy.'

Ryan was close to screaming: 'They was kids! Fucked-up kids with no mum and no dad! I gotta do this. You gotta pay.'

'For the last time, Danny, give me the gun and piss off home before it's too late.'

'Troy – please . . . For Christ's sake, he's going to shoot you!'

'No, he's not.'

'I gotta do this. It's family. Family. There's got to be blood.'

Danny held the gun at arm's length, as steady as he could, and aimed it straight at Troy's head. He stepped forward, far too close, far too squeamish, closed his eyes as his finger tightened on the trigger – and Troy snatched the gun from his hand. He flipped out the magazine, threw it one way, threw the gun the other, and decked Danny with a left hook to the jaw. For a big man and an ex-boxer he went down with remarkable ease, crashing to his knees in front of the *chaise longue*.

Troy turned to check on Kitty. She was quiet, goose-pimply, the merest shiver flickering across her torso, gazing past Troy to look at Danny, the green eyes as wide as saucers. Troy knelt down in front of Danny. 'Danny. They were pigs. Neither of them were worth your life or mine. Do you hear me? Pigs.'

'My kid brothers,' Danny said softly.

'Pigs, Danny. Pigs. I've saved you from spending the rest of your life looking out for those two, explaining them, apologising for them, covering up for them and in the end disowning them. If family and blood really mean anything to you, then hold them in your head as they were just before you joined the army in 1940 or when you got out in '46 – and forget everything since.'

Danny took his eyes off the carpet and looked up at Troy. 'Like they was toddlers, like they was eight yearsold?'

The image of a cherubic child, eight years old, reckless beauty, a hand-tinted photograph flashed into Troy's mind. 'Exactly,' he lied.

'But . . . brothers . . . brothers . . . blood.'

'Brothers . . . blood . . . bollocks. You want blood, have some.' Danny was bleeding from the lip where Troy had hit him. Troy reached out, smudged the lip with his thumb and held it up to him. 'You want blood, you got blood. But it's all you're getting.'

He wiped the blood off on Danny's lapel and Danny wept.

Troy had never seen a man weep like this before, but it had been a year of weeping. So many had crouched on the floor in his sitting room in just this position and wept – invariably for themselves. Masha, Foxx, and now Danny. Even Kitty had wept once, had wiped a tear from her eye when first mentioning her mother's death. But she had not wept since and she wasn't weeping now. She was still staring at Danny, but with what Troy took to be pity rather than her usual scorn. They'd been lovers. All summer long they had been lovers, and she stared and did not move. No arms to hold him, not even a healing hand to touch his and let him know he was not alone in the world. She stared and she stared, and did not move until Troy picked up the phone.

'Troy no! You can't! For God's sake, don't turn him in. He's harmless, can't you see that?'

Troy said, 'Could I have a cab to the corner of Goodwin's Court and St Martin's Lane? About five minutes? Fine. Where to?'

He turned to Kitty, 'Where does he live?'

'Narrow Street. He lives in Narrow Street.'

Troy rattled off the address and put the phone down. 'Help me get him up.'

Kitty and Troy each took an arm. Danny felt like the world's largest rag doll, a Looby Loo of grief and inertia. He seemed not even to notice when Troy dragged one arm across his shoulder and hefted him out into the street. Danny's legs kicked in. He walked with Troy almost tucked under one armpit steering him towards the end of the alley. At the first corner, where Goodwin's Court dog-legged round the steps of the last house, Danny swung round to look back at Kitty standing on Troy's doorstep, naked, blank and baffled in the golden light of a streetlamp. Troy saw his lips trying to form words, the slight pout and wide spread of a hard consonant that would not come. Then Troy swung him back and out into the street.

It was less than a minute before a cab pulled up at the kerb.

'What?' said Danny.

'You're going home.'

'Home?'

'Home.'

'But I tried to kill you.'

'No, you didn't.'

Troy tipped him into the back seat, sprawled across the leather with his strings cut. The cabman looked at Danny, looked at Troy – naked from the waist up, barefoot – and leaned across to the window.

'Not pissed is 'e, guv'ner?'

'No,' said Troy. 'See he gets into the house safely. OK?'

Troy found a fiver in his trousers pocket and pressed it into the man's hand.

'Say no more,' said the cabbie.

And Troy sincerely hoped that no one would.

§ 118

It was the last night Troy spent with Kitty. They lay on their wide shores of the bed not touching. The spreading puddle of their intercourse an ocean between them. The only words Kitty had spoken since Troy had sent Danny home were 'That's it. I'm done in, absolutely knackered.' And they'd gone to bed simply to sleep. When he was certain that she was sleeping, Troy slipped from the sheets, went downstairs to the telephone, asked for the international operator and placed a person-to-person call to Washington DC. Frederick Troy to speak to Dick Goldblatt.

§ 119

A couple of days passed. Kitty came and went, came and went. Not her usual pattern, of vanishing all day and turning up in the evenings trailing bags from Harrods or Selfridge's, scrounging change off Troy to pay the taxi. She'd appear in the morning or the middle of the afternoon and showed no inclination to stay the night – Troy thought that perhaps she was simply picking up on his wants and wishes – until the third night, when she came in so late, the intention, to be there by 'accident', was obvious.

'I haven't seen him since, you know.'

Troy had nothing to say to this, so said nothing.

'It's over. It had to end some time, after all.'

To say anything to this was to invite a discussion along the lines of 'And you and me? Are we over?' Troy wanted no such discussion. He had made up his mind days ago.

'Get me a drink, will you, Troy? A vodka. A large vodka. I really need a drink right now.'

He was rummaging under the sink when the telephone rang and Goldblatt's voice said, 'Mr Troy? Dick Goldblatt. I'm at Claridge's. There should be a black cab at the end of your street by now. I have Mrs Cormack's cases packed. The man in the cab will escort her straight to Heathrow.'

Troy went out into the court, looked over his shoulder and called to Kitty. 'Kitty, a moment, if you would.'

'What? Can't it wait until I've had a drink? What's so . . . ?'

Troy walked off towards the end of the alley. Kitty followed, high heels clacking on the paving stones, saying, 'What are you up to? Troy, what's going on?'

There was a black cab, the driver standing by the luggage space where the passenger door should have been. When he saw Troy approach he opened the back door and stood by it uncomfortable, unsure of his pose, neither cabbie nor footman.

'Troy?'

'Get in the cab, Kitty.'

'Eh?'

'Get in the cab.'

Kitty stared at the cab, stared at Troy, and said a simple 'Bollocks!'

She turned and took a step back into Goodwin's Court. Troy seized her hand intending merely to stop her rather than pull her back, but it was she who pulled. One swift jerk on his hand and they had swapped places – Troy with his back to the court, Kitty with her back to the cab; the streetlamp, perched on its iron bracket high on the corner wall, cast a dim yellow light upon her.

Another swift tug and she had him by the shoulders, another and her hands held his head, straining against the light to see his expression.

'What? What do you want?'

He knew she could not see the look in his eyes. He could see hers clearly. Big green emeralds fit to burn holes in his skull. Betrayal.

'What? What do you want from me, Troy?'

And a voice within the cab spoke. 'Kate.'

Kitty's head jerked as though she'd been stung – just a fraction, a movement almost electrical, as though resisting looking over her shoulder – then her head bowed, her forehead touching his. Her hands retraced their ascent, slid to his shoulders, from his shoulders to his arms, gripping tightly as though she was about to shake him as Alice shook the Red Queen. The final onset of reality.

A long, long sigh.

'Oh, God, Troy what have you done? What have you done?'

She wrapped her arms round him. He could not but reciprocate. She whispered in his ear, voice cracking, 'You silly sod; what have you done?'

She kissed him on the ear. It really *was* a kitten after all.

He could not have prised her off, but the strength left her. She left him. Turned her back on him and walked to the cab. Stood stooping, staring into the black interior.

'Kate. Get in. We're going home.'

Troy looked over the curve of her back. Calvin Cormack sat on the edge of the seat, one arm outstretched to Kitty. Troy had not set eyes on Cormack since the war. He'd lost all his hair now, gained a few pounds in weight – and the sadness in his eyes matched the sadness Troy had found in Kitty's the day she had turned up on him in London all those weeks ago.

'Kate. Please get in.'

She took his hand. Delicately, none of the ferocity with which she had held on to Troy – fingertips barely touching. It was like ballet: he pulled on the invisible thread, she flowed in beside him. There was no embrace. She took her seat next to him, looked once at Troy then turned her head away. Cormack, too, looked at Troy, the sadness overwhelming now, smiled once, seemed about to speak but didn't. Then the cabman closed the door, muttered, 'Evenin', guv'ner', and in seconds the cab rolled away down St Martin's Lane. Troy watched it as far as Trafalgar Square. As it passed the Duke of York's theatre half a dozen bulbs burst in the illuminated sign, showering the cab in a fine rain of broken glass.

Troy went home. Put the vodka back under the sink. Lifted the piano lid and played through Brubeck's 'Blue Rondo A La Turk'. Note-perfect. For the first time. Note-perfect. But what was note-perfect in jazz? Lifeless. No brilliant corners. It don't mean a thing if it ain't got . . . He recalled his wife's definition of jazz – 'Bum notes that work' – and closed the lid.

§ 120

Troy liked the open door. It was a characteristic he'd inherited from his mother. Once the weather was tolerably warm the door to the house would be propped open. She'd even done this with the Hampstead house in his childhood, oblivious to the risk. He supposed he did it to let light and air into what was, after all, a poky little house forged out of the structure of a Georgian shop – indeed, it still had the shopfront – but part of him wanted the serendipity of street life, to see who might pass, who might look in, who might drop in. It was the natural nosiness that had made him a copper in the first place.

He was organising himself early in the evening of 8 October to drive out to Mimram and vote. He had never registered in London and always voted for his brother. For a year or two after the war he had even been a member of the Labour Party out of nothing more than loyalty to Rod. What he could never dare to tell him was that he'd let his membership lapse. He was searching for his car keys when he heard a footfall on his doorstep, and turned to see his sister Masha, a large shopping bag of groceries at her feet, a nervous smile upon her lips. It was unlike her ever to buy anything so practical as food. She shopped, but always for clothes, always for herself. Troy could see a tin of baked beans in tomato sauce on top of the bag. He'd never known Masha to buy baked beans in her life. It was prosaic. It was dull. It was ordinary. Masha didn't do ordinary.

Curious.

'Expecting rationing to make a comeback, are we?'

'I have a larder to fill. A family to feed.'

And curiouser.

'Eh?'

'I'm taking Lawrence back.'

'Really?'

'I'm taking Lawrence back. Good bloody grief, that's the wrong way round, isn't it? I drive him away. He has an affair, the only affair of his married life, at a time when I think I've lost count of all my infidelities to him. But that's the way it is – he's asked me to take him back. I should be begging him to take me back.'

'So he and Anna have—'

'I didn't ask what had happened. But I rather think it's been over for a week or two. Do you think she'll take it badly?'

'I wouldn't know,' said Troy.

'Ten or more years of an on-off affair and you don't know how she reacts to breaking up?'

Troy said nothing.

'I'll try to make it work. I'll try to be everything I haven't been these last twenty years. A wife to my husband, a mother to my children. Do you know, it never occurred to me to think how the kids reacted to my behaviour? Lawrence had to walk out before I saw the look in their eyes. Katya's fourteen now. I doubt there's much about her parents' behaviour that escapes her. I've been so bad, so very, very bad. It amazes me that she doesn't pass judgement on me. Although there was implicit judgement in her words when Lawrence left. "Don't worry," she said. "Daddy's not like you." If I'd been using half my brain when she said that I should have been scalded. Once I knew what she meant, how she saw me, I was scalded. I've done rotten things, you know.'

Of course he knew.

'I rather think it's part of being one of two. Together Sasha and I were capable of things we might not have dared separately. I suppose I should have seen the writing on the wall long ago. She and Hugh drove each other mad. He was barking long before the end and she's not much better now. I think I conspired with her to make him mad. All the lies I told for her, all the lies she told for me, all the times I pretended to be her. But, you know, Freddie, she isn't me. I knew that once and for all at the poor bugger's funeral. I just couldn't admit it. We who were one weren't any more. I could feel her peel away like a snake sloughing off the old skin. Perhaps she'll spend the rest of her life on the fragile branch of her own lunacy. Perhaps Lawrence and I still stand the chance she and Hugh never gave each other. Perhaps I had to do something so completely rotten, so utterly unspeakable that it would be enough to make me stop. To make me see myself for what I am.'

'The road to Damascus?' said Troy.

'No, that was St Paul and seeing God and all that, wasn't it?'

'I don't think there was much that was saintly about the man until that moment.'

'Then perhaps that is it. Road to Damascus it is. And you?'

'I haven't seen the blinding light, if that's what you mean. I haven't heard Jiminy Cricket chirp in my ear either.'

'Really, Freddie? After what you've just done?'

'When you said we shouldn't tell anyone I agreed with you. Silently, but agree I did. I also rather thought that meant we wouldn't be discussing it either.'

'I wasn't talking about the night we spent together, Freddie. I can only blame myself for that. You, as ever, were passive in your consent, as I often think you are in all your morality. Your trick is to let things happen. To let things take their course. I've known quite a few of your girlfriends say exactly that over the years. "Freddie doesn't try too hard", "Freddie never comes to you, you have to go to him" – that sort of thing. I wasn't talking about us at all. I was talking about those two blokes you killed in the East End.'

'As I said, Masha, I have seen no blinding light. If I live to be a hundred I doubt my conscience will ever twinge about the Ryans.'

When she'd gone, kissed him sisterly upon the cheek and left with her new burden, Troy scribbled a note to Anna at her house in Bassington Street and dropped it into the pillar box in Bedfordbury: 'Get over him. And when you do, call me. T.'

§ 121

Troy drove out to Mimram. It was the first time he'd driven without Mary McDiarmuid since the night Rork had been killed. It was not like riding a bike – he had forgotten so much of what natural drivers liked to take as instinct. He heard himself crunching through gear changes, and learned from the honking of half a dozen motorists on the North Circular Road that his steering was none too good either. But it had symbolic value – to be back at the wheel of his own car, with no need for glasses and to drive as badly as the law allowed.

The polling station at which his card told him to present himself was the Blue Boar in Mimram village. The political machine had taken over the snug, a room scarcely big enough for the job – a good queue would see people lined up into the street, just as there were now. He found himself standing behind Frank Trubshawe, clutching his helmet as if it was a flowerpot full of something precious. Troy peeked over – it was full of leeks, freshly dug and caked with earth. Trubshawe had been harvesting them. They were early this year. Troy's didn't look as though they'd be ready for Christmas. Trubshawe turned to see who was being so nosy, looked at Troy, looked up at the gathering clouds in the dusky sky and said, 'Looks like it's finally breaking.'

Troy looked up. He was right. The heatwave and the Indian Summer that had blended almost seamlessly into it were coming to an end with the brewing of a mighty storm, a burgeoning mass of bulbous nimbostratus, glowing silver at the edges, that threatened at any moment to form a face to huff and puff with.

'Never known a year like it,' Trubshawe said, then added, 'Of course I have, roaring summers, baking summers, but you know what I mean. It's been a year this has.'

'Indeed I do, Mr Trubshawe. It has been a year.'

Troy wondered if Trubshawe would make any reference to the matters they might be deemed to have in common, the 'ambergooities', which had made the year what it was far more than the weather had, but he didn't. He was off-duty, and it was typical of Trubshawe to have a clearly defined sense of on and off duty. When Troy suggested they move round to the public and have a drink Trubshawe, being off duty, agreed, and they passed an hour discussing what little else they had in common: the cultivation of the leek – Trubshawe had taken first prize with his leeks at the last Mimram horticultural show, and Troy had managed the feat the year before; the husbandry of the pig – Trubshawe lined up with Lord Emsworth in keeping Whites; and the quality of the local brew, in which Troy successfully faked an interest.

Troy wondered if the taking off of the copper's helmet had not been just for a handy receptacle, not just the mereness of symbolism, whether Trubshawe might not have developed a trick Troy had never managed at any point of his life both before and since he had become a copper: could out of sight really be out of mind?

He was home well before ten. He knew the way things were going for Labour, and thought better of putting on the television. It was still 'new' and he had not and never would get used to it. He lit a fire in his study, switched the wireless to the Third Programme – a concert recorded the month before at the end of the Henry Wood Proms, snippets of Delius, *A Song of Summer* and one of those things he wrote in Florida that still sounded more English than American, that made Troy think of that last, lazy, casual, illicit, erotic night with Foxx – no, out of sight was almost never out of mind. He settled back in an armchair, saw the black clouds roll by his window, heard Delius drowned in thunder, rain pelting down like shrapnel on the rooftops, waited for the greater storm to burst within the hustings.

Cid came in just after midnight. 'I've had enough. I made my excuses and left.'

'I'm sure Rod can stand on a podium without you.'

'I feel rotten about it. You know, loyal wifie at his side as he makes his victory-cum-thank-you speech and all that. God knows, I've done that every time since – when? 1950? But not tonight. Not the mood he's in. I left Nattie behind with a rosette and told her to look supportive. In a bad light the press might even think she's me. You know, it's at times like this it crosses my mind – how much more of this can I put up with? I have fantasies of "Nice day at the office, dear?" "Oh, yes, Spiggot and I ordered a job lot of paperclips and Wiggins has been promoted to regional manager," and I say, "Jolly good darling. It's Cook's day off so I caught the 12.15 into Chipping Bumley, had lunch at the Kardomah, changed my library books, bumped into Mary Moppet, bought a leg of lamb, came home and made shepherd's pie. It'll be ready in half an hour." And then I put his slippers on for him and he does *The Times* sodding crossword over a dry sherry and the whole world starts to look like the closing scenes from *Brief Encounter*, "Oh, Cid, you're such a silly old sausage" – anything, anything so mundane, anything so cripplingly, mind-rottingly normal would be better than having to go through all this . . . all this . . . all this fucking shit.'

It was so unlike his sister-in-law to speak 'Troy'. She had wrestled with the words before giving in to them, and when she had she reminded him of no one quite so much as Kate Cormack. 'Would you like a drink?'

'No, Freddie. I'd like to go to bed and wake up to find we're in power at last. But that isn't going to happen so I'll settle for a good night's sleep instead. They're expecting a result before three. If you're staying up, try and keep Rod up until rage has given way to guilt. Let normal service resume. He's always more amenable when he's feeling guilty.'

'You married the right brother. I don't do guilt.'

'So you tell me. Night-night, Freddie.'

Rod came home in fury at two-thirty in the morning. 'We're going to lose. We're going to fucking lose!'

'But you're OK? You won?'

'I won, Labour's lost. What bloody use is that?'

Troy had a bottle of Château Margaux Grand Cru 1945 uncorked and breathing by the fire. He handed a glass to Rod. 'Drown your sorrows.'

Rod took one swig and kept right on course. 'Three victories in a row, and each time the buggers increase their majority. That's – that's unprecedented. What the bloody hell do we have to do to get elected? What do we have to do? If we promise them jam tomorrow then we're tight-fisted Reds asking them to pay for a future they can't even imagine. If we say jam today, then they tell us we're cooking the books and can't possibly pay for jam today without asking them to pay higher taxes. What do the British want? What do we have to do?'

'Have you thought of changing your name to "the Conservative Party"?'

'Freddie, if all you can do is take the piss I'm going to knock your fucking block off!'

'No, there's two things I can do. I can pour wine and I can vote. I came up to vote for you, if you recall.'

Rod swigged, handed his glass back to Troy, said, 'Fill 'er up, waiter,' and flopped into an armchair, wrestling with his tie. When it came loose he leaped up again, tore off both tie and jacket, stamped on both and flopped back down with his hand out for the wine glass. 'And I'm grateful, believe me, I'm grateful. It's just that's it's all so . . . fucking deadly.'

Troy sat down opposite. It was too good a claret to swig. He rolled it around on his tongue, hoping Rod would slow down and get rat-arsed at a more civilised pace.

'You know – it was Ike. He fucked it for us. Macmillan got a joint telly broadcast. All I got was a lawn littered with fucking golf balls. Ike made him look like . . . Like what, for God's sake?'

'A statesman.'

'That's it. A statesman. What every sodding PM wants to be – more than a politician, a statesman. And Ike handed it to Mac on a plate.'

'Perhaps next time you should get the President to come over and root for you.'

'Next time. 1964? Good God, Freddie, that's like a science-fiction number. 1964 isn't five years away, it's an age away. We'll all be bloody robots by then – tin hearts, tin brains, tin cocks. 1964 – Jesus Christ! Do you know, I can still remember the first year I was conscious of having a tag to it. I was five. I'd drifted through life, the longest part of life, it seems, with the outside world scarcely touching me. Knew it was there, out there on the horizon somewhere, things like the King dying – the old man took me to watch the parade . . . Can't remember a sodding thing about it, wish I could, the Kaiser was there, the Tsar, all those Balkan monarchs who got kyboshed – but, no, the first year I can remember as a year is 1914. I remember asking him, "Dad, what year is it?" and the answer, "1914, my boy. The second of January." '

'Hardly a year to forget.'

'Quite. But I'm telling you now that all that pre-1917 stuff seems to me a damn sight closer than the prospect of 1964. What a preposterous bloody date.'

Rod reminded him of Kate Cormack. He was sure she'd said something very like this, some sad song of the creeping tread of time.

'You'd think the world would end before we got to a figure as crazy as that. Yet that's our next crack at getting into power. Unbelievable, un-fucking-believable. We'll still have Mac bumbling his way through his repertoire like George Robey on tour, a trunkful of daft hats and comic trousers – and the Americans'll have Cormack or Nixon. Men in their forties. A whole new generation. We'll look like fucking dinosaurs.'

'Well, it might be Nixon, if Ike comes out for him.'

'Ike hates Nixon. If Nixon were on fire Ike wouldn't piss on him.'

'But it won't be Cormack.'

'Aah, I see. You have inside information?'

Troy said nothing.

They'd got halfway down the third bottle, Rod very much the worse for wear, maudlin and dishevelled, well on the road to guilt, when he said, 'Shpoon.'

'What about him?'

'What do you intend to do? You're surely not going to leave thingsh as they . . . are?'

'It all depends if you win or lose.'

Rod waved a hand across the space between them as though cutting ribbons – slicing through the ambiguity. 'We've already lost. The country has gone to hell in a handcart. We are . . . bolloxed. Banjaxed, buggered and bolloxed.'

'You will agree – a spook, and at that a spook of dubious sexual mores, in opposition is one thing. In the Cabinet quite another.'

'Sho, you'll shay nothing?'

'Rod, let us agree – we both of us underestimated Ted Steele. We looked at the rubbish in the papers and we took him at face value. OK – he asked for that. He cried out to be "Lord Spoon" and we stuck it to him. He worked as hard at the image of the self-made man who knows how to spend money as he did at making the money in the first place. We all fell for the illusion he spun round the dreadfully vulgar wife and her twice-time vulgar car. But . . . there was more to him than that. He'd been through more than we either of us knew. More than we cared to imagine. And it didn't even dawn on me until the night I had him sitting in here, the evening of Ike's reunion, refusing to answer my questions. It had never occurred to me that this might by no means be the worst interrogation Spoon had suffered. Stupid of me. There he was, chatting to Mala Caan, and we both knew what her experience of the war was, we both know how she earned her VC. Spoon was far, far tougher than I'd ever guessed. Yet . . . the Ryans terrified him. He told me so when we went upstairs. He'd no idea they killed the boys they brought him just for sport. But he knew they'd kill him if they didn't get what they wanted. He was more scared of them than he ever had been of the Gestapo. He told me what they were up to, and then he made it perfectly clear he'd go to jail before he'd testify against them. He said he'd faced SS thugs armed with pliers and a blow-lamp and felt less scared. But it wasn't just words. It wasn't just what he was telling me. He rolled up his shirt and showed me the scar tissue down his spine where the Gestapo had taken a blow-lamp to him. Burns the size of half-crowns. Made his back look like the twelve spot in dominoes. And he took off his shoes and showed me the toes they'd broken with pliers. He spared me the dropping of his trousers to show me where they'd crushed one of his balls. I took his word for that. He said the only key to surviving was to convince them you knew nothing. He did. They stopped pulling him to pieces, and stuck him on a train to Belsen, from which he escaped. And when he'd finished telling me all this, he said, "What else can you do to me, Mr Troy? What can you do that is worse than the Gestapo, that is worse than Patrick and Lorcan Ryan?"'

Rod uttered a sotto voce 'Jesus Christ.'

'Now, in its way the same may be true of old Bobby Collington – they scared him shitless is the cliché – and what the deal was with Maurice, we'll never know. Maurice would be a hard man to intimidate, but we all have our breaking point. I saw Spoon's that night – I've never seen emotional collapse and self-control in such equal measures before.

'The upshot of all this is that the decision isn't mine, it's yours. Spoon has been a spy for someone all his life. It's his *modus operandi*. He doesn't know any other. In that sense he's no different from tens of thousands of others who lived through the war. What they did then has achieved the level of an addiction. They do what they do because they can do no other. I suspect the Americans don't think much of him as a spy, but it's enough of what used to be to satisfy the craving he has. You're a bit like that yourself. Part of you is still Wing Commander Troy. No bad thing at all. But it's perverse in Spoon. It's an addiction. To spy is what makes him what he is. It's become his identity. Money, fame, success – God knows he has all three aplenty – all those are insignificant compared to the sheer frisson of the secret life that spying confers upon him. I'd even venture, despite all the assurances I've had as to the reality of his homosexuality – he is no mere dabbler, after all – that the appeal for him lies in the fact that such sex must always be secret sex. He enjoys the clandestine world of the bugger and enjoys just as much the lies of a marriage lived in public. The presentation of a false front to the world. He's a foreigner who passes for English, the queer who passes for married, the member of Her Majesty's House of Lords who serves a foreign republic. A spy down to his socks. You and I used to joke that he was probably the only Labour MP who voted Tory. The joke's on us. Nothing about the man was real.

'There are still only half a dozen people who know he's a spy – you, Gaitskell and me, and three members of my team at the Yard who read the letter I showed you. The letter isn't in any Scotland Yard file, it's in my desk drawer just over there. Your secret can stay a secret. I have no case against Spoon that I would ever wish to bring. But it remains – he's a prime candidate for blackmail. Do you really think this mad scheme will work? Do you think Spoon is consistent enough or simple enough to be an unwitting conduit? Do you really want him anywhere near power? For that matter do you want him anywhere near your party? The ball, as the Americans say, is in your court.'

Rod said nothing. A rare enough event in itself.

§ 122

Troy woke to a nudging hand. The Fat Man was towering over him with a cup of black coffee held out to him. 'I made for both of you,' he said.

Troy looked across the room. Rod was slumped in the armchair by the last-glowing embers of the night's fire, mouth open, drooling and schnucking.

'It's the business. The ground-up stuff. None o' that instant muck you're too polite to say you don't like.'

Troy followed the Fat Man out to the verandah, and down in the direction of the pigpens. He looked at his watch – he had been too drunk to remember to wind it and it had stopped in the night. He looked up at the sky. It was ripe with the bulbous clouds of autumn. Not a hint of the sun.

'What time is it?'

'Half past eight.'

'Is anyone else up?'

'I think your sister-in-law's been up a while. I saw her pegging out some washing.'

'How did she seem?'

'She was singing "The Red Flag". Y' know "cowards flinch and traitors sneer" and blah-de-blah, but every other word was that f-word you lot seem so fond of. I don't think she meant any of it, 'cept the f-words, that is. I think it might be that irony thing you keep trying to explain to me and I don't ever seem to get the 'ang of.'

'I'm sure it was,' said Troy.

'You stayin' long, cock?'

'No. My suspension's over, but Onions has insisted on me taking a few days' compassionate. All the same, I have to get back today. Unfinished business, you know . . . that sort of thing.'

'Fine,' said the Fat Man. 'Don't tell me. See if I care. I've better things to do 'ere. Did I tell you the pig's learnt how to balance a parsnip on the end of 'er snout?'

'Thin end or thick end?'

'Thin end, o'course. This is a class act, this pig is.'

They arrived at the tree under which Cissie the pig habitually sat. The Fat Man delved into a capacious trouser pocket and pulled out a ten-inch parsnip, much in the same way that a beat bobby extracted his truncheon. He tossed it into the air, the pig watched it cartwheel through space, leapt forward and stuck out her snout to catch the parsnip and hold it balanced by the thick end.

'Ah, well,' said the Fat Man, 'Nobody's perfect.'

'Now, where have I heard that line before?' said Troy.

§ 123

Once it had begun to rain, it did not stop. October became a sodden vengeance for the summer heat, rain pelting down on London rooftops, rattling the sashes and filling the gutters. It had been raining like this the first night he set eyes on Foxx. Jeans and T-shirt. Soaked to the skin, banging on his door – just as she was now.

Troy took her by the chin as she stepped over the threshold. A black eye, a split lip, and a broken tooth.

The tears were silent tears – no sobs, no throwing herself on his shoulder. A simple 'If you feel like telling me what a fool I've been, now would be a good moment.'

'Christy?'

'Just when you think you've got to know a man . . .'

'Where is he?'

'Oh . . . on his way to Heathrow, he's booked out on the late Pan Am to New York.'

'Do you want a doctor?'

'No. And certainly not the Polish Beast. I'll see my dentist tomorrow.'

'It looks bad.'

'Flesh wounds, Troy.'

'Does it?'

'Ha-bloody-ha.'

Troy kissed the split lip. 'Go and clean up.'

When he heard the bath filling Troy called Swift Eddie at the Yard. 'Eddie, get on to the airport police. Tell them to arrest Vince Christy, an American booked for New York on the Pan Am late. Possible alias Cristofero da Vinci. Tell them to bung him in the cells overnight. No kid gloves. No favours. We'll sort out a warrant first thing in the morning.'

'And the charge, sir?'

'Oh . . . let's start with Grievous Bodily Harm, shall we?'

§ 124

In the middle of the night Troy got up for water and heard snoring from the sitting room. A large ginger man was stretched out on the sofa. In the middle of the floor was a tin leg. Taped to the tin leg was a note.

```
To my good fortune you forgot to lock
the door last night. Hence you find me
here.
    Don't dash off in the morning, there's
a couple of things we need to chat
about.
    The wife - obviously - but also what
you said the last time about 'You cannot
change yourself, you can only change.'
That was what you said, wasn't it? Or
was it the booze talking to me?
    Whatever - been giving it a lot of
thought, especially in the light of the
way you've just grabbed the headlines.
    We cannot change ourselves. You're
right, of course. But we change on
a daily basis, do we not? For what
is character, if not the sum of our
actions? We are what we do, and what we
```

do changes on the quotidian.

Suppose for a moment that there were no limits to a man's actions. Suppose you could get away with anything. A man without limits would become a monster. A Frankenstein unbound, remaking himself out of his own being. Not from the flesh but from the spirit. It does prompt the question, doesn't it? What are your limits, Troy?

Ho hum bum. Just a thought, really. I'll sleep on it.

Come to think of it, it all sounds a bit Faustian more than Frankensteinian, doesn't it? Be a good point at which to quote you a bit of Goethe but, truth to tell, I can't remember a single sodding word the bloke ever wrote.

Ah, well, tant pis.

Yrs

Angus

James

Montrose

Tobermory

Pakenham

Redhead of this Parish,

War hero

Chartered Accountant

&

Failed Parliamentary Candidate.

PS My hollow leg appears to be genuinely hollow for the time being – where did you hide the Talisker?

Troy read it, was about to bin it, but instinctively turned it over to see what was on the other side.

```
┌─────────────────────────────────────────────┐
│         Parliamentary Constituency            │
│          of Eigg, Muck, Rhum &                │
│          Ardnamurchan (North)                 │
│                    ☆                          │
│      Your Independent Jam Candidate           │
│             Angus Pakenham                     │
│                    ☆                          │
│             Vote Pakenham                      │
│             on 8 October                       │
│    The Other Blokes Are All Scoundrels!       │
└─────────────────────────────────────────────┘
```

. . . and there followed what appeared to be Angus's political manifesto, headed:

Jam Today, Jam Tomorrow, Jam Forever.

Troy binned it unread and went back to bed, back to the pale, pleasing curves of a bloody, broken Foxx. The living woman pressed flesh upon his flesh; all the dead ones pinballed full tilt through his mind.

Historical Note

The most important thing I've changed is no real change, it's something that just happens – time gets compressed. The plot of this novel takes from May to October 1959. In particular the weeks of August and September get telescoped. Ike's visit began on 27 August and lasted ten days. The Wartime Reunion is real enough but was given by Ike rather than for him, at the US Embassy. The next day when Ike had left Macmillan announced the General Election. Parliament was dissolved ten days later and the election held on 8 October – the first I can remember in any detail, and in which I delivered countless leaflets on behalf of a now defunct party that got hijacked by the talking suits in the 1990s, who, at the time of writing, have just led us into a third war in six years. (I had thought nothing would ever top the Macmillan government for lies, sleaze and backstabbing . . .) Where was I? Ah . . . What I describe as taking place after Ike's departure would take a matter of days not weeks. I'm not conscious of having changed anything else. It was a very dry summer, Russ Conway did make number one in the pop charts . . . and, from less than ridiculous to the certain sublime, Time Out did become the fastest selling Jazz record in history.

The most useful books I found in the course of research were Eric Rumsey's *The Dockland Gangs* (Weidenfeld & Nicolson, 1960), Rossi and Lambert's *Scotland Yard: Shoot to Kill?* (Eyre & Spottiswoode, 1959) and Race and Marks's *Teach an Old Pig New Tricks* (Werner Laurie, 1947).

Acknowledgements

I wrote most of this novel in the high, wet hills of Derbyshire and rewrote it on the New York Subway mostly back and forth between Manhattan and Brooklyn. If coffee and cake called, then bits of it got rewritten in the back room of *Ceci Cela* at Spring and Lafayette in Little Italy. Hence I think it fitting that I should acknowledge the witting assistance of . . . Zette Emmons and Sarah Teale (roof over my head), Gordon Chaplin (desk space), John Fagan and Linda Shockley (unflagging encouragement), Frank Lawton (whizzes and bangs), Clare Alexander, Ion Trewin and Anna Hervé (tweaks and turns) . . . and the unwitting assistance of the New York Metropolitan Transit Authority and the blokes who run *Ceci Cela* . . . Herve, Laurent *et* Dominic – and waitresses with the patience of saints.

Read on for a preview of

SECOND VIOLIN

VIOLIN

The next
INSPECTOR TROY
novel by

JOHN LAWTON

§

Under moonlight
a madman dances.

§ I

12 March 1938
Hampstead, London

Yellow.

It was going to be a yellow day.

The nameless bird trilling in the tree outside his window told him
that. He had learnt too little of the taxonomy of English flora and fauna
to be at all certain what the bird was. A Golden Grebe? A Mustard
Bustard? He took its song as both criticism and compliment – 'cheek,
cheek, cheek'.

Fine, he thought, if there's one thing I have in spades it's cheek. Do
I need a bird to tell me that?

He watched its head bobbing, heard again the rapid chirp – now more
'tseek' than 'cheek', and was wondering if he had a yellow tie somewhere
for this yellow day and whether it might sit remotely well with his suit,
when Polly the housemaid came in.

'My dear, tell me . . . what is this bird in the tree here?'

'Boss . . . there's bigger fish to fry than some tom tit–'

He cut her short.

'There, do you see? In the cherry tree. The one with the yellow
breast.'

'Boss . . . I'm a Londoner. Born, bred and never been further than
Southend. Sparrers is me limit. Just call it a yeller wotsit and listen to me.'

He turned. It was typical of her to be so casual in her dealings with him, untypical of her to find anything so urgent. It was as though she'd seized him by his lapels.

'Yes?'

''Itler's invaded Austria. It was on the wireless you know. The missis sent me to tell you.'

The missis was his wife. Time there was, and not that long ago, when he would have learnt of such things not by his wife sending in the maid, but by a phone call from his Fleet Street office at whatever time of day or night, deskside or bedside. On his seventy-fifth birthday he had told his editors, 'History can now wait for me.' Usually history waited until he had his first cup of coffee in his hand.

'Do you want me to turn the set on in here, Boss?'

'Yes, my dear. Please do that.'

It was indeed a yellow day. What other colour has cowardice ever had? It was all too, too predictable. Hitler had signalled his punches like a feinting boxer. He had had his editorial ready for a month now, ever since Hitler and Schuschnigg had met at Berchtesgaden in the middle of February for Schuschnigg's ritual humiliation – 'I am the greatest German that ever lived!' . . . so much for Goethe, so much for Schiller, for Luther and Charlemagne, for Beethoven and Bach. He'd listen to the next bulletin on the wireless, and if nothing forced a change upon him, and he doubted that it would, he'd take the editorial out of his desk drawer and have a cab take it to Fleet Street for the evening edition. All it needed was his signature . . . a rapid flourish of the pen and, in the near-cyrillic of his handwriting, the words 'Alexei Troy'.

§ 2

14 March
Vienna

The Führer took his triumphant time getting to Vienna. There was his hometown of Linz to be visited, embraced, captured on the road to Vienna. The town from which, as he put it himself, Providence had called him. He drove through streets gaily decked out with the National Socialist flag – red and black can be so striking in its simplicity – past cheering citizens, gaily decked out in green jackets and lederhosen.

In the second car SD Standartenführer Wolfgang Stahl, a fellow Austrian, wondered where they got it all from. As though some wily rag-and-bone man had been round the week before with a job lot of old coats and leather britches. It seemed to him to be parody, to be bad taste, to be Austria's joke at its own expense. All this, all of it, would be at Austria's expense. It was simply that Austria didn't know it.

It was past lunchtime on the following day before the entourage rolled into Vienna. Hitler was in a foul mood. The motorcade had broken down. Not just the one vehicle but dozens had ground to a halt with mechanical failure. It looked half-arsed. And the trick to invading without a shot fired, to taking a country that was all too willing to capitulate, was to look wholly-arsed, as though you could have taken them by force if you so desired. The Wehrmacht was untested in the field. Any failure now sent out the wrong signal to the fair-weather friends of Austria and Czechoslovakia. The world was watching. That nincompoop Chamberlain was watching. Entering Vienna, they crossed a bridge that had been mined. Schellenberg had inspected the device personally, taken a gamble with their lives, thought better of telling this to Hitler, and mentioned it to Stahl only as a problem solved. It was just as well. The bad mood did not lift. Hitler accepted the adulation of the crowds in the Heldenplatz, scowled through the reception at the Hofburg Palace and flew on to Munich the next morning. Country captured, country visited, Secret Police installed. Next.

Stahl stayed. The SS was already rounding up suspects, tormenting Jews and murdering discreetly as a preamble to murdering indiscreetly. Neither was his job. Himmler and Schellenberg had flown in ahead of the convoy at first light. Heydrich, flash as ever, had flown in in his own private plane, meditating on his plans for Austria's first concentration camp. They had gilded thugs aplenty, thugs in oak leaves, thugs in lightning, thugs in black and silver. Stahl was just an ornament. He'd been invited to Vienna, his native city, merely as part of the Führer's sense of triumphalism. He'd been presented to the Viennese as a prodigal son, someone not quite called by Providence, which only had room for one, but touched by it. The hand of fate that had grabbed Adolf Hitler, had brushed the sleeve of Wolfgang Stahl. Others stayed on simply because the pickings were too rich – not simply what could be stolen, but what could be bought. The department stores of Vienna were so much better stocked than those in Berlin. Stahl had in his pocket a handwritten note from Hermann Göring – 'Could you get me a dozen winter woollen underpants from Gerngross's, waist 130 cm?'

Stahl stayed because Vienna fixed him, fixed him and transfixed him as surely as if it had struck out, stabbed him and pinned him to the wall. He could not help Vienna in her suffering, and at the same time he could not resist watching as she suffered.

§ 3

14 March
Berlin

TELEGRAMME : TROYTOWNLON

TO : TROYTOWNBER

ATT: ROD TROY

MY BOY, DO YOU NOT THINK IT TIME YOU CAME HOME?

THIS IS, DARE I SAY, A JACKBOOT TOO FAR.

DO NOT WAIT FOR WAR. COME BACK NOW.

COME BACK TO YOUR WIFE AND YOUR FAMILY.

YOUR LOVING FATHER,

ALEX TROY.

Rod showed the telegramme to Hugh Greene in Kranzler's restaurant at lunchtime.

'I can't say I'm always getting them. But it's not the first and it won't be the last. Thing is … the old man never wanted me to come out in the first place.'

In 1933, when the Nazis had taken power, Rod had been just short of his twenty-fifth birthday and had been three years a parliamentary correspondent on his father's *Sunday Post*. He begged his father for the Berlin posting. In the September the old man had finally agreed and Rod had presented himself to the Press Office of the National Socialist

Workers' Party and the British Embassy as the new Berlin Correspondent for the Troy Press. The Germans had looked askance at his authentication, but said nothing. The embassy had said in one of those subtle walls-have-ears tones, 'You're taking one hell of a risk, old boy.'

Greene echoed the line now, 'Your father has a point. You don't have the protection I have.'

Greene had come to Berlin, via Munich, for the *Daily Telegraph* the February after Rod. He was younger than Rod by nearly three years, and taller by more than three inches. They had been 'absolute beginners' together, often sharing what they knew. Rod revelled in the languid mischief that Greene seemed to exude, the nascent wickedness of the man. It reminded him more than somewhat of his younger brother. Much as he was loth to admit it, there were times when he missed his brother. Even more he mised his wife. She had joined him a few weeks after the posting and, like the colonial wife in Nigeria or Sierra Leone, she had returned home for the birth of their first child in 1936, and was home now expecting the second.

'If I have to weigh that one up every time Hitler pushes the country to the brink, I might as well go home and become the gardening columnist reporting on outbreaks of honey fungus and the private life of the roving vole.'

'Questing vole, surely?' said Greene. '"Something something through the plashy fens goes the questing vole".'

Rod ignored this.

'What matters, what matters now is that I should be here. My father doesn't see that. I should be here. So should you.'

'Quite. Except, of course, that we should both be in Vienna.'

§4

Martha showed every courtesy to the SS thugs who had burst into her dining room. Gesturing to the table, where she had piled up her housekeeping money, she invited them to 'help themselves' as though it were a plate of sandwiches and they guests for afternoon tea. They stuffed their pockets like beggars at a banquet. Then they stared. They had probably never been in an apartment quite like this in their lives.

Could they feel the burden of dreams?

Martha's daughter, Anna, sensing that they would not be satisfied with the best part of a week's housekeeping, knowing that they undoubtedly subscribed to the Nazi notion that all Jews were misers and slept on mattresses stuffed with banknotes, went into the other room, beckoned for them to follow and opened the safe for them. 'Help yourselves, gentlemen' – to six thousand schillings.

Even this was not enough. They hesitated at the door to her father's study – she would have little choice but to step between them and block the way with her own body – when the door opened and a diminutive, white-haired, white-bearded man appeared before them, glaring at them silently with the eyes of Moses, the eyes of Isaiah, the eyes of Elijah. Behind him they could see row upon row of books, wall to wall and floor to ceiling, more books than they had ever thought existed. The old man said nothing. He was a good foot shorter than the biggest of the SS men, and still he stared at them. Did they know these eyes saw into the depths of man?

'We'll be back,' they said. And left.

Could they feel the burden of dreams?

§ 5

The next day Professor Nicholas Lockett, of King's College, London, a lanky Englishman so English his furled umbrella remained furled in the worst of weathers, a man possessed of size 12 and a half feet, a man passionate about his subject, arrived in Berggasse expressly charged by the Psychoanalytic Society of Great Britain to impress upon Sigmund the necessity of leaving. Sigmund needed impressing.

He stretched back on the wide, red chenille-covered couch reserved for his patients, stared at the ceiling and said.

'My dear Lockett, I am too . . . old.'

'Nonsense . . . you are . . .'

'. . . Incapable of kicking my leg high enough to get into bed in a wagon-lit!'

'You are Psychoanalysis. Where you are . . . it is. The Society is a moveable feast.'

'Alas, Vienna is not. It is quite securely fixed to the banks of the Danube. I've lived here since I was four. If at all possible, I'd like to die here. To leave now would be . . . like a soldier deserting from the ranks.'

Lockett did not hesitate to be blunt. Perhaps it was the prone, patient-like position that Sigmund had adopted.

'More aptly . . . to remain would be like being the last officer on the Titanic. If you stay, that end may come quicker than you might think.'

'Quicker than I desire?'

'I don't know. How fondly do you desire death?'

'One does not need to desire what is inevitable. It is a waste of desire. Desire what is possible, desire what is merely likely.'

'Very neat. Is that original or is it Marcus Aurelius?'

'Need you ask? I am desire's biographer.'

'But you'll come?'

'Where? The French will admit me, as long as I agree not to be a burden on the state and starve to death. The English . . .'

'. . . Will let you in.'

'The English have closed their gates on Europe.'

'No we haven't. It's not at all like that.'

'What are you saying, Lockett? That the indifference of the English is an aberration, a temporary aberration?'

'Yes. That's exactly what I'm saying.'

'Fine. Get me out. Get us all out.'

A dismissive wave of a hand in the air.

Now Lockett had cause to hesitate. It was not simply that the old man's assertion was unconvincing — he was far from impressed yet — there were the flaws in his own insistence too.

'It's not entirely straightforward. It's possible. It's most certainly possible. I'd even say it was likely. It's really a matter of who you know.'

'Was it not ever thus? When was it not thus?'

'I mean — who you know in England. Who you know who might be ... well, who ... who ... who might be in *Who's Who*?'

'My dear Lockett, you sound like an owl.'

'A few names I could approach on your behalf, perhaps?'

'Do you know Alexei Troy?'

'You mean Sir Alex Troy — the newspaper chap?'

'The same.'

'Where on earth did you —'

'A patient. You will understand, Lockett, that this is strictly between ourselves. You have read my 'The Case of the Immaculate Thief'?'

'Naturally.'

'That was Alex Troy.'

Lockett was silent — all he could think was 'Good Bloody Grief!'

'The Alex Troy of 1907–8. He had not been long in Vienna. He had landed up here after his flight from Russia. Or, to be exact, from the 1907 Anarchist Conference in The Hague. He turned up on my doorstep the day after it finished. I treated him all that winter. Indeed, he lay on this very couch. Shortly afterwards he moved to Paris, and I believe from Paris to London, where, as they say at the end of tuppenny novellettes, he prospered.'

Prospered, Lockett thought, was hardly precise. Troy was, and there was no other phrase for it, filthy rich. But then he had begun as a thief, as Freud would have it, an immaculate and far from filthy thief. One to whom not a speck of dirt could stick, either to the clothing or the conscience, it would seem.

'We did not keep in touch. Merely the odd letter from time to time — more often than not when an English translation of something or other of mine came out. His German was never good, after all. But I think I can safely say he is unlikely to have forgotten me.'

'Quite,' said Lockett.

'Will he do?'

'Well, he knows everyone. That's undeniable. I doubt there's a politician in England that would not take a telephone call from Alex Troy.'

§ 6

19 March
Leopoldstadt, Vienna

Krugstrasse was a street of tailors. Beckermann's shop stood next to Bemmelmann's, Bemmelmann's stood next to Hirschel's, Hirschel's next to Hummel's. The shop beyond Hummel's had stood empty for nearly a year now. Ever since old Schuster had packed his bag and caught a train to Paris. He'd tried to sell the shop, but the offers were derisory. From Paris he wrote to Hummel: 'Take the stock, Joe, take all you want. Take the shop, it's yours. I'd rather see it burn than sell it to some Jew-hating usurer for a pittance.'

Not that he knew it but Schuster would almost have his way. It would be Hummel who watched the shop burn.

The following week Schuster wrote, 'Forget the shop, Joe. Leave Leopoldstadt. Leave Vienna. Leave Austria. How long can it be safe for any Jew?'

The day before the German annexation the local Austrian SA had rampaged carelessly down the street of tailors, smashed Hirschel's windows and beaten up Beckermann's grandson, who was unfortunate enough or stupid enough to be out in the street at the time. Most people had more sense. Had the SA been less than careless they could have taken out every window in the street and looted what they wished. No one would have stopped them, but the rampage had its own momentum and, once it had gathered speed, roared on from one target to the next, glancing off whatever was in the way. Hummel and Beckermann's grandson helped Hirschel board up his window.

'Is there any point?' Hirschel had said. 'They'll be back.'

But a week had passed, a week in which many Jews had been robbed of all they possessed, some Jews had fled the city and some Jews had taken their own lives, but the mob had not returned.

At first light on the morning of the 19th, a German infantryman banged on the doors all along the street with his rifle butt.

Bemmelmann was first to answer.

'You want a suit?' he said blearily.

'Don't get comical with me grandad! How many people live here?'

'Just me and my wife.'

'Then get a bucket and a scrubbing brush and follow me.'

Then he came up to Hummel, shadowed in the doorway of his shop. Hummel had not been able to sleep and was already dressed in his best black suit.

'Going somewhere, were we?'

Hummel said, 'It's the Sabbath.'

'No – it's just another Saturday. Get a bucket, follow me!'

By the time he got back from the scullery every tailor in the street was standing with a bucket of water in his hand. Old men, and most of them were; not-so-young men, and Hummel was most certainly the youngest at thirty-one; men in their best suits, pressed and pristine; men in their working suits, waistcoats shiny with pinheads, smeared with chalk; men with their trousers hastily pulled on, and their nightshirts tucked into the waistband.

The German lined them up like soldiers on parade. He strutted up and down in mock-inspection, smirking and grinning and then laughing irrepressibly.

'What a shower, what a fuckin' shower. The long and the short and the tall. The fat, the ugly and the kike! Left turn!'

Most of the older men had seen service in one war or another and knew how to drill. Beckermann had even pinned his 1914–18 campaign medals to his coat as though trying to make a point. Those that knew turned methodically. Those that didn't bumped into one another, dropped buckets, spilt water and reduced the German to hysterics. Well, Hummel thought, at least he's laughing. Not punching, not kicking. Laughing.

He led them to the end of the street, to a five-point crossroads, where the side streets met the main thoroughfare, Wilhelminastrasse. In the middle of the star was a long-parched water fountain, topped by a statue of a long-forgotten eighteenth-century burgomaster. Someone had painted a toothbrush moustache on the statue – it was unfortunate that the burgomaster had been represented in the first place with his right arm upraised – and around the base in red paint were the words 'Hitler has a dinky dick!'

'Right, you Jew-boys. Start scrubbin'!'

They scrubbed.

When they had finished the message was still more than faintly visible. Gloss paint did not scrub so well. And they'd none of them been able to reach the moustache.

The tailors stood up, their knees wet, their trousers soggy.

'We can scrub no more off,' Hummel said as politely as he could.

'Who said anything about any more scrubbin'?' said the German.

He took a dozen paces back and raised his rifle. Bemmelmann sagged against Hummel's chest in a dead faint. Hummel heard the gentle hiss as Beckermann pissed himself. Heard Hirschel muttering a prayer.

But the rifle carried on upwards, drawing a bead on the statue's head, then the crack as it fired and chips of stone showered down on Hummel. The second crack and the stone head split open and two chunks of rock heavy enough to stove in a man's skull bounced off the cobbles behind him and rolled away.

'Right,' said the German. 'Pick your feet up Jew-boys. And follow me.'

Hummel roused Bemmelmann.

'Where am I?' the old man said.

'In hell,' Hummel replied.

§ 7

Hummel had no difficulty seeing himself and his neighbours as Vienna saw them from the early-morning doors and windows, in the eyes of women shaking tablecloths and in the eyes of unshaven men still munching on their breakfast roll, clutching their first cup of coffee. A raggle-taggle bunch of damp and dusty Jewish tailors led by a bantam-cock of a soldier, strutting while they straggled – a recognisably barmy army.

Every so often the German would try to kick a little higher, but, clearly, the goose step was not as easy as it looked and needed more practice than the man had given it, and was all but impossible whilst turning around every couple of minutes to urge on his charges. It might have been better to herd them like pigs or cattle, but Hummel could see the thrill of leadership in the way the man stuck out his chest and kicked out his legs. He'd probably never led anything in his life before. He shouted, they shuffled. Down to the river, across the Aspern Bridge, along Franz Josef's Kai and into the ancient heart of Vienna.

The German yelled 'Halt'.

Hummel was wondering why he could not just yell 'stop' – as though there was any particular military relevance to a word like 'halt' – when he realised where they were. Outside the Ruprechtskirche. Probably the oldest church in the city – some said it had stood twelve hundred years already. It was a small church. A simple, almost plain exterior. Not a touch of grandiosity in its conception or its accretions. What desecration now? Of course, the final desecration would be if this idiot, this tinpot Boney at the front, were to marshal them inside. Hummel had never been in this or any other Christian church.

A crowd had their backs to them. The German parted a way with his rifle and Hummel found himself on his knees once more, his bucket and brush set down before him, facing a large bright blue letter 'H'. Beckermann plumped down next to him, the bucket obscuring the letter. Hummel looked to his left wanting, for reasons that were inaccessible to him, to know what word he was obliterating now. The man next to him was hunched over, scrubbing vigorously, the letter already half-erased. Hummel knew him. He could not see his face, but he knew him. He looked at the blue wide-pinstripe of the man's back, and he knew the suit. He had made it himself not two months ago for a young violinist named Turli Cantor.

Cantor did not turn. Hummel dunked the brush, gazed outward at the mob and bent his head to scrub. They had an audience – a crowd of onlookers who seemed to Hummel to be neither gloating nor commiserating. He had heard that the mobs could be as vicious as the SA, jeering and kicking as rabbis were dragged from their homes to clean public lavatories. This lot showed no inclination. They were watching with the casual half-attention of a crowd watching a street entertainer who they found just distracting enough to pause for, but who would be off the minute the hat was passed. So that was what they were? Street entertainment. The Famous Scrubbing Jews of Vienna. Roll up, roll up and watch the kikes on their knees on the steps of a Christian church. He looked again. They were blank, expressionless faces. Perhaps they had no more wish to be there than he had himself. The troops standing between the Jews and the mob weren't ordinary soldiers like the one who had led him here. They were black-uniformed, jackbooted German SS.

Hummel was making good progress with his 'H' when he felt a change in the mood of the mob. He risked an upward glance. The SS were all standing stiffly upright – perhaps this was what was meant by 'at attention'? – and the crowd had parted to let through an officer in black and silver.

From his left he heard Cantor whisper, 'My God. Wolfgang Stahl!'

For the first time his eyes met Cantor's. 'I have known Wolf all my life,' Cantor said, his voice beginning to rise above a whisper, 'Surely he will save us?'

Cantor stood, clumsily, one foot all but slipping from under him on the wet stone flag and uttered the single syllable, 'Wolf.'

An SS trooper shot him through the forehead.

The crowd scattered, screaming. This was not what they had paid to see. Hummel rose – afterwards he assigned the word 'instinctively' to his action – only to feel the pressure of a hand on his shoulder, forcing him back down, and the sound of the German soldier's voice saying, 'Don't be a fool. You can't help him. You can only get yourself killed. You and all your mates.'

Hummel saw a boot push Cantor's body over, saw the black hole between Cantor's eyes, saw the click of the heels as the same boot came together with its mate and saluted the officer. Then he twisted his head slightly, enough to make the German tighten his grip, and saw the black leather of the officer's gloves drawn tight across his knuckles. Then one hand rose – the salute returned. The man turned and all Hummel saw was his retreating back and the movement of SS troopers across the steps, and then a voice was shouting 'Show's over', and someone he could not see at all was dragging Cantor's body away.

They scrubbed until the graffiti was washed away. They scrubbed until the blood was washed away.

Slouching home Hummel asked Hirschel what the word had been.

'Schuschnigg,' Hirschel replied. 'And it may be the only memorial our chancellor ever gets.'

JOHN LAWTON

THE INSPECTOR TROY SERIES

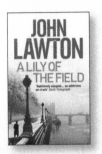
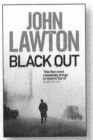

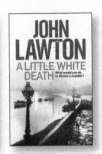

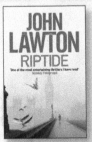

Grove Press UK

Also available as ebooks
www.atlantic-books.co.uk